ORDERS from ABOVE

J Merrill Forrest

This edition published by The Moon Tiger 2021

A CIP catalogue for this book is available from the British Library.

ISBN: 9780956795465

The Moon Tiger

www.jmerrillforrest.com

Angels
walk among us...

and sometimes
they cause mischief

Chapter 1
discovery

An hour before dawn, the headstones loomed charcoal and dove-grey before Topps as he strode through them to begin his first job of the day. He'd never understood why some people find a churchyard spooky, but then, he'd never been frightened by anything in his life. After hooking his canvas satchel over the wing of a small, sad-faced stone angel, he crossed to the shed, pleased to see that the vixen had eaten the nightly feast he left for her next to the compost heap. She had cubs to raise, and Topps had been lucky to see them playing rough and tumble once, until the vixen had smelled his scent and ushered them through the hedge and away.

He quickly loaded up the wheelbarrow with all the tools and paraphernalia he would need then, whistling tunelessly, he bumped the barrow over the uneven grass to the opposite end of the churchyard. He was eager to get started. With a short break for breakfast he could be done by lunch time. Never mind that the job would take a tenth of the time with a mini excavator or with a couple of helpers, Topps preferred hard, manual labour to taking the easy way with power tools. And he liked to work alone.

Flat cap pushed to the back of his head and shirt sleeves rolled to above his elbows, he spat into the palms of his huge, calloused hands and flexed his muscles. Raising the spade high, he brought it down so hard the sharpened edge sliced cleanly through the grass into the top few inches of packed soil. Then with booted foot, the veins and sinews of his arms and neck bulging, Topps worked it all the way in and so began the task of digging a new grave.

It wasn't long before his entire body dripped with sweat, but Topps, lost in the steady rhythm of digging, didn't pause even to wipe his brow. He dug deeper and wider, only becoming mindful of his surroundings again when the sun broke over the crenelated church roof in a blaze of scarlet and gold. It was going to be another scorching day.

Figuring he was about halfway done, Topps decided to take a break and eat. He rinsed his hands at the standpipe, gasping as the cold water hit the heated skin of his face and the back of his neck, then retrieved his satchel from the angel. His chosen place for breaks was in the shade of the far-spreading yew tree, leaning his back against the old stone wall, his feet resting on the grave of Gladys Edwina Ashburton. According to the lichen-covered headstone she had been born in 1817, died in 1901, and had 'dedicated her life to Nature'. Topps felt some affinity with Gladys because he also appreciated the natural order of things.

The only downside to Nature, he thought, was people. He didn't like people.

Ravenous after his labours, he made short work of two thick slabs of white bread smeared liberally with lard and wrapped round two mustard-covered cold pork sausages, washed down with swigs of dark, sweet tea. He contemplated eating the two blackened bananas he'd brought along, but decided to save them for later and get back to work.

In another four hours the digging was done and the mound of freshly-dug earth had been covered with artificial grass. Topps was preparing to lay out the webbing straps that would support the coffin as it was lowered by the pall-bearers, and something caught his eye. It was a mere glimmer in the packed, dark soil in the floor of the hole, but he wondered how he'd missed it when he'd smoothed the surfaces.

Curious, he jumped nimbly down to investigate, and used his penknife to prise the encrusted object free. He spat on it and cleaned away the dirt with the ball of his thumb, revealing a smooth-edged coin, a raised pattern on each of its faces. It was surprisingly heavy and he wondered if it could be gold. But no, probably not. It was more likely to be something worthless, if his previous finds were anything to go by. He'd once uncovered a beaded necklace, which had caused a lot of excitement, until the Heritage Museum in the city declared it wasn't at all valuable.

Topps slid the coin and his penknife into the back pocket of his shabby moleskin trousers and grabbed the spade to dig around a bit, but there were no more coins to be found. Disappointed that he hadn't discovered a treasure trove, he once again smoothed out the sides and floor of the grave. It took another hour to finish the preparations, clean and put away his tools, lock up the shed and grab his satchel. He was headed for the vicarage as the clock struck two.

Reverend Hartley Cordwell answered Topps' knock, his white hair like a dandelion clock atop his long, thin, jovial face.

"Good afternoon, Topps! Another fine day, isn't it?"

"Aye, sir, that it is. Just came to tell you that Jack's grave be ready, and I found this." He retrieved the coin from his pocket and held it out. "Couldn't find no more, though."

"Thank you, Topps. We're not destined to find riches in our churchyard, are we?" Hartley peered at the coin. "I'll put it in the safe until I've got time to have a proper look at it. Now, would you like a cup of tea? I've half an hour before I have to go out."

"No thank you, Reverend Cordwell, sir. I'd like to get the green watered, right parched the grass is."

"Well, if you're sure?"

"Aye, thanks all the same. I'll be getting back to work."

Topps wondered if the vicar would ever stop offering him refreshments. They must have been through this ritual hundreds of times, and, although he actually had more time for the vicar than anyone else in the village, never once had he accepted an invitation to tea. He simply loathed small talk or chitchat. The solitary nature of his job as village handyman suited him well; he did a good job for whoever paid him a fair wage and neither offered nor expected any conversation in return. After all his years doing odd jobs everyone had learned this and so left him well alone. Except for the vicar who couldn't seem to stop himself from offering tea.

Topps touched a forefinger to his flat cap and walked down the vicarage driveway, his mind on the grass of the village green turning brown and unsightly in the relentless heat. He caught a flash of colour ahead of him and narrowed his eyes as a man in red trousers burst from the rhododendrons and stared hard at him. Topps assumed he was on his way to see the vicar, but, without uttering a word, the stranger stepped smartly back into the bushes. By the time Topps reached the spot, there was no trace of him.

For the rest of the day he tried to put the red-trousered man out of his mind, but he couldn't shake off the feeling that he was being watched. Time and again he couldn't stop himself looking over his shoulder, but there were no more flashes of red, no mysterious figures diving out of or into shrubs or disappearing behind garden sheds.

His last task before heading home was to put food out for the vixen, but while he was doing so and then during the short walk to his cottage the feeling of being observed grew ever stronger and he looked back over his shoulder four times before giving himself a telling off for having fanciful notions. Who would want to spy on the likes of him? But the uneasy feeling persisted while he prepared and ate his dinner of rabbit casserole with green beans and tiny new potatoes grown in his own vegetable patch. He kept glancing at the window, half expecting to see a face peering in at him.

He passed the rest of the evening hand-washing his shirt and underwear in the sink and polishing his boots and then, at almost midnight, he put a pan of milk on the stove to heat it for his bedtime mug of cocoa. A tawny owl hooted, and Topps, spooning cocoa powder into the milk, listened for its mate to reply; they were probably hunting and Topps wished them luck.

A sudden and loud thumping on his front door took him so completely by surprise that he jarred the pan and splashed the back of his hand with hot cocoa. He turned off the burner beneath the pan and went to see who could possibly be bothering him at this time of night. It was unlikely to be the vicar, as he always went to bed early. Besides, he only ever knocked very gently while calling Topps' name, this person seemed intent on battering his door down.

Feeling very angry at being disturbed, not to mention scalded, Topps yanked the door open, to find a tall man in red trousers grinning at him.

"You!" he barked, curling his fists at his sides. "I saw you skulking around earlier. Who are you and what do you want?"

With a cheeky wink, the stranger replied, "You would not believe me if I told you who I am. But what I want, my dear chap, is for you to take a little holiday."

"What? What are you talking about, you stupid man? Go away!"

Topps tried to slam the door, but the stranger swiftly pushed his way into the cottage with surprising strength. Topps, rooted to the spot, could only sputter a strangled protest as the stranger walked around the tiny room, his eyes roving from the stained armchair to the scratched pine table to the single bed in the far corner. The man studied the damp, clean clothes hung to dry, then pulled on the rope that worked the pulleys to raise and lower the airer from the ceiling, seeming to find it amusing. After that he picked up Topps' very shiny boots, and laughed out loud at the rounded reflection of his face in the toecaps. Finally, the intruder swung his gaze to the stove and exclaimed, "Oh, is that cocoa I smell! Wonderful!"

He turned the full force of his grin on a furious Topps and said, "I'll make some for both of us, shall I? Nice and sweet? Then we'll talk about your little holiday."

Chapter 2

be careful what you wish for

Perched at his desk, hands busy straightening steel paper clips for the sake of having something to do, Nigel grew increasingly irritated by a couple of fat bluebottles buzzing and beating themselves to death against the grimy window. "You got in, so why can't you get out the same way?" he grumbled. "I can't open the window for you." He wished he could, both to rid the office of flies and to let in some fresh air, but they had long been sealed shut by grime and layers of sloppily applied gloss paint.

The printer continued to spit out copies of the photographs he'd taken during the previous night's surveillance. There was a 'ping' and Nigel groaned to see a warning flash up on the laptop screen informing him that the printer was running out of ink. He just had to hope and pray that there would be enough to finish this job, because he didn't have any more cartridges.

He loosened his tie, undid the top two buttons of his shirt, and wiped his face with a tissue. It shredded into tiny flecks on a patch of stubble on his left cheek, and, not for the first time, he wished he'd remembered to put a proper handkerchief in his pocket. Would this heatwave never end?

He uncapped a black felt-tipped pen to write the name 'Bingley' across the front of a grey folder. The pen had dried up. Less than half an hour into the day and he wondered if things could get any worse. A new felt pen he could just about afford, but print cartridges, essential for his job, were so blasted expensive. The water and electricity bills would arrive any day, as would the rent demand. His credit card was racking up ridiculous interest fees, and, worst of all, the monthly maintenance payment to Tansy, his avaricious ex-wife, was a week overdue.

"Damn it," he said out loud to the room. "So much for a new start. I hate this heat, I hate this job, I hate not having any money!"

"But you love me, I hope."

Nigel gave a rueful grin as his wife of one glorious year and two wonderful months came in, a vision of fresh loveliness in her strappy lime-green summer dress and white sandals, her dark-chocolate hair swept back in a glossy, swinging ponytail. Her flawless skin positively glowed, and if he weren't so horribly sweaty he would cheer himself up by taking her slender body in his arms and kissing her oh-so-kissable lips.

"I bring iced lemonade to cool your fevered brow," she said.

"Are you going to throw it in my face, then?"

"Ah, wry humour! That's good. You were looking so gloomy I was worried you were beyond help." Amelia set the glass of lemonade down and watched Nigel spread out the newly printed photographs. The last one was a bit stripy.

"Mr Bingley, I presume?"

Nigel nodded. "You know, it's one thing having to take pictures like these, at least then I'm concentrating on getting the light and the camera angles right rather than on the subject, but it's quite another having to study them in full-blown colour. This poor chap's soon going to be in very deep doo-doo with the terrifying Mrs Bingley."

He shuddered as the image of Mrs Bingley wormed its way into his head, her flabby face a deep, mottled red, chins wobbling with indignation, her mean, mud-brown eyes piggy with righteous rage.

"Still," said Amelia, picking up one of the pictures, "it looks like he had a good time last night. She's a stunning woman, I must say; goodness knows how she can even move in those heels and, and... goodness, what *is* that she's wearing? I wonder why she doesn't invest in some curtains. I bet she charges quite a bit for her services."

"She does. And that's how Mrs Bingley got suspicious, because she checks the bank statements and noticed how much cash was being taken out every Tuesday."

Truth was, Nigel felt rather sorry for Mr Bingley, because his wife truly was a frightful woman, with no social graces whatsoever. However, it was Mrs Bingley who was paying him and he desperately needed the money, so he gathered up the evidence of Mr Bingley's adulterous escapade, scribbled a quick note about hours worked on the case, and put everything in the file.

The phone warbled and Amelia, who thought it helped Nigel if it sounded like he had a receptionist, reached across him to answer it, pressing the loudspeaker button so Nigel could hear both sides of the conversation.

In a bright, musical voice that made him smile, she said, "Good morning! Nigel Hellion-Rees Detective Agency, how can we help you?"

A woman answered with equal brightness, "Good morning, dear, it's Dora Dash. I'm just calling to tell you that you can stop following my husband. This time I caught him red-handed myself!"

"Oh, Dora, what happened?"

She chuckled, "The silly fool had too much to drink at the Hunt Ball and bragged to everyone about his latest conquest. I had to save face, of course, so I hit him over the head with a champagne bottle, vintage Dom Pérignon, naturally. He promised never to stray again and to replace the practically *priceless* Aubusson rug that was spattered in blood from the gash on his forehead, and I get a brand spanking-new Mercedes."

Nigel rolled his eyes as Amelia replied, "Um, well, we're glad that's all sorted out, Dora."

"Now be sure and send me your bill, add a little retainer, and I'll be in touch the next time some daft floozy catches the ever-roving eye of Mr Dash. I hope it won't be too long, because I need to replace my entire wardrobe. Goodbye now, dear, and do please give my warmest regards to your delightful husband."

Nigel leaned forward, wincing as his shirt stuck to his chair then peeled away to damply reaffix itself to his skin. "I'd really hoped for more money from that one, Amelia, I've got nothing else coming in. It's just getting worse and worse."

"I know. But Dora will settle up quickly, she always does, and she's happy to keep paying a small retainer for next time, so it's not a complete loss."

Nigel pushed both hands through his hair, and blinked with irritation as it flopped forward again into his eyes. "Do you remember when we first met Dora? She swept in here, swathed in furs and jewellery, that tiny little dog peeking out of her handbag, stopping dead in her tracks because she hadn't known we'd taken over the business."

"I'll never forget it. You know, the last time she hired you I asked her why she didn't divorce her husband if he couldn't be faithful for longer than a week."

"Oh? You didn't tell me. What did she say?"

"She said that she had no intention of leaving him, only of enjoying herself with his money. I was appalled at her mercenary attitude, but she explained further." Amelia paused while she puffed out her chest and raised her chin before continuing in a voice that was a perfect rendering of Dora's breathy, little-girl voice, "It may sound callous, dear, but I'm not broken-hearted by the affairs because I really and truly don't care, and my husband knows it. It's a kind of game for us, you see, and for some extraordinary reason, it works. We both get what we want!"

"So it works because he has affairs, she pretends she's outraged, he gives her money and gifts. I find that sad."

Amelia nodded. "Oh, so do I. But Dora said it's because when she was young love broke her heart and poverty almost broke her spirit, so she decided that it's easier not to be in love and to have lots and lots of money." Amelia put the breathy, lispy voice on again and gushed, "You know that song that says diamonds are a girl's best friend? Well, believe me, sweet girl, they certainly are, and I've got *lots* of diamonds!"

Nigel laughed, but he couldn't stop himself giving a wistful glance at his wife's engagement ring, its tiny diamond chip the one and only precious stone *she* owned. It couldn't even begin to compare with the lowliest of the many rings that adorned Dora's fingers, certainly not with the enormous square-cut emerald chosen by his first wife even before he had proposed. His shoulders drooped and he said, "Perhaps you should divorce me and marry someone rich."

"Oh, Nigel, really! I won't even grace that comment with an answer." She marched to her own desk and shuffled some fabric samples around. Even her work as an interior designer was being affected by the long, influential tentacles of Tansy's father, with fewer and fewer jobs coming in.

Nigel knew he'd have to apologise. Amelia hated it when he went on about how he couldn't give her the things he'd been able to give Tansy. He knew absolutely that she loved him regardless, and he was damned lucky to have her. But just for a minute, maybe two, he wanted to wallow in self-pity. He pictured Dora Dash swanning around the showroom picking out her new car, the salesman fawning over her, as she demanded every extra gadget and gewgaws available. Maybe even 24-carat gold cup holders and a mink-lined bed for her puffball of a dog.

He'd had a Mercedes once. Silver. Dark grey leather seats, walnut dashboard, rain-sensitive headlight wipers, a roof that folded majestically up and down at the touch of a button.

He stopped the thoughts in their tracks. What was the point in going over what he no longer had? What was the loss of a mere car compared to the gain of the most wonderful woman in the world, who in about seven months' time would be the mother of his first child?

Shame-faced, he went over to Amelia and said he was sorry.

She smiled and his heart skipped a beat as she laced her slender fingers with his. He raised her hand to his lips and kissed the underside of her wrist. Her skin smelled of vanilla.

"Do you have any idea how much I love you?"

Amelia nodded. "Yes, Nigel, I do. And you know I love you too. More than anything. But you really hate this business, don't you? I know you thought it would be more about heroically searching for missing persons than chasing after cheaters and thieves. If there's anything else you'd rather do, you know I'll always support you."

"But what else can I do? The only career I want is closed to me, at least until Tansy remarries and her father stops using his money and power to keep me out of property development. I'm an architect, Amelia, I want to design buildings and then see them get built."

Amelia wiped the bits of tissue from Nigel's cheek and affectionately brushed his floppy fringe out of his eyes. "Well, according to the gossip columns, your ex-wife has someone very firmly in mind, doesn't she?"

"Yes, but we've been there twice before! She gets our hopes up sky high, and then she dumps them and we're rock bottom again. No, I'll believe I'm rid of her when she actually has another man's wedding ring on her finger. Just think, Amelia, I'd be able to get a job that would actually pay the bills. And there would be no more maintenance payments!"

As if on cue, the door crashed open and there was a jolly "Helloooooooo there!" A large man barrelled into the office, followed by two even larger men in brown overalls that strained across their beefy arms and chests.

"Greetings from the ex-wife, Nige, me old mate! You're a week overdue; I don't suppose you have the money?"

This was a monthly event that always played out the same way.

Nigel shrugged and the big man shook his bald head in mock sadness. "Dear oh dear! So what shall we take in lieu this time, eh? Nothing worthy in reception, that I do know." Whistling, hands on hips, he swept his eyes around the office then pointed to the items his cohorts should remove.

Nigel and Amelia stood by the window until the three men trooped out again, the boss wishing them a cheery goodbye until the same time next month, his henchmen grunting under the weight of Nigel's desk. They knew they could touch nothing in Amelia's half of the office, so the shelves of interior decorating books, wallpaper and fabric samples were safe.

Amelia said, "We could always bring in the kitchen table for you to work on."

"And, what, eat off the floor at home?" With a resigned sigh, Nigel dropped to his knees and started to gather up the files, papers and general detritus from his desk drawers that the men had strewn all over the grubby, worn carpet. The laptop had been unplugged and lay in one corner with the printer next to it, the digital camera perched on top. Nigel supposed he should be grateful that they weren't allowed to take anything that would prevent him doing his job.

"This is ridiculous!" he exploded. "I can't keep on like this, we'll soon have nothing left. Tansy only takes it out of spite. And it's high time we had a bit of cash to spend on ourselves. Everything you earn, Amelia, goes on rent and food." He stood up and took Amelia in his arms. "I want us to have a decent house, with a garden for our children and the dog we'll have one day." He raised her left hand "I want to give you a proper engagement ring."

Amelia laughed and said brightly, "Oh Nigel, all that will come in time, you know it will. And don't you dare try and replace my precious ring, do you hear me?"

She covered it up well, but Nigel knew that she was dreadfully disappointed that the aftershocks of his short, disastrous marriage to Tansy just kept on rumbling, affecting her as much as it did him. Her commissions were definitely fewer since she'd become his wife, and soon she would have to stop work, at least for a while. Then they would be a family of three living on the mere pennies he managed to earn through this dreadful business.

He sighed. "We won't be free of her until she finds herself another husband, and she seems in no hurry to find one, does she? Two broken engagements in less than a year! How many more, I wonder?" Nigel pushed his fringe out of his eyes; it flopped straight back down.

Beneath the charming and deferential veneer Tansy was ruthless, either because she'd been born that way or she'd learned it from her father. Nigel had begged for a clean break settlement, but he could not afford to hire a lawyer savvy enough to take on his father-in-law's legal team and win.

When they'd been married, Nigel had had to work longer and longer hours designing exclusive health complexes and mansions for multi-millionaires to earn the money to pay for his wife's extravagant spending. When he'd discovered that Tansy had been unfaithful to him with her personal trainer, their gardener and the young chap who mucked out the stables where she kept her horse, he had, with some relief, demanded a divorce. She'd agreed on the condition that Nigel allowed her to divorce him on the grounds of unreasonable behaviour so that her reputation would be untainted. If he'd only known what giving Tansy her own way meant for his future, he would have fought her tooth and nail, and told her doting daddy the truth about his conniving, perpetually unfaithful daughter.

But would that have made a difference, really? Knowing her father, he'd never believe his daughter capable of wrongdoing and so the outcome would still have been the same.

Nigel would still have lost his job, but his integrity would have been intact.

The only good thing to come out of the whole mess was Amelia. She had happened to be there discussing a project the day Nigel had been fired, and they'd ended up together in the nearest pub, a cardboard box of Nigel's personal effects from his office on the floor between them. She'd offered emotional support to Nigel as he'd struggled along in short-term and unsatisfactory jobs, and in a matter of weeks they had fallen in love with each other.

A short while after their low-key but utterly delightful wedding, a cousin of Amelia's had offered to sell Nigel his PI business, assuring him that he'd make pots of money. But however the cousin had made his money, Nigel soon learned it definitely hadn't been through honest means. Not long after he'd taken over and had his name painted on the door, he had had to turn away some very shady people. The cousin, meanwhile, had fled to a country that didn't have an extradition agreement.

Amelia continued with her own business, happy to run it from Nigel's office as she always went to a client's premises rather than have them visit her, so she'd been there when Nigel had had some very frightening moments with characters that could have been straight out of a gangster movie.

Nigel forced his mind back to the present and looked sadly at his beloved wife. "I'm so sorry, Amelia, I seem to have made rather a mess of things."

"Oh, don't go all maudlin on me." She kissed him and stroked his fringe out of his eyes. "We'll get there, you'll see. Now, I'm going to get the scissors and cut that blasted fringe of yours."

Nigel picked up a paper clip to unbend while Amelia rummaged in her desk drawers for a suitable pair of scissors. Truth was, in career terms, he was broke, trapped, bored and terrified. He loathed having to follow adulterous husbands and wives with his camera and recording equipment at the ready, writing reports about their seedy goings-on. This rundown office and his second-hand suits and worn out shoes depressed him. Not being able to buy for Amelia all the things he'd so easily and thoughtlessly bought for Tansy depressed him even more. And now there was a baby on way, and he was terrified that he'd fall short as a father just as he had in everything else.

Tansy had taken everything from him, *everything*, and even though she didn't need a bean from him she was still determined to bleed him dry.

Amelia told Nigel to look up at her and keep really still. As she snipped at his fringe, he closed his eyes tight and said, "I just wish something would happen to change our fortunes."

As he spoke the sentence, there was a sudden chill in the room and he shivered.

Chapter 3
orders from above

"Oh, look, the watercress in my sandwich is absolutely *wilting*. Why are we out here in this heat? It's much more comfortable inside." Gabe glared at his brother when there was no response. "Nick, are you listening?"

"Yes, I heard you! Why don't you go back inside, then?" Irritated, Nick flapped his hand at Gabe. "Scurry back to your air-conditioning, why don't you? You're such a wimp, even in winter you moan that it's too hot for you."

"And it's never hot enough for you, is it? Even the fires of Hell…" Gabe's whingeing tailed off as a short man dressed in the medieval uniform of a court messenger came scurrying towards them.

"You'd think," Nick grumbled so the little man was sure to hear him, "that they'd at least let us have lunch in peace."

Gabe tutted at Nick and beckoned the man over. "Hello, Herbert, what's up?"

Herbert, eyes darting nervously to Nick and away again, removed his floppy hat and smoothed one small hand over the thin ginger strands carefully combed from ear to ear over his shiny pate. He bowed slightly to Gabe and said, "Your presence is required on the top floor."

"Both of us?"

"Both of you, yes, sir. Um… immediately, in fact."

"Okay," said Gabe. "We'll be along in two ticks, Herbert, there's no need to wait."

Herbert rammed his cap back on and hurried away.

Frowning, Gabe packed up the half-finished sandwiches. "We haven't been summoned upstairs for ages. What have you been up to, Nick?"

"Me? Why assume it's me?"

"Because it always is! It's what you do!"

"Well, yes, but it's what I'm *supposed* to do! Trouble is my business. The more trouble I get involved in, the better my performance figures, you know that. And my figures have been exceptional this month. No, it must be something *you've* done."

Gabe thought his brother might be right, but couldn't for the life of him think what transgression he might have made. He said, "My figures are good too. My team has been working flat out, I really can't think why he wants to see us."

Nick tutted. "We'll find out soon enough, won't we? Let's go before he gets impatient and sends another of his minions out to fetch us."

The brothers hurried across the lush grass of the private garden at the back of their office building, an edifice of glass and steel that was taller and more architecturally magnificent than any other building around it. They strolled through a short, dimly lit corridor and pushed through a pair of heavy doors that led into the rear of a cool, bright, air-conditioned reception area. As they crossed the gleaming floor, Gabe saw Nick give a sly wink to the young receptionists, two beautiful women and one handsome chap, who sat behind the vast croissant-shaped desk. They all simpered and patted their hair. One of them, Gabe couldn't tell who, even giggled and he rolled his eyes at the sound. If he, Gabe, smiled at someone, they just wanted to pat him affectionately on the shoulder and straighten his tie. He couldn't understand it. He was just as good looking as his brother, with the same dark curly hair and grey eyes, they were the same height and build, they both dressed *very* smartly indeed. And yet…

The security guard rose from his chair and gave a faultless salute to the peaked brim of his cap then rushed ahead to summon the elevator for them.

The doors slid open with a quiet *swoosh*. The operator inside clicked his heels and stood to attention by the polished brass panel, chest proudly out and forefinger poised, ready to press the required button. Before entering, Nick muttered quite audibly about the necessity of having *quite* so many uniformed employees and Gabe, speaking over him, politely said, "Top floor please."

As they ascended, Gabe tried to keep his anxiety at bay, but a summons to see the Michael, aka Head of Global Operations, aka the Boss, was rare, and it usually meant a ticking off about something. He racked his brain, trying to think of anything that he might have done wrong. Next to him, Nick was impassive, giving the outward impression that he wasn't worried. But Gabe knew his brother, knew that he was afraid of nothing and nobody, except Michael. Oh, and spiders.

The doors opened with another *swoosh* and the brothers both gasped when they saw that it was Michael himself, grave-faced, waiting for them. This was really serious, then.

"Well," Michael said, putting one hand on Nick's shoulder and the other on Gabe's, "it's big news, boys. The DISC has finally turned up. Let's go to my office."

He led the way through wide, silent corridors to a vast room with floor to ceiling windows, a trembling Gabe and nervously grinning Nick at his heels. His personal assistant rushed to open the door into a private inner space, snapping on a switch before withdrawing. Table lamps flickered and settled with a soft, creamy glow as the three men entered.

Gabe swallowed hard. Rare as it was to be in The Boss's office, even rarer was to be shown into this inner sanctum. The rest of the building was sleek and modern, all very 21st century, but this room… well, this was like stepping back into a gentleman's private library within the walls of a grand house circa the Edwardian era. It was an intimate, windowless space that contained a huge bookcase filled with leather-bound books tooled in gold, an exquisitely carved coffee table, and two large sofas covered in dark red, crushed velvet either side of it. In the centre of the table was a tray set with coffee pot, cups and saucers, milk jug and a silver platter of cream cakes, which in a normal situation would have made Gabe's mouth water. But this situation was far from normal and his appetite, usually hearty, had totally deserted him. So the DISC had been found! Suddenly feeling boneless, he sank onto the sofa nearest the door.

Nick came over and sat close beside him. "Gabe? Come on, bro, you must have been prepared for this?"

Gabe, putting as much distance between himself and Nick as the sofa allowed, replied, "Yes, of course, but it's… it's too soon."

"Too soon? Oh come on now, that's hardly reasonable, is it?"

The Boss interrupted. "Let's not get into a quarrel. Gabe, I know you never wanted this day to come, but it has. The DISC has been found and the Agreement must be honoured. This is the biggest event in our history since… well, since the very beginning of our history."

Nick spoke, his voice steady, though Gabe could feel his brother's body vibrating with excitement, "When was it found? How?"

"It was discovered last week, in a vil—"

Nick interrupted, "Last week! Why are we only hearing about it now?"

"Because my team needed time to investigate and to develop a strategy so that we can set the Grand Plan in motion."

"So where was it found?" Nick demanded.

The Boss glared at him. "If you'd let me speak I shall tell you! It was dug up in a village churchyard, by the gravedigger preparing for a burial. I had Uri on the spot within minutes and he's now hidden in plain sight to keep an eye on the proceedings."

"And where is the DISC now?" Nick, all hyped up, leapt to his feet and paced up and down, filling the small room with his excitement.

"The vicar has it in his safe. No-one has paid much attention to it yet, they've been too busy with the funeral; the deceased was a very popular member of the village. We need to retrieve it, obviously, but for now it's well protected and we'll recover it before anyone gets a chance to examine it. What's important now is that the Plan is put into action as soon as possible."

Gabe looked imploringly at his brother, "I know how long you've been waiting for this, longing for this, but… but, Nick… I just don't think I'm ready!"

Nick spun on his heels to confront Gabe, and his voice was sharp, bitter, when he replied, "I can tell you to a *nanosecond* how long I've been waiting, and we'll just have to *get* you ready." He closed his eyes and clenched his fists, visibly reining in his impatience. When he spoke again, his voice was soft, cajoling, "Now, come on, bro." He glanced at The Boss, eliciting his support, "Orders from above and all that, eh? You signed up to this, so…"

"Yes, yes," The Boss agreed. "Let's get on with it, shall we?" He picked up a remote control and a map of the world appeared on the smooth white wall opposite the door. A few more clicks and it narrowed to one particular country, and then zoomed in further to one particular county.

"Wiltshire," he said, as he continued to zoom in, "in England. And this is the village where the DISC is."

There were a few photos of typical village scenes: a pub, a green, a row of thatched cottages, a church. "Fortunately for us it's a real backwater. As I've said, Uri is already in position there and reports he's good to go. My scouts have checked the place out and they've come up with a cover to get you in, retrieve the DISC, fulfil your obligations according to the Plan, and get out with no-one the wiser."

Gabe, dismayed by how far along things already were, could only whisper, "What do Nick and I have to do?"

"You *know* what we have to do, Gabe!" cried Nick, his eyes blazing with fury and frustration. "We have to implement the Grand Plan!"

With a click the picture changed to an old, very dilapidated building and The Boss continued, "Nick is right, Gabe. But we've never known when and how the DISC would be found, so you both need a way to work it to suit the time and circumstances we now find ourselves in. Here's what we've come up with. He pointed to the picture on the wall. "You are to buy this old water mill under the pretext of doing it up and turning it into a restaurant. This will allow you to come and go without arousing suspicion."

He switched off the slide show. "Nick, we've been through your list of suggested witnesses, and I believe we have selected the perfect candidate." He placed a photograph on the coffee table, a headshot of a personable but worried-looking man in his thirties.

Gabe had known about the requirement for a Witness if the Plan was ever to be executed, but not that Nick had been actively looking for one. He'd been feeling well and truly put out by proceedings already, but now he felt even more well and truly put out!

Nick rubbed his hands together, very smug. "Oh yes! I like this one, he's just ripe for the picking! And there's no need to glower at me like that, Gabe. Unlike you, I've always made sure I'd be ready for this day."

The Boss produced a sheet of paper and scanned the closely typed lines on it, saying, "To fill you in, Gabe, Nigel Hellion-Rees is an intelligent, honest, decent man trapped by a punitive divorce settlement. He's an architect, but thanks to his influential and very rich ex-father-in-law he cannot get work in that field and is currently working as a private investigator, a job he hates. He deeply loves his current wife, is about to become a father for the first time, and he desperately needs a helping hand to get his life back on track. That will be his reward for being our Witness."

Nick interjected, "I'll go and see him, shall I? Get the ball rolling?"

"Yes, of course, the sooner the better," said Michael. He put the typed sheet and the photograph into a brown Manilla folder, thick with other sheets of paper, and handed it to Nick. "The full strategy is in here. You will tell Hellion-Rees to purchase the mill on your behalf and draw up the plans for its conversion. He will then project-manage the build, and observe you two as you initiate the Plan." The Boss, his brows lowered, looked from Nick to Gabe and back again. "I leave it up to you to decide the right time to inform him of what it is he is witnessing and what his role will be when it's all done. Just be careful how you do it."

Gabe looked at the folder in Nick's hands, his eyes blurring as he read the large white label on the front with despair. He couldn't believe it, but this was really happening and he had no choice but to acquiesce. As Nick had said, he had signed up to the Grand Plan a long time ago, and just like Nick, he knew it inside out and back to front. It's just that he'd never thought they'd ever actually have to implement it. His whole body slumped and he had to swallow hard as he felt ridiculously near to tears.

Nick, on the other hand, was quivering with joyous expectation. He poured himself a cup of coffee and added milk and three sugars. Then he selected the largest, squashiest éclair and licked the cream from its middle before devouring it in two large bites.

There were times when Gabe really, *really* disliked his brother, and this was one of them. Thanks to the discovery of the DISC, Nick was about to get everything he wanted, while he, poor old Gabe, felt like he was going to Hell in a handcart.

Which wasn't too far from the truth, actually.

Chapter 4
introducing the good citizens of Ham-Under-Lymfold

Hartley Cordwell, Vicar of St Peter's Church in the village of Ham-Under-Lymfold, passed through the lychgate and strode up the gravelled path with a speed that belied his years. He'd hoped to be safely inside the church before Stanley arrived, but there he was, just outside the porch, his foul odour getting stronger with each step Hartley took. The black and grey shaggy dog, often mistaken for a wolfhound but actually of unknown parentage, rose to his four huge paws, calmly regarding Hartley's approach with his extraordinary golden eyes. Eyes that Hartley was sure could see right into one's soul.

Old Stanley respectfully bowed his head and rasped, "'Ow do, Your Reverendship, sir, 'ow do!"

The vicar had given up trying to get Stanley to address him in any other way. He replied, "Good morning, Stanley," trying not to inhale through his nose. "I see you have a new hat."

Stanley touched the bobble hanging from the left earflap of his knitted hat. "Aye, Olive Capsby gave it me, said it were to keep me warm come winter."

Hartley indicated Stanley's overcoat, worn year-round, and said, "Well, it's far from winter now, Stanley, aren't you a bit, er, warm?"

"I'd say I be comfortable, Your Reverendship. Now then, what do you think on this?"

Stanley reached behind him for his home-made sandwich board. He pulled it over his head and settled it on his shoulders, saying, "It be a new message, d'ye see?"

Hartley couldn't help smiling to himself as he read Stanley's latest offering, scrawled in garish green paint:

Wen you get run over by the buss of life,
call for Jesuses ambulunse.

"That's a very nice sentiment, Stanley."

"Well, seems ter me everyone these days has summat to worry about, don't they, Your Reverendship, I'm just offerin' 'em summat to think on that might help."

"Oh, yes, indeed, well done, Stanley. Will you be joining us for the service?"

"Nay, sir, nay. I won't be a-comin' in. I'll just pay my respects from out 'ere, and 'ope I don't cause no offence by it."

Hartley assured Stanley that no-one would mind if he stayed outside. In fact, he thought to himself, Stanley would cause far more offence by taking his pungent bodily odours inside the church than by keeping them outside in the fresh air. No, better that he stayed by the porch, as he always did before and after every service, be it funeral, wedding, christening or Sunday Service. He greeted everyone by name and furtively pocketed with hands encased in greasy fingerless gloves any loose change that was offered. Sometimes he was given tins of dog food, too, which he accepted with good grace on Digby's behalf.

Digby, who clearly thought he'd waited patiently long enough, took a pace forward and pushed his long nose into Hartley's hand, insisting that his rough head and velvety ears be thoroughly scratched. Hartley, remembering when he'd been a tiny puppy, a scrap of a thing, thought he'd grown yet more since the last time he'd seen him. Where or how Stanley had acquired the dog he'd never said, but it was hard to imagine one without the other now.

Stanley chuckled and rummaged in the pockets of his overcoat – really, how he could wear it in this heat Hartley had no idea – and produced a large, bone-shaped biscuit, which the dog accepted and ate with the utmost dignity.

"I must get on, Stanley. I'll see you later."

It was blessedly cool and peaceful inside the church. Hartley, keen to wipe away the smell of Stanley that clung to the hairs in his nostrils, breathed deeply the familiar aromas of incense and fresh flowers mingled with medieval stone, brass polish, wax candles and damp wool. How he loved his little church, every stone, every gargoyle, every nook and cranny of it. In six centuries it had witnessed so many events, and now it was ready for yet another, the funeral of old Jack Heavysides.

But there was no time to linger as he so often loved to do, it really wouldn't do for the mourners to arrive before he was appropriately dressed.

Once ready, he went and stood facing the altar to gather his thoughts for the imminent funeral. As he raised his eyes to the beautiful stained glass window, a sudden tap on his shoulder made him jump in fright. Hartley wheeled around, one trembling hand over the region of his thumping heart. "Oh, Topps, I didn't hear you come in." His eyes travelled down to the gravedigger's feet, which were usually encased in muddy steel-capped boots, but he had taken them off and was standing there in his socks. Thick red ones, with holes in both big toes. His flat cap was clasped to his chest with both hands.

"I'm going on holiday."

Hartley raised his eyebrows in genuine amazement. "A holiday, Topps? You? You haven't taken a holiday in all the years I've known you, despite my begging you to do so."

"Aye, but I'm taking one now."

Hartley peered closely at the man; his eyes seemed a little glazed. "Is everything all right, Topps?"

"It's just a little holiday. Don't know how long for. My cousin will stand in."

"Your cousin?" Hartley was having trouble processing this conversation. It was not only astonishing that the handyman was going away, but also that he already had a replacement lined up. "Don't you think I ought to meet him first? I mean, what is his name? And does he have credentials, testimonials?"

Topps' expression didn't change, and he spoke as if he was half asleep. "I will introduce you after the funeral, Reverend. His name's Uri, and there's no need to worry about his credentials, I can vouch for him right enough. He'll stay in my cottage and he'll do all my jobs just as fine as I would."

"Right, right." Hartley's mind continued to race. These were probably the longest sentences Topps had ever uttered, but Hartley knew from experience that he'd get no answers to his questions. And if he was going to be away for some time, a stand-in would certainly be needed and Topps had saved him the trouble of finding someone. "So when will you be going? And where, if you don't mind me asking?"

"I'll be going today, if you please, to my sister's in Cornwall. After I've seen to Jack's grave, of course. My cousin is already here."

He turned on his heel and Hartley could only watch, perplexed and worried that something was amiss, as Topps pulled his boots back on and stomped outside. He certainly didn't seem like a man going on a jolly holiday, and this was the first time Topps had ever mentioned having a sister. In fact, now he came to think of it, Topps had never mentioned any member of his family.

But moments after Topps left the church, a crowd of people came flowing in, pushing all thoughts of the taciturn handyman out of Hartley's mind. Soon every pew was packed, about five times more people than attended regular services these days. Hartley was not surprised, as the late Jack Heavysides had lived all his long life in the village, and had once been the jovial proprietor of The Blacksmith's Anvil. If only, Hartley thought, he got as many regulars in his church as The Blacksmith's Anvil did, he would be a very happy vicar indeed.

He couldn't help but smile as he waited for the colourful congregation to settle. Everything had been arranged according to Jack's own wishes, which had been written in heavy black biro on pale green beer mats and thrown carelessly into the top drawer of his kitchen dresser. One mat stated that everyone was to dress in their loudest, most colourful clothes, another listed the hymns he wanted, a third gave instruction that every person who attended his funeral be given a pint of ale at the wake, which was, of course, to be held in The Blacksmith's Anvil.

The slow crunch of car tyres on gravel heralded the arrival of the hearse, and the congregation fell into a respectful silence. Heads turned as the coffin was carried in on the shoulders of four burly, grey-suited, top-hatted undertakers. When it was settled on the bier the four men bowed their heads before respectfully withdrawing back outside.

Hartley welcomed everyone and announced the first hymn, "We begin with 'All Things Bright and Beautiful'. Please turn to page 138 in your hymn books."

There was a loud rustle as pages were hastily turned. A quietly weeping Olive Capsby played the opening notes on the organ, then tremulous voices began to sing, quietly at first but soon growing louder until the church was filled to the rafters with glorious sound.

The regular worshippers were dotted among the rest of the mourners, and Hartley sought them out one by one, thinking how he had seen more than a few of the village's inhabitants through from christening to wedding with a funeral or two in between.

The hymn came to a shaky end, with Olive keeping her fingers on the keys a beat too long so Hartley had to repeat the opening words of his carefully prepared sermon.

As he spoke, he gave a gentle smile to Carmen, Jack's daughter, resplendent and elegant in a fuchsia-pink dress with a dainty matching hat, its little spotted veil covering the top half of her face. Her lipstick was the same colour and Hartley couldn't help but think of a stick of Brighton rock. Carmen was a sincere and devout worshipper who never missed a service, and, what's more, arranged the weekly cleaning and took care of the flower arrangements. He would miss her when she and her husband left the village to join their son in Australia, leaving The Blacksmith's Anvil in the care of their only daughter, Cynthia.

Cynthia sat pale-faced beside her mother in a sleeveless dress of emerald-green and sea-blue swirls with a necklace of large green and gold beads and matching earrings like chandeliers. In her thirties, she had never shown any signs of leaving home, and certainly wouldn't go anywhere now that she had charge of The Anvil. Hartley knew that the villagers had some misgivings about this, though, because they loved their traditional pub and Cynthia seemed determined to 'Introduce New Things'.

In the pew behind Jack Heavysides' immediate family sat the very unpopular Violet Cattermole, a woman who had never been heard to say a good word about anyone. She had plenty of money, but she was mean with it, and wouldn't even pay for a set of dentures that fitted her mouth. When she spoke her false teeth clattered like Scrabble tiles in a cloth bag. She was glowering at Carmen's back, who she had more than once inferred had trapped her husband into marrying her. Sour as she was, though, Violet had perhaps the finest singing voice in the village.

He searched the sea of faces for Hilda Merryvale, Violet's kind and gentle younger sister – the very opposite of Violet in every way imaginable – and found her several rows back. She was gazing up at Hartley with her big friendly smile, which he acknowledged with a gentle incline of his head. Whenever he read a sermon he would see her lips moving as she repeated his words a split second after he'd uttered them. Hartley was flattered to know it was because she simply relished every word. She loved all the hymns too, and sang them loudly and jubilantly, having no need to glance at her hymn book for she knew them all. Unfortunately, she was tone deaf.

Behind Hilda sat the Fordingbridge family. Freddie, the son, was a very clever, ever cheerful, extremely polite, skinny, spotty, twenty-one-year-old who looked more like a young teenager. He had an amazing memory, never forgetting anything he saw or read. Ask Freddie what day of the week a certain date was and Freddie would tell you without hesitation. His dream was to become a television celebrity, so he applied for all the game shows on all the channels. While he waited for the call that he was certain would one day come, he worked stacking shelves in the out of town supermarket.

Hartley's eyes continued to roam, and he was pleased to see his lovely niece, Lorelei Dove, smiling back at him. Despite the family connection, Lorelei was not, sadly, one of his flock. Indeed, he would classify her as a bit of a New-Ager, and they often had fierce debates about their respective beliefs. But Hartley forgave her for her quirks because she was a wonderful human being. The only thing he wished for her was that she would meet and fall in love with a decent man. Her last two romances had been short-lived and disastrous and she'd been left utterly broken-hearted both times.

Next to Lorelei sat Glen Perkins, owner of the bakery and café, resplendent in an orange and sky-blue Hawaiian shirt. His wife Gwen was gripping the hand of their pretty, very shapely, eighteen-year-old daughter, Debbie. Debbie, it was known by all except her parents, had a crush on Freddie.

It was time for Hartley to call Jack's best friend, big-hearted Arnold Capsby, husband of Olive and owner of the Post Office and General Store, to come up and deliver his eulogy. He'd been sobbing uncontrollably into a large white handkerchief from the time he'd entered the church, and now he stumbled to his feet and staggered forward like a man going to the gallows. Olive rose from her seat at the organ to stand behind him, her hand rubbing his back, whispering that he could do this. But Jack couldn't do it. For twenty minutes he howled, hiccupped, snivelled and stuttered in a manner that made it impossible for anyone to understand a thing he said. By the time he'd finished, the whole congregation was sobbing along with him, except for Violet. Violet was finding it hilarious.

When Arnold finished with "J-J-Jack was m-my best frieeeeeeeeeeeeeeeeeeend," the last word ending in an anguished wail that seemed to echo round the stone walls, Olive led Arnold back and sat him down, providing him with a fresh handkerchief, before she returned to her place at the organ to play for the last hymn, 'Angels From the Realms of Glory'.

It seemed odd to be singing a Christmas hymn at a funeral and in the middle of one of the hottest summers on record, but it must have been one of Jack's favourites because it was listed on the beer mat. It was certainly one of Hartley's favourites, but most of the members of the congregation were now too choked up to sing it well, so he belted out the words in his fine baritone to encourage them. Carmen gave him a grateful, if watery, smile.

At last, the service was over, and the four undertakers in top hats, their grey suits making them look like pigeons in a crowd of peacocks, reappeared to heft the coffin onto their shoulders and carry Jack out to his final resting place.

Hartley spotted Topps over by the yew tree, well away from the grave, leaning on his spade and staring, slack-mouthed, into space. Beside him stood a tall, well-built man, wearing round, blue-lensed glasses and dressed like a model in a field sports magazine. Seeing Hartley looking at him, Topps' cousin Uri raised a finger to the brim of his flat cap.

Chapter 5
a new client

It was Friday afternoon and Nigel and Amelia sat side by side at the pine kitchen table, a replacement for the desk that had been taken during the last bailiff's visit. No new business had come in for either of them and they were wiling away the too-quiet hours with *The Daily Telegraph* cryptic crossword.

"Thirteen-across", said Amelia. "'Certainly, I start to notice every innermost thought'. Three words, two, three and ten letters."

"What letters have we got?"

"First word is something-N, so it could only be 'in', 'an' or 'on'. Second word A-something-something. Then in the third word we have C-something-N-something-C-then four blanks and it ends with an E."

Nigel scribbled this down on a scrap of paper, saying, "What's the clue again?"

Amelia repeated it and he gnawed the end of his already-chewed biro as he pondered.

"Got it!" He was triumphant, as it was usually Amelia who got cryptic clues more quickly than he did. She was better at general knowledge, too, he had to admit. "It's 'In all conscience'."

"Oh yes, so it is. Right, let's try three-down as we have a few letters for that. Er… are you okay?"

Nigel had jumped up, rubbing his shirt-sleeved arms. "Did it suddenly get really cold in here? It's not the first time and I've got chills all over."

"I don't feel anything. Someone stepping on your grave perhaps?"

Nigel frowned with distaste as he sat back down. "I've never understood that expression. How can someone step on your grave when you're still alive?"

Laughing, Amelia said, "Aha, dear husband, I know the answer to that one! It's an expression from the Middle Ages, meaning that someone has stepped on where your grave is going to be. Rather morbid, but there you go."

They both froze at the sound of the outer door opening and closing, then they exchanged wide-eyed, hopeful glances as Amelia rose and went to see who had come in.

She entered the tiny reception area as if she had all the time in the world, and was back in a few seconds, quietly announcing that a gentleman had arrived for his 11:30 appointment with Private Investigator Nigel. Her puzzled expression matched Nigel's, for he was not expecting any appointments today. Or any day in the foreseeable future.

As he riffled through the diary, fully expecting that day's page to be blank, he muttered quietly so only Amelia could hear, "But I don't have an appoi… Oh, wait. There is something…" He turned the diary towards Amelia. "You didn't put that in there, did you? How mysterious! Well, you'd better show him in."

Amelia whispered that she would make drinks and then go out so the client could have a private meeting with Nigel. Squaring her shoulders and widening her mouth into her warm, professional smile, she returned to the visitor.

Nigel heard her say brightly, "Please do go in. Can I get you a drink of anything? Tea, coffee, or would you prefer something cold, as it's so hot today?"

Whoever she was talking to murmured a reply that Nigel couldn't make out. He just had time to do up the top button of his shirt, tighten the knot of his tie and shrug on his navy-blue jacket, which almost but did not quite match his trousers, before the visitor strode in. Tall and imposing, oozing confidence and authority, his presence filled the room.

Behind him Amelia made wide eyes and a shrugging motion, miming that she had no idea who this man was.

Nigel swept his eyes over the stranger, easily recognising sharp dressing when he saw it. He'd worn couture clothes himself not so long ago. But he could tell that the garments this man wore were in another league entirely, and Nigel's teeth ached just at being in such close proximity. He longed to know the identity of the man's tailor, clearly a genius with cloth and cut. And, surely, only a master craftsman with a lifelong love and deep understanding of leather could have made those highly polished, soft-as-butter shoes, not to mention the fine burgundy leather briefcase?

He thought with a sharp pang about the bespoke suits and shoes he'd once owned. All of them, as well as his cashmere sweaters, silk ties and handmade shirts, had been cruelly and horribly vandalised by his ex-wife with bleach and scarlet nail polish, slashed to ribbons and left in a tragic pile on the thick cream carpet of his walk-in wardrobe. He'd had to recover his shoes, belts and underwear from the ornamental fishpond.

As he rose to greet the visitor, Nigel's nostrils caught the unmistakable scent of Amouage Gold Pour Homme, the same brand of aftershave Tansy had bought him for their first Christmas together. That had ended up in an explosion of lead crystal, aimed, fortunately inaccurately, at his head. The bottle had smashed against the bathroom wall, showering him with bits of broken glass and the potent amber liquid. The glass he'd been able to wash out of his hair, but the Amouage clung onto his skin for days afterwards.

The visitor smiled and spoke in a deep, melodious voice, "Good morning, Mr Hellion-Rees. How do you do?" He clasped Nigel's outstretched hand and shook it, once up and once down, very firmly, but he did not give his name and Nigel's brain churned trying to phrase the words to ask it. After all, what would the man think if he were to admit he had no recollection of this appointment? He'd lose the job before he even knew what it was, and he couldn't afford to lose it. Really, he couldn't. He just had to hope that things would become clear once the meeting was underway.

He beckoned the stranger to be seated on the one decent piece of furniture in the office, and glanced again at the diary. No matter how hard he tried, though, he could not make out the name scribbled there in a bronze-coloured ink, ink he was quite sure had come from none of the cheap office pens.

The visitor sat down and Nigel's eyes caught the gleam of scarlet silk lining as the man undid the buttons of his exquisite jacket. He was wearing a tie of deepest midnight blue, patterned in various shades of deep orange and red that seemed to flicker like flames in an open fire, and Nigel found himself transfixed by the illusion as the man settled himself. It's just a trick of the light, he told himself, trying to concentrate instead on the bright white shirt that would do a washing powder commercial proud. Nigel saw a glint of gold and rubies in the cuffs, and his teeth ached some more.

A deep voice, tinged with amusement, whispered, "Tut, tut, thou art coveting!" Nigel's skin instantly contracted into a thousand goosebumps, just like it had moments before the stranger had arrived, and he shivered and blinked in bewilderment. He had distinctly heard the words, but the visitor's lips hadn't moved.

He was the most strikingly handsome man Nigel had ever seen, and he could well imagine how women would swoon and blush and act all silly when they met him. The stranger, a knowing smirk on his perfect face, stroked his fingernails with his index finger one by one, first the left hand then the right. The nails were short and manicured, buffed to a soft sheen, yet the image of long, pointy talons came unbidden to Nigel's mind and he had to give himself a mental shake. The self-satisfied smirk widened to a disconcerting grin.

Nigel was immensely relieved when Amelia came in with two cups of coffee, for her arrival seemed to break some kind of spell. Nigel watched to see if she simpered at the visitor when she gave him his cup, but all she did was politely ask him to excuse her.

He felt cool grey eyes on him, and their expression made Nigel's scalp tighten and prickle. It was as if the man knew exactly what Nigel had been thinking. As if, indeed, he'd taken the full measure of Nigel Hellion-Rees and found him wanting, in an amusing kind of way. He again desperately tried to remember how this appointment had come about, but all he encountered in his perplexed brain were vacant pockets where the information should be. Maybe, he consoled himself, he was coming down with flu. Or something even nastier.

He pulled a pad towards him and picked up a pen, giving himself some time to gather his scrambled thoughts. He cleared his throat to speak, intending to take the initiative and regain some sense of control, but the potential client beat him to it.

"I am here to hire you to do a job in Wiltshire. We wish to purchase a disused mill there, which you and, I hope, Mrs Hellion-Rees, will renovate and convert to a top-class boutique hotel and restaurant."

For a moment, just a teeny tiny moment, Nigel felt like jumping up and dancing round the room. A construction job! A chance to get back into the work he loved! And interior design for Amelia! But reality hit him with a cold splat and he sputtered, "But, sir, you need an architect, and although I—"

The words dried in his mouth as the man held up his hand, palm towards Nigel, in a gesture of complete authority.

"I haven't finished!" The man paused, visibly reining in his impatience, and continued in a more conversational way, "While you are project-managing the work, you will also be using your PI skills for getting to know the locals – their hobbies and talents, likes and dislikes, their relationships, things like that. Easy enough, I would have thought. However, the first thing we need to do is secure the mill. It belongs to a woman called Violet Cattermole. She doesn't have it on the market, but she'll sell it to us once you put the proposition to her."

"I see," said Nigel slowly, though he didn't see at all. His mind raced, aware of just how much he needed the job, but knowing, too, that he'd have to turn it down. "Sir, this sounds like a job I would truly love to do, but you see there are problems and, for reasons I do not wish to go into, I am unable to take on work of this nature."

The man leaned back and regarded Nigel for a long moment. "Mr Hellion-Rees. Or may I call you Nigel? Good. So, Nigel, let me lay it out for you. You need this job. You were a highly respected and extremely well paid architect and property developer, work you loved and were exceptionally good at. You married the boss's daughter and she gave you the run-around, but would only grant you a divorce if you took the blame. This you graciously did, only to have her daddy fire you from his firm believing that you had mistreated his precious daughter."

Nigel sputtered, "How do you know all this?"

The man ignored the question and went relentlessly on, "Despite agreeing to her terms, your ex-wife vowed that she would make your life an utter misery. Her lawyers proceeded to take you to the cleaners and they continue to make it virtually impossible for you to even make ends meet. And on top of all that, her father used his considerable influence to make sure no other architectural practice or construction firm would take you on. Your wife's business is also detrimentally affected by his influence. How am I doing so far?"

Speechless, he could only stare at the man who seemed to know far too much about his predicament. And he hadn't finished.

"The divorce agreement, if you can call something so blatantly one-sided an *agreement,* ensured that not only were you stripped of practically everything you owned at the time of the divorce, you are now locked in to handing over a percentage of your earnings, or any items of value in lieu of earnings, until your ex-wife remarries."

He tapped the pine table and said, "Do you know that your fine desk is gathering dust in a warehouse? Your leather chair is there too, along with all the other items she has taken instead of money she doesn't need. Your ex-wife is doing this out of sheer spite." He grinned, real amusement twinkling now in his grey eyes. "But, hey, Hell hath no fury and all that."

Nigel felt helpless. His swivelling, reclining leather executive chair had indeed been taken, and his case files were now piled in a corner because they had also robbed him of his filing cabinets. But how did this stranger know all this? Stunned by the conversation, he pinched the bridge of his nose and said, "It's somewhat ironic, but it seems you have had a private detective investigating me?"

"I apologise if I have embarrassed or shocked you, but you must understand that this project is of global importance; we had to be sure we had the right man."

"*Global* importance? Converting a derelict mill into a hotel and restaurant? I don't understand."

"You don't need to understand at this stage, just do as we ask and all will become clear in good time." He sat back in his chair and brushed a non-existent piece of lint from his thigh, then he leaned forward and dropped his voice to a conspiratorial whisper, "And I promise you, you will be very well rewarded."

He named a sum just as Nigel took a sip of coffee to relieve the dryness in his throat. When Nigel, eyes watering, had recovered from his choking fit and mopped up the spilt coffee with tissues, the man repeated it and slid a bulging brown envelope across the desk.

"And to show our good faith, here's a little something to get you started. Hard cash, so you can buy all the equipment you need to draw up the plans for the mill without your ex-wife knowing about it."

Nigel eyed the envelope but didn't touch it. How delightful it would be to go out and buy stuff, but Tansy's henchmen would simply take it all away again when they came the following month and saw it in his office. The thought was unbearable, and he wished for the thousandth time that some other idiot would take her on and so set him free.

"Ah, yes," said the man, clearly and disconcertingly reading his thoughts, "you'll have to keep any new equipment well-hidden, won't you? We'll put our minds to the situation and see what we can do about that."

The way he said it sounded so sinister, Nigel started to object, but he was silenced by the expression in the man's eyes. His mind inexplicably danced with images of carnivorous creatures like wolves and hyenas and vampire bats. Okay, the man had white, even teeth and charming dimples, but there was definitely something a little... *dangerous* about him. The wolves and bats disappeared from his fevered brain, only to be replaced with visions of sinister men in fedoras and heavy overcoats, machine guns hidden in violin cases.

Of one thing he was certain: this was someone you didn't mess with.

The new client took a slim folder from his briefcase and handed it to Nigel. "Everything you need to know is in here." He rose from his seat and buttoned up his jacket. The tie still flickered. He put his hand out to seal the agreement, and said, "So, Nigel, we will sort something out so you can work in complete privacy and then you can apply your finely honed skills to the matter without fear of disruption. We are most confident that you and your lovely wife will do an excellent job." He paused as Nigel didn't speak or move. "I take it you *are* going to do the job?" He held out his hand for Nigel to shake and so seal the deal.

"Good man!" The client's perfect white teeth gleamed. "Here's my card. You will be so kind as to contact me only when you've got something useful to tell me. I shall not expect to hear from you until then."

Nigel nodded and took the thick white card. At last, he would know the man's identity and the name of the outfit he worked for! Nigel would have some clue as to what type of business he was about to get involved in. He glanced down. There was certainly something printed on the card in fancy raised copper-coloured lettering, but, try as he might, he couldn't read it.

When the stranger reached the door, he turned back, his hand resting on the handle, and said, "It was a pleasure meeting you, Nigel. And your charming wife." Then he was out of the office and Nigel could hear his and Amelia's voices as they talked. Amelia must have just returned.

He mulled it over. The building renovation sounded simple enough, and it was, he admitted to himself, something he'd be thrilled to do. And Amelia would certainly jump at the chance to do the interior decor. No, it wasn't the actual job that bothered him. It was the snooping around the people of the village for an unknown reason, and it was also the nature of the man. Something about him was deeply disturbing. Gave him the creeps in fact, though Nigel couldn't articulate why.

Some instinct told him he should have refused the job, but he'd circled the pound sign and the number written after it again and again, and he knew he couldn't possibly let this opportunity slip away. More importantly, he rather thought that this man simply would not accept a refusal. He pictured himself wearing concrete shoes and being thrown over a bridge.

Then an even more horrifying image came to him, of Amelia, gagged and bound to a chair in a dark, damp cellar, held captive until he agreed to do their bidding.

The air in the office felt supercharged, and Nigel felt... *peculiar.*

Had the meeting lasted half an hour or half a day?

His workaday watch, bought at a street market to replace the Patek Philippe the bailiffs had taken some time ago, told him it was 12:05. He felt distinctly tired and even a little sick. The business card was still clutched in his hand, but he couldn't make out the words printed on it no matter how hard he squinted. He held it up to the light, but although he could see what he thought was a series of letters, they seemed to shift and change as he stared, until he could swear that what he was seeing were tiny bugs criss-crossing the card.

He most definitely had the flu.

He jumped when Amelia suddenly came marching in and stood in front of him with her hands on her hips, angrily demanding, "Whatever possessed you to tell that man that I'm pregnant?"

Nigel's mouth moved but nothing came out.

"Before leaving just now he took my hand and congratulated me. He even asked if I knew whether we were having a boy or a girl! How could you, Nigel, we haven't even told Mum and Dad yet?"

"I… I didn't tell him! Honestly, Amelia, I didn't!"

"Then how did he know, huh? How?"

Nigel came round the desk and tried to pull Amelia into his arms. She kept herself stiff and unyielding, but Nigel held her firmly and kissed her cheek. "I didn't tell him, Amelia, I swear I didn't. But he knows an awful lot about me and the situation with Tansy, so maybe… well, I don't have an explanation, but he knows far more than I'm comfortable with."

"Okay, so he has supernatural powers, is that how he had an appointment that we knew nothing about?"

"I really don't know how that happened, either, believe me."

As she opened her mouth to speak, no doubt with more sarcasm, at which she was extremely talented, Nigel showed her the number he'd written on his coffee-stained pad and the envelope stuffed full of ten, twenty and fifty pound notes.

"Amelia, look at this. Whoever they are, they certainly have money to throw around."

"Wow! Well, we really can't turn this down, can we?" Her face softened as she looked at him, and she said, "You're very pale, darling, maybe you should take some aspirin?"

Relieved that the storm was over, Nigel nodded and sat down again. He noticed that the stranger had not touched his coffee, so he downed it himself, hoping another hit of caffeine, albeit tepid, might help him think. Sweetness hit the back of his throat, making him sputter once again. He didn't take sugar, and he reckoned he'd just swallowed a heaped tablespoon.

He slowly swung the typist's chair, salvaged from a roadside skip the day after his executive chair had been taken, and faced the window to gaze through the dirty glass at the wall of the decaying warehouse opposite. The sight of the familiar brick wall was strangely comforting, because somehow, and it was an uncomfortable feeling, Nigel wouldn't have been surprised to find that the view had changed. A spooky mist hovering over Highgate Cemetery maybe, or moonlight glinting eerily above the ruins of Machu Picchu.

Amelia asked him to fill her in about the man who'd just left. "Sexy chap, I must say. So, I ask again, how did he get an appointment without either of us knowing about it?"

"I really don't know. I thought *you'd* made the appointment until I saw the look on your face. I certainly didn't." He turned the diary so she could read it. "Look. That isn't my writing."

Amelia leaned forward. "No," she agreed. "And you know it isn't mine either. I can't even read what it says. Who is he?"

"I've no idea. Didn't he give his name when he came into the office?"

Amelia shook her head. "I know this sounds crazy," she ventured, "but is it possible that someone just walked unnoticed into the office and wrote the appointment in the diary?"

Nigel exhaled noisily, "How could someone possibly manage that? Either you or I are here, or the door is locked. And all it takes to make an appointment is a phone call."

"But there was no phone call," Amelia pointed out. "There's no sign of forced entry or we would have noticed, and neither of us wrote that in the diary. But anyway, putting aside the odd way this came about, and I'm sure there's a reasonable explanation, we have a new client, he's offering pots of money, so what does he want us to do for it? An investigation into a wayward wife?" She laughed, "Though I can't imagine any woman playing around if she had *him* for a husband!"

Nigel scowled and she leaned across his desk with a saucy smile to pat his cheek. "Don't worry, my darling husband, you know I have eyes for no-one else but you." Then the expression in her hazel eyes changed from flirtatious to thoughtful. "Actually," she said, "I felt there was something not quite right about him. Something that made me a little… uneasy."

Nigel was relieved to hear it, as it confirmed his own misgivings, but he didn't want to mention words like *mafia* or some other terrifying criminal organisation to Amelia, although he was sure he was on the right track. He outlined the content of the meeting, showed her the dossier, in which there was no mention of any names, company or otherwise, to tell them who they'd been hired by, and finished by asking, "Are you sure we should take this on? We both think there's something a bit suspect, don't we?"

Amelia nodded, "Hmm, maybe, but, Nigel, we need the money, especially with the baby coming, and they are offering an awful lot of it. I suggest we at least make a start, and see where it takes us. You go to… what's the place called again?"

Nigel searched for it in the documents. "Ham-Under-Lymfold."

"What a pretty name. I wonder if it's as quaint as it sounds. Anyway, I suggest you go there on Monday and get things underway. At least you'll be doing something you love, hmm?" She stood up, then exclaimed, "Oh, Nigel, is that a business card? Why didn't you say he'd given you one?" She held out her hand for it. "Now we can find out about our new client, and if anything looks at all dodgy or dangerous, then we'll have to withdraw."

Everything she said made sense to Nigel, but then Amelia always saw things so clearly. He gave her the card.

"What is this? I can't read what it says!"

"Neither can I. It's just like the writing in the diary, same colour and illegible." He shook his head. "This is really weird, Amelia."

Amelia brought the card close to her eyes then squealed and threw it on the floor. "Ugh! It's like tiny ants are crawling all over it. Oh, wait a minute. I think I *can* read it." She picked it up again and held it at a distance, squinting until her eyes were almost comically crossed. "Yes, it says... 'di Angelo Corporation'. There's more, but I can't make it out."

Nigel winced at the Italian name, thinking again about the possibility that they were dealing with the Mob.

Amelia came round and sat on his lap so she could tap out the name on the computer keyboard. The flimsy chair creaked but held their weight.

The search engine found di Angelo Corporation, and a picture of an ultra-modern building. Its frame was silvery steel, it had acres of mirrored glass, and the tall, thin upward-pointing icicle shape reminded Nigel of The Shard, the London building with an amazing ninety-five floors. But there were marked differences: the building was rounder, the glass appeared to be black, and there was a silvery ring around the building about three quarters of the way up. Nigel was puzzled that he didn't recognise it, because it was the sort of construction that would make the cover of most if not all of the architectural magazines he still read.

"Well, their office is impressive, but this doesn't help us much, does it? There's no menu or anything to tell us anything about them."

"You know, I've just had a crazy thought," Amelia said. "It sounds ridiculous, but do you think it could be something to do with espionage? You know, MI5 or MI6! A top secret mission, and they need us to do this thing as a cover for something?"

Although it was alarming, Nigel liked Amelia's speculation a whole lot better than his own. "It's a possibility, I suppose. It would certainly explain a few things, wouldn't it? Okay, I'll go to Wiltshire on Monday. Let's hope we find some answers there."

Chapter 6

Nigel on the case

Nigel left London very early in the morning so he could get onto the M4 well ahead of rush hour. Dipping into a bag of boiled sweets he'd contentedly driven along, allowing the satnav to guide him. After miles of dual carriageway, he'd made a turn onto a B road, driven through several pretty little villages of mellow stone and mullioned windows, and then taken a spur onto a very narrow, winding, twisting road. Sunlight flickered and strobed through the high hedges, forcing Nigel to blink and screw up his eyes.

At last he saw a dilapidated 'Welcome to Ham-Under-Lymfold' sign, some of the words and the little image of a church above them in need of repainting. He drew the car to a stop alongside the village green. He and Amelia had tried to find some information about the village, but they'd only come across one small paragraph on The Wiltshire Tourist Board website that mentioned a 12th century church, a pub and a café.

It was too early to go to the pub, so Nigel went into Perkins' Bakery & Café, setting a small brass bell tinkling above his head. The young lady behind the counter hastily put whatever she was reading out of sight and sashayed out to greet him. Beaming at Nigel, she adjusted her tight, low-cut leopard-print top and breezed, "Hello I'm Debbie what can I get you?"

Nigel chose to sit by the window, pleased to see the checked tablecloth was fresh and clean, and sat down. "Hello, Debbie. Can I see a menu, please?" He was hungry and rather hoping for a full English breakfast to fill his stomach before beginning his exploration of Ham-Under-Lymfold.

"Oh I'm sorry," said Debbie, taking a pad and pen from her frilled apron pocket, "but there's no point in giving you a menu as we're very limited today 'cos of it being Sunday yesterday and there was a power cut early this morning so my dad only got one batch of bread done." She adjusted her top again, revealing a tiny bit of scalloped black lace. "They're out shopping now and things will be back to normal tomorrow though they're both still sad after the funeral and our microwave's on the blink so I may as well just tell you what I can do."

Nigel could only gape up at her as she reeled off the choices with minimum punctuation, "Sandwich roll tuna ham or cheese or any combination of those white brown or granary bread coffee and walnut cake or Victoria sponge." She paused for a moment, eyes raised to the ceiling, pencil tapping a fast beat on the pad. "Of course you could have a baguette or a toasted sandwich if you'd prefer or a buttered crumpet or teacake because we use the grill thingy for them and that's working okay."

She talked so fast that Nigel, keeping his eyes firmly on her face, had to concentrate hard to follow what she was saying. He was disappointed that he wouldn't be getting much of a meal, but he was hopeful that this young, chatty girl would give him valuable information about the place and its inhabitants. He asked politely, "Funeral?"

"Oh yes old Mr Heavysides he is or rather I should say he was the landlord of The Blacksmith's Anvil then his daughter took over as landlady when he retired and he helped out a bit but he was squashed by a load of old beer barrels because of the great flood." She paused for breath. "The flood was years ago of course and lots of people almost drowned in their beds can you believe it but people said the water got into the wood of the cellar shelves and rotted them over the years until they couldn't hold the weight and poor Mr Heavysides was in the wrong place at the wrong time he was nearly a hundred which is really really old but it was very sad just the same."

Nigel, who'd been holding his own breath in wonder at Debbie's ability to speak so fast and without intonation or pause, gratefully exhaled.

But Debbie wasn't quite finished. "I heard people say that he'd only need a flat coffin on account of being squashed which would save some money but I saw the coffin in the church and it looked normal size to me."

Nigel peered at Debbie's pretty but heavily made-up face to assure himself that it was an attempt at a rather poor joke, but she looked perfectly serious. Either she was extremely good at leg pulling, or she was the type that took everything she heard literally.

She waved her pad. "Have you decided what you'd like to eat?"

Nigel ordered a pot of tea and a tuna mayonnaise sandwich, brown bread, not white. She carefully wrote it down, muttering 'tuna on brown', and bounced away, calling brightly over her shoulder, "It comes with salad and homemade coleslaw it'll just be a tick there are newspapers in the rack by the door if you want one it can be awkward eating by yourself can't it."

Nigel glanced briefly around the clean but rather dull interior of the café. In the far corner was a bakery counter, all the shelves lined with paper but containing just two round loaves and half a dozen baps. He moved his gaze to the window, which was clean on the inside but dusty on the outside, not quite seeing the row of cottages on the other side of the green because his mind was busy. He wished Amelia was with him now, but she was suffering a little from morning sickness and had decided to stay behind in the office, so he was on his own with not much idea of how to go about doing what he'd been hired to do.

Debbie appeared with his food, and he was gratified to see that the plate was piled high with a thickly filled sandwich, and what appeared to be homemade crisps, as well as the promised salad and a glass dish of coleslaw. He could smell that the bread was freshly baked. While Debbie placed the plate, cutlery, teapot, milk jug and cup and saucer in front of him, Nigel asked, "Perhaps you could tell me what places of interest are around here?"

She crossed her arms under her magnificent chest. "Oh well there's not much actually." She gave it some thought. "I suppose the church is nice enough it's very old." She considered some more, her head on one side. "And Merryvale Farm is quite nice too if you can stand the smell of manure you can buy eggs there and manure for your garden and you used to be able to get vegetables too until poor Mr Merryvale had a heart attack and fell into the grain silo took ages for anyone to find him now that was a lovely funeral so I'm told with Bluebell following the coffin right into the church."

Nigel swallowed quickly, almost choking on a chunk of bread, so he could ask the burning question, "Was Bluebell his daughter?"

"No silly!" Debbie laughed and flapped her hand at him, "She was Mr Merryvale's favourite cow. Anyway Mrs Merryvale runs the place now with the help of an old chap who should've retired years ago and sometimes agricultural students from the college they don't stay long though." A breath. "She can't pay them enough and the farmhouse roof leaks and there's no central heating neither and she stopped growing vegetables she's ever so nice is old Mrs Merryvale and I'm sure she must be lonely since her husband died and her sister hasn't had anything to do with her for years and years now." Breath. "Oh and you must go up to the old water mill just drive until you reach the river you can't go any further or you'll be in the water and that wouldn't do your car any good now would it?" Breath. "You can cross the river to the mill there's a stone bridge at the back of the village hall it's a bit of a wreck now but it's still safe enough to walk over and it's a lovely spot for picnics."

Nigel had only stopped himself from bursting out laughing by taking small bites and chewing furiously as he listened to all this. When he had to, he swallowed very carefully, not daring to take a sip of tea to wash it down in case she said something that made him spit it out all over the red and white checked tablecloth. He wished again that Amelia were with him, because she would have enjoyed it enormously.

When the food had been eaten and the pot of tea drunk dry, and the offer of a slice of cake regretfully turned down, he paid the bill and left a generous tip on the table. Debbie called out a cheery goodbye and went back to her magazine.

Fetching his camera from its hiding place under the rear seat of the car, Nigel strolled past a slim-trunked crab apple tree towards a solitary bench at the furthest edge of the green. He sat down so he could take a good look at the place. It was the quintessential little English village, a mix of charming cottages and houses, some thatched, some tiled with grey slate or moss-covered red tiles. A few were rendered white or cream, the rest were yellow and grey stone with dark brown window frames. All very chocolate-box pretty. He knew he needed to get up and walk beyond the green, perhaps visit the church, certainly locate the mill, but the long drive, the warmth of the sun and the weight of the food in his stomach was making him drowsy. He decided to just sit awhile longer and enjoy the peace.

It was probably just a few seconds before a loud snort startled him awake. It was a few seconds more before he remembered where he was and realised that, with his belly full and his face warmed by the sun, he'd dozed off and it was he who was the snorter. He rubbed his face to get himself fully awake and was in the middle of a good, long stretch when he heard a voice with a thick country burr call out, "Digby! You'm come 'ere, boy, and not be botherin' the gen'leman."

A very large, very shaggy dog came from behind him and sniffed around his feet. Nigel put out a hand and the dog sniffed that too before licking his fingers and then dipping his handsome head to rest his chin on Nigel's knee. He scratched the friendly dog's soft ears and caught a surprising waft of lemons coming from its fur.

"So you're called Digby, huh boy?" he said. "Suits you."

An old man, dressed as if for winter and strapped into a hand-painted sandwich board, ambled over and touched his fingers to the peak of his cloth cap in greeting.

"Apologies, sir. Digby likes people, y'see. And mebbe you'm got some food about you?"

Trying not to laugh at the image conjured up by the words painted on the board of Jesus driving an 'ambulunse' to aid those 'run over by the buss of life', Nigel replied, "Er, no, I'm afraid I haven't. Maybe he can smell the tuna sandwich I had a little while ago in the café?"

"Oh aye, mebbe that's it." He narrowed his eyes. "Not seen ye afore, not lost are ye?"

"Not lost, no. Just looking around."

"And why would that be?"

Taken aback by the directness of the question, Nigel wasn't sure how to answer. Two curious pairs of eyes were pinned on his face, the golden, appealing and rather wise ones of the dog and the pale blue, miss-nothing ones of the old man. The odour emanating from the man was eye-wateringly pungent, like raw garlic and onions and something else he didn't want to put a name to. Wanting to bury his nose in Digby's lemony fur, Nigel wondered when was the last time his owner had washed his body or his clothes, and thought it must be like a sauna inside the shabby coat and the wooden boards. After extensive rummaging in his pocket, the man produced a pouch of tobacco and a blackened clay pipe. He pointed the stem at Nigel and said, "Be 'appy to show ye round, for a small consideration, like."

It was a good and useful offer, but Nigel wasn't sure he could stand the various smells that were fighting each other to be the strongest and the most noxious, especially now a far from aromatic smoke from the pipe curled and wafted towards him. On the other hand, though, he needed information quickly, and this might be a good and efficient way of getting it. But what, he wondered, was meant by 'a small consideration'?

As if Nigel had spoken his question out loud, the man gestured to the pub and said, "The price of a pint o' mild over in The Anvil, now, that'd do me just fine." He unstrapped the boards and set them against the back of the bench. Now more of the filthy overcoat was revealed, Nigel saw that most of its buttons were missing, and the belt was no more than a frayed piece of string knotted round the man's middle. The man whipped off his flat cap and bowed from the waist, announcing, "Stanley Hubertus Invincible Trout at your service, sir. Lived 'ere all my life, as did my forefathers goin' many generations back."

"Well, Mr Trout—"

"Stanley, if you please, sir. Now, ye see that there?"

Nigel followed the man's grimy finger to a small, round, stone building on the far edge of the green. He'd noticed it already and wondered what it was. It had a domed roof, a tiny barred glassless window, and a rough wooden door studded with large, rusty nail heads. He reckoned maybe five or six people would be able to squeeze in and stand up inside it.

"That be the Blind. You be seein' the like all over the area, sir."

"Blind? What's it for?"

"Not used any more, sir, and there be some diff'rences of opinion as to their original purpose, but this'n was used fer chuckin' the drunks in to let 'em sleep off the booze and their foul tempers. My grandpappy used to spend a lot of time in there, that 'e did."

Not knowing how he should react to that bit of news, Nigel could only mutter, "Really?"

Stanley chuckled and there was pride in his voice, "Oh, aye. Grandpappy Trout were a ton of trouble." He indicated the centre of the green with a sweep of his arm. "Used to be a duck pond right there. But Grandpappy, now, 'e fell in it one night after a mighty long drinkin' session at The Anvil and bloody-well near drownded 'isself. Most Saturday nights 'e was thrown into the Blind, because my granma didn't want 'im 'ome till 'e was good 'n sober 'cos she said 'e snored like a pig when 'e wus drunk. But on this day, seems 'e left earlier than usual, and nobody noticed. Weren't till next mornin' 'e was found lyin' in the pond, with a bloomin' duck perched on 'is face. Lucky fer 'im he hadn't landed face down or 'e would've been a goner, that 'e would."

Stanley chortled, clearly relishing the telling of the story. "Mind you, everyone said it would've been the perfect way for 'im to go, soakin' drunk and oblivious, like, but the scare made 'im gave up the drink and so 'e lived a good few more years. But 'e still snored like a pig and they filled in the pond anyway so there'd be no chance of someone stumbling in and gettin' drownded, and that there crab apple tree was planted in 'is memory. Only us old-uns remember the pond were ever there. Shall we move on to the church, then, sir?"

Digby lifted his hind leg against Trout's memorial tree then trotted after the two men. Nigel had to walk quickly to keep pace with Stanley and was quite out of breath when they reached the Church of St Peter. Stanley told Nigel to go on in and look around. "Take yer time, sir. Digby and me'll wait out 'ere."

It was comfortably cool inside. The stained glass windows were rather fine, the silver candlesticks on the altar gleamed and tapestry-covered kneelers hung neatly from hooks on the back of the wooden pews. All around the walls were plaques of different shapes and sizes, dedications to village inhabitants who had passed on a hundred years ago or more. The same name appeared a few times, probably, thought Nigel, the members of some old squire's family, for there was bound to be a manor house attached to a village like this.

He strolled over to the church organ and paused to read a beautifully etched brass plaque placed on the wall to the left of the great grey pipes.

THIS ORGAN IS DEDICATED
TO THE MEMORY OF
WALTER SIDNEY HOPKINS
WHO DIED HEREIN AGED 15 YEARS
WHEN AN ORGAN PIPE
DID COME LOOSE AND FALL ON HIS HEADE
GOD REST HIS SOUL

Nigel read it twice to make sure it really said what he thought it said, then photographed it. There had certainly been some extraordinary accidents in this place.

When he re-emerged into the daylight, prepared to breathe through his mouth again when in close proximity to Stanley, he was led around the churchyard. It was impossible to miss the signs of a new grave, and while Stanley whipped off his cap to show his respects, Nigel quickly scanned the cards on the many wreaths that covered the freshly turfed mound. How many of those names, he wondered, would he get to know in the coming months… and for what purpose?

Back out on the road again, Nigel tried to get his bearings. The green was behind them and out of sight, to his left the road continued round a sharp bend, and in the distance ahead of him were steep rolling green hills dotted with black and white cows. The cattle, Stanley informed him, belonged to Merryvale's, a farm which ran in a long strip almost bordering the entire east side of the village. He pointed up at the high and brooding hill that loomed over the place, its surface creased and contorted in places by geological folds.

"That be the Lym, and as you can see, sir, this village bein' at its feet explains where the name Ham-Under-Lymfold come from."

Nigel, aware that time was getting on, nodded and said, "Debbie, the young waitress in the café, she mentioned an old water mill? Is it possible to see it?"

"Oh, aye," chuckled Stanley, refilling and lighting his pipe. "That just 'appens to be where I was a-takin' ye next."

They walked along at a steady pace, following the line of a very high, probably ancient stone wall.

"Is there a manor house behind there?" asked Nigel.

"No, sir, not any more. Burned down years back. Lightnin' strike ye see, and the fire spread so quick the whole darned property was lost. There be nothin' to see nowadays, just a few stones scattered 'ere and there. Used to 'ave magnificent gardens but Hilda Merryvale puts 'er animals in to graze sometimes, so there's nuthin' left o' them no more."

"And the house wasn't rebuilt?"

"No-one left to see to it. Owner was the last of the line, so it passed to some distant cousin twice removed who lives abroad. He ain't never even been to see it, far as I know, and people do say it will never be rebuilt cos o' the curse."

Nigel raised his eyebrows. "Curse?"

"Well now, silly superstition more like, but this place do get hit by lightnin' rather reg'lar. Did ye note them fuel pumps on the way in to the village?"

Nigel remembered them well. Just past the white 'Welcome to Ham-Under-Lymfold' sign, right at the very edge of the road, three old-fashioned petrol pumps stood like old sentinels, rusty and of no use except as a museum exhibit, or something convenient for passing dogs to pee on. Behind them was a wreck of a single-storey brick building with boarded up windows, its roofline jagged and open to the skies.

"Well," Stanley continued, "that be old Malky Blackstock's garage. Struck by lightnin' in 1965. Old Malky got out with nothing but the nightshirt he was wearin' and left the village never to be 'eard of again. Miracle, it was, that Blackstock was a-waitin' a fuel delivery otherwise them pumps would've gone up and taken out half the village, I reckon. Church's been struck a few times, too, but it's got one o' them lightnin' rods, so there's been no harm done. But then, o' course, the earthquakes do loosen the masonry."

"Earthquakes?" squeaked Nigel with disbelief.

Stanley chuckled. "Well, not earthquakes exactly, more like tremors. We get more than a few o' them. There were tremors the night my grandpappy fell into the pond, so seems ter me it weren't just that 'e were too drunk to stop hisself from topplin' in. And they're still 'appening, and it be said that's what did for old Jack Heavysides at The Anvil too."

Unable to credit that this little village really suffered from regular lightning strikes, floods and earthquakes, Nigel said, "But Debbie told me that the shelving had been affected by a flood?"

"Oh aye, there's truth in that, 'cos fer sure the racks would've been weakened by the water. But I think it were the tremors that caused the whole darned thing to collapse."

Having nothing to say to that extraordinary story, Nigel walked on, his eyes on Digby who was now trotting well ahead of them, stopping here and there to investigate a smell of particular interest in the grass verge and then pee on it. But Stanley wasn't quite finished with the lightning stories yet.

"And all them thatched cottages along the green? Can't tell you 'ow many fires we've 'ad along there. Seems to me that them things are to blame for what's become of this village."

"What do you mean?"

"Oh, well now. Used to be so much goin' on all the time: events on the green and craft fairs in the village hall. The hall was also used as a nursery, but now there aren't enough little'uns, and they 'ave to go along all the way to Monkton Ridge. The church 'ad a wonderful choir, my great aunt ran the Women's Institute, there was a Book Club, a Writin' Group." Stanley sucked on his pipe. "All gone now. Oh aye, it were plenty different. But then, if you ask me, the floods, the fires, the tremors, talk of a curse, all that put the wind up people and so whole families upped and left and the life got sucked out of the place." Stanley shook his head in sorrow.

When the wall took a sharp turn to the left, Stanley led them on until the road ended in a car park in front of the village hall. Even as they approached, Nigel could see that the hall was in a neglected state. It wasn't falling down, far from it, but the peeling paint, weeds and uncut grass to the sides gave it an air of disuse, which was a shame because it was a charming building. He walked around it, noting with his architect's eye the fine arched windows and the attractive red and cream brickwork, then he studied the surroundings.

He could see that unwary tourists who entered the village in the hope of finding *Ye Olde Tea Shoppe* or some such, would quickly find they had come to a dead end and had no choice but to turn around here. Not to do so, as Debbie had so eloquently explained, meant ending up in the fast-flowing river.

"This be called the Turnaround," explained Stanley. He pointed his now empty pipe at the building on the opposite bank. "And that there be Angel Falls Mill, so called 'cos of the waterfall there."

Nigel watched Digby lope over the narrow stone bridge that linked the two riverbanks. The dog disappeared inside the old and long-disused building, the very building that Nigel had been sent to purchase.

The mill had more holes than tiles in its roof and nature had all but taken over its interior, but Nigel fell instantly in love with it. As he photographed the old building, noting that the waterwheel still looked pretty sound, plans for its renovation and eventual resurrection as a boutique hotel and restaurant set his mind spinning with possibilities. He could hardly believe that he'd landed the job of buying and restoring it, and Amelia would oversee the interior decor! But he told himself he mustn't jump ahead, he had yet to make the purchase, and there was a long way to go before he'd have the joy of drawing up plans and hiring builders and other tradesmen.

He knew from his mysterious client the name of the woman who owned it, but thought it would be imprudent to say so to his sharp-eyed, self-appointed tour guide. Still clicking away with his camera, he said, "Stanley, do you know who owns this?"

"Oh, aye, sir, that be Miss Violet Cattermole."

Nigel didn't miss the disdainful curl in the old man's lip as he said the name, but it didn't dim his excitement.

"Could you tell me where she lives, is she in the village?"

"Aye, she still be 'ere. I'll take you back to the green and show you 'er 'ouse, if you like?"

Hardly able to believe his luck, Nigel grinned and replied, "That would be excellent, Stanley, thank you."

The old man whistled for his dog and the trio retraced their steps to the village green. Stanley strolled over to the bench and swiftly strapped his sandwich boards back on. When they were settled on his shoulders he said, "I'll leave you 'ere, sir, if I may. That there be Miss Cattermole's place, the one with the green door."

Nigel, his mind bent on what Violet Cattermole might have to say to his proposal, put out his hand to offer a friendly shake but remembered in time the unhygienic state of Stanley and hastily shoved both hands in his pockets. "I'm so glad we met, and I'm sure we will meet again as I'm certain to be back again soon."

The old man, making no move to bid Nigel farewell and walk away, pursed his lips and fixed his beady eyes on Nigel's face. Digby daintily stepped forward and pushed his long nose into Nigel's leg, as if reminding Nigel of something important.

"Oh! Oh, I do apologise, my mind was... well, sorry..." Nigel pulled out his wallet, not sure how much to give his guide. He had very little change and only £10 and £20 notes, so it would have to be a tenner. It would go on his expenses, anyway. "This is for that pint of mild, and perhaps you could get a tin of something nice for Digby?"

He leaned down to stroke the dog's ears. The dark coat flecked with grey was far softer than it looked, and the pure black ears were like velvet. Digby gruffled with pleasure as

Nigel scratched, then as if hearing an unspoken word from Stanley, he ran to his master and Nigel watched them amble in the direction of the church.

Chapter 7
the hub of all the gossip

Before going to see if Violet Cattermole was at home Nigel decided a large glass of something cold would be just the thing after his long walk round the village. But when he got to The Blacksmith's Anvil, a fine old building with two bay windows either side of the half-glazed double doors, he was disappointed to find it closed. He read the black-edged sign on the door announcing the pub would re-open the next day, and remembered that the recent funeral had had some connection to the landlord.

It would have been a pleasant place to while away an hour or so before seeing Miss Cattermole, and also a great place to meet a few of the good citizens of Ham-Under-Lymfold, but clearly that would have to wait for another time. In the window were several notices, one of them saying that they had rooms to rent, shared bathroom, meals extra. Nigel made a note of the telephone number then read the printed menu: chicken and chips, ham and chips, pie and chips, sausage and chips, ploughman's lunch with Stilton or Cheddar cheese, chips an optional extra. Such simple fare certainly wouldn't offer any competition to the high class restaurant Nigel envisaged his client would offer at the mill.

With a sigh, Nigel decided not to return to the café and more of Debbie's breathless and unpunctuated speech, so he trudged to Violet's cottage. Maybe she would invite him in and offer him a cup of tea?

It was a handsome cottage, slate-roofed where it must once have been thatched, original diamond-paned windows, oak-timbered, the planes and surfaces of the walls charmingly uneven. Just the sort of cottage Amelia would love, Nigel thought, as he rapped sharply on the dark green door and waited.

And waited.

Deeply disappointed, he glanced around, but there was no-one to ask where Violet might be. He rooted in his pockets for pen and paper to write her a note.

"Would you be looking for Miss Violet Cattermole?"

Startled, for how could someone have appeared so suddenly, Nigel fumbled and dropped his pen. "Er, yes. Yes, I am." He retrieved the pen and smiled sheepishly back at the grinning man in the sharply creased red trousers and plaid shirt who had addressed him. There was something familiar about him, something in his stature and bearing, the curly dark hair and perfect teeth, only Nigel couldn't place it. The eyes were hidden behind blue lenses, but Nigel could tell that the man was amused by something. By him? Gosh, that expression, that feeling, was so familiar, but try as he might, Nigel couldn't remember where he'd seen it before. It was as if the knowledge slid away from his mind before he could grasp it.

"She's most likely in the shop," the man informed him. "It's the hub of all the gossip, so you might want to go and see if she's there rather than wait on her doorstep. I'm going that way myself."

Nigel thought the little village store and Post Office would be a good place to go, not only in the hope of meeting Miss Violet Cattermole, but he could also buy a local newspaper and some sweets for the journey home. He fell into step beside the red-trousered man.

When they entered the shop the woman behind the counter glanced with curiosity at Nigel, then beamed at his companion and cheerily greeted him, "Hello, Uri! How are you?"

Nigel watched Uri stroll to the back of the shop to get whatever he'd come in for, still racking his brain as to why he found him so familiar. It was like a brain-itch he just couldn't scratch.

A poke in the ribs brought his attention back and a gravelly voice rapped out, with strange clicking noises that reminded him of Scrabble tiles in a cloth bag, "You're not from around here. I saw you walking about with that tramp Trout. Where you from, eh?"

Nigel looked a considerable way down onto a black straw hat with a plastic flower of a rather garish lime-green on one side. Beneath the brim two eyes, as small and black as currants, glared up at him. He smiled and gave his rehearsed speech that he was searching the locality for a property to develop, and he'd just seen the old ruined mill.

The woman pursed her thin lips, as if she'd just sucked a lemon. "Is that right?"

Nigel had an uncanny feeling that this was the woman he sought. "You wouldn't be Miss Cattermole by any chance, would you?"

In the face of an implacable stare, much like Stanley's, Nigel waffled on, "Only I was told that the mill belonged to a lady called Violet Cattermole."

"There're some would question that she's a *lady*," the woman cackled. "Interested in the mill, then, are you?"

"Well yes, I'd certainly like to discuss the possibilities."

By now two more women had come into the shop and they and the shop owners behind the counter were listening with interest to this exchange.

"And just what would you do with it?" The old lady rummaged in the large brown bag looped over her elbow and pulled out a wrapped toffee. She removed the paper, popped the sweet into her mouth and started ferociously chewing and sucking on it with a lot of unpleasant noises.

Nigel, fervently hoping this formidable old biddy was not the lady he'd have to do business with, addressed the little group that had formed around him, saying, "Well, as I said, I'm a developer. I've been hired to locate a suitable building for a top-class restaurant with a few luxury bedrooms. I'd need to do some surveys, of course, but from what I've seen so far the mill has lots of potential and is in a magnificent location."

"A restaurant?" the old lady barked, as if he'd said he was going to open a brothel. She swallowed the remains of the toffee, then sucked on the remnants stuck to her front teeth.

"Naturally, it would be sympathetically restored and renovated by local craftsmen. The waterwheel looks as if it could easily be restored to working order. It would offer employment, and bring visitors to the village who might also spend their money in the shops here." Nigel found himself getting excited just talking about it.

A man introducing himself as Arnold Capsby, owner of the store, spoke up, "The café does food, and so does the pub, as well as bed and breakfast. Wouldn't you be taking business away from them?"

"Well, I've eaten in the café and I've seen from the pub menu that it provides good, traditional pub grub, which I'm sure is wonderful, and which many people will continue to want. But the restaurant would offer a very different kind of menu. And the café is closed in the evenings, so there would be no loss of customers to them. There'd be just a few rooms, which would suit tourists who want to visit all the wonderful places around here. After all, Bath isn't very far away, or Salisbury, but there will still be those who'd prefer bed and breakfast in a pub. So, now I've explained, could someone please tell where I might find the owner of the mill?"

There was a murmur among them all, then Arnold said, "Violet, why don't you introduce yourself and tell this nice gentleman what he needs to know."

Violet planted her feet far apart and folded her arms across her chest in an adversarial posture, which worked very well despite her tiny stature. "I am indeed Violet Cattermole, and I own the mill."

Nigel, trying not to feel rattled by her black, rather calculating gaze, bowed his head slightly. "I'm delighted to make your acquaintance, Miss Cattermole."

She said nothing. She didn't even blink.

"Er… right, then. My name is Nigel Hellion-Rees. I have to get back to my office in London now, and I'll need to consult with my client, but perhaps you would be kind enough to give me your number so I can telephone you to discuss things further?"

"Well, you're polite, I'll give you that." Violet turned to the plump woman standing next to Arnold at the counter, "Olive, write down my address and phone number." She did not say please or thank you, that clearly wasn't her way, but Olive did as she was asked. Everyone followed the piece of paper as it was handed to Nigel and stowed in his wallet, then Violet harrumphed and stalked out of the shop. It seemed to Nigel that the atmosphere immediately lifted with her departure. Nigel selected a local newspaper, a bar of chocolate and a small bag of pink and yellow pear drops and took them to the counter. Olive took his money and counted out his change.

"A restaurant?" she said, with a friendly smile. "It would certainly be nice to see that old mill brought back to life, wouldn't it, Arnold?"

Her husband nodded, "Aye that it would." He turned to Nigel. "It's one of the oldest buildings in the village, apart from the church. Violet and her sister were born and raised there. Violet never married, and when Hilda got wed and moved to Merryvale's Farm, it was agreed that Violet should have the mill."

Olive finished the story: "Unfortunately its upkeep was beyond her, and Violet felt isolated on that side of the river, especially when the bridge all but collapsed. Then the mill was so badly damaged in the hurricane of 1987, Violet had to move out, and she bought a cottage in the centre of the village. Since then the mill's been left to nature, sorry to say."

Arnold took up the story. "I don't think she's ever been back there since she moved out. We've all said at one time or another what a shame it is that a piece of history should be allowed to decay like that, but no-one's actually done anything about it. Too expensive, I suppose."

Olive leaned forward on the counter. "And you really think you could make something of it?"

"Oh yes," said Nigel, making a mental note to check out the hurricane and all the other strange disasters that had befallen this little village. "Something wonderful could most definitely be done with it. So I'll be seeing you again, I'm sure."

As he left the shop, someone grabbed the door before Nigel could close it and Uri stepped out into the street close behind him. He was so close Nigel could just about see his eyes through the blue lenses, and knew for certain that the man found something, probably Nigel himself, rather amusing.

"Sounds like you got what you came for?" He stuck his hand out. "Name's Uri. I'm mostly in the employ of the church, but also the general handyman in the village. Gardening, household repairs and such like. So, if you buy the mill I assume we'll be seeing quite a lot of you in future?"

Trying to make out the eyes behind the blue lenses, Nigel couldn't help but notice how soft the man's hand was as he shook it. Glancing down, he also couldn't help but notice the manicured nails, not a speck of dirt on them or ingrained in the cuticles. The clothes, too, looked as if they'd been newly unwrapped from cellophane that morning.

His eyes travelled back up to Uri's face and he realised with a start that he'd let the silence go on a beat too long. "Nigel Hellion-Rees," he stammered. "Architect and property developer. And, um, yes, I'll be here frequently if all goes to plan to er, um, project manage and um, renovations."

Uri grinned and for a microsecond of a second Nigel almost got who Uri reminded him of. But, like a mudslide after heavy rains, it was gone.

"Come, my man," said Uri, laughter in his voice, "I'll accompany you back to your car."

Chapter 8
STARdust

A song from a Vaughan Williams opera began on the radio and Reverend Hartley Cordwell turned the volume control hard to the right. As the music surged into the small vicarage study, filling the room and shaking the old leaded-glass windows, he filled his lungs, opened his chest, and sang along in his rich baritone voice, relishing every word.

He was sitting at his leather-topped bureau, polishing with a soft, damp cloth the coin Topps had found in the churchyard. It was a very fine piece of work, and as he scraped and buffed the grime away he was getting more and more certain and more and more excited that what he held in his hands was gold. The one side he'd already cleaned was exquisitely patterned with a fantastic bird of paradise perched on a branch of a blossom tree, wings outspread, long tail plumed with curling feathers. Now he was working on the other side.

The dirt on this surface was well ingrained, so he had to use his thumbnail loosen it. Eventually the image emerged of another bird… no… not a bird at all, more like a… yes, it was like a pterodactyl, with a horned head and bat-like wings outstretched, ending in sharp talons. Not a pleasant thing, thought Hartley, singing louder as he turned the coin to polish its smooth edge.

But the words abruptly caught in his throat as the coin started to vibrate, sending a startling sensation to swiftly rise from his thumb to his palm then through his whole arm and into his chest. Hartley cried out and the coin fell, bouncing off his desk and onto the floor. Eyes wide and shaking and flexing his still-tingling hand in an effort to get rid of the pins and needles, Hartley followed its progress as it rolled across the floorboards until it came to rest in front of the filing cabinet.

Gingerly, he rose from his chair and walked the three paces to the cabinet. Hands on hips he stared down at the coin, the hideous creature upwards, as still as an inanimate object should be, then he bent down and flicked it with his fingertip. A low humming sound started to emanate from it as soon as Hartley's skin made contact and Radio 3 crackled with static which was painful to the ears. Terrified, Hartley dashed to switch the radio off, hardly daring to take his eyes from the gold piece that now seemed to be talking to itself.

It said:

"Heads, *I* stay," in one voice, and at the exact same time, a different, lighter voice said, "Tails, *I* stay."

There was a long silence, then a gentle tinkling sound followed by a short silence. The first voice peevishly exclaimed, "Damn and blast!"

Hartley stood with his finger still pressed on the off button of the radio. After a few seconds of silence, he carefully lifted his hand and cocked his head. Nothing. He looked around the room, but all was as it had been before.

Before what, exactly?

He lowered himself onto the chair, all the while staring at the golden disc. It lay on the carpet like a… well, like it was an ordinary coin that had fallen from a pocket, not at all like something that hummed and talked and *hurt* when you touched it.

It clearly was not a valuable artefact, like he had hoped, but a modern and sophisticated device. Some kind of electronic toy perhaps. Yes, that made sense. A toy that when you played with it vibrated and hummed and said 'heads' and 'tails'.

Remarkable technology, really.

Disappointed that it wasn't gold and probably worth very little, he bent to pick it up again. It scorched his fingertips and he snatched his hand back in pain and fright.

The coin started to vibrate again.

Fascinated and wondering what else it could do, Hartley waited to see what would happen next. A continuation of the heads and tails game perhaps?

But the coin seemed to grow bigger and bigger and blacker and blacker, until the... the... *creature* burst from it with an ear-splitting screech, making Hartley yelp in terror and throw his arms over his head in protection.

Like a cat-sized, horn-headed bat it flew around the room, coming so close to Hartley that he felt the breeze from its flapping leathery wings ruffle his hair. Heart pounding, he grabbed the edge of his desk to keep himself from fainting.

At that moment the telephone rang. The noise seemed to distract the creature, and it flew down towards the coin. Hartley watched, frozen now with fear and disbelief, as the creature was sucked back into the coin, feet first, razored beak last.

He let the telephone go through to the answering machine.

For a long moment he stared at the coin, toy, whatever it was, almost daring it to activate again, and then someone pounded the knocker on the front door.

Hartley's first thought was how he was going to get past the coin to go and answer it. His second thought was to wonder if he was going mad.

Another knock, louder and longer, galvanised him into action. He scooped his leather-bound Bible from the desk drawer and, holding it up in his right hand, he swept the coin up with his left hand and tossed it clear across the room and into the open door of the safe. Any other day he would have missed at such a distance, but he was too terrified to congratulate himself on such an accurate throw.

Two men stood on his doorstep, one fat, one thin, wearing blue sweatshirts that carried a gas company logo. The thin man thrust a laminated identity card in front of Hartley's face.

"Sorry to bother you, sir, but can you confirm that you are Reverend Cordwell and your boiler was recently serviced?"

"Yes, indeed. Is something wrong?"

"I'm afraid, sir, that we've been informed by the manufacturer that a faulty part may have been used. We need to check it out and, if necessary, change it. No charge, of course."

The thin man put his foot on the threshold. "I'm sure you don't need telling, sir, that gas boiler faults can be deadly."

Hartley let them in, showing them into the kitchen. "The boiler's behind that cupboard door. Would you both like a cup of tea?"

The thin man started to say no, but the fat one intervened. "That would be very nice, sir, thank you. Milk and two sugars for us both."

Hartley set about making a pot of tea, while the thin man removed the cover from his boiler. He hummed and ha-ed for a bit, then said, "Yep, you've got one of the faulty valves all right."

The fat man announced he needed to fetch the replacement part from the van, excused himself, and left the room.

"Well, that's a relief, I must say," said Hartley, pouring out the tea. "It's very good that such a thing can be put right so quickly."

"Oh, there's no time to waste when it comes to gas, sir."

His colleague returned and the two men set to work. Hartley's telephone rang, and although there was a handset in the kitchen, he didn't want to take the call there in case it was a private parish matter. He hurried to his study to take it there.

He paused when he saw that the safe was slightly open, for he was certain that he'd closed it. His scalp prickled and, feeling shocked to the core yet again, Hartley spun round to find the two men coming slowly into the study, looking like menacing burglars now instead of cheerful boiler repairmen. He exclaimed, "You're not from the gas company!" He hesitated and then slapped himself on the forehead as he exclaimed, "I don't even have gas! That's an electric boiler. Who are you? How dare you—"

The thin man darted forward and grabbed Hartley, pinning his arms to his sides. He demanded of his colleague in an urgent whisper, "How could you be so careless?"

The fat man, clearly rattled, whispered back, "I wasn't! The safe mustn't have locked properly."

"The Boss is going to be furious. We'll have to use the Dust, it's the only way to salvage the situation. Quickly."

The telephone stopped ringing at last, and Hartley's answering machine clicked on.

The fat man, looking extremely unhappy now, sprinkled something resembling a shiny blue salt shaker onto a large white handkerchief. When the cloth was clamped over Hartley's nose and mouth, he was forced to inhale a sweet smell he couldn't put a name to and the last thing he heard before everything went black was, "I'm so sorry about this, sir, but it's only STARdust. It creates an alternative reality and is really quite harmless in small doses. You'll wake up and not remember that any of this happened."

~~~

Hartley sat up in bed and opened his eyes to utter darkness. His bedside clock glowed 3 am.

He had a dull headache and a strange, perfumey smell in his nostrils. He sneezed twice. Then again. He had no memory of going to bed. Or of having any dinner before going to bed. He searched his memory and was dismayed not to be able to remember much about the previous day at all. There were fragments, vague foggy images, of what he had done, who he had spoken to, but nothing concrete.
~~~

He fought it, but sleep took him back into oblivion. When he woke up again at his usual time of 6:30, he leapt out of bed, hungry and full of vitality, his earlier confusion forgotten.

After a hearty cooked breakfast, his plate wiped clean of egg yolk and ketchup with a hunk of bread and put into the sink to wash later, Hartley settled down in his study to work. There was one message on his answering machine from yesterday afternoon, which surprised him as he'd been home so how could he have missed it, but it wasn't of great importance.

Once the minor matter had been dealt with, Hartley switched on the radio, and set about cleaning the coin that Topps had found with a soft, damp cloth. The grime came off easily and as he buffed away he became more and more certain and more and more excited that the coin was gold. He fetched his *Antique & Collectible Coins and Medals* from the bookshelf and flipped through it until he spotted a picture that very much resembled the coin in his hand, a florin from the reign of Edward III. It was exceptionally rare, he read, and could be worth a lot of money. He could barely breathe with excitement, thinking what he could do for the church with the windfall the coin might bring.

He heard the back door open and close, followed by footsteps on the tiled kitchen floor. He smiled at the sounds of his washing-up being done and then the kettle being filled at the tap, then moments later Lorelei popped her pretty head round the door.

"Hello, Uncle. Kettle's on and I've brought some scones and clotted cream."

"Wonderful," answered Hartley. "I'll be right there." He put the coin back in the safe.

By the time he entered the kitchen, Lorelei had placed a pot of tea, jug of milk, plates, knives and spoons on the table with the scones, and was pulling off the lid of the cream carton.

"Lorelei—"

"Have you got any jam, Uncle?"

"Um, no, only marmalade, I'm afraid. Look, Lorelei, there's somethi—"

"Oh, marmalade's no good. Let me have a look in the fridge." Lorelei crossed the kitchen to the huge, ultra-modern American-style fridge, so out of place in the old-fashioned kitchen with its mismatched drawers and cabinets. She moved a few jars about, muttering, "Ploughman's relish... pesto... tomato purée... mustard... ah, this'll do!" She pulled out a jar of cranberry sauce and peered at the label. "This isn't from last Christmas, is it?"

He decided he'd have to wait until she was less distracted to tell her about the coin. "No, no, it's quite fresh. I like it with ham."

"Ah, well, it's sweet so I can't see why it won't go with scones. Tuck in, Uncle, I'll pour the tea."

Hartley took a scone. He didn't think he'd have an appetite after the sausage, eggs and bacon he'd had, but found he was ravenous and devoured one of the scones in short order. He drank some tea, then reached for another scone and liberally coated it with cream and a spoonful of cranberry sauce. "I must say, this makes an excellent substitute for strawberry jam."

Lorelei was still nibbling at her first scone. She was always popping round with cakes and goodies, but she barely ate any of them herself. Lorelei interrupted his thoughts as she said, "Something's up, Uncle, I can see it in your aura."

"My aura? Oh, Lorelei, really!" Hartley frowned as he always did at Lorelei's New Age notions.

"Well it's true! I *can* see auras, you know." She narrowed her eyes and traced the outline of his head. "And yours is most definitely excited. I'm right, aren't I?"

He grinned. "As it happens, I am rather excited about something. But you don't need to see auras to know that, Lorelei, I've been trying to tell you since I came in here."

She laughed. "Sorry, Uncle, you have my full attention now. Tell me what it is that has your aura glowing so brightly."

She fixed him with her beautiful green eyes, and Hartley decided not to get into one of their debates. They had opposing ideas, and sometimes it was easier to each let the other believe what they believed. "I think the coin that Topps dug up may be gold, and very valuable if my book is anything to go by."

"Oh, that's wonderful! I do hope you're right, Uncle, you'd have some money for church repairs and it would please Topps no end that he's found something of value after all these years."

Hartley replied, "Oh, yes, Topps would be delighted. Well, I *think* he would be, I've never actually seen him display a happy or cheerful emotion. Remember those bits of pottery he found last year? He hovered over me while I cleaned them, and then I found a maker's mark, which clearly said, 'Made in China'. I couldn't help laughing, but he just stomped off in a huff."

Lorelei giggled. "I can just imagine it. Can I see the coin, Uncle?"

"Of course, my dear. Let me fetch it from the safe."

He returned with the coin and the book and handed them to Lorelei, holding his breath as she compared the coin to the photograph he pointed to.

"Gosh, yes, that might be it. A Double Leopard. Oh, it's beautiful, isn't it? Such a shame it's the only coin found, though."

"Topps explored all around the area where he found it in case it turned out to be a hoard of buried treasure, but this was it. The Heritage Centre will be able to tell us what it is and what it's worth. When will you be going into town, could you take it in for me?"

"Thursday afternoon." Her eyes gleamed with humour as she held the coin up to the light and said, "Hey, do you think I'll need an armed guard?"

"Heavens, wouldn't it be wonderful if it were that valuable? We could get something done about the damp in the vestry before we're growing mushrooms in there. Now, how about another cup of tea, is there enough in the pot?"

While Lorelei poured, she asked, "How's the replacement Topps getting on? He seems very friendly, quite unlike our Topps. I saw him outside digging up the rose bed and he called out a cheery hello."

Hartley smiled, "I do rather like him. He plays chess, for a start, and very well at that; I haven't been able to beat him yet. He has his own set, a beautiful thing of all kinds of wood that he said he'd made himself. And he *talks*."

"He certainly sounds the opposite of our taciturn Topps." She sipped her tea. "What's his name again?"

Hartley chuckled. "Uri. Sounds Russian, doesn't it? I've asked him about himself, but he's rather adept at not giving much away, so I don't know where he's from or if he has family other than Topps. He wears these blue-tinted glasses that make it difficult to see his eyes, and that makes a person very hard to read, don't you think, if you can't see their eyes?"

"I'll have a close look at his aura next time I see him, you can't disguise that, Uncle."

Hartley ignored her. "He's very well read. I was talking about Sunday's sermon with him last week, and it turns out he knows as much about the Bible as I do. And he has some fascinating ideas on all sorts of subjects: history, science, art. I must say, though I probably shouldn't as it's not very charitable, I'll miss him when Topps comes back from his holiday."

"I'm glad it's worked out, then; I know you were worried about losing Topps even for a short while because he does work hard." Lorelei glanced at her watch. "Oh no, look at the time! I really must be going. I've got someone coming about a pet portrait, a golden retriever this time, which will be lovely after that African rock python. And I want to get to the shops first."

"Righto, just let me wrap the coin up for you. Mind you keep it safe, now, it could be worth a lot of money."

Lorelei looked affronted and Hartley apologised.

She kissed him on the cheek, and he watched her while she walked the short distance to her cottage by the green.

Hartley's attention was then caught by the arrival of dozens of colourful and noisy birds landing on the beautiful feeders that Uri had made. He'd told Hartley that woodwork was his hobby, and, if the vicar didn't mind, he'd like to equip the old workshop behind Topps' cottage so he could work there. Having seen the bird-feeders and also the garden bench fashioned from a single piece of burr oak, Hartley had had no hesitation in agreeing.

Uri was still outside, vigorously digging the borders with a large fork. Birds were cheekily hopping on the newly turned soil, pulling up worms. As if he knew Hartley was looking, he turned his head and touched his forefinger to the flat cap perched on his thatch of black curly hair. For no reason he could discern, Hartley shivered.

Chapter 9
the other one

"All done, sir. We'll be off now."

Bemused, Nigel watched the team of workmen troop out of his office. They had been sent by his still-mysterious client to make a space where he could work on the mill project in total secrecy.

The main office looked just the same as before, as the workmen had knocked through into a void behind the wall and created just enough space for Nigel to work in there with the equipment he needed. The dividing wall was now covered by paper patterned with thin, multicoloured vertical stripes that made his eyes water. Stuck up with drawing pins at each corner was a poster of a Caribbean beach scene, its cerulean blue sky and saffron sand clashing with the stripes behind. Nigel tentatively touched a small white seashell at the bottom left-hand corner of the poster, and a door slid soundlessly open.

Lights automatically flickered on as Nigel stepped in and looked around his secret room with a mixture of wonder and disbelief. He ran his fingers over the top of the large monitor of his new computer, excited to know that the very latest software had been installed. In the corner was a state of the art printer atop a low, steel filing cabinet suitable for storing large plans and blueprints. With all this in the tiny area, there was barely enough room for Nigel to squeeze in and sit down at the desk, but he loved it all the same. And it was blessedly cool.

Amelia hadn't seen the secret room yet, but any moment she'd arrive with a bag of fresh, warm croissants and a carton of fresh milk for their morning coffee. Nigel stepped back into the main office and closed the door with another touch of the seashell.

When Amelia breezed in, her cheeks rosy from her walk in the sunshine, it wasn't only milk she carried, for she had bought a glossy magazine. Nigel saw it was called *Haut Monde*. Curious, he remarked, "That's not the kind of thing you usually read."

"I saw it on the newsstand and just had to buy it. Look at the centre pages!"

Before opening it, Nigel glanced at the front cover to see what had caught Amelia's eye. His ex-wife stared out at him from a colour photograph, beneath which, in bold, white type, was the line, *Inside Exclusive: Tansy Hellion-Rees, daughter of construction magnate Hugh Wutherington-Parker, explains why she is happy to be alone again.*'

"Not good news for us, is it?" said Amelia. "This must be the third millionaire Tansy's driven away."

Nigel sighed as he opened the magazine. "I'm beginning to wonder if we'll ever be able to get her out of our lives."

Resisting the urge to scribble a bushy moustache and round spectacles on Tansy's surgery-perfect face, he quickly scanned the article. The accompanying photograph showed her sitting on a huge dark green sofa, two glossy black Labradors at her feet. Nigel recognised the room as the largest and grandest of the four reception rooms in her father's glorious country retreat.

In fact, Tansy was sitting on the very settee where he had sat, waiting to ask her father for her hand in marriage. He found it hard to believe now that he had been so bewitched by her and unable to believe his luck that such a beautiful woman was his. If only he'd known what a cold and deceitful heart lay beneath that alluring exterior! But of course he'd no inkling, he'd thought she was the perfect woman, and he'd downed two large tumblers of whisky in quick succession for courage. His boss, soon to be his father-in-law, had laughed at Nigel's slurred speech as he'd stammered how very much he loved Tansy and wanted to marry her.

Consent had been given followed by a hearty slap on the back and the promise of a hefty pay rise, but, shortly after the wedding, it had all gone horribly wrong and Nigel had very quickly begun to wish that Tansy's father had marched him off the premises for being a drunk not worthy of his daughter. Tansy morphed practically overnight from a sweet, adoring and adorable woman into a demanding and unreasonable harpy. Too late, Nigel had discovered just how she operated. He was but one of many men to have their fingers burned by her, but he was the only one foolish enough to have married her.

Thoroughly fed up at the unhappy memories, he threw the magazine in the waste bin. "Oh, let's forget about her! Come and see this."

Amelia gasped as he opened the secret door. Peering inside, she looked around and said, "This whole thing is amazing. I would never have guessed there was so much space behind this wall. And it's so lovely and cool." She stepped back and touched the seashell to close the space. "It's all very peculiar though and, I think, rather scary. Who *are* these people, Nigel?"

He shrugged. "My guess would be something like the British Secret Service, like you suggested, operating in the guise of a business corporation. I hope we're doing the right thing, taking on this job?"

They hadn't heard from the client since his visit, and when Nigel had tried to get information from the workmen while they created this new workspace for him, they'd neatly brushed him off and he'd learned nothing more at all.

The phone rang then and Nigel, who was nearest, pressed the loudspeaker button.

A woman's voice, smooth and soft as warm caramel, purred, "Good morning, Mr Hellion-Rees, this is the di Angelo Corporation calling."

Nigel raised an eyebrow at Amelia, who made a face at him and mouthed, "Spooky!"

"I'm just calling to let you know that a car is on its way to collect you and Mrs Hellion-Rees, sir."

"I— what? I mean, sorry, did you say a car? On its way?"

"Yes, sir. To bring you to your meeting here with Mr di Angelo. We will see you soon."

"But we don't have a mee—"

The call was disconnected, leaving them staring at the silent phone in disbelief.

"Can you believe that?" Nigel said to Amelia. "Didn't even bother to ask if it was convenient!"

"Well, darling, maybe we're about to find out at last who we're really dealing with."

The outer door opened and closed and two seconds later a short man in the traditional uniform of a chauffeur appeared in the doorway of the office. Nigel took in the shiny-peaked cap, the navy jacket with its double row of brass buttons and the jodhpur-style trousers tucked into leather black boots and wondered. Unless the di Angelo office was right round the corner, the driver must have been well on his way even before the phone call.

The long, sleek, silver-grey limousine looked terribly out of place in the narrow, litter-strewn street. The driver held the door open for Amelia and then walked round to open the other side for Nigel to climb into the immaculate interior. They were soon underway, gliding smoothly into the busy London traffic. Nigel glanced at his watch and murmured to Amelia that he wondered where they were going.

The soft leather seat seemed to wrap itself round him like a comfy armchair, bringing back memories of the days he'd sometimes been chauffeured around by his mega-rich clients. The windows were darkened so the passengers could see out, but yet were hidden from curious eyes. Nigel recognised that they were driving slowly in heavy traffic along Bond Street, then New Bond Street with Tiffany's, Cartier, Chanel. They turned into Conduit Street, and there, on the right, was Savile Row. He'd once thought nothing of spending a day in these streets, spending money he'd worked so hard to earn, though mostly on Tansy rather than himself. The thought depressed him, so he sat back and closed his eyes.

He jerked awake when he felt that the limousine was going down a steep incline, and noticed that Amelia was just waking from sleep too. How long had they been out of it? He looked out of the window and saw that they were driving down a ramp to an underground parking garage, which he assumed was beneath the icicle-like building of the website.

He grabbed his briefcase and stepped out of the car. The garage, low ceilinged and dimly lit, was vast, but this was the only vehicle in it.

"If you take the elevator over there, sir, madam, the operator will take you to Reception."

Nigel and Amelia did as they were told, and were soon wondering which of the two stunningly beautiful receptionists and one extremely handsome man they should approach. But the man had already noticed them and greeted them with a wide smile.

"Mr and Mrs Hellion-Rees, welcome to the di Angelo Corporation. If you would be good enough to take a seat over there, someone will come and take you to the meeting shortly."

Nigel followed Amelia to one of the large red settees that were placed in clusters around the airy space, sat down and looked around with his architect's eye. The reception area was as clean as an operating theatre, all gleaming white marble and travertine, with steel fixtures and fittings. The ceiling soared above him, criss-crossed with heavy steel beams held together by giant bolts. Spiralling light wells ensured the ultra-modern, ultra-smooth, ultra-expensive space was well lit and ventilated, and he loved it.

Expecting to have to wait a little while, Nigel looked over Amelia's shoulder at a magazine she'd picked up, but he'd barely had time to register the title of the publication when a polite 'Ahem' alerted him to a man in a well-cut suit and very shiny shoes standing in front of him.

"Good morning, Mr Hellion-Rees, Mrs Hellion-Rees. Would you please allow me to take you to Mr di Angelo's office?"

Right, thought Nigel, helping Amelia up and following Shiny Shoes, I wonder if this will turn out to be the man I've already met?

The three of them rode up in a silent elevator with the same silent operator, and when the doors pinged open on the 108th floor, his companion indicated that they should follow him. They walked down a very long, thickly carpeted corridor, its walls covered with huge canvasses of modern art. They turned a corner, and ahead of them was a glass wall through which he could see a very, very large and very, very smart office.

Shiny Shoes opened the door, announced Nigel and Amelia, and handed them over to an elegant personal assistant. She told them her name was Sarah and asked if they wanted coffee, tea, or anything else.

"Um, coffee would be lovely, thank you," replied Amelia, and Nigel said he'd have the same.

"Filter? Or do you prefer cappuccino, latte, macchiato, espresso? We even have Kopi Luwak, if you'd like that?"

When they both looked blank Sarah laughed and explained, "It's also known as civet coffee. It comes from partially digested coffee cherries that are eaten and defecated by the Asian palm civet. It's the most expensive coffee in the world and if you'd like to try it…?"

Nigel shook his head. "Oh, I think filter would be just fine for me, thank you."

Amelia agreed.

"Excellent! We have our own blend, which I'm sure you will find most enjoyable. If you'd like to go through to Mr di

Angelo's office I shall bring it through." She pointed to where they should go.

This space was even bigger than the one they'd just left, and was beautifully decorated in pleasing shades of blue and green. The wall facing them was floor to ceiling glass, and the stunning view, so incredibly high above London, made Nigel feel almost dizzy. But he still couldn't get his bearings because the view was all wrong. Surely he shouldn't be able to see The Gherkin *and* The London Eye *and* Tower Bridge? Oh yes, and over there to his left was The Shard. Impossible.

He was totally distracted by this conundrum until he noticed the outstretched hand of a man who was so like the one who had visited him in his own premises, but wasn't.

"How do you do? I am very pleased you could both come today."

"Um. Mr di Angelo?" Feeling somewhat wrong-footed because of the confusing view, Nigel shook the proffered hand, and looked closely at the man's face. Very, very similar indeed to the man who had visited his office. He cast a quick glance at Amelia, and could see she was thinking the same.

"I'm Gabe. It was my brother, Nick, who came to see you at your office. He hopes to join us later. Ah, here's the coffee. Thank you, Sarah, we'll see to the cream and sugar ourselves."

When Sarah had closed the door behind her Gabe grinned at Nigel and Amelia and laughed at Nigel's grimace when asked if he'd opted for the Kopi Luwak.

"We have a running bet that no-one will ever choose it." He lifted his cup and said, "I have to tell you, it's delicious, but I do appreciate that a drink made from beans that have passed through an animal's intestines isn't to everyone's taste." He looked from Nigel to Amelia, his eyebrows raised, "So, can I tempt you? Either of you?"

Nigel shook his head then swivelled in surprise to Amelia as she said, "I'd be willing to try it."

"Oh, excellent! Well done you! I'll just tell Sarah to bring you a cup."

Gabe helped himself to a generous amount of cream and added four crumbly cubes of brown sugar with the tiny silver tongs, saying, "Not good for you, I know."

He noticed Nigel looking at the view and laughed.

"Fantastic isn't it? It's the very latest technology in glass, and what you are seeing are holograms of every major landmark in this wonderful city. In fact I can change it to any capital city in the world with just the touch of a button."

Incredulous, Nigel found himself staring out at the New York skyline. At night.

"So," said Gabe. "I hope I may call you Nigel and Amelia? Lovely, do call me Gabe. What do you have for us? How's our little project going?"

There was a short interruption as Sarah came in and handed Amelia her cup of Kopi Luwak. To Gabe, she said, I've just heard from Nick. He sends his apologies."

Gabe thanked her and Sarah withdrew. To Amelia he suggested she add cream and sugar if that was what she normally did.

Both he and Nigel watched carefully as she picked up her cup.

"Oh!" she exclaimed after she'd smelled it and taken her first sip. "It's delicious! It's kind of… nutty and caramelly and… chocolatey. I like it!"

"Good. I shall ask Sarah to ensure you receive a bag of beans so you can make it yourself at home." He spoke over Amelia's protestations, "Now where were we? Ah yes, Nigel, an update if you please."

"Ah, um. Well, um… Gabe. I believe everything is going to plan." Nigel lined up the photographs on the table so they were facing Gabe. "The mill has been abandoned for many years, as I'm sure you know, but I think it could be restored into something quite stunning." He pulled some plans out of his briefcase. "Here are some ideas we've been working on, exterior and interior."

Gabe picked up the first couple of drawings, pencil sketches of a renovated façade, and then a colour palette for the restaurant décor prepared by Amelia, but Nigel had the impression he wasn't really interested. Maybe the other one was the driving force, but there was as yet no sign of his arrival.

"These look excellent. Now, have you arranged accommodation for yourselves while you're working there?"

"Well, Amelia won't need to be there until the build is quite far along, so I shall be staying in very comfortable rooms above the local pub. And there is a nice hotel for you and the other Mr di Angelo in nearby Monkton Ridge, for when you come to visit." He sipped his coffee, the most delicious he had ever tasted, and waited for a reaction. Gabe seemed to be deep in thought for a moment, then he shrugged his shoulders as if coming to some sort of private decision, and leaned forward.

"Okay, so tell me about the village. Is it very small? Remote? Is it the sort of place that gets tourists pouring in to snap thatched cottages with pretty streams running through the gardens?"

"Well, no. It's a very pretty village, if a little run down, but any tourists would just pass through really, as there's nothing there to encourage them to stay. The pub offers basic food, as does the café, and I think both are in need of updating and refurbishment."

Amelia chimed in, "I haven't been there yet, but from what Nigel tells me, the mill would have to be strongly marketed as a destination place for people visiting the nearby places of interest, like Longleat and Bath."

Nigel nodded in agreement, waiting for Gabe to make some comment. When he didn't speak, Amelia said, "I wonder if you can tell us what this is all about? I mean, we appreciate the work, we really do, but, well, your brother said there was a larger agenda, of global importance, and there are so many strange things going on…"

Gabe smiled at last, and his clear grey eyes sparkled with genuine amusement. "Of course you find this whole thing strange, and I don't blame you." He leaned back in his chair and shook his head in apology as he said, "But I can't tell you anything more at this time, I'm sorry."

"I see," said Nigel, picking up his paper-thin, gold-rimmed china cup and putting it down again. "So are we ever to know what it is you are hoping to achieve there?" *And*, he thought to himself, *please don't let it be anything illegal.*

The dimpled grin flashed again, but was quickly gone and Nigel thought, not for the first time, that Gabe di Angelo was troubled about something. It showed in his eyes. But he replied amiably enough, "You will be told, I promise you, and soon, once my brother and I have got things organised. I'm sure Nick will have told you, and so I will reiterate, you will do very well out of this. And you can rest assured that you will not be asked to do anything that is against the law."

Nigel wondered if this man was a mind reader, but he was relieved to hear that everything was above board.

Gabe glanced at his watch. "Well, I think we've covered everything. I do apologise that Nick wasn't be able to join us as he'd planned, because he was looking forward to seeing you again. I hope you don't mind being dragged across London for such a short and probably unsatisfactory meeting, as I'm unable to enlighten you at this time."

"Oh, well, we're glad to have met you, and very grateful for your trust in us."

"Good, good!" He slid a sealed brown envelope across the desk. "Now, here's our authorisation for you to act on our behalf. Get whatever and whomever you need. You'll have fun with the mill, I know, and there will be no difficulties with its renovation." He turned to Amelia. "You're just the team we need, Amelia, your husband's a private investigator and architect and you're an interior designer. I hope you both enjoy yourselves."

Amelia graciously smiled and said how thrilled they both were for the opportunity to work on such a prestigious project.

When she finished speaking Gabe rose, looking very serious as he said, "Please make no mistake, this is a very important undertaking, and your part in it is significant. Now then, I suggest you get yourselves well established in Ham-Under-Lymfold. I think the pub is an excellent place for you to be, actually, as it's central to the village and you're sure to meet a lot of the locals there. When we come, my brother and I will stay at the mill."

"But you can't!" exclaimed Nigel, urgently pointing to the photographs again. "The mill is a complete wreck!"

"Oh, we'll manage, don't you worry. We'll pitch camp there and be perfectly comfortable. You'll see."

He offered his hand first to Amelia and then to Nigel. The resemblance between the di Angelo brothers was remarkable, Nigel thought, but whereas one sensed that Nick had a dark and somewhat sinister side to him, Gabe seemed open and really, genuinely, very pleasant.

The elegant secretary escorted Nigel and Amelia to the elevator, and told them the car was waiting in the basement garage to take them back to their office.

But Nigel wanted to see the remarkable building from the outside, so he asked the operator to stop and let them out at Reception. The little man looked uncertain, but he pressed the button when Nigel firmly asked him again. He wanted to see for himself this upside-down icicle and to know where, exactly, he was. There was a revolving door to the right as they came out of the elevator, and he guided Amelia towards it, intending to go outside.

"Oh, Mr Hellion-Rees!" It was the receptionist who had greeted them when they arrived. He was hurrying towards them, an anxious expression on his face, and Nigel had the feeling that he was trying to head them off. "I do apologise, Mr Hellion-Rees, Mrs Hellion-Rees, but the car is waiting to take you to your office, and it's needed back here immediately. So, if you wouldn't mind…" He had his hand on Nigel's arm now, gently but firmly guiding him away from the revolving door, giving Amelia no choice but to follow.

The security guard, his mouth set in a straight line of disapproval, stood by the elevator, holding the doors open. The little operator was cowering at the back, and once Nigel and Amelia were inside, it was the guard who leaned in and pressed the button for the basement. They were carried down to the garage.

The silver-grey limousine was no longer alone in the vast underground space, for there was a black one of the same make and model parked next to it. Nigel just knew that this was Nick di Angelo's car, and wondered how long he had been back and why he had not made an appearance at their meeting.

They were soon settled on the soft leather seats again and on their way, but he and Amelia were even more baffled about the whole thing than they had been before. They'd been to an office he hadn't known existed, that had holographic windows that he'd never heard of. They'd learned nothing new about the job, so still didn't know what they were getting themselves involved in. But they had a gorgeous old mill to renovate and enough money in the bank up front to pay the maintenance due to his ex-wife for several months to come, and that, at least, gave Nigel something to be happy about.

He patted the large bag of beans that sat on the seat between him and Amelia and she sighed, "I didn't have the heart to tell Gabe that all we have to make coffee with is a kettle!"

Chapter 10
a fateful meeting

Three o'clock on a Thursday afternoon and the high-spirited group of schoolchildren were being herded by their teachers to board the coach outside. In an upstairs room historian and archaeologist Dr Stephen George heard them leave in a cacophony of scuffling feet, shouts and laughter, then all was blissfully quiet. For the past two hours he'd been scribbling notes for his forthcoming lecture on excavation techniques to university students and it wasn't coming together. Several A4 sheets were scattered across his desk, covered with his untidy writing. The scrawl was scribbled-out here and there and double-headed arrows shot from one paragraph to another where he couldn't decide whether to swap them round. When the intercom buzzed he gladly threw down his pen, grateful for the interruption.

"Yes, Stella?"

"Miss Dove is here to see you."

"Oh, yes, the coin found in the churchyard at Ham-Under-Lymfold. I'll be right down."

The first thing that caught his attention as he entered from the stairwell was a cloud of shiny, dark red curls. The second thing was a very trim figure. The third, fourth and fifth things were the dazzling smile, creamy skin and pair of luminous eyes the colour of cinnamon. By the time she spoke, softly introducing herself as Lorelei Dove, Dr Stephen George was utterly lost. It even seemed, in the moment that he took her outstretched hand and didn't want to let it go, that the usually dim, cool interior of the Heritage Centre reception was suddenly very bright and very warm.

"Miss Dove." Had there ever been such a beautiful name? "I'm Stephen George. Won't you come up to the lab?" It all came out in a rush, and Stephen didn't miss Stella's raised eyebrows and knowing smirk as he led the way back upstairs to his first-floor office.

"Here we are, please do go in."

She preceded him with another dazzling smile that made his heart pound like he'd just run a marathon in world record time. Why had he never met her before this? Where had she been all his life?

"The last discovery was brought in by your uncle, I hope he is well? I was very sorry to have to tell him it was of no value," he said with a voice half an octave higher than usual.

"Uncle Hartley is fine, thank you. It was easier for me to come this time as I work just up the road, at the Art College."

Just up the road! And he had never seen her.

"Have you worked there long, Miss Dove?"

"Please call me Lorelei."

Her name sang in his brain. Lorelei. Lorelei Dove. A perfect name for a perfect woman. Would she one day be Lorelei George?

She was answering his question, forcing him to wrestle his mind back from his ridiculous reverie and give his full attention to this vision of loveliness.

"It's been just over a year, actually," she said. "I moved from Reading when my aunt died and left me her cottage in Ham-Under-Lymfold. I was lucky enough to get a teaching job here straight away, so…"

Maybe it could be lucky for me, too, Stephen thought, coming over all daydreamy again.

Lorelei said, "I saw a group of schoolchildren leaving as I came in, and it reminded me of a school trip to London, a long time ago. We went to look at a Bronze Age collection, but I was fascinated by a display of crystals in the foyer, and a huge amethyst geode in particular. I really loved that, probably because purple is my favourite colour," she laughed and swept a hand over her T-shirt, fringed scarf and long skirt in various shades of purple. She then waggled her fingers to show off glittery lilac varnish. "I had to save up for it, but I have a super geode in my living room that's almost as tall as me."

Stephen cleared his throat so he could speak properly. "Oh, we have geodes here, too. You must see them before you go. But let's have a look at this coin, shall we?"

Lorelei pulled a small, bubble-wrapped lump from her shoulder bag and placed it on the table. The bubble-wrap unravelled to reveal another lump, this time of cotton wool. Inside that, the coin gleamed under the overhead lights.

Stephen fetched a magnifying glass from a drawer and leaned on his elbows to study the uppermost face of the coin, a crowned king sitting on a throne.

But he was distracted by the nearness of Lorelei, by the scent of her, her unwavering gaze and air of curiosity and anticipation. He didn't want to bother with the artefact, he wanted to talk to her. To find out everything about her. To find out if she would have dinner with him. Soon.

She smiled at him, frightening Stephen into believing she could read his mind, but she said, "Uncle Hartley has a book about coins, and he thought this resembled a gold florin. It was called, um, a leopard something, I think."

Inwardly giving himself a firm shake to make himself concentrate, he traced with a fingertip one of the two leopard heads near the king's elbow and felt excitement stir. "It could be that your uncle is right. There is a coin called a Double Leopard, and if this is one of those it will be pretty valuable. Let's have a look on the internet."

He went to a dusty laptop and typed in 'Double Leopard coin'. Within seconds, he had a picture of one on the screen, and Lorelei leaned in close as they both studied the actual coin and the large, clear picture in front of them. He breathed in the apple scent of her, and longed to reach out and touch her hand, her hair, her face.

"It looks just like it, doesn't it?" she breathed. "And look, it says it could be worth more than a hundred thousand pounds!"

"Yes, indeed. But let's not make assumptions. I'm not an expert in coins, ancient pottery is more my line, so I'd like to suggest that we send this to an expert I know in London. Would that be all right, do you think?"

"Of course! Please feel free to do whatever you think necessary. Oh, Uncle Hartley will be over the moon."

She was picking up her bag. She was going to leave. Desperately, he rooted about in his brain to find something to say that would really impress her, something intelligent, scintillating and witty. He blurted, "Oh please, don't go!"

Lorelei looked a little startled, and he inwardly groaned that he was behaving like an idiot. Taking a deep breath, he started again, "I'm sorry, what I meant was, please stay while I photograph and document this. And I need to give you a receipt for it."

She smiled and put her bag down again, and as he looked into her golden-brown eyes he felt the floor tilt beneath his feet.

For the next quarter of an hour, Lorelei stood patiently by while Stephen photographed the coin, measured and weighed it, made notes about it.

The high-windowed room started to heat up, and Stephen couldn't help but stare at her as she removed the fringed scarf from around her soft, white neck. Her fingers were long and slender, the lilac nails quite short. Stephen, wanting to kiss those fingers very badly indeed, noted the absence of a wedding or engagement ring, but surely such a lovely woman was already taken? How could he find out?

He shook himself before she caught him gazing at her, wrote out a receipt and handed it to her, saying, "That's as much as I can do right now. It could be a week or two before the expert I have in mind is available to take a look at it, so may I, that is, may I take your, er, your telephone number to let you know when we have the, the, er, the results?"

Good grief, he thought, *now I'm stuttering like a lovesick teenager!*

Lorelei stated her home number, twice, very slowly, and leaned over to watch him write it down. Was it her incredible hair that smelled of apples, or was it her skin?

"If you, er, need to, um, ask me anything, Miss Dove... Lorelei... then do call. I'll be here most days, unless I'm lecturing at the university. But anyway, I shall telephone you the moment I have any news. Or before, if I need to ask you something. About the coin, I mean."

"Right. Yes. Fine. Well, I'm sure you're busy and I have to get going, so..." Lorelei wound the purple scarf round her neck and picked up her handbag.

"I'll show you out—"

"Oh, there's no need. Really. I can find my way."

And she was gone. Too late, Stephen remembered that he'd offered to show her the geodes downstairs. Bereft at the missed opportunity to spend more time with the enchanting Miss Dove, he stared at the doorway until Stella appeared there, her sleek blond bob blotting out his memory of Lorelei's auburn curls tumbling down her slender back. Stella was looking at him with a knowing expression.

"Lovely young woman," she said, barely able to contain her laughter at Stephen's dumbstruck expression. "I hope you got her telephone number."

"I did, as a matter of fact. But don't you go getting any ideas, Stella. She might be married, or engaged, or—"

"Nope, you have no worries there. I happen to know that she's free as a bird and looking for her soulmate."

"How?" he croaked. "I mean, how could you know that?"

"Because I know her uncle, and I saw him just a couple of weeks ago. He told me that she'd just come out of another disastrous relationship and he wished with all his heart that she could meet a nice man." Her face full of mischief, she said, "*You're* a nice man, Stephen. A very nice man."

"Now, Stella, I think we're getting a bit ahead of ourselves."

"Stephen, you *are* nice. You're kind, intelligent, you have a great sense of humour and on top of all that you're very good-looking, a veritable Indiana Jones. And from the rapturous look on her face as she left here, I would say she was rather smitten too." She turned on her heel. "I'll make some tea."

Stephen wanted to punch the air for joy at even the possibility he might be of interest to the wondrous Lorelei Dove, and debated with himself how soon he should call her.

What would be the right amount of time to wait? Two weeks? No, no, far too long. One week? Yes, he thought a week would be about right.

Chapter 11
coup de foudre

After making himself wait the entire agonising morning of the following day, it took an even more agonising three attempts to dial the right number. After apologising twice to a gravel-voiced man who clearly did not like being telephoned by stuttering strangers, he punched the numbers out slowly and extra carefully then paced up and down while he waited for this vital call to be answered.

A woman, sounding rather breathless and distracted, said, "Yeff?"

His heart sank. He was sure he'd dialled correctly this time. Had he read the signs of her interest wrong and she'd deliberately given him the wrong number? It wouldn't be the first time that happened to him.

"Er, sorry, I'm not sure I have the right number. Is Lorelei Dove there, please?"

"Yeff, thiff iff fshe,"

He didn't remember her having a lisp.

There was a light clatter, then she spoke again in the lovely voice he remembered, "Yes, it's me. I'm so sorry, I had a paintbrush in my mouth."

Stephen, heartbeat accelerating, punched the air with joy and danced a little jig in his narrow hallway. It was her, it was really her!

"Are you there?"

"Yes, sorry. Hello! It's Stephen George here. I hope I haven't called at a bad time, are you doing a landscape painting or are you decorating?"

"It's an animal portrait, actually, a side-line of mine to supplement the rather meagre teaching salary. I'm doing a gorgeous African rock python that's eighteen feet long."

"Gosh, I hope it's not there posing for you!"

Her warm laugh trickled into his ear. "No, I'm working from a photograph. She's called Betty and I'm painting her coiled up with her forked tongue coming straight out of the picture at you. It's a retirement gift for one of the keepers at the zoo. So, Dr George, any luck with my uncle's coin?"

Stephen leaned against the wall because her voice was doing strange things to his insides. "Do call me Stephen. I've spoken to a coin expert about it, and he's very excited. I… um… I hoped to be able to discuss things with you over dinner. I mean, are you free for dinner? Tonight, maybe?"

"Oh good golly yes!" laughed Lorelei, making Stephen punch the air again because she sounded so very keen to see him. Or maybe she was just excited about the coin?

"Great," he said. "Will your uncle want to join us, do you think?" He hoped she could hear how reluctantly he offered the invitation.

"Oh, I shouldn't think so. Uncle Hartley likes to eat very early. I can report back to him."

"Terrific! Do you know The White Lion in Monkton Ridge, opposite the monument?"

"Yes I know it, but I've never been inside."

"It's very nice, and they do excellent food. Shall I pick you up at 7 o'clock?"

"Oh, are you sure? I'd be happy to meet you there."

"I wouldn't hear of it. Just tell me where to find you."

She objected a little more, saying she didn't want to take him out of his way, but his persistence won the argument. He scribbled down the directions she gave him.

"See you later, then, Stephen. Goodbye."

Stephen put the phone down. She had sighed, definitely sighed, and he was sure it was with pleasure. Now, how lucky was he that she happened to be free this evening? And how could he occupy himself for the four hours in between now and the time he would, once again, be gazing at the heavenly Lorelei Dove?

He rushed upstairs, impatiently pulling off his clothes as he went. He left them in a straggly line on the stairs and the landing, and dashed, naked, into the bathroom. A hot shower and a shave should use up some time.

Ten minutes later, still damp from the shower and dressed only in socks and tartan-patterned boxer shorts, Stephen rushed to his wardrobe and started grabbing trousers and shirts off their hangers, flinging them on the bed. When he had an unsatisfactory heap with still no idea what to wear, he started on his shoes, scattering them across the floor.

"I need help," he said out loud.

He ran downstairs and keyed in a number on the phone. It was answered almost immediately, and he didn't give the person at the other end a chance to even say hello.

"Stella! Stella, it's me. Stephen. Help!"

Stella's husband laughed, "An emergency, eh? Just a minute, I'll call her."

Stephen tapped his foot impatiently.

"Yes, Stephen dear, what can I do for you?" Stella said, amusement very evident in her voice.

"Stella, listen. I've got a date with Lorelei Dove. You remember her? She came to the Centre with that coin? Of course you remember, you remember everything. You probably already know that I'm crazy about her! Did you notice her hair? Her eyes? The freckles across her perfect nose?" He ran out of breath and stopped.

"And?"

"And what?"

"Is that what you called to ask me? If I remember all her many lovely attributes?"

"Uh? Oh, sorry, I'm all over the place. Stella, listen…"

"Stephen, dear, I *am* listening, and you are babbling. I'm delighted that you have a date with that lovely young woman. I suppose you don't know what to wear, is that it?"

"Stella, you are amazing."

"I know, dear, I know. Where are you going?"

"The White Lion." He felt panic rising. "Gosh, Stella, is that a good place to take her? Should I be taking her to a swanky restaurant in Bath instead?"

"No, dear, I think The White Lion is a very good choice for a first date, it's cosy and informal; the state you're in you wouldn't be able to handle all the cutlery in a posh place. Now then, is that pale blue striped shirt you bought last month clean and pressed? Good. Now, how about the dark grey flannel trousers I picked out for you at Mason's? Good. Wear those. Your black brogues, polished of course. Leather jacket. Don't overdo the aftershave. Okay? Well, have a wonderful time, and I look forward to hearing all about it tomorrow."

Stephen heaved a sigh of relief and rushed upstairs to dress as instructed. He was buttoning his shirt when the phone rang again.

"Hello?" he said, out of breath from the dash back down the stairs.

"Stephen, dear, I forgot two things. First, your hair. Don't forget to comb your hair, it can be rather wild."

"Hair. Okay, right. And the second thing?"

"Grey socks, Stephen. Not your novelty ones. Lorelei needs to get to know you better before you start wearing those."

"Gosh, Stella, you're a witch and I don't know what I'd do without you."

In his room, he hopped on one leg as he tore off first one sock decorated with Indiana Jones-style hats and then the other before frantically searching in his sock drawer for a clean pair of plain, grey ones.

With one last look at himself in the mirror, he grabbed his car keys and set off for what he hoped would be a life-changing evening.

He found Lorelei's delightful little cottage easily and she came outside as soon as his car drew up beneath the lamp post. He couldn't remember what they talked about on the short drive, but it seemed to take no time at all before they were settled at a table in front of the inglenook fireplace. Stephen, having consulted Lorelei for her preference, asked for a bottle of red wine to be brought over immediately so they could have a drink while they perused the menu. Now that they were seated opposite each other instead of side by side in his car, conversation seemed awkward. Stephen felt ridiculously tongue-tied, and it appeared that Lorelei felt the same.

"So," said Lorelei, eventually, when the small talk had been exhausted, "what did your colleague, the coin expert say? I've been dying to know if it's something special."

Stephen gave her a rueful grin and held up his hands, palms outwards. "Confession time, I'm afraid, as I've brought you here under false pretences. Ambrose Alt, the expert I want to assess it, can't come to the Centre so I've arranged to take the coin up to him next week. But I'm pretty sure you have got something special and I've emailed him a set of photographs and some detailed notes." He swallowed a mouthful of wine for courage. "So, I can't enlighten you at the moment, I'm afraid, but I did so want to see you again. I hope you're not cross at the subterfuge?"

"Cross? Oh no," breathed Lorelei, her gorgeous green eyes softening in a way that made him feel like he was melting inside, "I'm not at all cross."

"Good, um… oh… good."

They gazed at each other.

Stephen was the first to blink, and he squeaked, "Have you decided what you'd like to eat?" He cleared his throat and said it again, melting even more at Lorelei's warm laughter.

She chose a vegetable lasagne and rocket salad, and refused the bread when a basket of rolls was brought to the table.

"I'm sorry, I should have asked, are you a vegetarian? Will my eating steak be a problem for you?"

She laughed. "I don't mind what *you* eat," she said. "But yes, I am a vegetarian. I'd be vegan, only I like cheese and eggs too much. And, of course," she held up her glass of wine, "some food and wines you might think are vegetarian actually aren't and I'm too lazy to check the labels, so I guess I'm not really a committed veggie."

When their food arrived, Stephen immediately tucked in, and was worried when Lorelei took just a few bites then pushed her lasagne round the plate.

"Isn't it any good?"

"It's delicious. It's just that I don't have much of an appetite. My mother says I eat like a bird, and Uncle Hartley always says that I must be a cheap date." She blushed at that and apologised. "I didn't mean… well, this probably isn't a date, is it?"

"I'd like to think it is, Lorelei, and I'd buy you the most expensive item on the menu. Except I think that might be the lobster, and you wouldn't want that."

"I certainly wouldn't!" She shuddered. "Boiling the poor thing alive." She placed her knife and fork on her plate and took a sip of wine.

"Ah. Well, I shall remember never to order lobster."

"Thank you," Lorelei laughed. "Does that mean we'll be having more dinner dates then?"

Stephen grinned happily and clinked his glass to hers, "Oh, I do hope so!"

By the time Stephen was driving Lorelei home, he was deeply, irrevocably in love, and the signals he'd received from her were giving him cause to think that she felt something for him too.

When he escorted her to her door and said goodnight, she reached up on tiptoe and kissed him on the cheek. He so badly wanted to crush her to his chest and kiss her lips, but forced himself to settle for a promise that she would have dinner with him again very soon.

It was with great reluctance he walked back down her garden path and to his car.

An hour later, sitting on his sofa with a cup of tea, he replayed every minute of the evening. She was perfect in every way. Her name. Her voice. Her figure. The colour of her hair. The scent she wore. He loved her company, the way their conversation had moved easily from subject to subject once they got started.

He wondered if he could wait another three days to call her.

No. He definitely couldn't wait that long.

"Hello?" her voice was husky.

"It's me."

"Hello me."

"I couldn't wait to hear your voice again."

"It's lovely to hear *your* voice again."

"Lorelei?"

"Mmm?"

"Do you believe in love at first sight?"

She laughed, a sound that trickled down the phone wires and into his ear like warm honey. "A *coup de foudre*? As a matter of fact yes, I do."

"Lorelei, can I see you again?"

"Oh yes. Yes, please!"

"I'll call you. Very soon. Good night, Lorelei. Sweet dreams."

With the phone clutched to his chest, Stephen fell back against the cushions, heart racing. He didn't recognise himself. He'd never, ever felt like this before, and he'd never, ever done anything like this before. But then, he'd never met anyone like Lorelei before.

As he drifted off to sleep he wondered if calling before breakfast tomorrow would be too soon.

Chapter 12
settling in

Nigel stowed his underwear, vests and socks in the top drawer of the pine chest, from which came the faint odour of mothballs and lavender. His coat, shirts and shoes were next put away neatly in the wardrobe and his dressing gown hung on the back of the bathroom door. Finally, having set his book and toilet bag on the nightstand, he considered himself once again ensconced in the largest of the guest bedrooms at The Blacksmith's Anvil.

His room had a firm double bed, brown faux-leather two-seater sofa with comfy cushions, and a drop-leaf table with two chairs in the bay window, where he could sit and view the green. He had a small television, tea-making facilities and a tiny fridge. There was a warm, clean bathroom next door, which was shared by the room on the other side. Nigel didn't mind this, and anyway, it had so far turned out on each visit that he was the only guest.

He'd stayed here several times now, to be on hand as the contract for the purchase of Angel Falls Mill had been finalised, to take measurements for his architectural plans, research local building contractors, and also to fulfil the other, more mysterious part of his task, that of getting to know the inhabitants of Ham-Under-Lymfold. They were a friendly bunch, so it wasn't proving too difficult.

The di Angelo brothers had said they were coming for an update, and he was to meet them in the bar later. They had taken ownership of the mill a month ago, at too high a price as far as Nigel was concerned, but they had insisted the sale be agreed upon without haggling.

As far as Nigel knew, the brothers had arrived early in the morning. He was nervous about the meeting because no matter how he tried, he couldn't shake his hunch that not everything was above board. He decided to have a walk and get some fresh air ahead of the meeting.

Autumn was coming and the evenings were beginning to draw in. Nigel strolled along the picturesque High Street, admiring the cottages that lined the opposite edge of the green. The buildings were all different in some way, whether it be a thatched roof or a slate one, a green solid door or a half-glazed red one, leaded windows or modern glazing. At this time of day, the kidney-shaped village green was ringed with cars, as the owners of the houses had no space in their tiny front gardens for driveways. Cooking smells pervaded the air, and Nigel wondered wistfully what meals were being cooked behind the closed curtains. Then he wondered even more wistfully what Amelia was doing. She'd decided to stay in London and let Nigel do this trip alone. She would come regularly once things were far enough along for her to begin her own part in the project

In the distance, the sky was blackening swiftly, something additional to the oncoming night. Nigel sniffed the air, sure he could smell rain. A streak of lightning lit up the sky over the hills, making him shiver as he recalled the tales of gloom and doom Stanley Trout had told him on his first visit here, a visit that now seemed to have taken place a very long time ago.

Large, cold raindrops began to splash on his head and spatter the ground around his feet, so he turned up his collar and hurried back to The Blacksmith's Anvil, going straight up to his room to fetch his plans for the mill conversion.

When he entered the bar ten minutes later, he nodded and waved to Stanley, who was nursing a pint of milk stout at his usual corner table. Digby lay at Stanley's feet, his eyes closed and body relaxed but his long, shaggy tail thumped up and down in recognition of Nigel's voice. The fire in the beautiful inglenook fireplace was set but not yet lit. He hoisted himself onto a bar stool and ordered a gin and tonic for himself and another milk stout for Stanley.

"Settled in all right?" Cynthia asked as she tonged ice and a sliver of lemon into a glass.

"Yes, I have, thank you. I'm beginning to feel very much at home here."

"I'm so glad. And I look forward to seeing Amelia here again soon. Is she okay, not still suffering from morning sickness is she?"

Nigel frowned. "It's been more like all-day sickness, but she is getting better."

"Oh, I'm happy to hear that. Here you go, then." She placed the glass, which he knew had a very generous measure of gin in it, and an open bottle of tonic, on the bar. "On the house. To welcome you back as our guest." She poured the stout and said, "I'll take this over to Stanley."

"Thank you, Cynthia, that's very kind of you."

With rising anticipation he tipped the tonic into his glass, relishing the sound of the gentle fizz and the sharp whiff of juniper and lemon. He closed his eyes and took an appreciative sip, savouring the sensation and taste on his tongue.

The Capsbys and Fordingbridges arrived in a clamour of voices and claimed one of the larger tables, each calling out hello to Nigel. They were shortly followed by Glen and Gwen Perkins, who pulled up extra chairs and joined them, the volume rising as everyone talked at once. Five minutes later, a clap of thunder boomed right overhead, making everyone jump. Olive Capsby shrieked in fright then giggled with embarrassment. Another boom, even louder, shook the windows and reverberated around the room, just as the door opened and the di Angelo brothers sauntered in. Nigel felt the hairs on the back of his neck bristle.

The brothers seated themselves at the table in front of the fireplace, and Cynthia bustled over to light the fire. Soon, orange and yellow flames merrily flickered, instantly raising the ambience, and she asked what they'd like to have. Nick asked for two pints of Speckled Hen and two packets of smoky bacon crisps.

Nigel ambled over to their table and said hello. Nick merely inclined his head, but Gabe said warmly, "Nigel! Halloo to you! Have you got a drink? Oh good. Take a seat and let's have a chat."

Nigel remembered that when he'd first met Gabe he'd thought he was so like Nick that it would be difficult to tell them apart physically. Now he had spent a little time with both of them, though, it was simple: Gabe was a paler version of Nick, or Nick was a darker version of Gabe. Personality-wise, it was even easier to tell who was who: Gabe was warm and friendly, Nick wasn't.

As soon as the crisp packets were opened, Digby rose onto his long legs, shook himself vigorously, and trotted over. He rested his handsome head on Gabe's thigh and stared fixedly up at him through his shaggy grey eyebrows.

"Ooh, lovely doggy! What's your name, boy, eh?"

"It's Digby," supplied Nigel, as Gabe fed the grateful dog some crisps.

Digby, making that strange, gruffling sound that indicated his pleasure, transferred his attention to Nigel. "I haven't got anything, Digby, sorry."

The dog turned his head to Nick, who curled his lip and muttered, "What a scruffy animal, should it be in here?"

As if ashamed of himself, Digby tucked his tail between his legs and actually backed away from the table.

Gabe tutted. "That was mean, Nick."

"You don't like dogs, then?" asked Nigel, feeling sorry for Digby as he squeezed himself under Stanley's table and laid down, his huge shaggy head on his huge paws, his golden eyes fixed balefully on Nick. Nick shrugged.

"Hey, Nigel," said Gabe. "So what's been happening around here, eh?"

"Well, mostly it's all talk about the mill. Everyone's speculating how much Violet Cattermole got for it, and how it will look when we've renovated it."

"Talk of the devil," grinned Nick, pointing his thumb at Violet, who had just arrived.

She stalked across to the bar and ordered a port and lemon. Nigel had been there on the day the sale was agreed, had heard Glen Perkins loudly say wouldn't it be a wonder if Violet bought a round of drinks to celebrate her good fortune. But she hadn't. She'd only ordered her usual port and lemon and announced that she had no plans to move to a bigger house or buy a new television or three-piece suite. No, she'd insisted, she was fine where she was and perfectly happy with the things she already had, thank you very much. The money would go in the bank and she'd treat herself to a few luxuries now and then.

Stanley had commented to Nigel, "It's not right that that woman should have all the money from the mill, 'twas her sister's childhood home, too, y'know, but I doubt Hilda's seen or ever will see a single penny, despite being in dire need of help. She's a fine lady, is Hilda, 'tis hard to believe they be sisters." Nigel, having by then met Hilda, had to agree, because so far, to the obvious disappointment of the locals, Violet had been true to her word and shown no signs of flashing her new-found wealth about.

"Have you settled into your room?" Gabe asked politely, bringing Nigel's attention back from the grumpy old lady, who had seated herself as far away from Stanley as was possible.

"Oh yes, I arrived about two hours ago. It's basic but very comfortable; I've had the same room each time I've been here, so it's getting to feel like a home from home."

"Is Amelia with you?"

Nigel explained that she'd start coming with him once the build was well under way and she could start on the interior design.

"Are you two having a bite to eat?" he asked. "I'm going to have ham and chips and a glass of wine."

"We've eaten," said Nick, draining his glass. "But another two pints would go down well." The way he said it made it clear that he expected Nigel to go fetch.

Like Nigel, the brothers were dressed casually in jeans and sweaters, but unlike Nigel's, their jeans and sweaters were expensive brands. Two coats, one chocolate-coloured suede and one biscuit-coloured cashmere, had been piled rather carelessly on a chair nearby. They were expecting to see Nigel's initial plans for the conversion of the mill, so before going up to the bar, he handed the file of drawings to Gabe. Gabe placed it on top of the coats, saying they'd look at them later.

Nigel noticed then that the pub had filled up but was unusually quiet. Word must have spread that the two strangers were the ones who were going to do up the mill and open a grand restaurant. He had talked it up on each of his visits, insisting that the development would bring jobs and visitors, people who would spend their money in the village pub, the café and the general store. It was a Very Good Thing, he assured them, his fingers crossed behind his back in case it turned out to be a disaster, and they said they were looking forward to welcoming the di Angelo brothers and offering any help needed.

Nigel placed his food order, but before he could order the drinks, Arnold Capsby appeared at his side. In a loud voice, no doubt so everyone would be aware of his generosity, Arnold told Cynthia that whatever the di Angelos were drinking, he was paying.

The brothers inclined their handsome, curly-haired heads in thanks to Arnold, and Arnold self-importantly puffed out his chest. The other men present ignored him and Nigel smiled wryly to himself, thinking that they were probably kicking themselves for not thinking of it first.

He picked up his glass and returned to the table, putting the question to the brothers that he'd been dying to ask, "So where are you staying? Did you check into the hotel I recommended?"

"No, Nigel," drawled Nick, speaking as if talking to a halfwit, "we're staying at the mill."

Eyebrows raised in shock, Nigel exclaimed, "But how? How can you possibly manage? There's no electricity, no hot water…"

"We're fine, Nigel, all settled in," assured Gabe. "Come round tomorrow morning and see for yourself. You'll be surprised at what a little, uh, *effort* can achieve."

Baffled, but seeing he would have to wait until tomorrow to see their living arrangements, Nigel asked, "So what happens now?"

Gabe took a long pull from his beer and burped quietly. "Beg pardon! Marvellous stuff, this. We'll fill you in when you come tomorrow."

Nick chimed in, "Now is not the time and here is not the place." He leaned forward and tapped the side of his nose, his fine grey eyes gleaming with amusement. Or was it malice?

Nigel shivered, and turned around to find that everyone's attention was fixed on them. Most people hastily dropped their eyes, or turned to their neighbour and started chattering. Only Violet didn't look away. Her port and lemon raised partway to her mouth she seemed mesmerised by the men who had unexpectedly brought her so much wealth. Nick raised his glass in a salute to her, but Nigel sensed it was a mocking gesture. Cynthia bustled over then, bringing Nigel's ham and chips. Eyelashes fluttering, she looked only at Nick, even as she asked Nigel if he wanted ketchup and mustard.

Hungry, he picked up his knife and fork and tucked in. Digby, ever the hopeful hound, was soon back by his side.

"It's a nice village, this," said Gabe, "I'm keen to visit the church, I've heard it's very fine. Have you been inside, Nigel?"

"Oh, yes, in fact the first day I came here." He recounted the story of Walter Sidney Hopkins and his unfortunate run-in with a loose organ pipe.

Gabe, visibly upset, exclaimed, "Oh, the poor boy!"

Nick snorted into his Speckled Hen and laughed out loud, making Digby scamper back to Stanley.

Gabe snapped, "You have no feelings *whatsoever*, Nick!"

"And you, dear brother, are a wuss."

They bickered like children for a few minutes, much to Nigel's amazement, then as suddenly as it had flared up, it was over and Gabe's good humour restored. He turned to Nigel, "We ought to be going. We'll see you in the morning, Nigel. Come about 11 o'clock for coffee."

Within a moment they'd donned their coats and were gone.

Nigel declined Cynthia's offer of dessert and went upstairs to his room. He didn't want to get drawn into conversation with any of the people in the bar, who were clearly bursting with curiosity.

He was curious himself. How could those two men possibly be staying at the mill? How could they offer him coffee in a place that had no kitchen and no power?

Then it came to him. Of course! They were in a caravan, a luxury caravan, parked somewhere near the mill, probably in the village hall car park. Yes, that would explain it. Happy he'd thought of it, he turned on the television to watch the news.

Chapter 13
the impossible truth

The next morning Cynthia was busy with an early delivery from the brewery, so Nigel told her he'd get his breakfast in the café. Gwen Perkins took his order, Glen Perkins fried the eggs, bacon, sausages, black pudding, tomatoes, mushrooms and two thick slices of bread fresh baked that morning, and Debbie Perkins brought it to his table, with a large brown pot of tea that had a small chip on the spout.

"There's enough to feed a small army here!" Nigel declared.

Debbie giggled and said in one breath, "Well you just eat what you can and leave the rest nothing goes to waste all our leftovers go to West Haven pig farm as pigs eat absolutely anything now do you need tomato or brown sauce we have both or mustard maybe we have three different kinds?"

When he declared his preference she brought a red plastic squeezy bottle over and Nigel liberally poured ketchup over everything on his plate, before picking up his knife and fork and tucking in with relish. Chips last night and full English this morning, not good for his waistline, but oh so tasty. He didn't think he'd manage half of it, but it was all so delicious and he was so hungry, he found himself asking for another slice of Arnold's scrumptious bread to mop up the remains of yolk and ketchup. After draining the pot of tea, he put his napkin on the table and sat back with a happy sigh.

The three Perkins stood in a line behind the counter and grinned at him. "Another happy customer," trilled Mrs Perkins, wiping her hands on a blue tea towel.

The *only* customer, Nigel thought to himself, as he left the steamy warmth of the café. They could do so much with the café, give it a lick of paint and replace some of the tables and chairs, make it more enticing. Then more people would come and discover a place that made wonderful bread and cakes and served excellent home-cooked food.

He planned to spend an hour in his room going over his copy of the plans again before his appointment at the mill. But the prospect of coffee on top of all that tea and breakfast made him feel queasy, so he hoped they hadn't gone to any trouble. Well, he hoped Gabe hadn't gone to any trouble, because he was certain Nick wouldn't bother.

Out on the pavement, he pulled his collar up. It was a chilly day, but at least it was dry. As he passed the Post Office, Arnold Capsby waved at him through the window and he waved back. It gave Nigel a warm glow to think that he'd been in the village just a few times and already he was accepted with warm smiles. So different to life in London, where the pace of life was so fast, too fast for a cheery hello from anyone. Here, people had time for a chat, and he loved it. In fact, it hadn't been at all difficult finding things out about people, because everybody talked so openly about themselves and each other.

"Hey, Nigel! Wait up!"

Nigel turned to see who was calling him. "Uri! Hello. How are you?"

"Just dandy, Nigel, just dandy. Are you on your way to the mill? Mind if I walk with you?"

Nigel glanced sideways at his unexpected companion. He and Uri had talked a few times on his previous visits and he found him very interesting. He was knowledgeable about so many subjects, and made such superb things out of wood, Nigel wondered why he chose to be a gravedigger and handyman in an insignificant little village like Ham-Under-Lymfold.

"I'm surprised to find you're still here, Uri. I thought I'd heard that your cousin was only taking a short holiday?"

"Originally, yes, but some family business came up and he needs to stay away for a while longer. I'm happy to stay on as long as needed, though, so here I am!"

They reached the Turnaround. Nigel was expecting to see a huge gleaming caravan parked there, maybe an American Winnebago or something like it. But there was no caravan, luxury or otherwise. He scanned the area around the mill in case they'd somehow managed to get something over the narrow stone bridge, but there was no sign of anything habitable beside, behind or anywhere near the crumbling building.

Uri's head was turned towards Nigel. The eyes behind the blue lenses seemed to be watching him closely.

"Are you, er…?" Nigel pointed to the mill, not at all sure why Uri would be going there.

Uri nodded. "Yep. Shall we go over?"

They crossed the bridge and walked up to the door of the decrepit mill. Like the church door, it was made of thick oak planks studded with black, dome-topped nails. It was severely warped by time and weather and hung loose on its rusting hinges. Nigel heard voices inside, and Uri called out to announce their arrival.

A face appeared at the unglazed window above their heads, and Gabe cried, "Good morning, Nigel! And there's Uri with you, excellent! Come on in."

Nigel knew there was no staircase inside and couldn't imagine how Gabe had got up there. He pushed the door open very carefully in case he dislodged him from a ladder or something, but what he saw when he stepped over the threshold made his blood freeze then go hot, as if he'd been dipped in an Arctic ice-hole and then a vat of boiling oil.

Feeling dizzy he clutched the doorframe to keep himself upright, aware that the muscles in his jaw could not hold his mouth closed. His eyes darted madly about, right to left, left to right, up and down, down and up.

This. Could. Not. Be.

There was a staircase. A very wide staircase with a beautiful, curving banister painted the colour of clotted cream. A burgundy wool runner covered three quarters of the width of the steps, held in place on the shallow treads with shiny brass stair rods.

Down the staircase tripped Gabe, beaming in welcome.

Nigel gingerly let go of the doorframe and stepped forward onto a polished parquet floor. A floor that, last time he'd looked, had been dusty, crumbling concrete. His stunned brain registered the very large open-plan space, which should have been exposed to the elements, but there was a smooth white-painted ceiling above his head, hung with two enormous crystal chandeliers. On his left was an area tastefully furnished with two large multi-cushioned sofas, one cream, one red, two armchairs likewise, a glass-topped coffee table, a walnut bookcase and, on another low glass-topped table, a very high-spec music centre. On the wall was a flat-screen television, the biggest he'd ever seen.

To his right was a carpeted dining area. The huge oval table was set with gold-rimmed white china and gold cutlery, and twelve high-backed chairs made of a gleaming honey-coloured wood were set round it. Beyond that he could see a kitchen with all the latest gadgets, including a coffee maker any specialty coffee house would be proud of. Somewhere at the back, he just knew, there would be several large bedrooms, each exquisitely decorated and furnished. Each with an en suite bathroom, piles of fluffy white towels warming on heated rails. Of course the sinks, bathtubs and showers would have gold taps.

His ears buzzed as if a swarm of bees had taken residence inside his skull and he thought he was going to pass out. He stumbled as he stepped forward, and felt Uri's steadying hand grasp his elbow.

Even with a vast army of workmen, how could they possibly have done this in the short time Nigel had been away from the village since his last visit?

Gabe stood before him and patted him on the shoulder. "A shock, I know, old bean. Take some deep breaths and come on into the kitchen for a cup of coffee. I know you don't care for the most expensive coffee in the world, so instead so I've got some of our special Italian blend on the go, and a slice or two of Battenberg cake fresh from the splendid Perkins' bakery. I trust your breakfast has gone down enough now to allow room? The delightful Debbie told me you had the full fry-up with extra bread."

Dazed and still unsteady on his feet, Nigel allowed himself to be led by Uri to the breakfast bar and placed on a swivelling chrome chair with a red leather seat. Nick appeared, seemingly from nowhere, and took the seat next to Nigel without saying a word. Gabe filled four mugs with fragrant hot coffee and cut four large slices of the yellow and pink sponge which he put on gold-rimmed plates. He handed everyone a gold cake fork and a linen napkin, then took the seat on the other side of Nigel. Looking from one to the other, Nigel felt like the filling in a sandwich. Uri leaned against the sink, just like he usually did in the vicarage kitchen, and Nigel had the uncomfortable feeling that he was finding this whole scenario highly amusing.

"I suppose," said Nick, "now you've seen this, we'd better give you an explanation?"

Nigel could only give a small nod. He was feeling quite nauseous now, and it wasn't because of the black pudding still sitting in his stomach. No, it was because he knew that if he were to step back outside and look at the mill, he'd see an old, wrecked, empty building. He knew too that if anyone else should come to the mill for any reason, they too would only see an old, wrecked, empty building. And even if someone were to venture inside, they wouldn't see all this. Oh no. Only Nigel was allowed to see this. He didn't know how he knew, but he was absolutely certain that he was right. And obviously Uri was connected to the di Angelo brothers. His replacing Topps must, in fact, be part of the plot.

But what was the plot? Maybe, at last, he was going to find out.

He looked at Gabe, beseeching wordlessly to be put out of his misery.

Gabe grinned back at him. "We're angels," he said, cheerfully and with immense pride. "Archangels actually. I'm Gabriel, obviously, and Nick here is Lucifer. We call him Nick as no-one on the planet is called Lucifer, and Luke would confuse him with Luke the Evangelist. Maybe you'd worked that out?"

The brothers waited for a reaction.

Worked it out? Were they mad?

Nigel could only able shake his head, opening and closing his mouth like a fish that had unwittingly leapt out of its bowl.

"And this," said Gabe, pointing to Uri, "is Uriel. He's here at the Boss's behest as an observer."

Uri removed his blue-tinted glasses and Nigel gasped. Now he could see that his eyes were exactly the same unusual grey as Nick's and Gabe's, framed with the same thick, long, very black lashes. "If I didn't wear these," explained Uri, tucking them in his shirt pocket, "people would soon notice the similarities between us, and that could raise awkward questions."

"Yep," said Nick, taking up the explanation. "Twins you humans accept easily, but not so much triplets. You mere mortals get very excited about triplets."

Gabe, laughing at Nigel's expression, said, "Angels really do walk among you! You and Amelia thought we were spies, didn't you? The Boss was thrilled at that, let me tell you."

"And the Boss is?" stuttered Nigel.

"Why, Michael of course! He of the flaming sword."

Nick put his fork down on his now empty plate with a clatter and drawled, "And I'm the villain. The bad guy. Old Nick. Satan. The Dark Lord. Tempter of Humankind. But it was somewhat forced upon me, and a Promise was made at the beginning of your, and by that I mean Humankind's time, that one day I would get my turn to be the good guy again."

Uri spoke, raising the hair on the back of Nigel's head, "That day is now."

Gabriel leaned forward and touched Nigel's arm. "It would be impossible for us to explain it to you, so we thought we'd *show* you."

"Show me?" It came out as a croak. "Show me what?"

"How it came about. How Lucifer came to Fall into Hell, and The Promise that was made at the time."

Nick took up the story. "What you'll see and hear will just be like watching a film at the cinema. It's what happened to us and it will explain things far better than we could if we were to just tell it to you. The human imagination is rather limited, I find."

As he listened incredulously to this nonsense, Nigel realised he was now feeling woozy as well as nauseous. Dimly, he wondered if they'd put something in his coffee.

"Don't worry," comforted Gabe, patting his arm. "You're perfectly safe. Come and sit in this armchair over here. That's right. Now just watch and listen and then we'll talk some more."

A large white screen slowly and noiselessly descended from the ceiling and flickered to life with a grainy black countdown from ten to zero. Sweat beading on his forehead, Nigel sat staring at it, bemused and befuddled by the strange turn of events. Everything else in the mill, including Gabe, Nick and Uri – had they *really* said they were angels? – seemed to recede from his vision. The sound of a hundred trumpets boomed from concealed speakers, forcing Nigel to clamp his hands over his ears to prevent his eardrums bursting.

"Sorry, sorry," cried Gabe, hastily pressing buttons on a remote control to turn the volume down. "Is that better?" He gently pulled Nigel's hands away from his ears. "I said, is that better? Here, have some popcorn."

A huge red and white striped cardboard bucket was placed on Nigel's lap. Nick leaned over and grabbed a handful for himself.

The screen turned a sparkly pale blue while a deep voice announced: "*Welcome to the Great Hall of All Angels.*"

There was another trumpet volley, and the camera panned through billowing clouds to a colossal white building. The great, gilded doors, more than twenty feet tall, parted and swung slowly inwards, revealing a hall of breathtaking proportions. At the far end, a staggeringly beautiful stained glass window glowed in jewel colours. The scene panned over a golden altar on a high platform, at each end of which were candle holders eight feet tall bearing huge creamy candles. Large silver bowls overflowing with bunches of grapes and other fruits of all shapes and sizes covered the altar's surface. Nigel registered the sounds of birdsong and tiny, tinkling bells as he gazed at the amazing scene opening up before him.

The narrator continued, and Nigel felt as if it was specifically directed at him: "*If you could have been there, which you couldn't, of course, because you didn't exist then, you would have been dazzled by the light and laughter of ten thousand angels.*"

And he was indeed dazzled.

"Aaaaagh! My eyes. You've burned my eyeballs!"

"We always forget, brother," drawled Nick, taking another fistful of popcorn from Nigel's bucket, "how weak is the flesh of mortal men. Give him a pair of sunglasses."

Nigel wiped his streaming eyes and put on the dark glasses handed to him by Gabe.

"I'm so sorry, Nigel. Are you okay now?"

Nigel managed a strangled yes and focused again on the screen.

A throng of shimmering figures milled about.

"That's us," said Gabe wistfully. "All of us. The whole hierarchy of angels. We're waiting for Michael."

A bell rang, nine deep, solemn tolls. Nigel felt the reverberation rise through the soles of his feet to the hair follicles on his scalp. A figure, a head taller than all the others, stepped up onto the platform and raised a huge, gleaming sword. The blade burst into flames.

"There, that's Michael," whispered Gabe, and Nigel didn't miss the awe and respect in his voice.

"Doesn't wield that sword much these days," muttered Nick.

Gabe shushed him and touched Nigel's arm. "Now, pay attention. I'll explain things as we go along. Popcorn okay, is it? Sweet and salty, absolutely the best!"

Dumbstruck, Nigel shoved some popcorn into his mouth for something to do that felt vaguely normal while he watched this extraordinary movie unfold. The babble of indistinct but animated conversations dropped and then fell away to silence. The angels' wings and bright white gowns shimmered and quivered as a huge shadow with a glowing edge appeared above, below and around them.

"That's the Angelic Aura," whispered Gabe, clasping his hands and sighing with happiness. "You can't see it as it really is, of course, because it would be too much for your fragile mind, so it's kind of represented here in light and shadow."

The buzz of excited voices and laughter started up again and reached a crescendo, before dropping once more to sibilant whispers. Nigel spotted Gabe, or Gabriel as he should think of him up there on screen, among the crowd and Nick, no, *Lucifer*, next to him.

Gabe placed himself in front of the screen and pointed out various angels.

"That's Zadkiel. And those two giggling together are Cassiel and Raziel. Ooh, and there's you, Uriel!" He tapped Nigel's shoulder and said in an almost whisper, "Uriel is Michal's right-hand angel."

Michael waved his sword and there was a lot of loud shushing until all the angels fell absolutely silent again and they all stood in alert stillness.

"You can't hear Michael's voice as it really is," said Nick with obvious relish. "Or ours. It would *literally* fry your brains."

"That's right," chimed Gabe, throwing his brother a warning look. "Michael believes it does us good to change roles every hundred thousand years or so, so what's happening here is, as he calls our names, we step up to the altar to receive our new orders. See? And once they're given, you'll note that the angels kind of… dematerialise? Well, they *re*materialise in that part of the cosmos to which they'd been assigned. Exciting isn't it?"

Nigel numbly took another handful of the sticky popcorn and pushed it into his mouth. A particle in his bemused brain registered that the popcorn was absolutely the best sweet and salty he'd ever tasted.

The scene of the angels going up to the altar and disappearing went on for a quite a while, until Nick snorted with impatience and picked up the remote to fast-forward the film. "Honestly, we'd be sitting here for decades if we were to watch every single assignment."

Nigel had to look away, for the speed of the film made his head spin. At last, Nick stopped the fast-forward at a point where just two figures stood before Michael in the Great Hall.

"Gosh," said Gabe, stuffing more of Nigel's seemingly bottomless bucket of popcorn and speaking with his mouth full, "I remember this so well. I got more and more excited as the places I really *didn't* fancy were assigned to others." His face took on a dreamy expression. "I was wondering, would I get Hephterion, with its silver skies and twin purple suns? Mazhtesh, which is entirely covered in ocean the colour of topaz? Either would have been very nice, thank you, but I really, really hoped it would be Eshmerien, which is populated with cute and cuddly, chirrupy creatures that live harmless lives in beautiful magenta-leaved trees."

"You mean there are such places?" asked Nigel incredulously.

Nick pressed the pause button and, his voice dripping with sarcasm, said, "Nigel, what humans know about the universe wouldn't even make a microscopic dot on the most microscopic of microscopic things."

The figures on the screen started to move again. Despite the dark glasses, Nigel's eyes burned because he was finding it impossible to blink. Gabriel and Lucifer, larger than life against the brilliance of the screen, had turned and were looking at each other in confusion.

"Ah, now, you see us there? We've just been told that our destination was right where we're standing now… Earth!" Gabe clapped his hands, clearly enjoying himself. Nick glowered.

Planet Earth, thought Nigel desperately. The blue planet. I'm on Earth. I am an Earthling. This is not happening.

Gabe started prattling again. "You humans think that Earth must be the most wonderful planet in the whole wide universe, but it isn't really. Oh yes, the design of its geography and geology, its flora and fauna are the work of pure genius, but they're not unique in the cosmos. Far from it! Angels have been on Earth since its beginning, of course, watching over what you call the primordial soup and on through the arrival of the great beasts that walked the land, flew in the air and swam in the oceans, followed by the new, improved and much smaller versions of birds, insects, sea creatures and plants that have appeared through the millennia."

Nick stepped up in front of the screen to take over the story. His countenance was sorrowful, an expression Nigel would never have expected to see, as he said, "I was so innocent then."

Nigel flicked his eyes from the two brothers standing near him, to the two, shimmering, quivering, winged creatures in the film.

Nick explained, "We were the only ones left and we knew at this point that we had been chosen for Earth. Then we were told about a new species. Humans."

Gabe, who had been bouncing on his heels with impatience, butted in, "We found out that humans had been perfected after eons of frustration and many failed experiments, but, apart from a little niggle here and there, Father was pleased with the end result and expected great things of them. Of you." He pointed at Nigel. "The male gender of the species handsome and strong, the females beautiful and placid. Of course, these attributes were not guaranteed in their offspring, but there's only so much that can be achieved at first pass."

Nick said, "Michael explained that humans – the likes of you, Nigel – had been granted the entire planet to play in. It was thought you'd largely avoid the freezing area, at least until clothing had been invented, and the oceans would cause a few problems because you don't have gills. The most unfortunate part of this design, though, was that you were given brains that could operate beyond pure instinct."

"In other words," interjected Gabe, "you were given the capacity to *choose* your actions in a way a wild animal can't…"

"If you don't mind, Gabe, *I'm* telling this part of the story. Now, where was I? Oh yes. All other creatures so far created lived purely by instinct, they didn't really think beyond where their next meal was coming from, and where it would be safe for them to sleep so they wouldn't, in turn, become a meal for something bigger and meaner than them. But a human can think great thoughts and make decisions and take responsibility…"

Gabe couldn't help himself and butted in again. "It was something new and untried, and *we* had been specially chosen to be your guardians!"

There was such pride in Gabe's voice, but for the first time Nigel wanted to slap him rather than Nick. It was all too much.

And it wasn't over yet.

"Specially chosen, my eye! I'd say we drew the short straw," Nick declared. "See us up there? Gabriel and Lucifer, full of joy and happy anticipation, anticipating what Michael was going to say! Listen to him now."

On screen, Michael addressed the two figures Nigel knew as Gabe and Nick.

"Archangel Lucifer, Archangel Gabriel, hear me! You are hereby charged with the care of a new species: humans. They will have an intellect way above anything else so far created, for their unique brain biology will enable them to choose their actions and be accountable for them. But our projections predict that although most of them will live exemplary lives, doing good works, helping others, there will be those who will choose to do bad things. So, for the former, as a reward when their lives are done, we will offer them Paradise."

The air around the angels turned from a white nothingness to an azure blue sky dotted with fluffy, gold-rimmed clouds above lush green, flower-bedecked fields. Unseen harps played beautiful music.

Beside Nigel, Gabe sighed, "Isn't that just lovely!" but Nick shushed him as Michel continued. "Yea, there shall be Paradise for the good, and for the evil there will be… HELL!"

Lightning flashed and flickered on the screen and Nigel watched Lucifer and Gabriel jump into each other's arms, white-faced and clinging to each other like frightened children. The camera zoomed in on their terrified faces, then out again to show the whole scene.

The ground beneath their feet changed to a roiling grey surface littered with rocks and scree. There was a deep rumble and the rocks reared and rolled and they had to let go of each other to keep their balance as the ground in front of them groaned and split with a mighty crack. It yawned open into a gaping, smoking hole.

The angels gingerly tiptoed forward, holding tightly on to each other's sleeve, and peered over the ragged edge. The scene zoomed in for another close-up, this time to show bright red molten lava bubbling and burping far below, a veritable pit populated by menacing black figures wielding pitchforks. Flames like solar flares leapt upwards and singed the tips of the angels' glorious wings.

The camera focused on the angels again as they both jumped smartly back from the brink and turned to face each other, their expressions mirroring pure, blind panic.

"What you see is representative, of course," drawled Nick now. "There isn't *actually* a stinking hole in the ground, Hell is far more sophisticated than that! But let's move on. The bottom line at this point was, one of us was to be the good angel and help humankind to be, well, *good* to each other, and the other one would have to be, as it were, the bad angel taking care of the *evil* side of things."

"Yes," Gabe's voice was tinged with sorrow, "and Michael said we had to choose."

For the first time, Uri came forward and took up the story. "Neither Gabriel nor Lucifer dared be the first to speak. Or move. They both understood the concept of 'selecting a volunteer', i.e. if no-one immediately puts their hand up to accept the mission, then the first one to blink, cough, scratch or fall to the ground in a dead faint, gets picked. They stood there like statues for, oh, I don't know how long. Michael went away to do other things, and left me to watch over them until they'd come to a decision. But they neither spoke nor moved a muscle. Not for a long, long time."

Gabe chimed in, "Michael got so exasperated with us, of course, and Uri suggested there must be some other way to make the decision. It was decided that we'd flip for it, so our destiny was hinged on the toss of the Divine Instrument for Settlement of Conflict. The DISC. See?"

A large golden coin filled the screen. It flew high into the air, paused as if enjoying the view from up there, then tumbled down again, glinting and sparkling as it spun over and over in the bright sunlight.

Nigel heard Lucifer say, "Heads, I stay."

And at the exact same time Gabriel said, "Tails, I stay."

The camera panned in to give a close-up of the DISC as it landed on the floor of the Great Hall, puffing up a small cloud of silvery dust. It teetered on its edge, turned slowly seven times, then tipped over and fell with the merest *tink* of metal on stone.

The angels clutched each other's sleeve again while Uri stooped down to see how the DISC had landed. He announced the result and a long silence followed.

It was broken by Lucifer exclaiming, "Damn and blast!"

The words 'The End' appeared on the screen before it went blank and rolled silently up into the ceiling. Uri announced that he would make some fresh coffee and Nick suggested Nigel might benefit from a slug of brandy first.

Nigel downed the brandy in one gulp, gasped, and croaked, "So you lost on the toss of a coin and went to Hell?"

In his heart of hearts, he still didn't believe any of it, but felt he had no choice but to behave as if he did. These individuals were clearly deranged and he wanted to get out of there in one piece.

"Yep. End of my innocence, as you can imagine. I didn't think it was fair, though. I mean, it should have been best of three at least, don't you think? But that's by the by, it was a long time ago. The thing is, I had no choice but to accept my destiny. I asked only one thing."

"And that was…?"

"When good and evil had been thoroughly tried and tested, all the kinks ironed out, analysed and fully understood by all concerned," he paused to take in air, then ended with a rush, "then Gabe and me would swap. I would return to the golden angelic hierarchy and Gabe would take my place and don the mantle as Lord of Eternal Darkness."

"Yes," said Gabe, rather sourly. "I didn't think Michael would listen to any *conditions*, but he actually chuckled and agreed to it. To my utter dismay, I might add. Uri transported the DISC to Earth and it was buried deep. We weren't allowed to know where. There it remained for thousands of years until it was dug up here, in the churchyard, thereby triggering the swap."

Nick took over. "At the time of the DISC's burial, Michael, Defender of Goodness and Chief of all Archangels, devised the Grand Plan which we are honour-bound to implement. But you see, in order for us to prepare for our new roles, we have to have a little *practice*. Uri is here to oversee it all."

"Yes," said Gabe. "Nick has to tempt a bad person into doing something good."

"And Gabe has to tempt a good person into doing something bad. And then we will swap jobs." Nick patted Nigel's shoulder. "You're the Witness."

Nigel, seriously beginning to wonder if these madmen would let him live to see another day, stammered, "Er, W-witness?"

Gabe sighed. "People will have to *know*, Nigel! You'll have to inform the world that Lucifer has returned to the Heavenly Hierarchy and that I..." He choked, unable to go on, and his grey eyes filled with tears.

Nigel leapt up and whirled to face Nick and Gabe, his tormentors. "This is insane!" he yelled. "I don't know what your game is, but I want no part of it. Angels? It's preposterous! You eat, for a start. Surely angels don't need to eat?"

"Of course we don't," snapped Nick, as if talking to a halfwit. "We eat because we enjoy it. And don't think for a minute we have digestion systems like you do." He shuddered. "Stomachs and intestines. Eugh! Doesn't bear thinking about."

"B-b-but... you... you... *can't* be angels! You don't even have wings!"

There was a soft sound, no more than a sigh. A light breeze ruffled Nigel's hair, and before his very eyes a pair of giant feathery wings sprouted from Gabe's back as Uri appeared with cups of coffee and slices of chocolate cake on a tray.

"I must say, my man," said Nick, clapping Nigel heartily between the shoulder blades, "you've gone awfully pale."

Not knowing what else to do, Nigel crammed a big piece of sponge into his mouth.

Uri laughed at his bulging cheeks. "When you've finished that I'll walk you back to The Anvil. I don't think you can take any more at the moment!"

Almost weeping, Nigel swallowed the cake, drank the coffee, and allowed himself to be led from the room.

Back at The Blacksmith's Anvil, Nigel asked Uri, "What did you mean when you said I couldn't take any more? Is there seriously more to this story?"

"I suggest you go up to your room, Nigel, and have a rest. I'll be back in an hour to tell you what happened when the DISC was found. Then you'll know it all, as we stand so far."

Nigel went up the stairs with a weary tread, but he didn't rest.

He just sat and stared at the wall until Uri returned, wondering how he was going to tell Amelia this incredible story that they had become a part of.

Chapter 14

seven virtues, seven sins

"… and the screen furled itself back up to the ceiling and I half expected to find myself sitting in the middle of a row of red plush chairs with empty cartons and sweet wrappers swirling round my feet."

Exhausted at relating the long and complicated story, Nigel took a deep draught from the glass of iced water and looked at Amelia, waiting for her reaction. For days he'd agonised over this conversation, but now they were together in Ham-Under-Lymfold to meet with Gabe and Nick he couldn't put it off any longer

"Angels," Amelia said now, with a measured and somewhat dangerous calm. "You expect me to believe we've been employed by angels?"

"Archangels, actually."

"Gabe is Gabriel and Nick is Lucifer?"

"Yes. And Uri is Uriel, who's here as an observer for Michael."

"And that would be *the* Michael, would it, the guardian and protector with the flaming sword and all that? Oh really, Nigel! I've never heard anything so ridiculous. You're having a joke, right? So stop being so silly and tell me what really happened!"

Nigel swallowed hard. If only he could tell Amelia it was all in jest. She probably wouldn't laugh, but at least the world would return to normal. With a sigh he said, "I just told you what really happened! It's not a joke, it really isn't. I wish it was."

"Did they give you something, put drugs in your coffee, or something in the cake, that made you hallucinate?"

Nigel sighed. "I thought of that, but why would they drug me? On my honour, I've told you the absolute truth. When I challenged them Gabe sprouted wings before my very eyes! And how can you explain what they've done to the mill? When I left there with Uri, and looked back, what I saw was the wreck of an old building with its door hanging off the hinges."

"Like I said, some kind of hallucinogenic drug."

"I can only say that it seemed very real to me at the time, and it still does."

Amelia looked deep into his eyes, as if hoping to read his mind and find the truth there.

"Okay," she said eventually, "I'm going to play along. Setting aside the number of times we've met Gabe and Nick and they've behaved like perfectly normal human beings, we are now to believe that they are really Gabriel and Lucifer and they have to change angelic roles because some sort of disc has been dug up?"

"The Divine Instrument for Settlement of Conflict, yes."

"Which has been found in Ham-Under Lymfold?"

"In the churchyard by the gravedigger. He gave it to the vicar."

"But the gravedigger has been replaced by another angel?"

"Uriel, yes. The villagers know him as Uri."

"So why hasn't this great coin discovery hit the news? I mean, a – what did you call it again?"

"The Divine Instr—"

"Oh, never mind. The thing is, if something like that were dug up, surely there'd be some hue and cry about it? I mean, the thing must be incredibly valuable!"

"Yes, I know." He dropped his head into his hands and rubbed his scalp. She was not going to believe this next bit either. "Apparently, the vicar cleaned it and activated it somehow and this gargoyle-like thing flew out of it and—"

Amelia rolled her eyes to the ceiling. "Oh, Nigel, please!"

"I'm telling you what they told me! So, Michael sent two men in the guise of gas boiler repairmen to swap the DISC for a real gold coin, something went wrong, and they had to knock out the vicar with an amnesia dust. He doesn't remember the DISC at all and he's now in possession of a genuine and very valuable English coin."

There was a long silence, and Nigel could tell by the tightness of Amelia's jaw that she was holding her temper in check.

Eventually she said, sarcasm in every word, "It just gets better and better."

He put his hand out to stop her rising from the sofa. "Okay, okay, I can understand your scepticism, but you weren't there! I'm telling you, Gabe and Nick—"

"You mean Gabriel and Lucifer, don't you?"

"Yes, precisely! It's so hard to explain, Amelia, but it was *real.* I've been over and over it a hundred times, but it's as if I understand the truth in some part of my brain that I didn't know I had."

"Hmm. So, you're telling me that all this is so that Lucifer gets to sit on a fluffy little cloud in Heaven strumming a harp, and poor old Gabriel turns into a creature with horns and hooves and takes up the dark throne of evil?"

"That about sums it up, yes, but only metaphorically speaking. I don't think clouds, harps, hooves and horns come into it."

"But Gabe sprouted wings, you said!"

"Only momentarily."

She ignored that. "But before any of it can happen, they have to, what? *Practice?*"

"That's right," said Nigel wearily. "It's been so long, you see, Gabe needs to get acquainted with sinners so he can run Hell efficiently, and Nick has to learn to be nice so he can return to the hierarchy and behave like a good little angel. I suppose they want to get close to ordinary people and, um, study them."

"They could do that in their own office, surely? They must employ thousands of people. Nigel, surely you know how ridiculous this sounds?"

"Oh, yes. I know *exactly* how ridiculous it sounds. But, the thing is, Amelia, even the office must have been an illusion. You try and find an office block in London that has 108 floors. Not only that, but their building has an impossible view, and I don't believe for a moment it's due to holographic windows! Can you tell me how a wrecked mill that's been abandoned for years can become a fully furnished mansion inside a week? Can you explain how that appointment that started all this got into the diary and how we were given a business card we couldn't read until *they* wanted us to be able to read it? And what about—"

"All right, all right!" Amelia held up her hand for him to stop. She chewed her bottom lip. "I don't know. But Nigel, just think for a minute. If these… these people… or whatever they are… can do all these fantastic things, why are they hiring you to renovate the mill? It seems such a…" she waved her hand in circles as she searched for the right words, "…such a *pedestrian* thing to do."

Nigel shook his head. Explaining the impossible was extremely tiring. "I didn't ask them. Perhaps you can."

"I'm not going there, not after what you've told me!"

"I know how crazy it sounds, Amelia, believe me. I saw it all, and it still sounds utterly mad. But we have a meeting with them in less than hour, and maybe you can see that blasted film for yourself, ask your questions, and then we'll be able to talk about it properly and decide what to do."

He waited. Amelia sat with her arms folded, her legs crossed, her whole body emanating utter confusion. Then she unfurled herself and sat up straight, and Nigel knew he'd won, at least for now.

"Alright," she said, raising her chin in a challenging manner. "Let's go, if it'll put a stop to this nonsense." She glared at him and stood up, then sat down again. "There's something else, isn't there? I can tell by your face."

Nigel hesitated before telling her, then blurted, "I've been chosen to be their Witness."

Amelia gave him a long look and Nigel saw her jaw tighten again as she said, her voice witheringly icy, "Witness?"

"You know, like, um, like the Gospels. I'm to inform the world that Lucifer has returned to Heaven and Gabe has—"

He ground to a halt as the look on Amelia's face turned dangerous. It was pointless telling her any more, she would just have to see it for herself. He held her jacket up and helped her shrug it on, and they walked in silence to the mill.

"There it is," he announced when they reached the Turnaround. "Angel Falls Mill, just as you last saw it. And that name can't be a coincidence!"

"And you're asking me to believe," replied Amelia, "that inside that wreck is a luxury house and the di Angelo brothers are living in it?"

"Yep, and you're about to see for yourself. Come on, I can't wait to see your face when you step inside."

Before they were halfway across the little stone bridge Gabe came rushing out of the door of the mill, which was still hanging off its hinges. He grabbed Amelia, kissed her heartily on both cheeks and then gathered her into a hug, crying, "I'm so delighted you could come!"

"Thank you, I'm pleased to be here. Nigel has told me all about it, but nothing beats seeing the real thing."

Nigel thought her tone was a tad sarcastic, but Gabe didn't seem to pick up on it. With a happy grin he said, "Nick's inside, won't you come in?"

Nigel entered the mill behind Amelia so he couldn't see her expression, but he certainly heard her gasp and had to move smartly to one side to avoid her foot coming hard down on his as she staggered backwards in shock.

"Good morning! Lovely to see you again, Amelia, and positively blooming, if I may say so." Nick had taken her hand

and was leading her across the vast space to the white sofa. "Nigel," he muttered over his shoulder, a dismissive hello if ever he'd heard one.

"I wouldn't worry," whispered Gabe, "Nick seems to be very attractive to women, and he plays up to it, but your Amelia only has eyes for you. Besides, we may look like men to you, but we're angels, and angels are asexual beings."

Nigel started to laugh, but realised that Gabe was serious. "Is Uri coming?"

Gabe shook his head. "I'm afraid not, he's busy at the vicarage."

Amelia, sitting down now, was staring around her in wonder. "Nigel told me about this, but I didn't believe it."

Nick, who had sat himself close beside her, his arm across the back of her cushion, said coolly, "And he told you about us being angels, but you don't believe that either, do you?"

"Would you like to watch the film?" Gabe was like an eager puppy. "It might make things easier. And we've got excellent popcorn, all sorts of flavours."

Amelia slowly shook her head. "No, it's all right. Really. Nigel told me every little detail."

Nick, a gleam in his grey eyes, said, "But you still can't accept it, can you?"

"What I really don't understand," she declared, "is why you're going to the trouble of hiring Nigel and me to do up this mill? I mean, look at the place, it's fabulous! Why don't you just leave it as it is?"

"Amelia, Amelia," tutted Nick, sliding his arm down the cushion so that it rested on her shoulders. "This isn't the mill!"

This was news to Nigel, and he swung round to face Gabe. "How can it not be the mill?"

Gabe smiled at them both. "I will explain. We're using the mill as a portal, you see. When you step through the door you step out of your reality and into ours. Well, our reality in that we've made it accessible to you, if you see what I mean. No-one else would see this, only you two."

"Is your office the same? A portal?" asked Nigel.

"Yes, it is. We create something that you can understand, that's all."

Nigel struggled to process this. He thought of the reception, the elevator with the little uniformed operator, the long carpeted corridor to Gabe's fantastic suite of offices Okay, he hadn't recognised the building and he'd been prevented from going outside, but that had been because the limousine was urgently needed. Wasn't it?

Nick stood up and paced across the room. "The office, as you see it, is both Heaven and Hell, but you couldn't possibly comprehend the reality. It's a representation, like the film we showed you."

"But you asked about the mill, Amelia," said Gabe. "Doing it up and making it into a going concern is our gift to the village for their unwitting involvement in the Grand Plan. You and Nigel get the pleasure of doing the things you both love, the workmen you hire will be well paid and also get enormous job satisfaction, and once it's up and running, it will bring employment and visitors willing to spend money into the village. So there you have it. Everyone wins."

White-lipped, Amelia whispered, "I don't believe it. I don't believe any of it."

Nick sneered, "Perhaps you'd like a little more proof? Are you sure you don't want to see the film? No? Then perhaps I should summon my mascot!"

"Nick—" there was both a warning and a plea in Gabe's voice as the air rapidly chilled and their ears were assaulted by a horrid, ear-piercing shriek.

Nigel quickly crossed to the sofa and sat beside Amelia, pulling her into his arms as a huge and monstrous shape shimmered in front of them. The sight of it made his skin crawl, and his nostrils twitched as an unpleasant smell pervaded the room. Amelia's hand flew to her throat. With another terrible screech, the thing fully formed and stretched its bat-like wings with a noise like a rug being heartily thwacked with carpet-beaters. Its great head was horned, its beak hooked with razored edges, its powerful body covered in leathery scales. It was truly a dreadful, terrifying thing that surely belonged in the Prehistoric Age.

"On second thoughts," drawled Nick, his eyes like flint, "I really don't think this is a good idea: he looks hungry."

The creature flickered and flared briefly before fading away to nothing, and the smell of raw sewage instantly, thankfully, went with it.

"How about my mascot then?" chirped Gabriel, desperately trying to lighten the atmosphere.

Another bird, much smaller, appeared in the same place in front of Nigel and Amelia, but this one had brightly-coloured plumage and was breathtakingly lovely. It flew on sapphire blue wings tipped with white, its long tail feathers fluttering like golden ribbons, and landed on Gabe's outstretched hand.

"My bird of paradise," he said softly, stroking its scarlet breast.

Amelia sighed, "Oh! It's gorgeous."

The bird immediately flew to her and sang a song of such haunting beauty that her eyes filled with tears.

"Enough of this," barked Nick, spoiling the mood. "Let's get to business."

The bird disappeared in an instant, leaving in its trail the scent of roses and mint which Nigel and Amelia gratefully inhaled.

Nick disappeared for a while, then came back pressing buttons on the remote control so familiar to Nigel. The screen came down from the ceiling. Under his arm, Nigel could see that Nick carried the buff folder that he and Amelia had prepared, the folder that contained brief profiles of everyone he'd met or heard about in the village. Their jobs, skills, hobbies, their likes and dislikes.

"Are we going to watch another film?" asked Nigel, hoping the answer would be no.

"Nope. This screen also serves as a whiteboard. We can write on it and rub it off." He waggled a packet of coloured pens, selected the black one and drew two vertical lines so the screen was divided into three columns. They were perfectly straight and perfectly spaced.

Gabe was quiet, but his body language shouted that he didn't want to participate in whatever was coming.

"Right." Nick, now cheerful, held a red felt pen in his hand, poised to write. "Who can name the Seven Sins?"

Nobody answered.

"Come on, come on! How about you, Nigel? Just one or two to get us started?"

Having not the faintest idea where this was leading, Nigel blew out his cheeks and came up with Pride and Envy.

"Good, good, I like those." Nick wrote them up. "I well remember how you envied my sartorial elegance the first time we met. How about you, Amelia?"

Nigel thought she wouldn't join in, but she seemed to have decided to rise to the challenge.

"Gluttony and Lust, I think. Wrath is another one. And is Greed the same as Gluttony, or a different sin?"

"Oh well done!" Nick pranced around like a game show host, clearly enjoying himself. "Gluttony and Greed are, I grant you, closely related, but they are different sins. Gluttony is all about wanton self-indulgence, whereas greed is about selfish and uncharitable acquisition. So, that's six. And I'll add the seventh, because we don't want to be here all day."

He wrote the word 'Sloth' on the whiteboard then read through the list, eyes aglow, pronouncing each sin with relish.

He stepped back and they all regarded the seven words written neatly in the column on the left-hand side. Nick took the blue pen from the pack and held it out to Gabe. "The Seven Heavenly Virtues, brother."

"Oh, that's easy," smiled Amelia. "Faith, Hope, Charity, Fortitude, Justice, Hope—"

"Duh-uh!" said Nick. "You said Hope twice. Shall we play charades to give you a clue?"

"Okay, okay, Nick! Let her think." Gabe spoke sharply to his brother, but his eyes were soft on Amelia.

She said, "I can't think of the others, sorry."

Gabe wrote the remaining two on the board. "Temperance and Prudence. Don't hear them much these days, but they're such wonderful words, aren't they?"

Now there were two lists on the screen, in identical, neat calligraphy. The centre column was still blank.

"Right, Nigel, who's the most unpopular person in the village?"

Something in Nick's tone made Nigel highly suspicious, but though his mind raced he still couldn't guess what they were up to and couldn't find his voice to ask.

Amelia, with narrowed eyes, posed the question he hadn't been able to form in his mind, "Why do you want to know?"

"Now, now, Amelia, this is all part of what we're paying you for. Nigel has been here getting to know the residents for a reason. You're about to find out what that reason is."

Gabe jumped in. "There's nothing to worry about, I promise you. This is the good part."

"Okay," said Nigel, trusting Gabe in a way he would never trust Gabe's brother. "Well, then, I'd have to say Violet Cattermole."

Gabe wrote her name up in the middle column. "Yes, that's what we thought."

"Is there anyone else?" demanded Nick. "What about Freddie Fordingbridge?"

Nigel was surprised. "Freddie? No, he's very nice and extremely popular. A lovely young man, I'd say, always polite."

"Ah, but according to your report he spends hours playing violent war games on his Xbox, the bloodier the better—"

"But that doesn't make him bad," Amelia said. "Lots of lads play games like that and that's all they are – games."

"Well how about Stanley Hubertus Invincible Trout, then, he's—" and, to everyone's amazement, Nick collapsed into a fit of giggles.

They looked at him with raised eyebrows. "I heard something about our Stanley Trout," he gasped, wiping his eyes. "Apparently, some youngsters used to play a version of hopscotch out in the street. One would throw a pebble into a chalked grid and as they hopped to the pebble, the chant would be..." He continued in a sing-sing voice, "Stanley-Hubert-us-Invin-cible-Trout, take his ini-tials-and-shout-the-word-out." He looked from Nick to Gabe to Amelia but they stared back blankly. "They'd all scream SHI—"

"Okay, okay, we get the drift," said Gabe.

Nigel chuckled and said, "Everyone likes Stanley actually. He's knowledgeable and great fun to talk to. You just need to be able to hold your breath for a long time. No, I think I would have to say it's Violet. Everyone here is so pleasant, that one sour old lady really stands out like a sore thumb. She's bad tempered and rude, and very mean to her poor sister, Hilda, something to do with Hilda taking Violet's boyfriend way back when. They haven't spoken since Hilda married him."

Gabe circled Violet's name on the screen. "Well, you said it when we saw her in the pub. She has money, her sister doesn't, and Violet has no intention of helping because she's still harbouring a grudge. So, I think it would be fitting to tempt her with Charity." He turned from the whiteboard. "Nick? Do you agree?"

Nick nodded, but didn't sound very enthusiastic when he replied, "It's as good as any, I suppose."

"Well, that's agreed then. Let's have a coffee break shall we? Amelia, let me show you around the kitchen."

Nigel watched Amelia as she wandered around the amazing kitchen in open-mouthed wonder. Anyone would admire such sleek, clean lines and all those gadgets, especially someone like Amelia who loved cooking but only had the most basic kitchen in their tiny flat. Gabe, getting more and more excited, showed her how everything worked, in between making and pouring copious amounts of their special-blend coffee. Nigel suspected the angels were addicted to it.

Every time Nick suggested going back to the screen and getting on with things, Gabe would pour everyone another cup and hand round slices of one of Glen Perkins's Victoria sponge cake. Nigel, beginning to shake after so much caffeine and sugary cake, had the distinct impression that Gabe was deliberately delaying going back to that screen and those lists.

When they could drink no more coffee and the cake was gone, and everything in the kitchen had been admired twice over by Amelia, Nick actually grabbed Gabe by the arm and dragged him back into the living room. Nigel couldn't help but notice how Gabe's demeanour drooped when Nick let him go.

Nick picked up the red pen. "Now then, Nigel. Who would you say is the most popular person in the village?"

A sound issued from Gabe's throat that was like a suppressed sob. He sank down on the sofa next to Amelia and grasped her hand. His other hand went to his mouth, and he started chewing at a fingernail.

Amelia's expression was one of dawning realisation.

"Nigel?" Nick stood by the screen, his grey eyes, very dark now, fixed on Nigel.

"Um, it's hard to answer that one," Nigel hedged. "As I said before, there are so many nice people here."

"Indeed. But one or two must stand out, I would think?"

Nigel stared at the words on the screen. On the right were the Seven Virtues. There was Violet Cattermole's name with an arrow pointing to Charity. On the left were the Seven Sins. He had a horrible, nauseating feeling he knew where this was going.

He squared his shoulders and held his hand out for Amelia. "We don't want any part in this."

"Don't you?" The words exploded into the room from Nick, and he seemed to grow a foot taller as he blocked their exit. "You think you have a choice now? We told you what this was about! We told you we needed to practice before we could change over."

"Yes, you did, but I didn't know that meant you would start meddling with lives like this!"

Gabe put his hands up and said, "We didn't make the rules, but we have to abide by them. We've been in our roles for an awfully long time and I don't know how it feels to tempt someone into sin, and Nick doesn't know how it feels not to do it. So you see, the Boss demands that we experience a reversal of our current roles in order for us to prepare for our new ones."

"Well we won't help you choose who gets the bad deal, that's too much to ask," exclaimed Amelia.

"You've already done it," said Nick carelessly, pointing to the file. "I was just hoping to inject a little fun into the proceedings."

The blood drained from Nigel's face as he looked wildly from Nick to Gabe and back again.

Gabe pulled a large handkerchief from his pocket and swiped at the tears filling his eyes. "It wouldn't matter who you said, Nigel, because he's already decided."

"Who? Who has he decided on?"

Gabe's voice was a mere whisper. "Lorelei Dove."

Amelia stalked over to Nick, fury on her face. "Do you mean to tell me," she said, her voice very low and dangerous, "that some poor, unsuspecting person is going to wake up one morning and find themselves afflicted with… with… wrath or lust or something else equally nasty?"

"And what's wrong with lust?" he leered at her. "You can have a great deal of fun with lust. But I notice you say nothing about the mean Miss Cattermole waking up to find herself feeling suddenly charitable towards her fellow men."

"Please, Amelia, please," cried Gabe. "It's not as bad as you think. We do have the power to make people do whatever we want, but really we are only allowed to tempt them. It's up to them whether or not to give in."

"But that's still not fair! You're still manipulating them and they don't know what you're going to do!"

Nick threw his hands up in exasperation. "Well, it wouldn't be temptation if we told them, would it? You don't seem to understand what that word means; it means lure, coax, beguile…"

"What if I told them, warned them what you're going to do?" she hissed.

"Well, you could, of course, but what, exactly, would you tell them? Do you think for a moment they would believe you? *You* don't even believe you!"

"Well, I'm fast getting there…"

"Yes, dear, because we have allowed it."

"Don't you patronise me!"

"You shouldn't let yourself get so upset in your condition, you know."

"How dare you!"

Amelia and Nick were now almost nose to nose. Amelia, breathing heavily, her fists clenched and eyes narrowed with fury, glared up at Nick, but Nick didn't glare back. He had tilted his head and was studying Amelia as if she were a rare and beautiful butterfly caught in a specimen jar.

Nigel could see Nick's admiration. He wasn't surprised. His wife was magnificent anyway, but even more so when she saw injustice and wanted to do something about it. Gabe, on the other hand, was still slumped on the sofa, a picture of utter dejection.

"Okay, okay, that's enough. Break it up you two," said Nigel, stepping forward and gently pulling Amelia away.

After holding Nick's amused gaze for another few seconds, and clearly having to fight the urge to slap his face really hard, Amelia finally relented and sagged into Nigel's arms.

"And to think," she said, looking sadly from Gabe to Nigel, "that we're involved in this."

Nigel didn't reply. It was true. He, especially, was involved. He'd used his private eye skills to find out what he could about the good citizens of Ham-Under-Lymfold and typed up the profiles he'd handed to the angels. It was really basic information, but he still felt horribly guilty.

"Amelia," said Gabe gently, patting her arm, "it won't do any good to interfere, you know. We have to do this, you see, and, we're hoping to tempt one person from being bad to good, don't forget, so things may turn out all right in the end. Let me explain once more. The bottom line is, Nick has to learn how it feels to be responsible for a person changing for the good, so he can remember how it is to be an angel rather than a devil—"

"*The* Devil," if you please, interrupted Nick.

"Oh shut up, Nick, I'm trying to explain things here. And I, well, I have to experience it the other way round. You know, lead someone into Temptation and all that."

"But doesn't a person get to choose whether they're good or bad?" said Nigel.

"Yes, Nigel, they do. I keep telling you, we can only tempt them. They can choose whether or not to be tempted. But one way or the other we have to achieve a result or the change can't happen, so if not Violet and Lorelei, it will be someone else and someone else again until it happens."

Nick snorted. "Yeah, but it won't come to that. Humans are weak. Easily led. It'll be a piece of cake. Which, as it happens, is a good metaphor, since I've chosen the sin of Gluttony for the luscious Lorelei Dove. And you, Nigel, your final act as our Witness, will be to explain to the world that I am the good guy loved by all and Gabe is the one wearing the dark mantle."

Amelia walked up to Gabe and peered into his eyes. Softly, she said, "You don't want it to happen, do you?" She returned to Nigel's side and pronounced, "As far as I can see, the biggest problem you're going to have in all of this is each other. Gabe, you're a lovely man... angel... whatever. It simply shines from you. Do you think you can really be another Lucifer?"

"And what about me?" snarled Nick. "Don't you think I can be a good angel?"

Her withering look said it all.

Chapter 15
charity

Gabe was in a very good mood, because today Nick was going to begin the process of tempting Violet Cattermole from being a rich, mean old lady into becoming a rich, generous old lady. He'd hummed all the way through breakfast, causing Nick to growl at him at a couple of times, and he'd taken great satisfaction in reminding Nick that he had to learn how to appreciate the Seven Virtues, not denigrate them. "You seem to forget, brother, that you must put the old Lucifer behind you, otherwise how are you going to return to the hierarchy as a reformed archangel?"

"Fsst!" or something like it was the sour reply.

There had been a light shower of rain during the night, but the day had dawned dry and bright. They spotted Violet sitting on the bench on the green, the black straw hat with the lime-green plastic flower on her head and a large bag of toffees at her side. She was chewing furiously while she monitored the goings-on in the neighbourhood.

"Now, Nick," whispered Gabe as they approached, "all you need to do is to entice her in the nicest and politest possible way to give you one of her sweets. I'll show you how it's done, okay?"

They sat down, one either side of Violet. With a 'tut' of irritation she snatched up her toffees before Nick could squash them. She eyeballed them both with her most haughty expression, but Gabe responded with a hearty, "Good morning, Miss Cattermole. Lovely day!"

"What do you want?" she snapped, false teeth clacking.

Gabe pointed to the colourful bag she clutched on her lap and said in the politest of tones, "I love toffees, may I have one?"

"No, you may not."

"Well that's rather mean," Nick grinned, and before she had time to slap his hand away, had grabbed a handful toffees from the packet. "Mint, nope. Butter, nope. Ah, treacle, that's more like it!" The red wrapper was off in a trice, the sweet popped into his mouth, and he started chomping noisily. "Mmm, delicious." That was followed in quick succession by a liquorice and then a rum & raisin, the wrappings carelessly dropped to the grass at his feet.

"Nick!" hissed Gabe. "Pick up your litter! And that's not temptation, that's force!"

Nick, making no move to pick up the wrappings, just laughed, "Yeah, but I've got a toffee and you haven't." He waved a green-wrapped sweet in the air. "Want this mint one?" Gabe huffily refused, so Nick nudged Violet and said, "See it all from here, do you, the goings on?"

The old lady pursed her lips like a drawstring bag and a malicious gleam came into her black, piggy eyes. "That I do. Lived here all my life, and I've watched people arrive, born in the village or come from elsewhere, and I've seen them go, either to pastures new or to the graveyard in a coffin. Way back I saw young Jack Heavysides sneak out of his father's pub to pay a visit to Carmen Watson, as she was then, who was obviously not the Little Miss Pious she liked to make herself out to be. Became Mrs Heavysides quick enough, because there was a baby on the way. Said it was premature when it arrived a month early!"

"Naughty Carmen," drawled Nick. "Who else did you spy on?"

"I watched Gwen Brown set her cap at Glen Perkins, brazen as you please, and she had him marching up the aisle within a year. And now there's that Debbie Perkins, nothing but a wayward teenager whose legs are obscenely long and skirts far too short."

"Ooh," said Nick, "Spiteful little cat, aren't you! What about Lorelei Dove over there, what do you think of her?"

"Nick," hissed Gabe. "Stop it."

"Oh, I'm sure Violet is more than happy to talk." He nudged her again, "Right, Violet?"

"The hussy has a new boyfriend." Violet pointed to Lorelei's tiny, one-bedroom cottage opposite. "Stays overnight he does. And some nights she doesn't come home, and there's no need to guess where she is. Puts a little case in her car, and off she goes with a silly grin on her freckled face."

She was glassy eyed now, as if in a trance.

"That's enough, Nick! Let's start again, and do it properly this time."

Gabe lightly tapped Violet's arm. "Good morning, Miss Cattermole. Lovely day!"

"What do you want?" she snapped.

"A toffee would be nice," said Nick.

"Then go and buy your own, young man. I'm a pensioner, you know!" She clutched her bag of toffees to her chest and tried to shrink away from the brothers.

But for the next hour they kept her there, held tight between them, while they chattered about everything from the narrow confines of village life where everyone knew your business to the political situation in Brazil. Nick kept asking for a toffee, and Violet kept refusing, not daring to open the bag to take any for herself in case Nick grabbed them all.

Gabe could see that what Nick really wanted to do was wrestle the bag from the old lady and scoff the lot. He wasn't even trying to come up with another way in to tempt Violet to niceness. He hissed at him.

Nick glowered back at them, then said to Violet, "See much of your sister, do you?"

Gabe shook his head with another warning, thinking that this was not a good opening gambit.

Violet sucked in her breath and fixed Nick with furious eyes, "What's me and Hilda got to do with you?"

Nick shrugged. "I just wondered. I mean, you've got your nice house and all this money, thanks to us, and she doesn't, so it stands to reason that you might like to help her out."

"I'll have you know, you cheeky devil, that my sister's house is far larger than mine!"

"Oh sure," Nick drawled, highly amused at being called a cheeky devil. "But I bet yours doesn't have a leaking roof, rotting floorboards and heating so ancient it gave up the ghost years ago."

This was met with a furious intake of breath and Gabe watched in alarm as Violet's face turned a mottled purple with indignation.

"Excuse me," he muttered, "I just need a word with my brother." He scooped up the discarded wrappings scattered on the grass, grabbed Nick's arm and pulled him away.

"Nick, you're going about this all wrong! You're not tempting her to do a good deed, you're just annoying her."

"I know, isn't it fun! She's such a splendid woman!" He looked back over his shoulder at her and sighed. "I like her just the way she is."

"Of course you do, but I must remind you yet again, brother, of your mission. It's Charity, Nick, and only Charity. And all you have to do is get a toffee given to you willingly. It could hardly be easier! Now let's try again."

Nick's lip curled as he went back to the bench and sat down, lightly touching Violet's arm before saying with a false joviality, "Good morning, Miss Cattermole. Lovely day!"

"What do you want?" Violet snapped.

"A toffee would be nice," he replied.

"Then go to the shop and buy some. I'm not a charity, you know!"

Gabe frowned at the irony of her choice of words. Clearly this was going to take a lot longer than they'd thought, and they were just wasting their time right now. "Let's go, Nick."

They traipsed back to the mill and sat at the breakfast bar in the kitchen, coffee and cake untouched in front of them.

"All you had to do was get Violet to give you a single toffee. But oh no, you had to steal a handful and then get her all worked up about her sister. Now we've got to think of something else."

"Bad habits are hard to break, bro."

"It doesn't bother me, Nick." He gave a careless shrug, trying not to show any sign that he was actually delighted at Nick's mess up. But Gabe was an angel and angels did not renege on their promises. And this particular Promise, one with a capital P, simply could not be avoided for long. He knew he had a duty to remind Nick of what was at stake, but he couldn't bring himself to look his brother in the eye as he muttered, "After all, it just means I get to stay in Heaven longer."

That made Nick sit up. "Blast it, you're right! I hadn't considered that!" He hopped off the stool and paced the floor. "All right, Gabe, while I work out my next move you can take your turn. All you have to do is tempt Lorelei Dove into having something loaded with calories. She was a greedy girl once who ate half a dozen cakes a day, so it should be easy. One mouthful of chocolate cake or whatever should trigger Gluttony, and then I'll make sure I sort out our delicious Violet Cattermole. Such a shame to have to meddle with a perfectly glorious sourpuss, but it has to be done!"

Gabe sighed. Why oh why did he have to be so honest all the time? Why couldn't he have kept silent and let Nick just bumble along, getting it wrong? Now, he was sure, his brother would not make the same mistake again, and the time was creeping ever nearer when he, sweet and gentle Gabriel, would have to accept the horrid, evil mantle of Hell.

Chapter 16
gluttony

It was time for them to leave, but Stephen really didn't want to move. He was too absorbed by Lorelei's face, her hair, the feel of her soft, warm body in his arms as she chatted about… well, he was too busy listening to her voice to take in the words. For all he cared she could be reciting train timetables, he'd still be as enchanted as he'd been when they first met. Tonight was their twenty-third date and they were going to celebrate with a candlelit dinner in his favourite place, a small and intimate Italian trattoria, just around the corner from his apartment.

"We need to go, Lorelei," he said with reluctance. "The table's booked for 7:30."

Lorelei leaned into him, but after allowing himself the pleasure of just a brief kiss, Stephen sighed and pulled himself away. "If we don't move right now, we'll never get out of here. We're going to be late as it is. Come on, let's go and eat and then we'll come back here and…" He waggled his eyebrows and did a lewd little jiggle with his hips, making Lorelei giggle.

"Do you think we'll get to eat dessert this time? Maybe we should share one."

It was a private joke between them that they'd never managed to stay for a pudding. From the moment they sat down, the heat between them would start to build, rising by the minute until it simply got too hot for them to eat anything else. Stephen, in a strangled voice, would ask for the bill, and they'd be out of the restaurant and entwined in each other's arms like lovesick teenagers. The last time this had happened, a passer-by had muttered, "Get a room, why don't you!"

Stephen held out her soft woollen wrap and kissed the tip of her freckled nose once it was settled around her shoulders. They made the short walk as if joined together from shoulder to hip.

They arrived twenty minutes after the time he had booked for, but it didn't matter, they were greeted warmly and led to a table in the corner.

The waiter handed them a menu each, took their drinks orders, and with a flourish lit the stubby candle in the wax-covered Chianti bottle. Lorelei looked so beautiful, Stephen began to wonder if they'd manage to get beyond the starter, let alone make it to a shared dessert. He fingered the box in his pocket and wondered when would be the best time to—

His thoughts were interrupted by a chocolate-brown voice drawling, "Good evening, Miss Dove."

Stephen blinked at the tall figure staring down at Lorelei as if he'd like to devour her. Slightly alarmed, he racked his memory… yes, it was one of the di Angelo brothers; he'd seen them once in The Blacksmith's Anvil and Lorelei had told him who they were. At first he thought the man was alone, but then saw that behind him was the other one, the brother, looking as if he was trying to hide.

Stephen blinked some more, and then, remembering his manners, raised his bottom a couple of inches off the chair and held out his hand. "Hello, I don't think we've been formally introduced? You obviously know Lorelei, and I'm Stephen George."

"Nick di Angelo," replied the man, giving Stephen's hand a brief but bone-crunching shake. "And this is my brother, Gabe."

The one called Gabe stepped forward with a shy smile and gave Stephen the merest nod of his head. He then took Lorelei's hand, raising it and grazing her knuckles with his lips and gazing deep into her eyes. When he let go, Lorelei seemed momentarily startled, and Stephen saw such a sorrowful expression on Gabe's face that he wondered if he'd recently had some very bad news.

There was an awkward silence as Stephen waited for the two interlopers to go to their own table and leave them alone before the romantic mood was completely broken. And he wanted tonight to be very romantic, more than any other night they'd spent together.

But Nick, directing a slightly malicious grin in his direction, rubbed his hands together, and said, "Well, isn't this nice. Hey! Why don't we all sit together?"

Before anyone could object – and everyone except Nick looked as if they really wanted to – he had ordered that two tables be joined up so the four of them could sit together.

Stephen was too stunned and too well-mannered to do anything other than pretend it was what he'd wanted all along. Perhaps Lorelei was better acquainted with the di Angelos than he'd thought and she was happy for them to share their table? But as Gabe took the seat next to her, his cheeks flushed and his eyes downcast, he could see that Lorelei was just as taken aback by this turn of events. Of the four of them, then, only Nick di Angelo seemed totally relaxed, and Stephen felt a resentful dislike for the man start to build.

The evening that followed was utterly surreal as far as Stephen was concerned. The velvet-lined box could not possibly be brought out from his inside pocket under these circumstances, even if the di Angelo brothers were to leave them alone after the meal. Maybe it was a sign, for Stephen believed in such things, that it was too soon to be thinking of marriage? They hadn't been together all that long, after all – but no… he'd known she was the one for him since their first date in The White Lion. And Lorelei constantly declared her love for him. She'd even told him that he had a wonderful aura, and had been surprised and delighted that he'd known exactly what she'd meant.

"You'll love my sister," Stephen had responded. "She's a family counsellor, but she does astrology for a hobby. She loves angel cards and psychic fairs, all that kind of thing."

"And you don't think it's silly?" Her green eyes had searched his brown ones.

"No, Lorelei, I don't think it's silly. My sister is one of the smartest and most sensible people I know, and her astrological readings have sometimes been of great help to me. She's longing to meet you."

Now he wanted to marry Lorelei as soon as possible. He'd told Stella, who had become very fond of Lorelei, that he planned to have the ring secretly placed in a glass of champagne and presented to his beloved, but she had replied, "That's very romantic, Stephen, but fraught with danger, bearing in mind you both go all to pieces when you're together. You'd have to hope she didn't knock her glass over or just gulp it down and choke on it! But really, dear, Lorelei strikes me as a woman who would prefer you to go down on one knee and present the ring in the traditional manner."

So that's what he'd planned to do, right here in this restaurant, but now he could only sit, fuming in silent frustration, as Nick di Angelo dominated the conversation. The subjects ranged from the narrow confines of village life where everyone knew your business to the political situation in Brazil and back again. Nick ate heartily, sometimes talking with his mouth full, but Stephen noted that Lorelei and Gabe merely picked at their food. He hoped they could make their escape after the main course, but when he tried to say that they had had enough to eat, Nick overruled them and called for the dessert menu.

A waiter brought over a blackboard with the desserts neatly chalked on it and left it on the table so they could take their time. Gabe, who'd hardly spoken a word, didn't even glance at it, muttering that he didn't want anything.

"Would you please excuse us for a moment?" said Nick. "I just need a quick word with my brother."

They left the table and Stephen watched in amazement as they walked out of the restaurant. Were they leaving him with the bill? But no, he could see them through the window, and they seemed to be arguing. Well, Nick was talking urgently and waving his hands about, a look of fury on his face, but Gabe was standing with his head down and his hands shoved in his pockets, looking like a schoolboy being admonished by the headmaster. Stephen looked ruefully at Lorelei and said, "I'm so sorry about this. I should have insisted at the start that we wanted to be alone."

Lorelei smiled at him, "No need to apologise. You were being polite and I rather think Nick wouldn't have taken no for an answer."

"They're a bit strange, though, aren't they? Nick doesn't stop talking!"

"Mm, and Gabe doesn't say much at all. Oh, shh, they're coming back. Let's say we're finished and need to leave."

The brothers took their seats, Nick grinning as he laid his napkin once more across his lap, Gabe looking for all the world as if he was holding back tears as he did the same.

"Lorelei," Gabe said, his shoulders still slightly slumped as he reached for the blackboard, "I do hope you're going to join me in having a dessert?"

"Er, no, thank you." She patted her stomach. "I'm far too full."

"Oh you can't be," said Gabe, his cheeks flaming for some unfathomable reason. "You hardly ate a thing! Now, how about chocolate mousse?"

Lorelei held up her hand. "No, really. I don't want anything."

"Raspberry roulade? Profiteroles? Crème Caramel?"

Gabe sounded a bit desperate and Stephen wondered why he was trying to force Lorelei into choosing a dessert. He decided to take charge, and tried to attract the attention of a waiter, saying, "I'm sorry, but we really do have to leave now. I'll get the bill."

Gabe implored, "How about rhubarb tart? Or ice cream? Gosh, says here they have six flavours."

Lorelei shook her head, and reached behind her to take her wrap from the back of her chair.

Nick, looking highly amused, said, "So… no desserts, then."

Gabe dropped his head, whether with frustration or relief Stephen couldn't tell, until he caught a smile that Gabe was trying to hide. What on earth was going on here?

What happened next was so astounding Stephen would later believe he'd hallucinated the scene. As Nick leaned forward and made to touch Lorelei's arm, Gabe gave a strangled cry and, to Stephen's mind, deliberately knocked over his nearly-full glass of wine. The liquid appeared to leave the glass in a solid burgundy ball which skimmed across the surface of the crisp white tablecloth before hurling itself at Nick, spattering the front of his pale blue shirt, his red silk tie, and the lapels of his jacket. Not a speck of wine landed anywhere else.

There was a stunned silence and nobody moved until two waiters converged on their table with napkins and started to dab at Nick's clothes. His face a picture of controlled fury, Nick pushed them away and told them not to trouble, then he calmly asked for the bill.

He insisted on paying. "After all, it was my idea that we all dine together." He ordered Stephen to put his wallet away when Stephen tried to contribute.

The bill was settled with a large pile of new twenty-pound notes and the brothers said their goodbyes. Stephen caught Gabe, who'd spoken not a word since knocking over his wine, cast a very strange look at Lorelei as he rose from his chair, one of profound sadness. They really were a pair of odd fellows.

But that was forgotten as with much relief Stephen gently escorted Lorelei away from the trattoria in case the dreadful

Nick di Angelo, despite his wine-stained suit, reappeared and insisted on dragging them to a nightclub or something.

Finally alone back at his apartment, they discussed what had happened. Stephen asked if she'd noticed anything odd about the wine-spilling incident, but she replied that her eyes had been on him so she hadn't seen anything.

"I can't explain why," she mused, "Gabe seems quite sweet, but I'm really not keen on Nick. There's something about him—"

He held up his hand to stop her speaking further. "Shh! No more talk of them or anyone else!" He slid down onto one knee in front her, took her left hand in both of his. "Lorelei, my darling, sweet Lorelei, will you marry me?"

Her eyes widened and she gasped, "Stephen, I—"

"I know it's early days for us, but I don't care! I love you, Lorelei, I know you are the one for me, and I want you to be my wife." He pulled out the velvet box and lifted the lid, revealing a delicate ring set with a round purple stone, two small diamonds sparkling either side. "Please say yes."

"Oh, Stephen!" she gasped. "It's beautiful! Is that amethyst?"

He nodded. "I had it specially made. I couldn't think you'd want any other stone." He removed it from its snug velvet bed and held it up to her. "It'll fit you, my love. I borrowed a ring-sizer from the jeweller and measured that silver ring you sometimes wear when you left it on the bedside table. But, Lorelei, you haven't answered my question."

She threw herself at him, knocking him flat on his back, crying, "Oh Stephen, the answer's yes! Yes please! Yes, yes, YES!"

Chapter 17
a new recipe

Gabe was not happy to be heading for the bakery at 4:30 in the morning, but Nick, who'd finally stopped sulking after the failed temptations of Violet Cattermole and Lorelei Dove, was determined that they would go together.

"Come on, bro," Nick cajoled. "It'll be interesting!"

"The only thing that interests me about baking is eating the result. How do you know that he starts so early anyway?"

"It's all in Nigel's profiles, which you would know if you bothered to read them. Perkins wakes very early without the aid of an alarm clock and leaves his warm double bed without waking his wife, who doesn't rise until four hours later. He tiptoes downstairs in his dressing gown, and into the kitchen, where the only sound is a loudly ticking clock. Laid out for him by Gwen the night before are his work clothes, a large, clean white apron, and a mug with a spoonful of instant coffee and two sugars in it. Then he gets dressed and-"

Gabe butted in, "Are you really telling me that Nigel's reports go into such fine detail?"

"Well, he hasn't done a bad job, but, no, he could hardly know all the really intimate details. So I've checked them out for myself."

"You mean you've been spying? Honestly, Nick, you really are struggling to be angelic, you know."

"Oh yes? And what about you at the restaurant with Lorelei? If you wanted to stop me touching Lorelei and resetting the scene you shouldn't have done it that way! I'm sure Stephen George noticed the trajectory of that wine!"

"Not that again! Of course he didn't notice! Humans see magic all the time but they don't believe their own eyes and brush it away. I didn't want you resetting the scene, Nick. I just couldn't do it, not that night." Gabe narrowed his eyes at his brother. "You do know what Stephen was intending to do, don't you?"

"No I do not know and I don't care! Unlike you, I was concentrating on the job in hand, not prying into his mind."

"He was going to propose, Nick!"

Nick's grey eyes narrowed and darkened to obsidian and he spoke through gritted teeth, "As you've so recently pointed out, it is only in *your* interest that neither Lorelei nor Violet succumb to temptation." He stabbed his finger into Gabe's chest, and continued to jab with each word while Gabe backed away step by step. "So you can be sure, *brother*, that I shall be watching you *very* carefully from now on."

Nick stalked off, leaving Gabe to trail along miserably in his wake.

Nick was right, of course. Gabe didn't want the changeover to happen, not now, not ever. But a promise was a promise, especially when it was with a capital P and made by archangels, so he had no choice.

He resolved to try harder next time, and maybe it would be easier because, surely, the engagement would have taken place. But then there'd be the wedding! He forced his bottom lip to stop wobbling and hurried to catch up with Nick.

"So why are we going to the bakery so early?"

Nick tutted. "I was explaining why before you interrupted me! He starts baking on the dot of 5 o'clock. By the time the ovens have reached the correct temperature he's got the proved loaves and rolls ready to go in the ovens, and he's measured out the ingredients for cakes he's going to make that day."

"That's all very fine, but as I've already said, as much as I love bread and cakes – particularly cakes – I have no wish to stand in a hot kitchen watching them get made. And what will Glen Perkins think, us just turning up unannounced and interrupting his work?"

"He won't mind, Gabe. And if he does, it'll be very easy to make him *un*mind."

"I still can't see why you're so keen to do this and why you have to drag me along."

Ignoring Gabe's remark again, Nick chattily passed on more information about the baker. "Our man Perkins used to sell high-spec kitchen equipment all over Europe. He and Gwen had a very fine house in Richmond, where Debbie was born. He made good money because he was good at his job, but when the company hit hard times, he took voluntary redundancy and used the money and his savings to return to the place of his and Gwen's birth and buy this little place. He'd had a dream of having his own bakery ever since his mother had shown him how to make sourdough bread when he was eight or thereabouts."

"Really?" said Gabe, brightening up as he loved to hear nice stories about people and, anyway, he couldn't hold a bad mood for long.

"Yes. And his wife, the magnificent Gwen, had been more than happy to move back to the village as well, thinking it would be a better place to raise their delightful young daughter. Ah, here we are." Nick peered through the darkened window of the bakery. "There's light at the back, let's go round."

They went down a narrow alley and through the wooden gate that led into the Perkins' tiny garden. The gate creaked on its hinges and Nick cursed as a big ginger tomcat yowled as it darted between his legs. The back door opened a crack, spilling light onto the dark lawn, and Glen called out, "Is someone there?"

Nick replied, "Good morning, Mr Perkins. I hope you don't mind me calling round, but you did say that I could watch you bake if I could ever get myself up in time. Well, this morning I awoke particularly early and I thought, aha! Today is the day to take Mr Perkins up on his word, and my brother decided to come along too!"

Gabe could see that Glen Perkins was struggling to remember promising any such thing to anyone, but he stood back to allow them both into his kitchen.

Nick stepped over the threshold ahead of Gabe, and rubbing his hands in anticipation, said, "I'm really excited about this, you know!"

Glen watched in bewildered silence as Nick walked over to where the ingredients and tins were laid out, studying them for a bit and then turning to the two large ovens, which were working themselves up to temperature. Gabe heard a strangled cry come from Glen's throat when Nick opened the door to one of the ovens, and stuck his head right in.

"Fascinating!" echoed back at them, then Nick withdrew his head, closed the oven door and turned to Glen, his beaming face scarlet from the intense heat, and trilled, "Let's get started then, shall we?"

Glen Perkins merely nodded, cleared his throat, and then, like a man in a trance, launched into an explanation of what he was about to do. "It gets pretty messy in here, what with the flour getting everywhere, so may I suggest you wear an apron? You certainly don't want flour or dough on your smart clothes, do you?"

He opened a small cupboard by the door that led into the café and took out two freshly laundered aprons.

Nick, more delighted than Gabe had seen him in a long time, shrugged off his leather jacket, hung it on a hook on the door, and donned the apron; Gabe more slowly followed suit. As Glen Perkins was more than double the size of both him and his brother, the aprons should have wrapped round them twice with room still to spare, but once he and Nick had tied theirs round their waists with neat bows at the front, they seemed to have adjusted themselves to a perfect fit.

Gabe stood beside Nick and they watched in absorbed concentration as Glen worked with the risen dough, knocking and shaping loaves and rolls before putting them into tins and onto baking sheets. Some were wholemeal, some brown, some white, but all quite plain.

Nick broke the silence. "Have you ever thought of making something a little, um, more interesting?" he asked, once all the trays and tins had been slid into the ovens.

Glen set about cleaning the work surface of flour and sticky bits of dough so he could start on the cakes. "No, Mr di Angelo, sadly there's no call here for exotic breads. The villagers like their loaves and rolls plain; they wouldn't buy bread with herbs and seeds in it."

"Are you sure about that?"

Clearly a little irritated by Nick's questioning of his expertise, Glen banged his bowls and utensils into the sink with too heavy a hand, causing one to crack and fall apart in two pieces. Glen said a very rude word before exclaiming, "That was my favourite mixing bowl. What a nuisance."

"Oh, I'm sure it can be fixed," cried Gabe. "Here, give the pieces to me. I promise you I'll bring it back good as new."

Behind Glen's back, Nick rolled his eyes, then went on the attack again. "Well, now, Glen, I wonder if you're right about the villagers not wanting fancy breads? I happen to know that Mrs Capsby buys sundried tomato and green olive ciabatta from the bakery in Monkton Combe every Saturday, and Mrs Fordingbridge buys cinnamon rolls there because Freddie loves them. The Reverend Hartley Cordwell is very fond of their walnut bread, so, you see…"

Glen, paying attention now, handed the pieces of his mixing bowl to Gabe, and faced Nick, who casually informed him, "I also happen to know that that very bakery is closing down soon as the owners are retiring to the coast. The new buyers are going to turn it into a gift shop, which will fill the residents of Monkton Combe and Ham-Under-Lymfold and many other villages with despair. Think about it. Where will Olive Capsby go to get her ciabatta and Freddie his cinnamon rolls then, hmm? Must the good vicar deliver his sermons without being fortified by his favourite sourdough? Why make them go all the way into the city when they could get what they want right here?"

"Well, I—"

It dawned on Gabe at that moment that Nick had just performed a Very Good Deed for Glen Perkins of his own volition, and that's why he'd wanted Gabe there, to be a witness to it. He beamed at Nick to show his approval, and said to Glen, "My brother is right, Mr Perkins. If they have to go into the city, they'd most likely buy *all* their bread there to make the effort worthwhile. But not if you start offering such things now. It's worth thinking about, isn't it?"

"And let's not forget that the new restaurant will be in need of plentiful supplies of fancy breads, and what would be better than for a local baker to be the provider? Good for them, excellent for you."

Glen slowly nodded his head. "Um, maybe you're right… I'd certainly enjoy making such things."

"Good man!" said Nick, patting Glen on the shoulder. "You mull that over then, but in the meantime let's do some cakes. We're particularly fond of cakes, aren't we, Gabe! In fact, I have a rather special recipe to share with you, if you've got some fine dark chocolate handy."

~~~

Back at the mill, Gabe immediately set about repairing Glen's mixing bowl.

"Feels good, doesn't it, brother?" he said.

"What does?"

"What you just did for Glen Perkins! You've just done something really kind by showing him the way to improve his business."

Nick shrugged his shoulders and a sly look came into his eyes as he said with studied nonchalance, "How about we count it as an achievement for Charity, and leave Violet to her wonderful, nasty little ways?"
~~~

"Oh, Nick, is that why you did it? But there was no *tempting*, and Glen is already a good person so there was no change of any kind! You performed a straightforward act of beneficence and you should feel proud of yourself, but Violet is still your target."

Nick shrugged. "Oh well, it was worth a try. And at least we'll get some decent bread and cakes around here now."

"Always an ulterior motive with you, isn't there?" Gabe held up Glen's bowl. "Good as new, with a little bit of glue and a touch of angel magic. I might go and return it to him now."

"No, wait! Before you go let's have some coffee and a slice or two of that divine chocolate cake. When the villagers get a taste of this, they'll be beating down Glen Perkins's door!" He grinned at Gabriel, a sparkle in his eye, "I could get used to doing good deeds, bro."

Gabriel could only snort in disbelief, but he accepted the coffee and cake.

Chapter 18
the master craftsman

It was yet again time to visit Ham-Under-Lymfold and Nigel set off with his usual reluctance. Since that horrible meeting about Sins and Virtues, he particularly dreaded an encounter with Lorelei Dove in case the angels had succeeded in with their horrible plan. It would all be so much easier if Amelia were with him, but she had a small interior design job to do and so had to stay in London.

As he drove to Wiltshire, he wondered what was happening at the mill and began to feel excited about seeing it again. When the angels had demanded the work be done to ridiculous deadlines, Nigel had retorted that if anyone in the building trade could start within days of asking it could only be because they were cowboys. This had been met with one of Nick's insufferable grins, and sure enough, as Nigel had found telephone numbers and made calls from his secret behind-the-wall space in his London office, everybody but everybody had said they were available to start on the date he specified. And for very reasonable rates too. Nigel hadn't missed how surprised they'd sounded by their own promises.

When he reached the Turnaround he saw that the old stone bridge had been widened and strengthened so it could carry vehicles. He drove across and parked in front of the mill, next to a white van. He could see on the dashboard two empty plastic cups stained with strong, orange-coloured tea, and a newspaper, carelessly folded to the sports pages.

Scaffolding surrounded the building, men in hard hats milled around, and a large skip was fast filling up. The clear, cold air rang with the sounds of hammering, sawing, drilling, whistling, occasional swearing and a commercial radio station that bellowed out appallingly bad local adverts after every third song.

Nigel put on his own hard hat and high-vis yellow jacket and looked up with approval at the reclaimed slate tiles that covered the roof and then strolled inside, trying not to remember the day he had stepped through the portal to the other, immaculate interior that Nick and Gabe inhabited.

He had a good scout around, stopping here and there to speak to some of the builders, satisfied to find that all was going to plan and the work was being done to an extremely high standard. It was all going so well, in fact, he felt confident that he could get some more tradesmen lined up so there would be no hiatus in the mill's progress.

Needing a quiet place to consult the plans and make some notes, he decided to leave his car where it was and take a walk to the café.

Gwen Perkins carried over Nigel's order of coffee and chocolate cake. On the plate was a generous slice of a rich, dark sponge, its top smothered with deep swirls of chocolate frosting. "A new recipe Glen came up with. He's trying to come up with a name for it," Gwen said. "It's got chilli in it, would you believe, but I promise you, it's absolutely divine."

She asked him if Amelia was well and if she'd be visiting the village again soon, and then, indicating his laptop and the papers he'd spread on the table, said she'd leave him in peace.

Nigel forked in a generous mouthful of the cake and almost swooned at how wonderful and delicious it tasted. He had an idea and called out to Mrs Perkins: "Why don't you have a little competition for someone to find a name for it?"

"What a wonderful idea! We could get a few leaflets printed and put a box here on the counter for customers to post their suggestions."

"And maybe the prize could be a whole cake to take home?"

"Oh, Nigel, thank you! I'll ask Debbie to go and talk to Freddie about producing a poster or two to put in the window here and in the pub. He's very good with computers." Gwen looked over her shoulder to check no-one else was in earshot, then lowering her voice, confided with a wink: "Between you and me, I think my Debbie is a bit sweet on him."

As she bustled off to put the suggestion to Glen, Nigel switched on his laptop and called up the section dealing with the restaurant's décor. Amelia had adored putting it all together, everything from the plaster finishes, the colour schemes, tables and chairs, soft furnishings, lighting, flooring, et cetera. The only thing she had not had any say in was the front decoration of the bar, for this was to be of hand-carved ebony, designed by Nick. It was to cover the full length of the bar, so Uri was to make it in four separate panels which would be seamlessly joined together.

Nick had provided Nigel with several detailed drawings, and he and Amelia had agreed that it was a fantastic design. Very intricate, very delicate, it took a lot of concentration, and not a little insider knowledge, to see that it was actually a metaphorical depiction of The Fall, as it had been shown to Nigel on that extraordinary film. The far left section showed a host of winged and robed angels surrounded by sunbeams. The next section showed Gabriel and Lucifer standing side by side, clutching each other's sleeve, staring down into a smoking pit. The third part was mostly a complicated pattern of loops and whorls, but, in its centre, there was a large disc, engraved with flowers. The far right section was of flames and writhing human figures being tormented by horned imps with pitchforks.

It reminded him of those puzzles that have to be looked at in a cross-eyed way in order to see a black and white 3-D picture emerge from a mass of coloured dots, and Nigel knew that it would only take a couple of people to work out the carving and it would quickly become a major talking point which would, very probably, bring in more people who wanted to see it for themselves.

Only Uri was deemed good enough by Nick to create such a thing, and Nigel was looking forward to seeing him to deliver the drawings as soon as he'd finished the wonderful cake. In fact, it was so wonderful he contemplated having a second slice, but his stomach was full so he reluctantly got up to leave. As he paid Gwen Perkins she said, "We'd like to thank you for your idea, so next time Amelia is with you please come and have tea and cake on the house."

It was drizzling with rain by the time he arrived at the old grey vicarage. Uri's tiny cottage could only be reached through a side gate into the garden, but this was locked so Nigel knocked on the vicarage door. Hartley, wiping his hands on a striped tea towel, beamed a very warm welcome when he saw Nigel on his doorstep.

"You're back with us, then? How are you?"

"I'm very well, thank you. Can you tell me how I can get to Uri's place, please? The gate is locked."

Hartley stepped away from the door and bid Nigel to come in out of the increasing rain. "Oh? I wonder why that is. Uri's in the garden, tackling the rhododendrons which have gone rather wild, but Heaven knows why he wants to be out in this weather. Why don't you go through to the kitchen and I'll call him in. Would you like some tea?"

"Er, thank you, but I don't want to put you to any trouble. I'll just go and find Uri, if you'll point the way?"

Hartley's blue eyes twinkled. "Heavens, there's no need for that! It's time he had a break and you can talk to him here, in the warm and dry." He lowered his voice, "I happen to know that Uri does not bother with heating in his cottage, hardly comfortable for a chat. No, much better in here, beside my Aga."

Nigel followed the vicar across the black and white tiled floor of the gloomy, high-ceilinged entrance hall to a very large kitchen that hadn't been updated since about 1958. There were no fitted units, just a miscellany of cupboards and drawers and a big pine table, its surface covered in scratches and brown rings from mugs of hot tea and coffee carelessly put down. The only modern thing in there, looking very conspicuous, was a huge, American-style double-door fridge. The lino on the floor was cracked and worn right through in places, its original sky-blue only visible in one or two spots under the table. The porcelain sink had a line of rust running down from the cold tap, and an old boiler fixed to the wall spat hot water through a long, lime-covered spout. But it was homely and the Aga threw out a welcome warmth.

Hartley gestured to him to take a chair, saying, "I think you know my niece, Lorelei? And this is her fiancé, Dr Stephen George. I'll just go and give Uri a call, then I'll make a fresh pot of tea."

Startled at coming into contact with Lorelei unprepared and so soon, Nigel took a moment to recover his wits and say hello, relieved that she didn't look any different. Dare he hope that the angels had decided to leave her alone after all?

Hartley, having yelled at the top of his lungs to Uri, who was working somewhere deep in the bushes that lined the long garden, asked Nigel, "Have you heard about the coin?"

"The one found in the graveyard? No, I haven't heard anything."

"Well, it's fantastic news! Stephen here took it to a coin expert, and it turns out be rare and worth quite a lot of money."

"More than quite a lot, Hartley," said Stephen. "Several thousand pounds is the estimate."

"Really?" said Nigel. "That's fantastic. Does the money come to you or to the diocese?"

"Oh, to the diocese I should think, but the village church will get a large chunk of it as the coin was found here. There's an auction fee, of course, but whatever we get it will be very welcome. The coin is going be sold in London, but not for a month or so as it's still being examined by various other experts. Stephen has kindly offered to take us to the sale rooms and watch it go under the hammer."

Nigel noticed that Lorelei never took her eyes from her fiancé, and Stephen George clasped her hand as if their palms were super-glued together. It was delightful to see two people so very much in love.

The handyman arrived at the door and removed his damp cloth cap, before unlacing and removing his muddy boots.

"Come on in, my good fellow, sit down with Lorelei and Stephen and get yourself warm. Here's Mr Hellion-Rees to see you. He says the gate is locked." As he talked, Hartley put a huge blackened kettle onto the Aga and dropped teabags into a battered metal teapot.

"It's not locked," said Uri. "I took the bolt off to scrub away the rust and oil it, so it must be that the heavy rain of the past few days has warped the wood. I'll see to it."

Uri didn't take Nigel's proffered hand, but held both of his up to show that they were very dirty and he needed to wash them. He scrubbed them well in the kitchen sink, and dried them on a small blue towel. Nigel surreptitiously watched him, wondering what the others would think if they were ever to discover Uri's true identity. And Gabe's and Nick's, of course.

There was a smaller table to the left of the Aga, with a wheelback chair on one side and a three-legged stool on the other. On the table a game of chess was in progress. Uri studied the board as he dried his hands, then moved one of the pieces.

"Oh, Uri, not the bishop, I hoped you wouldn't spot that!" cried Hartley, bumbling around with cups and saucers. He tipped an assortment of biscuits from a large tin onto a plate, then said to Nigel, "After tea you can use my office, if you'd like to talk in private."

"Oh no," protested Nigel, "that's very kind of you, but I'm only here to ask Uri if he'll do a piece of work for the mill, a carving designed by Nick di Angelo for the bar. I've brought the drawings."

"Oh, how exciting!" said the vicar. "Have you seen everything Uri's made since he's been here? Bird tables, fruit bowls, walking sticks, even a garden bench, and they're all magnificent. He's going to make a couple of wheelback chairs to match this one."

Uri gave a gracious bow of his head at the compliment. "Thank you, Hartley." He took the drawings Nigel handed him and pulled off the elastic band holding them in a tight roll.

"Shall we make space on the table?" asked Lorelei, the first time she'd spoken since Nigel's arrival, apart from saying hello.

Nigel surreptitiously glanced at her. Beside her, Stephen was helping himself to the chocolate-covered biscuits, but Lorelei didn't so much as look at them. Surely a good sign that she hadn't been blighted with Gluttony, Nigel thought.

Uri used their mugs to keep the corners of the drawings from curling up, and they all studied the pencilled designs.

"It's a very intricate pattern," observed Stephen, "and, looking at the measurements, rather big! That'll take some doing, I should think?"

Uri laughed, a deep belly laugh that resounded off the kitchen walls. "It's not just a pattern! Can't any of you see what it is?"

Hartley, Lorelei and Stephen all dipped their heads for a closer inspection. After a couple of minutes of deep silence, Hartley straightened up and admitted, "Um, I'm not sure what you mean."

"Each panel tells part of one well-known story," answered Uri. "And right up your street, I should say, Hartley!"

Nigel, thinking how long it had taken him to see it, watched the other three and wondered which of them would be first to recognise what the design depicted. He smiled to himself as they traced the drawings with their figures and murmured among themselves.

Suddenly Hartley yelped with excitement and slapped his hand on the table, making the mugs jump. "Good heavens!" he exclaimed. "You don't see it at first, but it's the Fall of Lucifer, isn't it! My word, this is beautiful, just beautiful."

Now the other two could see it as well and Lorelei exclaimed, "It takes you ages to see it, but once you do it's so clear and you can't unsee it! That's so clever!"

Uri drained his mug and went to the Aga to have another fill of the strong tea from the pot. Nigel could sense he was deep in thought and wondered what he thought of Nick's design. Would he want to make it?

Hartley offered Nigel the plate of biscuits and said, "So this is for the restaurant in the mill? Oh, I'm so glad the di Angelos decided to come here, they've sparked new life into the place. Gabe, now, he's a really nice chap, very pleasant indeed. He wanted to know about my ministries, you know, where I was before coming here, the history of the church, things like that, and we talked about some of the Bible stories. He's very knowledgeable about all religions, in fact. Just like you, Uri."

Uri merely inclined his head again in acknowledgement.

Hartley carried on, "I'm not so sure about the other one, though, that Nick. I'm a Christian man, of course, and I know I shouldn't judge, but there's something about him..." He trailed off, his cheeks tinged pink with embarrassment, and hurriedly turned away to pour out more biscuits.

Nigel wondered what Uri's expression was behind his blue-lensed glasses, but his face was inscrutable as he took another gingernut and dipped it in his tea. When he'd swallowed the biscuit, he indicated the drawing and said to Nigel, "I'll need some new tools for such delicate work."

"That's no problem, just tell me what you need."

"And I like to keep myself to myself when I'm working, mind. My workshop's private."

Hartley said, "No-one ever disturbs you over there anyway, do they, Uri?"

"True, Hartley, true. Forget I said anything." Uri took a lump of wood and a small knife from his pocket. Within minutes, the lump had been transformed to a ballerina en pointe, her pretty head tilted to one side, her hands held delicately beneath her chin, her eyes closed in the ecstasy of the dance.

"Gosh, that's really beautiful," Nigel exclaimed. "My youngest niece dreams of being a ballet dancer and insists on wearing her tutu absolutely everywhere."

"Then please take it and give it to her," said Uri.

"Oh no, really, I didn't mean…"

"Please, I'd be glad for your niece to have it if it will give her pleasure."

Nigel stammered a thank you and placed the figurine on the table so he wouldn't forget to take it when he left. "So, I can't think of anything else at the moment, Uri. We'll just need to get you the tools you need, and the wood. Nick suggested ebony."

Uri nodded. "That'd be right. I know where to get quality stuff." He rolled up the drawings and replaced the elastic band. "I'll leave these here for now, Hartley, if you don't mind, and collect them when I've finished in the garden."

"My dear chap, it's absolutely pouring out there now. Why don't you call it a day?"

"Thank you, but I'll not stop yet. A bit of rain never did me any harm. Besides, I don't think it'll last."

And as he said it, the rain stopped and a glorious rainbow arced across the sky outside the kitchen window.

Once Uri had gone, the vicar offered Nigel more tea, but Nigel said he had to be on his way. He put on his jacket and picked up the ballerina.

Hartley said, "That is an amazing little carving, isn't it? He did one for Lorelei of a dove, for her name, of course, and it's absolutely wonderful. I'm delighted that you've asked him to do The Fall of Lucifer for the restaurant, he'll do an excellent job."

Nigel said his goodbyes, noticing for the first time the unusual ring with a purple stone on Lorelei's left hand. Maybe because she and Stephen George had got engaged so recently, the angels had not tried to do anything to her. Maybe they'd picked on someone else. But that thought didn't cheer him up, not really, because it meant some other very nice person was about to have their world turned upside down. If it hadn't been turned upside down already.

On the doorstep, he pulled up his collar and prepared to dash through the rain, but Uri was waiting for him.

"Well done, Nigel," he said. "It wouldn't have done for the vicar to realise that we know each other so well."

"So you'll start on the carving soon?"

Uri grinned. "Oh yes, and with pleasure. I'm looking forward to it."

"Then you'd better give me a list of the tools you need. Or, I suppose it would be better for you to go and get what you need?"

Uri laughed. "I'm an angel, Nigel, I already have everything I need. I was just pretending for Hartley's benefit."

"Ah, yes," said Nigel. "Speaking of Hartley, do you know if anything has been done to Lorelei? I didn't see any sign of Gluttony in there, so I was rather hoping..."

Uri laid a hand on Nigel's shoulder. "I know what you were hoping, but I'm afraid she's still firmly in their sights. Gabe had a go at leading her into temptation, but the attempt failed. He's just biding his time to have another go, but Nick is getting impatient. He hasn't had any luck with Violet, either." He removed his glasses and fixed Nigel with his clear grey eyes. "It will be done, Nigel, because it *must* be done."

Chapter 19
anyone for cocktails?

By 8 o'clock Friday evening, Nigel had had enough of going over the building plans for the mill and decided he'd earned himself a pint. With each step down the staircase from his room, the noise from the bar grew louder and louder. Bracing himself, he opened the door and walked into Cynthia's first Theme Night.

Freddie Fordingbridge, in his debut as barman, was at the far end of the bar, rooting through a large ceramic bowl piled high with exotic fruits. Debbie, perched on a bar stool, watched his every move with rapt attention.

Skinny Freddie, whose skin still showed the signs of the acne that had plagued him since he entered his teens, had been dressed by Cynthia in a frilled red shirt, unbuttoned to show a white, hairless chest and an over-large gold medallion on a chain. The shirt was tucked into tight, shiny black trousers with a high waistband. Seeing this ensemble, Nigel couldn't help thinking that Freddie's legs resembled two strings of liquorice, the top ends tied in a knot. He had to fight to control his facial muscles as Freddie greeted him.

"Hello, Freddie! What's with the fancy gear then?"

"Um, well, it's cocktail night, Mr Nigel. What sort would you like?"

Nigel had asked everyone to call him by his first name, but young Freddie always addressed adults by putting the Mister, Missus or Miss in front of their names to be polite and respectful, as his parents had brought him up to be. Nigel wanted that pint of real ale, so replied, "I don't know anything about cocktails, Freddie."

"Gosh, neither did I, Mr Nigel! It's called mixology, you know, and Miss Cynthia gave me books about it and cocktail recipes, and I read them, and memorised them, and Miss Cynthia got loads of bottles of stuff, and now I can make anything."

"You *memorised* them? But there must be hundreds of cocktails, surely?"

Debbie swivelled to face Nigel and gushed, "Oh yes there are simply *hundreds* of cocktails with all sorts of weird names and ingredients like vermouth and schnapps and sambuca and crème di cassis but Freddie only has to read things once and he remembers everything cos he's got a photographic memory isn't that right Freddie and he's promised to invent one just for me."

Nigel marvelled as he always did at Debbie's ability to speak without commas and full stops. Freddie blushed and muttered that he was trying to think of a suitable name.

"How about 'Debbie's Delight'?" laughed Nigel, making Freddie's blush flare to a painful crimson hot enough to toast marshmallows. "I'll have my usual pint, please, Freddie."

"But won't you try something a little different, just this once? Tell you what, I know you like gin, so how about a Singapore Sling? Or a Blue Lady? Much nicer names, I think than what Mr Nick over there is drinking."

Feeling the skin on the back of neck crawl, Nigel turned and scanned the crowded room to locate the angels. He hadn't known they'd be in the pub tonight, and didn't have a particularly good feeling about it. "What is it?" he asked Freddie.

"It's an Exorcist. It's made with tequila, blue curacao, lime juice. Mr Nick's tried a Rob Roy and a Bloody Mary, but he says the Exorcist is the best so far."

"I bet he does. And what is the other Mr di Angelo drinking, Freddie?"

"Um, well Mr Gabe, he's got a pina colada now, but he's had a mint julep, a Manhattan and a tequila sunrise, which he says he likes especially because they're pretty. They're my best customers so far, I must say. Everyone else just wants their usual, like you. Are you sure you won't just *try* something?"

Debbie held up her large glass, half-full with something resembling custard. Sticking out of it was a small green and yellow paper umbrella. "I've got a Snowball it's got lemonade in it and a squeeze of lime juice and it's really nice and fizzy and sweet why don't you try one?" She removed the umbrella to show Nigel the maraschino cherry skewered on it. "This is to stir it with but I like the way they taste and I keep eating them so Freddie has to keep giving me more." The plump red cherry disappeared into her mouth and Nigel wondered if she realised how provocative it was. It seemed lost on Freddie, though, whose brown, hopeful eyes were still fixed on Nigel, awaiting his order.

Nigel tapped the beer pump, making Freddie sigh in submission as he dutifully pulled a pint exactly to the marker on the tall glass and set it in front of Nigel. He took a welcome sip, then asked Freddie what time the di Angelos had come in.

"Oh, about 6 o'clock. Said they'd noticed the blackboard out front announcing our first Theme Night."

"And they've had, what, four cocktails each in the space of two hours?"

Freddie scratched his head. "Well, Mr Gabe has had five, actually."

Nigel shook his head, and observed that the locals, though chatting animatedly among themselves, kept throwing surreptitious glances at the brothers. "It's certainly packed in here tonight, Cynthia must be delighted."

"Well, yes, Mr Nigel, I suppose she is. It was quiet to start with, but when the Misters di Angelos arrived, Miss Cynthia said that everyone was always interested in what they did, so she put the word out that they were here, and, well, you know, *enjoying* the cocktails, and people came flocking in." He leaned on the bar, looking for all the world like a seasoned barman, except for his youth and frilly shirt, and said, "Mr Gabe told me something interesting. Did you know that the older the whisky is, the more it will evaporate in the cask, and the evaporated stuff is called 'the angels' share'? Mr Gabe says it tastes wonderful, though I'm not sure how you taste evaporation."

Agreeing with Freddie's astute observation, Nigel paid for his drink, and walked over to join Gabe and Nick at their table. They were draining the last drops of their cocktails and discussing what to try next.

"Hey, Nigel, my man!" Slurring his words, Nick greeted Nigel with a hearty slap on the back, almost knocking him to the floor. "We're just about to have another li'l ol' drinkie. What'll y'have?"

Nigel wouldn't have believed it, but it seemed the evidence was before him. Angels could get drunk! He indicated his glass of beer and declined Nick's offer.

"Oh, tame, tame," sneered Nick.

Gabe, his eyes bloodshot and unfocused, tapped Nick's arm to get his attention, and slurred, "Never mind him, brother dear. He can have his borin' old beer! What d'*you* wanna try next, eh?"

Nick furrowed his dark brows in concentration, ignoring the fact that all eyes in the bar were fixed upon him, and all ears attentively listening to hear what he would choose to drink next. Wow, these di Angelos could knock back the booze!

"I'll have a, er, um, what d'yer call it, um…" Nick clumsily clicked his fingers, trying to remember.

"Oh, get on with it," drawled Gabe, leaning into Nigel, rolling his eyes and tutting with a 'he's an idiot' expression.

Nick's face cleared and he rose a couple of inches of his seat as he yelled, "SATAN'S WHISKERS!"

Everyone jumped at the volume of Nick's voice, then all eyes swivelled to Freddie.

"The man wants a Satan's Whiskers, Freddie, can you do that one without cribbing from the book?" challenged Arnold Capsby.

Freddie raised his eyes to the ceiling and tapped his forefinger on his cheek in concentration. "Hmm, Satan's Whiskers, well now… Oh yes, I've got it!"

He grabbed the cocktail shaker and called off the ingredients as he added them one by one, "Gin, sweet vermouth, dry vermouth, Grand Marnier, orange juice and… three dashes of orange bitters." He added ice cubes and the silver shaker rattled as Freddie performed a manic dance, the way he imagined a professional cocktail maker would. In one deft movement, he whipped off the top of the shaker, placed the cocktail sieve in its place, whisked a cocktail glass off the shelf, and poured the mixture from a great height, like a true showman. He selected a paper umbrella but decided against it, finishing his creation instead with a thin, twirled slice of orange peel decoratively draped over the rim of the glass. He held it up, and sang, "Tah-daah", as if expecting everyone to burst into applause.

But his effort was met with silence as the locals stared at the orange-coloured concoction before they turned back to the brothers. Gabe lurched up from the table and staggered to the bar.

"Ooh, tha' smells nice," he said. "Orangey-yee. Bu' I wan' somethin' diff'r'nt. Wha' d'you suggest, young Freddie?"

"How about a Bentley, Mr Gabe, sir?"

"Hmm. Car. Big thing. Posh," said Gabe. "Too 'xpensive for the likes of you, young Fr, Fre, Fr'ddie, m'lad!"

"I meant a Bentley cocktail, Mr Gabe, sir."

"Ah, cockt'l, tha's more like it. What colour is't?"

"Um, it's Calvados and Dubonnet, so it's pinkish."

"Pink!" Gabe clapped his hands in delight, and Freddie got to work again with his shaker.

The locals and Nigel, who by now had come up to the bar because he had serious doubts that Gabe could carry the two cocktails without significant spillage, once again marvelled at Freddie's fine performance. Nigel picked up the full glasses and returned to the table, followed by a weaving, giggling, hiccupping Gabe.

Once they'd sat down, the brothers immediately picked up and clinked their glasses, and each took a delicate sip of their cocktail, eyes closed to better savour the taste. Gabe held the brew in his mouth, pursing his lips and swishing it around. Nigel half expected him to spit it out, as if he were at a wine tasting, but he swallowed it and pronounced it delicious. His face beamed with a beatific smile that reached from ear to ear.

Nick gargled his drink as if it was a mouthwash before swallowing it, and it almost choked him. But he recovered, blinked his streaming eyes in ecstasy, then he slapped the table with his free hand, and gasped, "Oh, you beauty!" before taking another, deeper drink.

The spectators were spellbound.

Reverend Hartley Cordwell chose this moment to enter The Blacksmith's Anvil for his customary half pint of bitter. He stopped in the doorway, perplexed to see so many of his flock gathered there. Capsby was the first to sidle up to Hartley and put him in the picture.

"He's had *what* cocktails?" he said incredulously.

Capsby relished telling the vicar again that Nick di Angelo had been enjoying drinks by the name of Exorcist and Satan's Whiskers.

"Good Lord," said Hartley, gripping more tightly the pocket Bible he always carried in his jacket.

Freddie called out, "Good evening, Reverend Cordwell, sir," and placed his half pint on the bar, not holding any hope that the vicar would be so adventurous as to order an exotic drink.

Nigel wondered if he should invite the vicar to join them, as he'd spent time with him that afternoon, but couldn't help a little shiver at the irony, not to say risk, of inviting the parish vicar to sup with Lucifer! If only Hartley knew, thought Nigel, smiling weakly as he caught the vicar's eye, just who he was standing a mere few feet away from.

At that point Gabe suddenly had a serious attack of hiccups, and Nigel decided it was time to sort them out.

"Gentlemen," he said quietly, "is this wise? I hope you don't mind me saying so, but you don't seem to be used to alcohol."

"Oh, tush," said Gabe. "Of course we're us'd to alco'l. Nick has the finest cellar in, in, in…"

"The cosmos!" finished Nick, sticking his chest out with pride.

"Yup, s'right, you better believe it, s'best cellar in the cosm's."

"And we can certainly handle these," said Nick belligerently. "We're angels, ain't we?"

"Shh," hissed Nigel. "Keep your voices down, you don't want anyone to hear you, do you?" He indicated the other people, who fortunately were now losing interest and were conversing happily with each other over pints, half pints and one or two strangely coloured drinks with paper umbrellas. Only the gold-flecked eyes of Stanley's dog Digby continued to regard them with his steady, intelligent gaze.

"We don't have to shhhhhhhh," said Gabe, spraying spittle onto Nigel's sleeve as he swept the expanse of the bar with his arm. "'s'no probl'm, we c'n make 'em deaf if we want to!"

"Even better," said Nick maliciously, "we can make 'em *freeze*." He snapped his fingers and the pub suddenly fell utterly silent.

Everyone but the di Angelo brothers and Nigel went still. Stock-still. Glen Perkins had a glass halfway to his lips. Freddie was in the middle of putting an olive into a martini glass. Debbie's mouth, rimmed with pink lipstick, was open in an O, poised to receive yet another maraschino cherry. Stanley was scratching himself where he shouldn't and Digby resembled a taxidermist's specimen.

"What have you done?" Nigel squeaked, surveying the strange and, in some cases, embarrassing postures of all the customers.

Nick clicked his fingers again, and everyone moved as if nothing had happened. His narrowed eyes hard and graphite grey, there was no trace of a slur when he hissed, "Just to remind you, Nigel, that we are capable of doing many things if we so choose."

Gabe hiccupped.

Nick swallowed the rest of his cocktail in one go, went white, then pink, then white again before pitching forward, striking the dimpled, copper-topped table with a hard wallop. His arms dangled to the floor, and it was plain to see that Nick, aka the Devil, was out for the count.

Gabe giggled, "Ha! S'first time I've ever out-drunk *him*!"

At that point, Freddie left the bar to wipe up and pick up the empties. In the tight black trousers, despite being so skinny, he could only mince between the tables, and bend about two degrees to pick up all the glasses because of the high, constricting waistband.

Someone shouted, "Don't sneeze, Freddie, whatever you do, you'll rip those trousers to kingdom come, and probably your insides with 'em."

Everyone roared with laughter, and poor Freddie blushed deep red from neck to forehead. Nigel gave him a sympathetic smile, knowing all too well how it felt to wear hateful clothes because someone else was calling the shots.

But was Cynthia on the right track to get more customers from outside the village, as she hoped to achieve by having these theme nights? There had been rumours that she wanted to gut the lovely old pub and refurbish it as a wine bar, all chrome and glass and Halogen downlighters, but fortunately that was just false gossip. She'd make it clear that it would remain a typical village pub, but with occasional entertainment to cheer the place up.

Nigel thought about what Stanley Trout had told him, about the village needing life breathed back into it, so he could only cheer Cynthia on with her ideas.

He was brought out of his reverie by a cold, wet nose pressing into his hand. Digby had decided it was time for his evening round to see who had a bit of pork pie or ham fat going spare. Nigel patted him on the head, "Sorry, boy, I've got nothing for you yet. Come back later." Digby regarded him steadily for a moment, then snuffled softly and turned away to try his luck with someone else.

Nigel realised that he actually was rather hungry and perhaps he should order pie and chips now, as it was getting late. Nick, who hadn't shifted his position an inch, snored gently and mumbled something unintelligible.

Gabe was muttering about dogs. "Feed 'em, walk 'em, pat 'em on the 'ead, and yer average dog's perfickly happy."

Nigel opened his mouth to agree and to excuse himself to go and order some dinner, but Gabe clutched his sleeve and said in a conspiratorial whisper that could be heard across the street, "I like people, I really do, but sometimes, y'know, I think I prefer dogs." He let go of Nigel's sleeve and slumped back. "What d'ya think of that, eh?"

As if on cue, Digby materialised at Gabe's side, sat down, and elegantly placed a paw on his knee.

"Good doggie," said Gabe, stroking the velvet ears just a little clumsily. "No crisps t'night, I'm afraid." But Digby didn't seem to mind, and he lay down at Gabe's feet to put his ears out of reach, fixing his incredible golden eyes on Nick. If dogs could talk, thought Nigel to himself, Digby would be telling me he didn't like Nick. Not surprising, really, even a goldfish would sense it was in the presence of something... not altogether nice.

He made a second attempt to stand up, but Gabe grabbed him again and dragged him close, almost pulling him off the stool. Nigel's eyes watered from the wafts of alcohol emanating from the inebriated angel's every pore.

"We all love 'em, tha's why they'll always be safe. And cats, come to that. Cats are alright." His eyes glazed over as he thought some more. "Or, or, um, stag beetles and aardvarks, now I come to think of it. All creatures, really, but humans." He tapped the side of his nose, or rather tried to tap the side of his nose, and missed. "Humans, now, well, you're walking a fine line, let me tell you. Not safe at all."

Nigel, still held firmly in a very uncomfortable position, managed to croak, "Safe? Gabe, what do you mean? And could you let me go, please, you're strangling me."

Gabe let go of Nigel's shirt collar, laughed, hiccupped and burped all at the same time, which made his eyes fill. "Oops, pardon me! I think I need another li'l drinkie. A green one. FREDDIE!"

Conversation stopped and all eyes swivelled once more to Gabe and then to Freddie, who, still polishing glasses, froze.

"FREDDIE!! GIMME ANOTHER OF YOUR WUNNERFUL CACKTOLLS... COCKTALS... CICKTALS... OH, YOU KNOW, ONE OF THESE." He held his empty glass aloft and waggled it.

Nigel took the glass from him and set it down on the table. "I think actually what you need is coffee. Strong coffee. And maybe something to eat?"

Gabe shook his head, and wailed, "Noooo. Wanna green drinkie. FREDDIE!"

"I think you've really had enough alcohol. I'll get some coffee, you just sit tight a minute."

The angel giggled, "Well, I can do that all right, cos I'm sittin' and I'm certainly tight, ha, ha, ha."

Freddie took Nigel's order and said he'd bring everything over to their table. Nick still hadn't moved a muscle. Just as well. It was hard enough handling Gabe in his cups, let alone coping with a drunken Devil at the same time.

"Gabe, you were going to tell me about this humans not being safe business. And tell me *quietly.*"

"Was I? Oh, yeah, well all right. 's simple really, for ev'ry, well almost ev'ry, I already said about stag beetles and, and oh, other whatsits being, what's the word, exept? Exempt, yeh. But usually, uuuuusually, when a new species is created there's a way of wiping 'em out if they don't, um, come up to scratch. Y'know. A virus. Or a nat'ral disaster." He tapped the side of his nose successfully this time. "Which ain't ever nat'ral, if you know what I mean."

Nigel's brain was racing, torn between amusement and disbelief. "What about dinosaurs?" he asked. "Is that what happened to them?"

"Ah, yes, now, yer average *dinosaur*, well, it was so BIG wasn't it? Pteradactyls... well, you've seen one, right? Nick's horrible mascot?" Nigel wiped the spit off his face. "Brontosaurus, Stegasaurus..." Gabe shuddered and raked the air with clawed fingers. "All teeth an' claws and roarin' and shriekin' and slashin'. Awful things, they were."

"But we know that they were wiped out by climate change, or a meteor, or something."

"Well, there may well have been a meteor, my man. After all, there're thousands of 'em whirling in space out there so's obvious one or two would smash into this planet, little though it is. But what d'you think *causes* meteors to hit planets, huh? Or trigger climate change? Ya don't know, do ya!"

Nigel kept his eyes on Gabe while turning his face away from the alcohol fumes.

Gabe's mouth turned down at the corners. "I was rather fond of dodos, y'know, I was sooooo sad that they couldn't cut the mustard."

"Dodos?"

"Yah, they were really cute, with their funny beaks and big feet. But there was a design fault, see. They were so stoopid they simply couldn't work out how to breed, so that was that."

Nigel frowned and struggled to make sense of his jumbled thoughts. "But, Gabe, you make it sound as if humans, in our present form, were just, sort of, *put* here. What about the theory that we're descended from apes? That we *evolved* into what we are now?"

Gabe snorted. "Couldn't possibly comment on that sort of thing, Nigel ol' buddy."

"But, if I understand you correctly, you're saying that for every, well, almost every creature on this planet—"

"And all the planets in all the universeses."

"Okay, this planet and all the planets in all the universes, that a virus or a disaster is sent to wipe out any species that doesn't, how did you put it, come up to scratch?"

"Yup."

"And there's a danger of it happening to us? We could be wiped out, just like that?" He clicked his fingers.

Gabe giggled. "I'd say it's quite likely, the way you're carryin' on. I mean, dinosaurs were just mean and ugly, but your mistreatment of the rainforests, playing around with weird kinds of genetic engineering, eating those disgusting processed foods when there's perfickly good food available with all the vitamins you could possibly need. I mean, my man, the list of your carelessness and incomp… incompet… incompetenceses just goes on and on!"

"Okay, okay! So do you think something is likely to happen any time soon?

"Dunno 'xactly. But it'll be something sparkly, prob'ly, cos most of our stuff is sparkly. It'll just rain down on you from the skies some time 'n you'll all run outside and say ooh, how pretty. And then you'll die." He hiccupped.

"But is this really likely to happen, Gabe?"

"As I said, I dunno, 'cos me 'n' Luce, y'know my brother Luce, right? RIGHT?"

Nigel hastily nodded and flapped his hand to indicate that Gabe was too loud.

"We don't know what'll happen to you, we're too far down the, the watchamacallit, the angelic hierarchic-hic-cy. Only the Seraphim would know," he whispered the last bit as though afraid the Seraphim would hear him. "I mean, we archangels know it's quite likely, but not if or when'll it happen. All I c'n say, my friend, is that you'd better watch it!" He giggled and almost fell sideways off the stool.

The conversation had to stop at this point because Freddie had minced over with a large tray on which he'd balanced a place mat, cutlery wrapped in a red paper serviette, a plate of steak and kidney pie, chips and peas, and two cups of coffee. He carefully avoided looking at either Gabe or the top of Nick's head, and Nigel thought he was probably feeling guilty that he'd allowed them to get so drunk.

"Thanks, Freddie," said Nigel, trying to let him know that he didn't blame him.

At that moment, Uri came in and walked up to their table.

"Uri, me old mate, me old mucker!" cried Gabe. "Come and sit down with us. We're having a lovely time." He wrapped his arm around Nigel's neck, almost choking him, "Aren't we, Nige?"

Nick slowly sat up and tried unsuccessfully to focus on the room. His fringe was sticky where he'd lain in the spilled drink, and spookily stood up in two horn-shaped peaks. His forehead was dimpled from the beaten copper tabletop, and his eyes were bloodshot. Nigel had to stifle the urge to laugh.

"Gabe, Nick" Uri hissed. "You've both had far too much to drink. Let's get you out of here before you say something we shouldn't."

"But I'm enjoying myself—" wailed Gabe.

Nick winced. "Don't whine! I hate it when you whine."

"I'm not whining."

"You are too."

Uri raised his eyebrows at Nigel and said very quietly so only he could hear, "Before these two get into one of their childish spats, could you help me get them out of here? As soon as some fresh air hits them they'll sober up. Then you'll have to say something to the crowd in here; their eyes are out on stalks."

Sure enough, Cynthia, Freddie, Debbie, Stanley, Digby, and all the locals gathered in the bar watched them go, and no one said a word until the door was closed again, then their voices rose in excitement. Coming back in, Nigel heard things like, *Fancy that, drinking the night away until they were out of their cups?* And, *Did you see how many cocktails they had?* And, *I'm surprised they could stand up after that lot.* Olive Capsby said, *I think they were talking about dinosaurs.*

Nigel went to the bar and said to Cynthia in a very loud voice, "Sorry about that, Cynthia. Those two have been working far too hard, and I know neither of them had had anything much to eat all day. Just overdid the winding down, I think, and they'll be rather ashamed of themselves tomorrow."

Arnold called out, "Aw, haven't we all done it at some time or other?" and everyone else laughed in agreement.

Nigel went back to his table, unwrapped his cutlery, and tucked into his rapidly cooling pie and chips, wishing fervently that Amelia had been with him to see it all.

He felt a soft pressure on his thigh and two golden eyes gazed up at him. Digby loved steak and kidney pie.

Chapter 20

eavesdropping is never a sensible thing to do

It was early in the morning and Hartley was at the back of the church in a curtained-off area sorting through some old hymn books. He hummed no particular tune as he worked, dividing the books into three piles: definitely repairable, possibly repairable, beyond help. He tutted as he opened a book and saw obscene doodles inked in the margin. Who would do such a thing? It was added to the utterly-finished-and–only-good-for-the-wood-burner pile.

He heard the metal ring rattle then the heavy oak creaked door opened and slammed shut. Peeking through a gap in the curtain, Hartley saw Gabe di Angelo amble up the knave towards the organ. He wondered if he should cough to let Gabe know that he was there, but the man seemed to be deep in thought so Hartley decided to let him be. He often visited the church, and usually sat in contemplative silence just for a few minutes before leaving.

But the silence was interrupted by a strange tinkling sound, like distant wind chimes, and Hartley put his eye to the gap again. There was a sort of shimmer behind Gabe, and he watched in mounting disbelief as it solidified into a tall, bearded man with longish white hair, wearing a loose white tunic over baggy white trousers. *Extraordinary*, thought Hartley, *is it Glastonbury Festival time again?*

The man, his robe flapping and his flat-soled sandals slapping on the stone floor, strode to stand beside Gabe in front of Walter Sidney Hopkins's plaque.

"Hey there, Gabriel!"

"Peter! How nice to see you. How are things at the Gate?"

"Fine, fine, thank you for asking."

The visitor clapped a hand on Gabe's shoulder and leaned forward to peer at Walter's plaque. "Ah, yes," he said in a soft, marshmallowy voice, "I remember young Walter. Most unfortunate accident with this splendid organ." He turned and put his hand on one of the shining eight-foot-tall organ pipes. "This very pipe in fact, and it's not even dented."

"Is Walter all right now?"

"Oh yes. He was very accepting of his fate. Approached the Gates with wonder all over his young, grubby face and asked immediately if there were any jobs available."

"And did you find him something?"

"Got him into the Messenger Corps. He quickly rose through the ranks and works for the Dominations now. I don't think it will be long before he is promoted to the Thrones."

"I'm glad to know that."

"Yes, of course you are, you soft-hearted old thing. And, of course, there was a Mr Jack Heavysides joined us from here very recently. Nice chap, very cheerful," he wrinkled his nose, "but reeked of beer."

"It's very nice to see you, sir, but to what do we owe the pleasure?"

"Well, it's certainly nice to visit and find that one is in a Holy place named after one."

"Ah, but you have a very big chance of it, don't you, because *hundreds* of churches are called St Peter's."

"True, true, but it's most gratifying, all the same. But the reason I'm here is to ask about what's happening, Gabriel. It's chaos at the Gate! I mean to say, everyone knows that the Great Swap is in the offing, but nobody knows exactly what effect it's going to have when you and Lucifer actually do it. Do I continue to send the sinners down to Hell and the good people up to Heaven? Or are you swapping domains so that Hell is for good people and Heaven for bad? Do the good go up, or do they go down? Hmm?" His bushy white eyebrows beetled above his piercing blue eyes.

"No, no, nothing changes! I mean, yes, things will change, but not for the souls and not for you. Lucifer will take charge of Heaven, and I will go to Hell. We'll have to take some of our staff with us, of course, but not all of them."

The robed man laughed. "Well, well, an archangel going to Hell, I never thought I'd see the day."

Gabe pouted. "What do you mean? Lucifer's an archangel."

"Oh, yes, but that was at the Beginning, way before job descriptions were figured out. Lucifer grew with it, as it were, adapted as time went by and humans evolved, but you, Gabriel, you've only ever known Good. Are you up to it, do you think?"

The pout got poutier. "I've got no choice in the matter, have I! That's why we're here now, under orders from Michael and with Uriel keeping an eye on us. I admit I don't want to do it, but I'm getting a bit tired of hearing that I'm not capable. What about Lucifer? Do you think he can just neatly slot back into the hierarchy after all this time?"

Hartley had to clutch the curtain for support, then take a hasty step back in case he was discovered. What on Earth were they talking about? Well, he knew what they were talking about, but what could it mean? Was the man in the robe an actor in a Mystery Play or something? Were they rehearsing a scene where a character went to Heaven? But they'd been speaking about poor young Walter, hadn't they? The stranger had said that he'd met him.

The two men were still talking, so Hartley dared to creep forward again to watch and listen.

The man that Gabe di Angelo had called Peter had his lips pursed in thought. "Lucifer knew only Good before he Fell, because, as he likes to put it, he had no choice in the matter. You, Gabriel, have little or no personal experience of Evil. However, you must do what you must do and, now that I've established that nothing changes as far as I'm concerned, I must get back to the Gate. At least the strange deaths that have happened here might end now that Lucifer has his way at long last."

Gabe seemed startled. "What do you mean? Are you saying that Nick had anything to do with those deaths?"

"Well, I can't say for sure, but I certainly have my suspicions. I mean, there have been lightning strikes here far above the average for this country, and there was a terrible flood many years back. Quite a few souls have come to the Gate from this place under very strange circumstances, so you have to wonder. Think of Walter's demise. Then there was a Mr Trout, who drowned in a shallow duck pond, and Farmer Merryvale, knocked off his feet into a silo grain. And then Mr Heavysides arriving so recently…"

"But he was killed by falling beer barrels!"

The mysterious man nodded and scratched his beard. "Yes, indeed he was, but what caused the barrels to fall, hmm? Did you not know that the last four deaths I mentioned were caused by localised earth tremors?"

Beads of perspiration broke out on Hartley's forehead. He gripped the curtain with both hands and held himself stock-still. There was a long silence, then Gabe struck his forehead with his palm. "Lucifer did that? He caused the lightning and the tremors and the flood?"

St Peter put his hand on Gabe's shoulder. "My dear chap, I don't *know* that he did, I'm only surmising. Perhaps I shouldn't have said anything, and I'll say no more. I need to be getting back, anyway. Good luck, my dear Gabriel."

The man shimmered and disappeared with a faint 'pop' and Hartley at last dared to exhale, but quietly, as Gabe had grabbed a hymn book and was flipping through it as if searching for a particular page. "Oh, here it is," he exclaimed, "my favourite hymn!" With shoulders squared, he moved over to the organ and sat down. Hartley watched in amazement as he expertly pulled out a few stops, placed his feet on the pedals and his fingers on the keyboard, and began to play in a manner that would turn Olive Capsby green with envy. Hartley, also particularly fond of 'Onward Christian Soldiers' found himself joining in under his breath:

At the sign of triumph, Satan's host dost flee;
On then, Christian soldiers, on to victory!
Hell's foundations quiver at the shout of praise;
Brothers, lift your voices, loud your anthems raise.

"Well now!" Gabe exclaimed, stopping his playing and sounding rather wretched. "They'll soon be singing 'At the sign of triumph, *Gabriel's* host dost flee', and it will be *my* foundations that quiver."

Hartley could take no more. He slumped to the floor in a dead faint, ripping the curtain off its hooks as he fell.

When he opened his eyes again, he found himself looking up at Gabe di Angelo, leaning over him and fanning him with a large white handkerchief.

"Gosh, Reverend, you did give me a fright."

"You've rather given me a fright, too, Mr di Angelo."

"Oh dear. Have you been here all the time? How much did you hear?"

"I heard all of it, Mr di Angelo. That's why I fainted."

"Let's get you up. These flagstone floors are far too cold and hard for lying about on."

Hartley felt himself being hauled upright, untangled from the curtain and dusted down. "Okay now?"

"Not really, no," said Hartley. "What was all that about? How could that man just appear and disappear like that?"

Hartley felt Gabe's scrutiny, his facial muscles working as if he was trying to decide something.

"Well now, would you rather know the whole truth and then forget that I ever told you, or would you prefer it if I said no more before I make you forget what you've just seen?"

This choice completely flummoxed Hartley, so he wobbled over to a pew on shaky knees and sat down. "You mean, whatever happens next, I won't remember any of this. Is that what you're saying?"

Gabe nodded. "That's it, yes." He shrugged. "You've seen rather more than we'd like, really, and it's surprising how many people choose to *know*, just for a short while."

"Contact with *angels* and *saints*? You're an angel?"

"Uh-huh." He bowed. "Archangel Gabriel, at your service. Uri, the man who replaced your Topps, is Uriel. And the gentleman you just saw was St Peter."

"And your brother, Nick… he's, um, Satan?"

"He prefers Lucifer, but yes, he is."

"But he's been in my church! I've sat next to him in the pub! It's… it's not possible. Does anyone else know?"

"Nigel and Amelia Hellion-Rees both know the whole story. Nigel is our Witness, in fact. It's his job to tell the world about the change, when it happens."

"What change? What are you *doing* here? No, don't tell me. I really don't want to know any more."

"Okay, if you're sure. By the way, I believe you have seen Lucifer's mascot? From the DISC, I mean the coin, when you were cleaning it?"

Hartley felt perspiration prickle his upper lip. "I… don't remember. What mascot? What disc? All I've had is a coin that Topps found."

Gabe slapped his forehead. "Oh, I forgot! The DISC and all that were wiped from your memory. That means you've already had a dose of STARdust—"

"Stardust?" asked Hartley, weakly.

"Ah, actually it's a dust called Seraphic Tonic of Alternative Reality. We call it STARdust, or just the Dust. It wipes memories and, if necessary, replaces them with new ones. There're no side effects, except sometimes you remember a teeny, tiny little fragment of something, but not what it means. It's really and truly nothing to worry about. Look, let me remind you of a few things that have happened to you, some you were consciously aware of and some not, and it might help you decide."

Hartley dropped his head into his hands as images started filling his mind. Monsters rising out of coins. Satan raising a glass to him in the pub, malice in his eyes. St Peter in white robe and strappy sandals in his church. Archangel Uriel doing odd jobs in the vicarage garden. Archangel Gabriel talking to him right now. He held up his hands and begged it to stop. "Please, it's all too much. I don't want to know why you're here and why this is happening. I think you'd better dust me."

Gabe nodded his understanding. "Good man, that's probably the wisest course. If you would just come with me to the back room where you keep the hymn books? Good, good. Now then, let me think of an alternative reality for you. Ah yes!"

Hartley, feeling like he might faint again, watched Gabe produce from his pocket a white handkerchief and a small thing resembling a pepper pot. He sprinkled a sparkling dust onto the cloth and the room was filled with a sweet smell that Hartley couldn't put a name to.

"Right, just breathe this in, Hartley, there's a dear chap."

Hartley took the handkerchief and held it to his face. He inhaled with deep breaths and the dust tickled his nostrils and the back of his throat.

Gabe intoned, "You've just this minute popped in to the church to empty the donations box. Keep breathing into the cloth. Good, good. You came into this room and tripped on the curtain. Now, follow me back out. Keep taking deep breaths. Excellent. Stand here, if you please, and pick the curtain up off the floor."

Hartley sneezed once, twice, three times, then noticed Gabe di Angelo walking up the knave towards him, tucking a handkerchief into his trouser pocket and humming 'Onward Christian Soldiers'.

"Hello, Mr di Angelo," called Hartley, pleased to see the friendlier of the brothers in his church. "Would you believe I tripped on the curtain and pulled it right off its hooks? Just going to fix it, and then I must empty the donations box. Not that there's ever much in it. All right, are you?"

"Oh, yes, I just came in to have a quick word with Him upstairs."

"And this is the very place to do it," chuckled Hartley. "So, I'll leave you to your conversation with the Higher Powers."

Hartley climbed onto a little wooden chair and put the curtain back up, sneezing again at the dust that billowed from the folds of the thin, fraying fabric. Two of the hooks were broken, but there were enough to keep the curtain up.

With that done, he opened the donations box with its ornate metal key and was amazed to find twenty-five pounds in it, more than the usual amount by twenty-four pounds fifty. He emptied the notes and coins into a navy blue cloth bag, locked the box again, and left the church with a cheery wave to Gabe. On his way home he hummed 'Onward Christian Soldiers' and decided that he would include it in Sunday's service.

Chapter 21
big brother is watching you

Nigel and Amelia sat on the sofa in their room at The Blacksmith's Anvil. Amelia was relaxed, but Nigel was itching to get to the mill to check on the progress there. The Sunday papers were spread around them, and he was scanning the business pages just to keep himself occupied until the pelting rain stopped.

"There's something about my old firm in here," he said.

"Hmm?" Amelia, flipping through a magazine, didn't show much interest.

"They're bidding to design and build a prestigious new development in Hammersmith."

Amelia put her magazine down and looked sympathetic as she asked, "Do you mind? Would you rather be doing that than the mill?"

Nigel thought for a moment and was surprised at how he felt. He smiled. "Do you know, I can't think of anything I'd rather be doing than restoring that lovely building? I've really fallen for the place."

Amelia smiled back. "That's wonderful, Nigel, I'm so glad." She picked up her magazine and went back to reading an article about mothers of gifted children. She couldn't imagine how she would feel, or cope, if their baby turned out to be some sort of prodigy.

Nigel abandoned the paper after reading the same sentence three times and glanced out of the window, hoping to see an improvement in the weather. What he saw was the di Angelo brothers sitting on the bench on the green. Neither of them had an umbrella, nor were they wearing raincoats, yet their hair and clothes looked bone dry.

He stood and screwed up his eyes to get a better look. Oh dear. He'd have to go out there and talk to them.

"Amelia, I think our angels need a reminder that they are supposed to be behaving like human beings."

Amelia turned her head and followed his gaze to see what Nigel was referring to. "Oh, I see what you mean. You'd better go out there before anyone else notices, if they haven't already."

Nigel swapped his slippers for the wellies he used for going on site and pulled on his raincoat. Down by the main door, he selected a brightly coloured golf umbrella from the few kept in a tall, gaudily-painted ceramic pot for pub customers, and strode out to the bench where the two angels sat, idly chatting. They smiled when they saw Nigel approach. Well, Gabriel smiled, Nick sort of snarled. Nigel wondered for the hundredth time if Nick would ever get the hang of niceness. He rather thought not, which did not bode well for the forthcoming change of angelic role.

He planted himself in front of the brothers, water cascading from the back of his blue, yellow and red umbrella and splish-splashing on the sopping grass behind his feet.

The brothers sat companionably side by side, with the rain teeming down all around them but not actually *on* them. Rain dripped from the leaves of the tree, but not from the few branches overhanging the bench, and a wide patch of grass in front of the angels was also dry. It was as if there was a huge invisible waterproof canopy protecting them and their immediate surroundings from the weather. Nigel, he realised, was standing half in and half out of the protective shield.

He turned and waved towards the window of his room at Amelia, who was watching. The two angels leaned away from each other to peer round Nigel's body and his umbrella and they waved at the window as well.

"Is your lovely wife well?" asked Gabe.

Nigel ignored the question. "Gentlemen," he said, through gritted teeth. "I'm delighted to see that you two have made it up with each other at long last, but have you noticed that it's raining? Pouring, in fact?"

"Duh, like, yes of course we know it's raining," snapped Nick, glaring at Nigel as if he was an idiot.

"Well, the thing is, when you're pretending to be human beings, which I assume you still are, then you should remember that human beings, when rained upon, GET WET!"

He waited, watching the expression on their faces as they worked out exactly what he meant.

"Ah," said Nick at last.

"Oh," said Gabe.

And they looked guiltily at each other before peering sheepishly up at Nigel.

"I apologise, Nigel," said Nick, almost sounding as if he meant it.

"Do you think anyone else apart from you and Amelia have seen us?" Gabe asked anxiously.

"Let's hope not," said Nigel. "But I think you ought to leave quickly. Go back to the mill, or wherever it is you go."

At that moment a small, dark green van pulled up at the edge of the green and out of it climbed a small man in a dark green uniform. He reached back deep inside the vehicle and emerged clutching a clipboard in a white-gloved hand.

Hoping the deliveryman wouldn't notice the two brothers sitting in their cocoon of dryness, Nigel grew alarmed as it became obvious the little man was heading straight for them. He leaned forward to cover the two angels with his umbrella, shivering as cold rain slid down the back of his collar.

"Herbert!" exclaimed Gabe. "How nice to see you. I say, I like the new uniform."

Herbert bowed from the waist, first to Gabe and then to Nick. He did not, Nigel noticed, look directly at Nick, though he did give a shy smile to Gabe. His peaked cap bore a logo, the entwined letters AMC in gold surrounded by a circle of laurel leaves.

To Nigel, Gabe explained, "Herbert is a member of the Angelic Messenger Corp. Their uniform used to be in the medieval style; you know, floppy velvet cap, doublet and hose."

Nick snorted and went into peals of laughter, "And our Herb, here, has to have the skinniest legs you've ever seen. Quite a sight in doublet and hose, I can tell you!" He slapped his thigh and laughed until tears squeezed from his eyes.

Herbert blushed scarlet from his neck to the roots of his ginger curls and fumbled with an envelope held by the sprung metal hoop on his clipboard. He held it out to Gabe.

Gabe took it, opened the flap, and removed a small piece of thick, speckled cream paper.

While he read the note, Nigel studied the little messenger man, who had tucked the clipboard under his arm and now waited with his peaked cap held in front of him with both hands. His uniform consisted of dark green trousers with a narrow gold satin band down the outside seams and a blazer that was comfortably loose fitting and adorned with gold buttons. His shirt, the collar and cuffs just visible beneath the blazer, was a very pale green, set off by a dark green and gold striped tie. A badge pinned to the blazer's lapel announced his name, and the promise, in curly letters, 'we deliver, time no object'. On his rather tiny feet were polished brown leather loafers, which creaked like an old oak branch in a stiff breeze as he rocked forward onto his toes and back onto his heels. He was a bundle of nerves, Nigel could tell.

And then Nigel realised something else. The man, even though he was standing in the pouring rain, was bone dry, just like Gabe and Nick.

"Nick," Gabe said, saying his brother's name slowly. "It's from Michael. It says, 'Word has reached me that you two are getting careless'."

Nick stopped chuckling at the memory of Herbert's skinny legs encased in brightly coloured tights. In a second, his eyes changed from jovial to mean as they focused on

Herbert, causing the little man to take a hasty step backwards as he jammed his cap back on his head.

"If you would just sign here," he gabbled, holding out the clipboard and a pen to Gabe.

There was a crackling noise and the acrid smell of burning.

"Oh, dear," said Gabe. "Did you really have to do that, Nick?"

Nigel and the two angels, Nick chortling with malice, regarded the messenger's cap now lying on the grass, sporting a melted peak and a ragged, smoking hole where the logo had been.

Poor Herbert capered around, flapping at his singed ginger curls like a demented magpie that had landed on a live wire.

Gabe picked up the still smouldering cap and handed it to Herbert.

"I am sorry, old chap, really. You know what Nick's like. He can't help it."

Without a word, Herbert took the ruined cap and stomped off into the rain, muttering that the cost of a replacement would probably be taken out of his wages.

Gabe rounded on Nick. "Why did you do that? We've just had a reminder that we're being watched, and you have to go and pull a stunt like that. What if anyone saw?"

Nick shrugged. "I'm just having a bit of fun! Only Amelia saw, and, if I'm not mistaken, she's having a bit of a laugh up there too. Oh well, I suppose we'd better get wet, like poor mortals do in the rain."

Within seconds, the thick dark curls of the two brothers was plastered to their skulls and the pounding rain made them blink. Nigel, still stunned by Nick's ridiculously childish behaviour, did not offer to shelter them with his umbrella.

Nick spoke first. "Gabe, this is ghastly. Why are we still here?"

Gabe, shivering, replied, "Yes, it is horrid and I want to get back to the mill and have a steaming hot coffee. But I know for a fact that when we start walking these trousers will *chafe.*"

Nigel watched them squelch their way across the green and up the road towards the mill, then he returned with relief to the warmth of his cosy room in the pub. Once he'd shrugged off his coat and sat down, Amelia handed him a towel and a cup of tea. He could smell that it was laced with whisky and he eagerly anticipated the moment when it would be cool enough for him to take the first sips and warm him from the inside out.

Amelia sat down, stirring her own drink. "What was all that about then? Who was that funny little man?"

Nigel told her the whole story and Amelia echoed his own thoughts when she remarked, "I really can't see how Nick is going to make it as a *good* angel, can you?"

Chapter 22
second attempts

Gabe knocked tentatively on Lorelei's door, hoping she wasn't home. But she was and she gave him such a sweet smile when she saw him standing on her doorstep, he wondered if he would be able to speak his piece. But after a couple of false starts he gave his rehearsed speech and said, "Lorelei, I've come to apologise for my brother and me disrupting your dinner a couple of weeks ago. I do hope we didn't spoil your evening?"

"Not at all," she replied graciously, her splendid green eyes sparkling. "Perhaps you haven't heard, but Stephen proposed to me that night. Look!"

Gabe leaned forward to look at the amethyst and diamond ring on Lorelei's left hand. It was very beautiful, and it certainly suited her. Delighted, he said, "Oh, how wonderful! My heartfelt congratulations to you both. I couldn't be more pleased. That's... that's wonderful, just wonderful."

He knew he was gabbling. How could he try to tempt her now, when she was so happy? Yes, she could refuse to be tempted, but what if, in her state of blissful delirium, her guard slipped?

But there was an agreement. And archangels did not renege on agreements. The Plan *had* to be implemented.

He took a deep breath and held out the large box of chocolates he'd been holding behind his back. "These hardly seem adequate after such tremendous news, but, anyway..."

Lorelei looked at the box but made no move to take it.

Gabe straightened his arm so the box was inches from her nose. "These are for you. By way of apology for... you know... the dinner. That's, um, that's why I came."

"Oh, Gabe, how sweet of you! But I really can't accept them. Oh gosh, that sounds so ungrateful." A slow flush crept into her cheeks, putting Gabe in mind of a beautiful rose. "I have to watch my diet, you see. I can't risk even one chocolate, because I know I wouldn't be able to stop. I was very overweight when I was young, and… gosh, why am I telling this? You don't want to know about any of that, I'm so sorry."

She was so close to tears, Gabe was undone. He backed away. "No, Lorelei, I'm sorry. I had no idea." The lie did not sit easily. "Please don't give it another thought."

"Oh, Gabe, please. Look, I'll accept the chocolates with pleasure if you'll allow me to take them to the art college for my students. Would that be all right? It seems so rude of me as you went to all this trouble, and I can see that they are very special chocolates, but…"

"No, no, really, it was no trouble at all. By all means give them to your students." He handed over the enormous box and scurried back to the mill, where Nick was waiting.

"Well?"

"She has the chocolates, but she says she'll give them to her students."

"Well, she might yet be tempted by them. If not, you'll have to try again. We have an Agreement, brother, and I expect you to fulfil your side of it."

Gabe slumped onto the sofa. "I know, I know. But she's just got engaged, Nick. She's in love and planning a wedding. It seems so unfair."

"So? I don't see how that has a bearing on anything. I just hope you've done enough by at least getting the temptation into her hands. Now I'm going out to see if I can tempt Violet into giving me a little bit of charity."

Gabe winced as the door slammed behind Nick. But then he sat up straight and smiled to himself at the thought that his brother was about to do something good!

~~~

Nick had his prey in his sights, and quickened his pace to catch up with her.

"Hello, Violet, how nice to see you again."

"Hah!"

"Still eating toffees, I see." He gave her his most charming smile. "Are you ever going to offer me one?"

Violet stopped in her tracks and swivelled on her heels to face him full on. "Young man, the more you ask, the less likely it is that I will give you one of my toffees. Please go away."

Nick shrugged. "Off to the pub, are you?"

She didn't answer, but Nick kept in step with her and held the door of The Blacksmith's Anvil for her to precede him. She did not thank him and he grinned at her back.

Cynthia greeted them, saying to Violet, "The usual for you?" And to Nick, "And what are you having, Mr di Angelo?"

"We're not together," barked Violet. "He's paying for his own drink." She gulped at her port and lemon as soon as the glass was placed on the bar.

Nick patted his pockets, giving the air of an increasingly desperate man. "Oh, no! I've left my wallet in my other jacket. I'm so sorry, Cynthia." He turned to Violet. "Violet, could you please lend me a couple of pounds?"

"Certainly not. I don't lend money to strangers."

You don't lend money to anyone, Nick wanted to remind her.

"Don't worry, Mr di Angelo," said Cynthia. "You can pay me next time you're in."

Violet left after half an hour, and Nick stayed on for another twenty minutes, nursing his pint of bitter, racking his brains.

What else could he do to tempt Violet into an act of charity? Just the tiniest chink in her armour and she would be his.
~~~

He walked slowly towards her house, thinking hard. Then he had it.

Just before he reached her front door, Nick performed a spectacular fall. Splat, he went, onto the hard road surface, grazing his hands and tearing his trousers at the knees. Excellent.

He hauled himself up, tore his trousers a little more, and knocked on Violet's door.

She was far from pleased to see him. "What now? I'm beginning to think you're stalking me."

Nick held out his hands so she could see the cuts on his palms. "I tripped, Violet. Would you mind if I came in and cleaned up?"

She glowered at him, her mean eyes like flakes of jet.

"And my knees are throbbing… if you can spare a glass of water and an aspirin?"

Violet drew herself up to her full height of five feet nothing. "What do you think this is, a pharmacy? You have the cheek of the devil, and you are seriously getting on my nerves."

The door was slammed shut, and Nick couldn't help the wide grin that spread over his face as he healed the cuts and scratches. Violet Cattermole was a magnificent woman. Magnificent!

But free will be damned! His and his brother's failures now called for drastic action.

He rushed back to the mill, needing to rethink his strategy, glad when he got there that Gabe wasn't there to disturb him.

Chapter 23
time to rethink the strategy

Walking through the village for some fresh, early morning air, Hartley saw Lorelei's car and decided to see if she had time for a cup of tea. About to knock, he paused when he heard raised voices from inside. Oh dear, was Stephen there, and were they having a row? Hartley couldn't imagine it; even before their engagement they had been like little lovebirds, and since Stephen had proposed, they'd been even more lovey-dovey with each other. Hartley thought it was wonderful and was so pleased that Lorelei had found such a lovely man who truly adored her.

Standing there, trying to decide whether or not to knock or to go away and leave them to it, Violet suddenly appeared at his side, chewing furiously.

Her eyes gleamed with malice as she whispered, "She's got a man in there, and it's not her fiancé." Another toffee disappeared into her mouth.

"Violet, I don't think—"

There was a loud crash, then Lorelei's voice, raised in fury, yelled, "Leave me alone! Go away! I'll call the police!"

Hartley hammered on the door. "Lorelei! Lorelei! What's going on?"

"Always said she'd come to no good," Violet smirked.

"Violet, shut up."

"I beg your pardon?"

"I said shut up! Lorelei's in trouble. Go and call the police."

Before Violet could leave, however, the front door was wrenched open and Nick di Angelo was imperiously ordering them to come in.

Hartley immediately pushed past him, calling out to his niece.

"I'm all right, Uncle."

She was in the living room, chocolates scattered around her, their fancy box upside down on the floor at her feet. Pieces of a shattered vase dotted the rug in front of the fireplace, and Hartley spotted a couple of small pieces lodged in Nick's hair.

Hartley turned back in time to see Violet being dragged in by the elbow, struggling in vain against the big man.

When all four were in Lorelei's tiny living room, Hartley looked at their assailant and demanded, "What on Earth is going on here? Why was my niece screaming?"

Nick seemed a bit shaken as he looked from one to the other of his three captives, his eyes coming to rest on Hartley. "You weren't meant to show up." He paced up and down, as much as the small room allowed, muttering, "I need to think, I need to think."

"Call the police, Lorelei," ordered Hartley.

"No!" Nick barred the door. "No-one is going to do anything. Now be quiet." He paced some more.

Hartley was relieved to see that Lorelei was angry rather than frightened, and she didn't seem to be hurt. Violet was still chewing away, her black eyes darting from Lorelei to Nick, no doubt thinking the worst. Hartley had never disliked anyone more than at that moment. As for Nick di Angelo, he didn't know what to think.

"Did you invite him here, Lorelei?" he whispered.

"No, Uncle Hartley, I did not." She glared at Nick and said, "He just turned up here and barged his way in. He's been trying to get me to eat one of these chocolates that his brother brought round this morning. I threw that vase at him, and then I heard you shout."

"What is it with women and throwing things at heads?" said Nick, exasperated. "A good thing I have a very hard skull."

"You had better explain yourself," fumed Hartley. "You can't hold us all here against our will."

"It wasn't meant to happen like this," muttered Nick. He drew himself to his full height, his head almost touching the low, beamed ceiling. "Okay, you won't remember any of this by the time I've finished with you, so let me tell you something." He pointed first at Lorelei. "You, I notice, have silly things like angel cards and angel ornaments all over the place, so it will amaze you to know, I'm sure, that you have actually had dinner with two *real* angels."

"What?" she scoffed.

Nick nodded. "That's right, *Archangels*. My brother, Gabriel, and me, the dreaded Lucifer. And Uriel. He sent Topps away so he could take his place and keep an eye on things. And you, Vicar, you've also seen a saint, our very own Saint Peter, in your church." He placed his hand on his own chest and raised his chin. "So tell me, how does it feel for you, a man of the cloth, to have been up close and personal with Satan himself?"

Hartley, wide-eyed, gasped and whispered, "That's impossible. You're being ridiculous."

"His aura is black, Uncle, quite black."

Violet snapped, "What are you talking about, you silly fools?"

"Ah, Violet, Violet," sighed Nick. "You are a wonderful woman. If I was staying in Hell and not having to turn you into a good woman, I'd keep you by my side always so I could enjoy your mean and selfish heart." He closed his eyes for a moment, as if imagining it. "But here's what we're going to do. You, vicar, will please sit next to your niece. You, Violet, will sit in this armchair."

"I will not."

"You will, Violet Cattermole. And the sooner you do as I ask the sooner all this unpleasantness will come to an end."

Violet sat down, jaw set and arms crossed tightly across her chest.

"This is how it's going to be," said Nick, producing a small brown pot. "You will all breathe deeply, please, and pay close attention to my next words." With a flick of his wrist, a sweet-smelling powder filled the room. "Reverend Hartley Cordwell, I'm sorry to put you through this for a third time, but it can't be helped… you just popped in for a cup of tea with your niece. Lorelei Dove, you will eat those chocolates, every single one of them. And Violet Cattermole, there's no reason why you'd be having tea with Lorelei, so when this is done I'm going to take you home and you will offer me one of your sweets."

For some reason, the words of *Onward Christian Soldiers* came into Hartley's head, and he started to sing.

Chapter 24
food and cats

"Thank you for getting my groceries, Lorelei."

Lorelei, munching through her second blueberry muffin, replied, "Not at all, Uncle. Are you sure you won't have another cup of tea?"

"Thank you, dear, but I must get on. Bring Stephen to the vicarage soon, won't you?"

He stepped out of Lorelei's front door into the cold and started to walk in the direction of the vicarage, humming *Onward Christian Soldiers*, a tune he simply hadn't been able to get out of his head this past couple of weeks.

Hearing a door slam, he turned to see Lorelei rush out of her cottage and leap into her car. She drove past him without so much as a wave, and he worried that he had made her late for something and she'd been too polite to say so.

Then he heard an over-revved car engine whine up the High Street, and turned to see Violet's rarely-used old Citroen 2CV screech to a halt in front of her garden gate.

Violet got out of the car and waved at him, calling his name, so he had no choice but to go over to her.

"Hello, Violet."

"Good morning, Hartley. Or is it afternoon? I've been into town and rather lost track of time."

Hartley blinked. This polite person didn't sound like Violet at all.

"Do you need help with your shopping?"

Violet opened the rear door of the car and reached in. There seemed to be a momentous struggle before she wriggled backwards and placed first a bulging plastic bag and then a wicker basket on the ground. A furious hissing and spitting blared from the basket as it rocked from side to side. White-faced, Violet slammed the car door, grabbed everything from the pavement and marched through the gate.

Hartley hurried after her. "Violet, can I help you with that?" He was wondering if, for some extraordinary reason, she had brought home a puma cub.

"No, thank you, but if you would just open the door please?"

He took the proffered key and opened the door, stepping back so Violet could go in ahead of him.

"Just come from the cat rescue," Violet explained. "Have you time for a coffee, Hartley?"

Hartley stared at her. The teeth still clacked, but the tone of voice simply was not that of the Violet Cattermole he knew and found it hard to love, in the way a man of the cloth should love a member of his flock. The Violet Cattermole of his acquaintance would not speak in that pleasant, genuine way.

"Cat rescue? You mean you've adopted a cat?"

Violet snapped, "Well it wouldn't be a dog now, would it?" and Hartley couldn't help smiling, feeling he was back on safe ground again. *This* was Violet talking. But she quickly ruined it as, with a heartfelt sigh, she swept her hands over her heavily powdered cheeks and apologised again.

They were in the sitting room, the now silent but vibrating basket on the floor between them. Violet indicated that Hartley should sit in the armchair by the window with the view across the green, then she tipped up the plastic bag and emptied its contents onto the floor: a small fluffy ball, a fluffy mouse, a fluffy cushion, several tins of cat food and a rattling box of cat treats.

"I didn't know you liked animals, Violet."

"Nor me. I don't know what came over me, I really don't, but I was driving past that rescue place last week and, well, I just turned in and he was the first one I spotted. Been through all their questions and checks, and got a call this morning to say I could go and fetch him."

"Have you ever had a cat?"

"We had mousers when we lived at the mill, but they were right feral, wouldn't let you near 'em."

"Have you got trouble with mice here, then?" Hartley glanced worriedly around the skirting boards looking for holes and mouse droppings.

"Mice?" She looked horrified at the thought. "Of course not! This is a pet."

Well, well, thought Hartley, Violet Cattermole has rescued a cat from the shelter. Who'd have thought she, of all people, would make such a charitable gesture? The basket was still vibrating, though, and Hartley had a feeling it wasn't because the cat was purring with joy.

"Well, better let this one out to get his bearings in his new home." Violet fiddled with the buckles on the red leather straps holding the basket closed. Claws slashed at the spaces as the door was loosened, then there was an orange flash as an enormous tomcat shot out like a bullet from a gun and hid itself behind the aspidistra in the corner. Two gooseberry-green eyes glared at them from around the pot, then, obviously feeling that a large plant didn't offer enough cover, the cat darted under the sofa with an angry yowl.

Hartley risked a quick glance at his watch, hoping that Violet wouldn't notice. He had things to do and the day was passing.

"Hartley, I was thinking of coming to see you, but as you're here..." She tore her eyes away from the bottom of the sofa, where the very tip of a stripy ginger tail could be seen. It was flicking from side to side – Hartley had had no idea that a tail could exude such irritation – and a low, menacing growl was coming from deep within its throat. "I wanted to talk to you about the font."

She spoke so quietly and in a strange monotone he wasn't sure he'd heard her correctly. "Did you say something about the font?"

"I'm sorry, Hartley, I promised coffee, didn't I?"

"Oh, don't worry about it, Violet, I've just had tea with my niece. What about the font, Violet?"

"Well, it needs to be repaired, right? And because it's so old only a specialist stonemason could do it, and that would be expensive. Well, how expensive?"

"Heavens, I really don't know. I haven't looked into it because we simply don't have the funds. I'm still hoping the coin that Topps found will be worth as much as they think it is, but it might take ages to get it to auction and I can't rely on it. The font is hardly used anyway, sadly, because there are so few Christenings here."

"But if it isn't repaired?"

"It'll go on crumbling, I suppose, but it's been there for hundreds of years, I'm sure it won't disintegrate on us any time soon." He could not for the life of him think why he was having this conversation with Violet, of all people.

"I want… that is, I think it would be a good idea… well, perhaps I could, you know, um, pay for it to be repaired?"

Hartley didn't know what to say.

"I got a lot of money from the sale of the mill, as I'm sure you know, and I've decided to put it to good use." She glanced at the cat's hiding-place, where the very tip of a pink whiskery nose was now visible instead of the angrily flicking tail.

Hartley pressed his hands together as if in prayer, then interlocked his fingers, giving himself time to think. Violet's eyes were glassy, unfocused. She was like a ventriloquist's dummy, with some unseen person with ill-fitting dentures providing the voice and words for her.

"I could hardly say no, Violet, to such a generous offer. We could have a plaque with your name on it in recognition of your generosity."

"A plaque?"

Hartley watched as a fleet of emotions flowed across Violet's deeply lined face. At first she seemed pleased by the idea, because, just for a moment, there was a familiar avaricious gleam in her eyes. But then her smile slowly faded and she said in earnest, "Oh no! No, no! I don't want recognition. That's not what charity is all about, is it?"

"Right. Ah, let me see, then. You've quite taken me by surprise here, I must say. I suggest you let me get some estimates of repair, and then we'll talk again. Now," he stood up, "I have to be getting along home, I've got a few ecumenical matters to attend to, you know. It's really so very kind of you to think of the church in this way, very kind."

A ginger paw shot out from beneath the sofa and grabbed the little toy mouse. Within seconds it was in sorry shreds on the carpet.

"And I wish you luck with your cat. Does it have a name?"

The old lady laughed, a rusty sound that made Hartley's eyes widen with shock. "He's called Fudge. But I might have to change that to Fireball, don't you think?"

It was the first time Hartley had ever heard her make a joke that didn't have an element of spite in it.

She followed him to the door and murmured that she was expecting Hilda. "Haven't talked to her in years. Far too many years. But anyway, I won't hold you up, Hartley. Thank you for coming."

"Oh, thank *you*, Violet." And he was out and away.

He walked briskly in the direction of the vicarage, once again humming that hymn, wishing all the same that he could get it out of his head, while his mind fizzed and sparked with confusion. Was that really Violet Cattermole he'd just been talking to, or had an alien landed during the night and taken over her body?

"Hartley Cordwell," he scolded. "Shame on you! Do you not preach that a leopard *can* change its spots?"

"Aye, that you do, Vicar."

Hartley jumped at the unexpected voice, and Hilda Merryvale chuckled as she came abreast of him from the other direction. "Are you talking to yourself, or Him up above, Hartley?"

Hartley laughed. "To myself, Hilda, I'm afraid. How are you? How are things at the farm?"

She frowned, her small nose wrinkling in her homely face. "I can't pretend that it isn't getting harder and harder as I get older. The farmhouse is falling down round my ears. Four buckets I had on the landing in the last downpour. I sometimes think, you know, that the place is so damp I could make a better living growing mushrooms in it."

Hartley tutted in sympathy. Hilda was too old to be living in a damp house and managing livestock day in and day out.

"Anyway, I'm on my way to see Violet."

"And I've just come from there, she said she was expecting you."

Hilda looked sad. "You know, I've never been inside her house. Can you imagine that, with us living so close to each other? I can't think why she wants to see me now. I do hope she isn't ill."

"She looked fine to me, Hilda. In fact, I really think it might be good news. I do hope so, anyway."

"I can't imagine what you mean, Hartley, but I hope so too. It's been such a long time that I've almost forgotten we're sisters, but we are, aren't we? And you've always said that blood is thicker than water, and deep down I've always believed she'd forgive me in the end. It's not as if I had a happy marriage, so if you think about it, I saved her from that! Ah well. I mustn't keep you. It's my turn for the flowers on Sunday, so I'll see you again then. Cheerio, now."

How typical, he thought, that Hilda had not a word of censure for Violet's terrible behaviour over the years. And yet, from the day she had married Merryvale, having had no honeymoon or any other kind of holiday since, Hilda had worked her fingers to the bone on that farm. Up at the crack of dawn for milking, constantly cooking and making huge meals for her husband and the farm workers, never going anywhere that warranted getting dressed up, and probably not having anything nice to dress up in anyway.

And Violet had no reason to be jealous of Hilda, none at all. In fact, as was commonly agreed among the villagers, Violet had had a narrow escape when the farmer had switched his attention to Hilda, because it had turned out that he was nothing like his name suggested. There were many who said he should have been called Miseryguts rather than Merryvale. He had certainly made Hilda's life miserable with his dour, over-strict ways, and had even driven out their only son, Maxwell, when he was one week past his sixteenth birthday. After a flurry of postcards from far-flung places all over the world, communication from Maxwell had ceased, so Hilda didn't even know if he was still alive. As if that wasn't enough, after Merryvale's death Hilda had found herself in terrible debt and so had carried on alone with just a few farmhands to help her, always hoping that one day her son would come home and ease her burden.

But Hilda's first emotion on hearing from Violet was anxiety that her sister might be suffering ill health.

He stopped mid-step. Could that be it? She looked well, but that didn't mean she wasn't sick, did it? Maybe she was dying and wanting to make amends for all the nasty, hurtful things she had done, before it was too late? But then she would hardly take on a cat, would she?

Hartley shook his head and continued walking. He hoped, he prayed, that Violet would offer Hilda some financial help. Better, he thought, that any money Violet had set aside for charity should go to her sister, a flesh and blood sentient being, and not to repair an inanimate, little-used piece of stone.

For the second time, he set out on the short walk to the vicarage, but was interrupted yet again by the speedy arrival of Lorelei returning from wherever she had been. She parked in her usual place, then unloaded about half a dozen bags of shopping. Hartley couldn't understand it. She may have forgotten one or two things the first time she'd gone to the supermarket earlier, but now she was pulling out bag after bag. One of them tipped over, and out spilled several packets of biscuits and a packet of what looked like doughnuts. Lorelei loved sweet things, Hartley knew, but ever since she'd lost all that weight, she'd avoided sugary, fattening foods.

She did not seem to notice that her worried uncle was watching her as she hurried across the green to her cottage with bags in each hand, a large bar of chocolate, only half unwrapped, held between her teeth.

Chapter 25
the fall in ebony

Nigel strolled away from the mill, his head reeling with how fast everything was happening. The outside of the building was complete and the scaffolding had been dismantled and taken away, so everyone who came to the site could now appreciate the special beauty of the stone building. Plasterers, electricians and plumbers were working around each other on the inside from early morning to late afternoon, and the ground floor was already beginning to look like the interior of the grand restaurant it would soon be.

He couldn't help but laugh to himself when he thought about the bewildered builders and tradesmen working twice, no, three times harder and faster than they were used to, and doing top quality work at that, without having a clue as to why or how. This would probably be the quickest renovation in the history of renovations.

It was a pleasant day, cold but clear-skied. Smoke curled from the chimneys of a few of the houses and cottages, filling the air with the pleasant smells of seasoned wood burning in stoves and open hearths. Nigel thought that the village, nestling in the green folds of the Lym, looked very cosy. Amelia adored it, and they'd both agreed they'd love to live here or somewhere like it if they could, especially when the baby came.

He was on his way to see Uri, because he'd had a message to say that he'd finished the first of the panels for the bar and Nigel was keen to see it.

He passed through the gate into the vicarage garden, turned left and walked along the neat paved path and through the arch cut into the dense leylandii hedge. The first time he'd come to the cottage he had been shocked that the brick and timber building, surrounded by a vegetable garden, was so basic, and the workshop behind it even more so. He thought Uri would work some angel magic and create a portal through to something luxurious, but he hadn't seen any evidence of it. It seemed Uri was content to be in the rustic, cobbled-together space created by Topps.

Nigel knocked on the cottage door and pushed it open when Uri called for him to come in. He stepped into the single room that made up the ground floor, to find Uri standing before the two-ring stove boiling water for his pot of coffee. The furniture consisted of a camp bed pushed against the wall, two old armchairs, both with stuffing peeking out from the cushions, a tall white-painted cupboard, a rather attractive pine dresser and a small, stocky table with ornately carved legs. On the wall there hung an old tin bathtub, and to the right of that was a sink with a wooden draining board. The only homely aspect was a shelf full of Uri's wonderful whittled figurines and an open fireplace in the far wall, but the grate was always cold when Nigel visited. He imagined that the toilet was somewhere outside, although so far he'd not needed to find out.

"Hello, Uri," he called.

"Perfect timing, Nigel. I'll get the drinks made and we'll go over to the workshop. Bring the biscuit tin, will you?"

Nigel waited while Uri operated his state-of the art coffee machine, so incongruous set next to the ancient cooking range. As the milk was steamed with loud shushing noises his mouth watered in anticipation.

Going into the workshop was like entering a miniature sawmill. His feet sank into inches of sawdust and he had to wait for his eyes and nose to adjust to the dust-filled air. But he loved the smell of sawn wood, the mingled scents of pine and oak and mahogany. And now, he supposed, ebony was adding a new dimension to the dust and overall perfume of the place. At least two thirds of the workshop was taken up with a workbench with stacks of different types of wood beneath, boxes of tools and all sorts of works in progress, like bird boxes and small pieces of furniture.

It was Topps' workshop, but Topps did not use it to create works of wonder like Uri did.

Nigel helped himself to two biscuits from the tin. He had a way of eating custard creams and bourbons that infuriated Amelia, which was to pull the biscuits apart and scrape the custard filling off one side with his bottom teeth. The remaining half of biscuit was then dunked into whatever hot drink was in his cup and swallowed whole. If he dunked it for too long and it disintegrated in the hot liquid, he scooped the gloop into his mouth with a spoon, which Amelia found even more disgusting.

He sat on a high stool and settled in to watch Uri at work, quietly taking apart and eating his biscuits while Uri started carving. Not a word was spoken. There was no need. Nigel knew that Uri would stop carving when he was good and ready, and then they'd chat.

After a while, Uri straightened up and pointed with a chisel to the end of the bench. "First panel's over there," he said. Nigel had noticed it enticingly propped there, but hadn't wanted to go over to it until he'd been given permission.

He studied the detail of the design drawing pinned to the wall, then compared it to the actual panel as he stood before it, separating another custard cream so he could get at the cream filling.

Just as Nick had intended, the carving was like an optical illusion. At first glance it was nothing more than a chunky piece of wood with an intricate filigree-like pattern etched into it. Then, with an effort to make the eyes adjust and focus, suddenly the brain could decipher the host of angels, with their magnificent wings and halos, beautiful faces, long draped robes, all bathed in dancing sunbeams. It almost seemed to take on colour and movement, but of course it didn't; it was just very dark wood, beautifully carved.

Running his fingers reverently over the figures Uri had carved, Nigel began to wonder. He'd seen the film, he'd even seen wings on Gabe's back for a split second, but was this the truth? Did this really happen?

"What do you think, then?" asked Uri, bringing Nigel out of his reverie.

"I think it's magnificent. Really and truly magnificent. Just like the film, in fact."

"Ah, yes, the film. Are you okay, Nigel, with all of this?"

Nigel blew out his cheeks before replying, "I can't really explain how I feel, Uri. Part of me still doesn't really believe I'm mixed up with angels, but another part of me can't deny it."

"Ah, well, that's normal."

"So other people do know about you? I mean, really *know* and not just think they know?"

"Hmm, I suppose I ought to tell you..."

"Tell me what?"

"We don't allow most humans who have had direct contact with us to remember it, only those who can handle the knowledge and use it wisely. Hartley discovered our secret – purely by accident, I might add – and Gabriel had to use our Alternative Reality Dust on him."

"Is that what's going to happen to me? And Amelia?"

"Not necessarily, in fact I'd say it's unlikely as we know you can both be trusted. Let's see how the land lies when you've completed the work we've asked you to do." At Nigel's puzzled expression he reminded him, "The Witness bit, remember?"

Nigel nodded, "Oh, yes. Yes, of course. I remember all right, but I shove it to the back of mind as I've no idea how I'm going to convince the planet that Satan has left the building. But still..."

Uri laughed. "My advice is not to worry about it yet. Just enjoy rebuilding the mill, as anything could happen between now and the Great Swap."

Nigel went to say something more, but Uri forestalled him and said, "Help me wrap this up, would you. I want to put it over there against the wall, where there's no danger of it getting damaged."

Together they wound plastic bubble-wrap round and round the panel and taped it securely, before carefully lifting it and leaning it against the wall. Uri produced a felt-tipped pen and a piece of plain paper on which he wrote "Panel 1" in rather beautiful script, all curlicues and fancy twiddly bits. He stuck the paper on the bubble-wrap with a piece of tape, and grinned at Nigel with an expression of deep satisfaction.

They sat side by side on the stools at the workbench, and Nigel handed Uri his mug of sweetened coffee. It was surprisingly hot after so long, and a little sawdust floated on the surface. And Uri didn't seem to notice the sawdust floating on the top as he drank it down in two swallows. He then asked Nigel to help him carry out a fresh piece of wood so he could start work on carving the second panel.

"Are you going to start on it now? It's," Nigel looked at his watch, "getting late. But what am I saying? Angels don't need to rest, do they, Uri?"

"Nope. But I'm not going to do much more tonight, as Gabriel and Lucifer are expecting me."

Nigel shivered at hearing Nick's real name spoken aloud.

Uri didn't seem to notice. He took down the drawing from the wall and refolded it so that the illustration for Panel Two was visible. He removed his blue-tinted glasses and polished the lenses on his shirt, replaced them and studied the drawing for a minute before pinning it back up again. "Just a few nicks to get it started, that's all."

The second panel was to show Gabriel and Lucifer standing side by side, clutching each other's sleeve, gingerly leaning forward and peering down into a smoking pit, just like the scene in the film.

He hadn't seen Uri start the first panel, so didn't know what to expect with the second, but at the very least he thought Uri would sketch something onto the wood, maybe with chalk. But he didn't. He paced from left to right and back again, studying the wood from every angle, before announcing that it was the wrong way up and Nigel must help him turn it.

Once turned, Uri again paced in front of the panel, studying it intently, reaching forward occasionally to stroke a particular part with his fingertips. After about twenty minutes of this, in which Nigel felt a knot of keen anticipation form in his stomach, Uri reached into the tool belt strapped around his waist and withdrew a small pointed instrument with a well-worn red handle. He made a few deft scratches on the wood, and Nigel was amazed to see the two angels appear in outline form.

"Uri, you are truly a gifted man. I mean, angel."

Uri laughed. He stood back and regarded his work, head first on one side, then the other. "That'll do for now," he said, replacing the tool. "You know, with my powers I could just blink this thing into being if I wanted to. As could Nick. But I'm doing this the proper way, as a master craftsman should, as it's much more satisfying. Now, why don't you come with me to the Mill?"

They made the short walk in companionable silence and Nigel followed Uri through what he now knew was a portal into the luxury space that Gabe and Nick had created for themselves.

As his eyes took in the scene in front of him, he stopped in his tracks at the threshold, wondering if a hurricane had gone through it. Broken china lay scattered on every surface, two of the six dining chairs were on their sides, a third had its front legs broken.

In the middle of the room stood Gabe, trembling with what Nigel could see was barely containable outrage.

Noticing them, Nick cajoled, "Look, Uri's here. And Nigel. Come on now, Gabe, calm down."

"Calm down? Calm down? How dare you!" He hooked his fingers and for a moment Nigel thought Gabe was going to launch himself at his brother and gouge his eyes, but instead he dug deep into his own scalp and pulled on his black curls. The mirror in the living room cracked and shattered.

"Er, fellas, what's going on?"

"Gabe's just a bit upset, Nigel, nothing to worry about."

"A BIT upset? A BIT?" yelled Gabe.

Flakes of plaster fluttered down from the ceiling.

"Gabe, stop shouting and repeating yourself, you're practically incoherent. Nigel doesn't want to hear about our petty squabbles, so—"

"PETTY?" This time Gabe did launch himself at Nick, and Nigel watched in growing alarm as the angels wrestled on the tiled floor.

"Come on now, you two, break it up." His attempt at peace-making was rewarded with a painful, bruising punch on the cheek from Gabe's fist. Undeterred, he waded in with Uri among the flailing limbs and they tried to separate the warring brothers. After quite a struggle they got Gabe and Nick apart, and all four of them stood for a moment, gasping and panting.

Gabe was so angry his pale skin seemed to effervesce with rage, and his eyes were a thunderous black. It was a sight so unfamiliar and unexpected that Nigel seriously worried that the angel was going to spontaneously combust.

Uri seemed equally worried as he said, "Would one of you please tell us what's going on?"

"Nick is a liar and a cheat, that's what's going on."

"Of course I am! I'm the Devil! Come on, Gabe, what did you expect? It was taking too long."

"What was?" asked Nigel, looking from one to the other.

Gabe sagged into a chair. "The temptation of Lorelei and Violet. We couldn't do it, so he," Gabe threw a look of absolute venom at Nick, "CHEATED! And not just with the temptation. Oh no. Saint Peter mentioned something about him meddling here by creating earth tremors and worse, so I checked. Anywhere on this planet with 'angel' in the name has been disrupted by him looking for the DISC. Salto Ángel in Venezuela, Archangel in Russia, Los Angeles in the USA – hah, think of the earthquakes *they've* had! It was HIM!"

"Can you blame me?" Nick appealed to Nigel and Uri, "Seriously, if you were in my situation, wouldn't you try to move things along a little?"

"Um, I don't know. Maybe," answered Nigel. "But what have you actually done to Violet and Lorelei?"

Nick shrugged, trying to act nonchalant. "I just speeded up the inevitable, that's all."

Uri folded his arms, seeming to grow taller and broader. His skin started to glow like Gabriel's, as if lit from within, and Nigel understood that this was what a very angry archangel looked like. Uri's voice sounded deeper and more resonant than usual as he demanded, "I think you had better start from the beginning."

The story came out in fits and starts, Gabe and Nick hurling insults at each other as the whole sorry saga unfolded.

"You used STARdust on Lorelei, the vicar and Violet?" asked Uri when Nick had finished explaining what he'd done.

"I had to! I told you, I hadn't planned on Violet and the vicar turning up like that. I had no choice."

"Yes you did!" yelled Gabe. "The choice was not to CHEAT! If you hadn't gone round to Lorelei Dove's place to CHEAT, then you wouldn't have had to CHEAT with the others."

Uri held up a commanding hand. "All right, all right. Enough, Gabe. We've established that Nick has been dishonest, but we can hardly be surprised by that. What concerns me is that Hartley Cordwell has now had three doses of STARdust, which is two more than any human has ever had before. I only hope there's no lasting damage."

"There won't be," said Nick, sounding, for the first time, almost cowed.

"How can you know that, Nick?"

He shrugged again, not daring to meet Uri's laser-like gaze.

Uri started to pace the room and Nigel began to feel a fluttering in his stomach, a mixture of nervous energy and hopefulness. Surely, he thought, as Nick had used supernatural force on Lorelei and Violet rather than temptation, it negated everything? Would that mean Gabriel staying in Heaven, where he so clearly wanted to be?

"I know what you're thinking," said Uri, coming to stand in front of Nigel and putting his hand on his shoulder. It felt hot, even through Nigel's overcoat. "And maybe you're right. But it's up to Michael. I shall have to go and see him."

"We'll all go," said Gabe. "Except you, Nigel, of course, you don't need to be part of this."

Nigel wasn't at all sorry. He said his goodbyes and left the Mill hurriedly, not stopping until he was back in his room at the pub.

Chapter 26
the consequences of gluttony

Lorelei arrived at the vicarage at 12:30 and came huffing into the kitchen. Hartley thought she did not look at all well. Her usually glorious red hair was dull and matted, her once creamy, smooth skin sallow and puffy. Everything about her was puffy, and so startlingly dull, including her clothes. Where had his sparkling, colourful niece gone? He felt a headache start to nag at the base of his skull. First Violet appeared to be a completely different person, now Lorelei was changing before his eyes, but unlike Violet, not in a good way.

He kissed her on the cheek. She burst into tears.

"Oh, oh, heavens! Lorelei, Lorelei, my dear, what is it, what's wrong?"

The tears flowed harder. She sank onto a kitchen chair and laid her head on her arms on the table. Her whole body heaved with sobs.

"My dear, please, please! Tell me, are you ill?"

She shook her head.

"Is it Stephen? Has something happened between you?" He hoped not, because he believed with all his heart that he and Lorelei were such a good match. He'd even dared to hope that he might be asked to conduct their marriage ceremony once they'd set the date, provided Lorelei didn't want a New Age ceremony in a field rather than a traditional church wedding.

Her head came up and she held out her left hand. "I…" she gulped, "I… I've broken off the engagement." This was followed by another storm of weeping.

Hartley saw that her beautiful engagement ring was missing, and he noticed that her fingers were swollen. He took the chair opposite her and wished he had a handkerchief about his person that he could offer. Kitchen towel would have to do. He tore off a sheet and gently pushed it into her hand.

Eventually she sat up and took several deep breaths.

"I can't stop eating, Uncle."

"What? But that's no reason to break it off with Stephen, is it?"

"Look at me, Uncle Hartley. I mean really look at me." She indicated her hair and her clothes.

Hartley didn't know what to say. Did she expect him to tell her that she didn't look a mess? Well, it would be a lie if he did, but he couldn't think of anything positive to say either. She had been terribly overweight all through her childhood and early teens, and had suffered bullying at school because of it. On her sixteenth birthday she had announced that she was going on a strict diet and had successfully slimmed down. But Hartley knew she was always terrified of putting on weight again, so couldn't think what would suddenly make her start overeating now, especially when she was so happy with Stephen.

Lorelei reached over to grasp his hand. "I think I'm ill, Uncle. I think there's something seriously wrong with me."

"Oh, Lorelei. Why? What do you mean?"

"All I think about, from the time I wake up to the time I go to bed, is food. I eat and eat and eat. Anything and everything! Uncle, I've eaten *bacon*, for goodness' sake."

"Have you been to see Dr Tyler, dear? Maybe it's, I don't know, a thyroid problem or something?"

"Yes, I've seen him. I sat in his surgery and devoured a whole bag of jelly beans. *Jelly beans*, Uncle. Full of gelatine! He's running some blood tests."

"Well, then. You'll have to wait a day or two to see what they show. I'm sure it will be sorted out, and I know, dear, that Stephen loves you. He must be devastated that you've broken off the engagement, surely?"

Hartley began to think he'd said the wrong thing, because her shoulders sagged and her bottom lip wobbled even more. Her voice was barely a whisper as she told him. "He is. But, Uncle Hartley, I did something terrible yesterday."

"Oh, surely not, Lorelei. You, of all people, could never do anything terrible."

"But I did. To a child. In a cake shop. Oh, I hate myself!" The tears overflowed and she lowered her head onto her arms again and howled while Hartley looked on feeling utterly helpless.

~~~

"She's broken it off? Oh, Stephen, I can't believe it."

"Neither can I, Stella. But I can't believe a lot of other things either. I mean I love her, I really do, but she's changed. I fell in love with that vibrant, gorgeous, glorious creature the first moment I laid eyes on her here, and now she's… uh… I don't even know how to describe it. My Lorelei, the one I want to marry, is a kind-hearted, loving, funny, sweet vegetarian with a tiny appetite. This Lorelei, all she does, and I mean *all* she does, is eat. She even had a bacon sandwich for breakfast the other day. When I asked her about it, she threw it at me." He paused. "Then she picked it off my jacket and ate it."

"Perhaps it's a hormone problem, Stephen. I don't mean to be indelicate, but is there a possibility she could be pregnant? That does really odd things to the appetite."

"I thought of that, and I did ask her, but she said no. You know, when we first met we talked about anything and everything. Now the only subject she can talk about is food. And she was always neat as a pin. You said so yourself. Her dress sense was, well, a little eccentric, but it suited her. And she always smelled wonderful." He looked wistful again, thinking how he had loved to bury his face in Lorelei's cinnamon coloured curls that always smelled so delicious.
~~~

"And she kept her house immaculate. But now! Oh Stella, she's so unbelievably untidy. You should see her studio! I mean, okay, it was a bit messy before, but messy in a nice, industrious sort of way, with all the paraphernalia of art everywhere. But it was clean. Now it's heaped with dirty plates and food wrappers, and I don't think she's even doing much painting now."

Stella shook her head in sympathy.

Stephen continued, "She used to pick at her food a bit, you know, eat little bits of everything and stop when she'd had enough. Now she eats and eats, and if I left anything on my plate, she'd eat that too. And yesterday…"

The silence stretched out as Stephen relived the memory and struggled to find the words.

"Yesterday?" urged Stella, gently patting his hands, which were twisting on his lap in agitation.

"We met for a walk in the park. Lorelei had brought a picnic. I was surprised she could carry it there was so much stuff. She spread it all out then scoffed it item by item with barely a pause in between. I hardly got a look-in. Afterwards, when we were walking back towards where the car was parked, she decided she wanted a cake. After all that picnic stuff! Anyway, she wouldn't be put off, so we went into a cake shop."

Stephen paused, and squirmed in his chair. "We were followed in by a woman and her little boy. Lorelei asked for an iced bun, and the little boy piped up that that was what he wanted too. The girl serving said that there was only one left. Well, you'd think that Lorelei would say that the little boy could have it, wouldn't you?"

He shook his head and smiled ruefully at Stella.

"Well, I'm ashamed to say that she didn't. The old Lorelei would have. She would even have bought it herself and given it to the little boy with a beaming smile. But not this time. Stella, not only did she insist on having it, she leaned down in front of the little boy and ate it in three huge bites. Then she walked out of the shop, leaving him in tears."

"Perhaps she didn't realise, Stephen?"

"Of course she realised! Didn't I just say how deliberate she was in upsetting that little boy? But a little later she cried and cried and told me that she hates herself. She's really changed, Stella. It's not the weight gain, I really don't care whether she's big or skinny, it's her personality I fell in love with, but that's changed beyond recognition. She was like someone lit from within, but now... well it's as if the light has gone out. She's just not the same woman any more. She's not the Lorelei I fell in love with."

"But you do still love her?"

"Oh, Stella, yes, I still love her. But after that scene in the cake shop, she wrenched off the ring and threw it at me, screaming at me to go away and never contact her again." His whole body shrunk inwards in misery. "Oh, Stella, how can I get my Lorelei back?"

Stella clasped his hand and gave it a shake to emphasise her advice. "Don't give up on her, Stephen. I've seen the two of you together and your love for each other just shines out. Just be there for her, until whatever it is gets sorted out."

"And how will I know? She won't let me near her, she won't answer my calls. I'm at a loss what do to."

Stella's eyes were full of compassion as she reminded him, "It's only been one day, Stephen. Give her a little time."

Any further talk was interrupted by the shrill ring of the telephone. Stephen slumped into a chair.

"Good afternoon, Heritage Centre. Oh, hello Ambrose, how are you? Yes, he's here, I'll hand you over."

Stephen took the receiver from Stella.

"Ambrose, hello! Do you have news of Reverend Cordwell's coin? Well, well, that is excellent. Friday, you say? Well, it's short notice but I shall call the Reverend Cordwell and see if he'd like to come to the auction with me."

"So it is valuable, then?" queried Stella, when Stephen had ended the call.

"Yes it is, and Ambrose thinks it should fetch a nice tidy sum at the auction. Could you book me a train ticket for Friday morning, please? I need to get to the auction house about mid-morning."

"I'll do it right away. And you, of course, now have some excellent news and an invitation to deliver to Hartley and his splendid niece, do you not?"

Stella picked up Stephen's car keys and waggled them in front of his face. "But if you don't get a move on you'll be late getting to your lecture at the university, so I'll call Hartley and Lorelei and book their train tickets if they decide to go with you."

Chapter 27
a new arrival

People pushed past him on the street, elbowing him out of the way, treading on his toes, but Gabe hardly noticed. He trudged along, head down, until he reached the peeling, dun-brown street door of the building that contained the offices of Nigel Hellion-Rees, Private Investigator. For a few seconds he simply stood and stared at it before pulling his hand out of the pocket of his cashmere overcoat and pushing it open.

The stairwell smelled faintly of disinfectant and mould, and as he looked upwards into the gloom, he considered how easy it would be to simply materialise in the office. But it had been agreed that whenever angels walked among mortals they must use doors and stairs like everybody else, unless they were certain they wouldn't be seen or if there was a dire emergency. He trudged up the three flights one step at a time and into the office.

Amelia was watering a tall, leafy plant that stood on the filing cabinet, and she greeted him with a wide, welcoming smile, a smile that made his heart turn over. "Hello, Gabe, how lovely to see you! Nigel isn't here, I'm afraid, he's at the Mill."

"Hello, Amelia," he gently kissed her on each cheek. "I know he is. It's you I wanted to see."

"Oh? There's nothing wrong is there? Is Nigel all right?"

He hastily shook his head, "Oh, no, no, there's nothing for you to worry about. Do you have time for a chat, Amelia, or are you too busy?"

Amelia laughed. "Busy? We don't have a single client on our books at the moment. Other than you, of course. Without the Mill project we'd go under, believe me."

Gabe's shoulders sagged and he sighed. "I'm sorry, Amelia."

She regarded him for a long moment. "Gabe, this isn't the first time I've seen you like this. Look, take off your coat and I'll make some coffee and you can tell me why you're here."

He unbuttoned his coat and looked around for the stand to hang it on.

"You'll have to use the back of a chair, I'm afraid," Amelia told him. "Our coat stand was taken by the bailiffs. We're so grateful for the secret office."

Gabe tutted, and asked Amelia not to go to the trouble of making coffee, for he only wanted a glass of water.

She laughed. "Water? But you always want coffee, even if it's instant. You're addicted to it. What's going on?"

Gabe sat down in a creaking wicker armchair with a worn velvet cushion on the seat. "I'm punishing myself, Amelia. Ever since I found out that Nick cheated without me knowing about it, or even guessing that he would pull such a stunt, I've been punishing myself. I don't use my powers. I walk everywhere rather than use my limousine, I don't drink coffee or eat cake, I don't watch my favourite comedy TV programmes. I sat through a whole afternoon of the goings-on of your Parliament yesterday. Never been so bored in my life."

Amelia frowned. "Um, Nigel told me about your fight with Nick. And I'm sorry that Lorelei was forced into Gluttony, but it isn't too bad is it? I mean, she'll just eat a lot, won't she?"

"It's far, far more than that, Amelia. Food has literally taken over her whole life. She's selfish and unpleasant in pursuit of it. She's already stopped caring about her appearance and the state of her home. And, you know, she's met the love of her life but has broken off their engagement."

"Oh, that doesn't sound good at all."

"Precisely. I hate myself."

"But you didn't do it, did you? It was Nick. And on the plus side, he did do something good, didn't he? With Violet Cattermole, I mean. Can't you be pleased about that? And surely Michael isn't going to let it stand, if Nick cheated to achieve it?"

"Oh, I am pleased about Violet. She demanded far more than the Mill was worth, and now she'll be finding herself giving a lot of that money to the community. Part of her is trying to resist it, as Lorelei is trying to resist Gluttony, but because Nick cheated by using the Alternative Reality Dust, they'll find it much, much harder to fight. And Michael has ordered a tribunal, and they take ages."

"Oh, but maybe he will find in your favour? And anyway, Gabe, surely you can undo the Gluttony? Surely you can remove the, the, what is it? Spell? Hex? Whatever it is, surely you can remove it and let Lorelei return to her normal self? Can't you, I don't know, re-use that Dust stuff on her? I mean, if Nick can do it, why can't you?"

"I can't do anything until the tribunal has passed judgement. Nick and I had a long and very uncomfortable meeting with him, and he told us to get back here and get on with it in the meantime, because no matter what the outcome of the tribunal, the Swap would still eventually take place."

"I can see how much you are hating all this. I'm so sorry."

They fell into silence. Gabe had longed to unburden himself to someone, and Amelia had constantly sprung to mind. Now that he had told her, though, he realised that he had merely spread his unhappiness onto yet another human being.

"No, it's me who should be sorry, Amelia. I didn't mean to burden you with my woes. Let's change the subject. How's the little one coming along?" He gestured at her well-rounded stomach.

"Just two weeks to go, I'm so excited. But Gabe, let's go back to Nick a minute. Was he always bad?"

Gabe shook his head. "There's was no concept of good and bad before Humankind was created. I suppose you could say that we were neutral. But after such a long time looking after the sinners, I guess it rubbed off on Nick. He's finding it hard to adjust, but I don't think it's impossible for him to change."

"And you?"

"Ah. Yes. Me. I don't think I can change. I'll just have to… Amelia? Why are you groaning like that? Amelia! Are you all right?"

"I—" she clutched first her back then her belly. "Oh! Oh no! Not now, please not now!"

"What's wrong? My dear girl, why are you on the floor? What in Heaven's name is happening?"

Her face creased with pain and fear, Amelia panted, "Waters. Broken. I'm. Having. The. Baby." She huffed out short breaths, then started to cry. "Call. Ambulance. Call. Nigel."

"Oh, Amelia, the baby's coming?" Joy suffused Gabe's handsome face. "Oh, I love babies!"

"Gabe!" Amelia gasped. "Ambulance. Nigel. Now."

"Ambulance? No way, Amelia, you're going in style, in my car."

"You. Said. You'd. Walked. Oooooooooooow!" She grabbed Gabe's hand and gripped hard. "I'm frightened, Gabe, please, please get me to hospital."

"Breathe, my dear mother-to-be, breathe! Now listen carefully, Amelia. I'm Gabriel, right? You understand me? *Gabriel.*"

She nodded, alternatively sobbing and puffing quick breaths in, out, in, out.

"So, you have no need to worry about anything. Anything at all. My car will take you to the hospital and then it will get Nigel."

"Take. Too. Long." She puffed some more, short sharp breaths, in out, in out.

He took her hand. "Just lean on me and we'll get you down to my car. Come on, hold on to my arm. That's it. Now, you can't possibly manage all those stairs. You'll feel a bit of a tug in your solar plexus, but under the circumstances you probably won't notice and… here we are."

They were in the back of the limousine. Gabe tucked a blanket round Amelia's knees, and within minutes he was removing it again because they were at the entrance to the hospital.

"How – *hooo* – is – *hooo* – this – *hooo* – possible?"

"Good heavens, Amelia, it really does take a long time for you humans to be convinced, doesn't it? No, don't talk. Come on now. Look, here's a nice nurse with a wheelchair." He helped her into it, and she held on fast to his coat.

"Don't. Go. So. Scared. Need. Nigel."

"I won't be long at all, Amelia. You'll hardly notice I'm gone, and I'll be back with Nigel in a matter of moments."

"Wiltshire. Three. Hours. Away."

"There, there, Amelia. Trust me, Nigel will be here in time to hold your hand. You just concentrate on getting yourself ready to bring your precious little baby into the world."

The nurse asked Gabe if he was the father and when he said no she told him firmly he would have to remain in the waiting room. He had to gently uncurl Amelia's fingers from the lapel of his coat, but he knew that the touch of his skin on hers would relax her. She'd be fine.

Now, after making more assurances to Lorelei, he slipped away in search of coffee and a piece of cake. He found a vending machine in the corridor, but didn't fancy any of the chocolate bars or crisps. He wandered down onto the ground floor and into the café, but he could smell that the coffee they offered would not suit his taste. He sat down at a corner table and glanced around. When he was sure everyone around him was too busy or preoccupied to pay him any attention, he used a bit of angel magic to materialise a slice of walnut sponge and a steaming cup of fragrant coffee. Cream, three sugars. And not in a paper, plastic or Styrofoam cup, either, but a gold-rimmed china cup perched on a matching saucer.

When he'd finished he sauntered out of the hospital and straight into his waiting car, which he had summoned while he was picking up the last crumbs of his cake with his silver fork. When he explained why they needed to get to Nigel, the driver touched his fingers to his cap, and they were on their way.

In angel time.

When the car materialised mere moments later in the Turnaround, Gabe climbed out and told him to be ready to return to the hospital once they had Nigel safely aboard.

He found Nigel round the back of the building taking photographs.

"Ah, there you are, Nigel. I've come to fetch you back to London."

"Oh?"

"Amelia is having the baby."

There was a pause, then, "AMELIA'S HAVING THE BABY?"

"Yes, that's what I said."

"BUT THERE'S TWO WEEKS TO GO YET."

"Apparently not. And there's no need to shout, Nigel, my hearing is excellent."

Nigel rushed around in circles, gabbling that he couldn't possibly go to the hospital in his old work clothes and muddy wellies, and how would they make it in time, and was Amelia okay, and it was too early for the baby to be coming, and, and, and.

Gabe ahemed to get Nigel's attention. "There are clean clothes and shoes for you in the car. Amelia is in my care and everything will be fine, so take a deep breath… that's right… and another. Good, now let's go to the car."

"Okay. Great. Clean clothes and shoes, you say? Super. So what are we waiting for?"

Gabe had to run to keep up with Nigel as he hurtled himself across the bridge and threw himself head first into the open back door of the car. As they set off, he wriggled out of his muddy jeans and boots and changed into the clean clothes. Naturally, they fitted him perfectly.

The glass screen between the back seat and the driver slowly and soundlessly wound down and the chauffeur called over his shoulder, "You might feel momentarily dizzy, sir, just a little pull in the solar plexus."

~~~

"Congratulations!" Gabe held out a huge cigar when Nigel staggered, awestruck, from Amelia's bedside into the waiting room. "Not to smoke, of course, I know you don't indulge, and you can't in here anyway, but it is a tradition, and it is one of Cuba's very best, so put it in your pocket as a souvenir of this day."

"It's a girl, Gabe! I'm the father of the most beautiful girl in the whole world. Oh, you wait 'til you see her! Ten tiny toes, ten tiny fingers. Her hands are like tiny starfish, Gabe, and her eyes! Oh, her eyes are so beautiful."

Gabe grinned, so glad he'd been a part of this. It made up for Lorelei's misery, just a little, which he was sure anyway would be reversed just as soon as he could find a way to put things right.

The door swung open and a pretty young nurse peered round. "Your wife and daughter are all cleaned up and comfortable, and your wife says can you please come back in, and bring your friend with you."

Gabe followed Nigel back into Amelia's room. Amelia was sitting up with the baby in her arms, gazing down at the
~~~

tiny face of her minutes-old daughter. When she saw Gabe, she held out her hand to him.

"Gabe, how can I ever thank you? I'm so grateful you got Nigel here in time. Whatever doubts I had about you before are well and truly gone. You really are an angel."

Choked with emotion, Gabe kissed Amelia's hand and said softly, "Thank *you*, Amelia, those are the kindest words and they mean the world to me. Now, can I have a proper look at this little one?" He gently pushed the soft, white shawl away from the baby's face.

"Would you like to hold her?"

Stunned, Gabe could only dumbly nod, and he took the bundle into his arms with such care and devotion, Amelia and Nigel both sighed at the sight.

"Let me introduce you properly," said Nigel. He leaned over his daughter and kissed her forehead. "Gabe, I'd like you to meet Chloe Gabrielle Lucy Hellion-Rees."

Gabe's eyes welled up as he gazed down at her, and he said, "That's quite a name for such a tiny thing. Welcome to the world, Chloe. You have the most marvellous parents, and you're going to have a wonderful life."

"I would hope so," joked Amelia, "with an archangel for a godparent."

"Really? You'd like me to be godparent?"

"Of course. Do you think Nick will mind very much?"

Gabe sighed, "He probably will. But he knows how close we've become, and I'm sure he'll be pleased that you've named her Chloe Gabrielle *Lucy*. After all, she can hardly have Lucifer in her name." He handed Chloe gently back to Amelia, gazing at mother and daughter like they were the most beautiful things in the universe. But then his expression changed and he straightened up, smacking his forehead with the palm of his hand, "Oh, but Nigel! Amelia! This is all wrong! Surely it should be Nick that's godparent, not me? How can you possibly tell darling little Chloe that she has Satan for a godparent?"

Amelia smiled at him, "To us you'll always be the angelic Gabriel you are now."

As if to confirm it, Chloe Gabrielle Lucy reached up her tiny starfish hand, and when Gabe placed his forefinger in her palm, she closed her fingers tightly around it, bestowing a trust that brought a painful lump to his throat. He tearfully confessed that he'd never felt as happy as he did at that moment.

Chapter 28
how much am I bid?

Hartley followed Stephen into the auction room, and looked around with interest. He was disappointed that Lorelei had declined to come, but clearly not as disappointed as Stephen. She had been the only subject all the way on the train, Stephen going over and over what had happened, why it had happened, and how could he get her back again. It was only when they'd arrived at Waterloo that Stephen had apologised, and said he would speak of it no more that day.

As they climbed into a taxicab, Stephen said, "If you've ever been to an auction before, Hartley, you'll know how exciting they can be. Have you thought what you'll do with the money, or won't it be your decision?"

"I've only ever seen an auction on television, so although I know the format, I'm sure it'll be very different actually being there and being part of it. I haven't dared believe that the coin could be as valuable as you say, but whatever it fetches today will go towards church repairs."

"Excellent. We'll soon be there, and my friend Ambrose Alt, the coin expert I first contacted, is going to meet us.

The taxi drew up outside a plain red brick building, and Hartley saw that they had arrived at the auction rooms of R Spenkleman & Company. A large, round man hurried forward, and he and Stephen warmly shook hands.

"Hartley, this is Ambrose. Ambrose, this is Reverend Hartley Cordwell."

"Lucky man!" boomed Ambrose, his voice perfectly fitting his stature. "You're little find is going to do very well today, I can assure you. Come on, come on, let's get in there and get ourselves some good seats."

Hartley followed them in, his eyes roving with fascination all around the entrance hall, which was much grander than the plain exterior of the building gave one to expect. It was crowded, with people grasping catalogues milling about, calling out to each other. They crossed into a large room, where blue-velvet-covered chairs were set out in rows on a highly polished parquet floor. The auctioneer, in a navy blue suit with wide white stripes that looked as if they'd been chalked on, was already at the podium, studying his notes. Behind him, men in plain dark suits and narrow blue ties were arranging the lots coming up for auction.

A bell rang, and Ambrose quickly hustled Hartley and Stephen to seats at the front. The hall quickly filled, and Hartley turned to see that people were even standing along the back wall. Ambrose leaned past Stephen and said, "It's quite a special day today, with nearly all of the lots of major interest. Your coin is number ten on the list, but I'm sure you'll enjoy seeing how it all works before we get to it."

Hartley settled into his chair and decided to really concentrate on the proceedings so he could tell Lorelei all about it. Such a shame she had refused to come, but he couldn't help thinking that there would be pastry crumbs all around her chair if she did.

The auctioneer tapped his microphone and opened the proceedings by wishing everybody a very good afternoon in a surprisingly resonant voice. He was very tall and stick-thin, with just a few strands of grey hair swept across his scalp. Bony wrists stuck out from his shirt cuffs, and when he announced the first lot, his Adam's apple caused his burgundy polka-dot bow tie to bounce up and down.

And so the auction began.

Hartley couldn't believe how quickly each item was sold. The auctioneer spoke super-fast, pushing the bids up in hundreds and thousands, then fifties, and even twenties, as the bidding had obviously neared its peak.

A painting sold for three hundred and fifty thousand pounds, a tiny porcelain figurine, which Hartley thought hideous, went for even more. The prices being bandied about were eye watering, and Hartley began to believe, for the first time, that the coin might command the figures Ambrose Alt had said it would.

"And now we come to Lot Number Ten, a very fine Edward III Gold Double florin, also known as a Double Leopard."

There was a flurry of noise as people turned to their catalogues.

The auctioneer looked carefully around the room, then began his chant again to create even more interest. "Very few specimens have been found, ladies and gentlemen, and this one is in excellent condition. This is a unique opportunity to acquire a most important example of Medieval English coinage. I have ninety thousands pounds from an outside bidder, who will start me in the room?"

And it went so fast again, Hartley couldn't keep up. Next to him he could feel Stephen's tension mount, and hear Ambrose muttering under his breath, *come on, come on.*

Hartley heard the words, "All done at five hundred and fifty thousand pounds? Going once. Twice."

The gavel banged and Hartley jumped.

"Sold!"

Stephen helped Hartley up and guided him along the edge of the room and out into the entrance hall. Ambrose followed, and gave Hartley's hand a hearty shake. Hartley still couldn't find any words.

Stephen laughed. "I think our Reverend is in shock, Ambrose, shall we take him to the pub and try to revive him?"

"Absolutely, my friend. I think a brandy is just what's needed before you take him home."

Chapter 29
the gift

Nigel escorted Amelia over the beautifully restored stone bridge and stood with his arm around her shoulders in front of the imposing mill house. The repaired studded oak door was closed, but only as part of the show he had lined up for her. Of course she knew the interior very well, as she had designed it and sourced the materials for it, but she hadn't seen it since it was all put together, thoroughly cleaned until everything shone and sparkled, the tables laid with precision for the first diners.

She smiled up at him. Chloe, half asleep in the beautifully fashioned carrycot that had been a gift from Gabe, gurgled softly and they couldn't stop themselves from peering in to look at her. Her long lashes swept her rosy cheeks, and Nigel wondered if he would ever want to stop kissing her tiny button nose.

Poised now to open the door, Nigel said, "Are you ready?"

Amelia nodded, and Nigel grasped the heavy iron ring. It turned with a satisfying *clunk* and the door swung noiselessly open on its new hinges. Nigel, remembering the first time he had done this when the angels were in residence, waited for Amelia to precede him inside.

To their left was the cloakroom, where coats, hats and scarves would be safely stored while their owners feasted on gourmet food and fine wines. Just past that, on the right, was the tall oak lectern-style table where guests would be greeted by a gracious and elegant host or hostess, and their reservations checked in a huge book bound in rich burgundy leather.

Nigel led Amelia through a stone archway into the main restaurant.

Every time he saw it, even though he and Amelia had created it, it was a revelation. Three walls were smoothly plastered and painted the colour of clotted cream. Everywhere hung bright tapestries and original paintings. The fourth wall was floor-to-ceiling glass panels, and through it could be seen the immense waterwheel, churning the river into a white-foamed millrace. The rushing water made a pleasing sound that could just about be heard through the double-glazed glass, but not so that it would disturb intimate conversation. Volunteers from the village, including Nigel, had spent two cold, muddy, wet weekends clearing the weeds from the spokes of the huge wheel, and specialists had been called in to repair the damage and get it turning again. The dining tables nearest the wheel would be the most sought-after, of course, but most of the diners would be able to see it while they ate, or, in fine weather, step outside into the landscaped garden before or after their meal and enjoy it at close quarters.

"My goodness, Nigel," exclaimed Amelia. "I can't believe how fast this has all come together. Isn't it lovely, really, really lovely!"

"I know," said Nigel, unable to hide how pleased he was. "I think we and everyone involved have done a marvellous job."

As Amelia slowly swept her eyes around the room, Nigel said, "Are you happy with everything, sweetheart? I know how much you wanted to manage the interior yourself after all your hard work, but our daughter had other ideas, didn't she! Have we placed Lorelei's pictures correctly?"

She nodded, but mentioning Lorelei made them both sad for a moment, for they had had to practically force Lorelei to do the work. Every day they hoped Gabe would bring news that the curse of Gluttony would be lifted because of Nick's cheating, but so far there was no news of how the angelic tribunal was going.

Nigel lifted Chloe, wide awake now, from her cot and settled her against his chest. "Come, my darling wife, let me show you and our gorgeous daughter around so you can see the wonder that we have created here."

They wandered between the round tables of mixed sizes, adorned with the snowy white tablecloths, not a crease to be seen, and garnet-coloured napkins beautifully folded and each with a sprig of dried flowers tucked in them.

Nigel told Amelia to go behind the bar and she marvelled at all the bottles of wines, beers, soft drinks, spirits and mixers, the highly polished glasses of all shapes and sizes, the gleaming silver dishes that would hold salted nuts and lemon slices and glistening black and green olives.

They went into the kitchen, equipped with the very best of everything.

"What a coincidence that Glen Perkins was a salesman of kitchen equipment before he'd turned to baking bread and cakes," Amelia said.

"Yes, indeed. The equipment may have changed since his day, but the suppliers are the same and he seems to know them all and he's proved himself an excellent negotiator."

They went upstairs and Amelia inspected the deluxe bedroom suites for paying guests, and the wonderfully appointed apartment where the manager would live, pronouncing it all perfect, just as she had specified.

"So," she said, as they wandered into and out of the pretty Powder Room and the elegant Gentlemen's Rest Room and back into the restaurant, "what's happening now as far as we're concerned? Is our job here finished?"

Nigel was about to answer when, as if on cue, the two angels strolled in through the main door. Chloe gurgled and stretched out a tiny hand towards Gabe.

Nick scowled and said, "She's rather young to be showing such favouritism isn't she?"

"What are you doing here?" asked Nigel. "I thought you were still at the tribunal?"

"Oh, we did our bit ages ago," replied Nick airily. "They won't call us back until they're ready to give judgement. Uri is still there, and will deliver the decision when it is given."

"Ah," said Nigel. "And will that be soon, do you think?"

"Who knows?" Gabe replied. "Let's not worry about it now, not today. What do you think, Amelia, are you pleased to see the results of all your hard work?" His gushing enthusiasm made her laugh with delight.

"It's wonderful, really fantastic, and I've loved every moment of it. But there's still a lot to do before the opening, isn't there?"

"Oh yes, staff to be hired of course, supplies to be bought once the chef has devised the menus. I don't think there will be any difficulties with any of that, though. After all, it is in the hands of angels, and you'll get just the right people. But it needs a name."

"Oh? Are we to hire staff then?" asked Amelia. "And I thought it was going to be called The Mill. That's how everyone always refers to it."

Gabe nodded, "True, Amelia, true. But it seems that there are many restaurants called The Mill or The Old Mill. Should ours be the same as so many others, do you think, or should we come up with something a little more… unique?"

"Well, I rather like The Old Mill," Nigel replied, wondering why Gabe hadn't answered Amelia's question about hiring staff but not ready yet to go into it.

"Or perhaps The Old Water Mill?" suggested Amelia. "It evokes a bygone age, and clients will love it that the magnificent old wheel is turning in full view of the dining area. It gives such a special atmosphere."

"Hmm," said Gabe, nodding his head but his expression showing that he didn't entirely agree. "I wanted to call it 'Angel Food'. Now what do you think of that?"

Nick snorted. "I've already told you, brother, that a name like that might suit a twee little café or a catering establishment that has ideas above its station, but not a high class restaurant." He turned to Nigel and Amelia. "Don't you agree?"

Gently, Amelia gave her opinion. "I'm sorry, Gabe, but Angel Food doesn't go with this being a boutique hotel as well as a fine restaurant. In fact, it sounds like a cake mix to me."

"Oh," said Gabriel, crestfallen. Then his eyes sparkled and he giggled. "Oh, it does rather, doesn't it? But I'm not keen on The Old Water Mill, it's too…" he circled his hand as he searched for the word, "ordinary."

"Well," said Nick firmly, "it's up to you two, anyway, so don't listen to him. You can call it what you want."

"Why is it up to us?" asked Nigel curiously. "It's your place, you should decide what to call it."

Nick laughed, and it wasn't a pleasant sound. "My dear boy, what would we want with a restaurant? Have you forgotten? It was just a cover while we did what we had to do. And we've just about done it, so soon we'll be returning to Heaven and Hell – that's me to Heaven and him to Hell, ha-ha – and we won't be back here again for some time, if ever, I can assure you."

It seemed to Nigel that the nearer they got to the Great Swap, the more unpleasant Nick got, and he didn't understand it. Wasn't the whole idea of this time in Ham-Under-Lymfold to get Nick to be more like Gabe? And, for that matter, Gabe was showing no signs of becoming even remotely devilish. How could they make the change if they themselves hadn't changed? And surely there was still a small possibility that Michael and the tribunal would decide to void the deal because of Nick's cheating.

Gabe voiced Nigel's thoughts and said, "You're jumping the gun, aren't you, brother?"

The two angels glared at each other and Nigel prepared to step in to prevent another spat, but Gabe broke eye contact first and exclaimed, "But this isn't about us! It's about you and Amelia, Nigel, and darling little Chloe. Your future!"

"Oh?"

Gabe started skipping from foot to foot like a gleeful child. He even clapped his hands, causing Chloe to swivel her head towards him. "Yes, yes! What my brother is trying to say, and not doing it very well, is that this place is *yours*. Don't you see? It's your reward for all you've done! And yes, Amelia, it is all above board. You don't have to pay for it, it's yours and Nigel's lock, stock and barrel – or maybe I should say lock, stock and wine cellar! So you won't be starting out in debt or anything. We know you love this village, and the countryside is a lovely place to raise children, so you won't mind moving here, will you?" His head swung excitedly from one to the other, but slowly his expression changed to one of anxiety and he repeated, "Will you?"

"I'm sorry, Gabe, I, we, that is, gosh, what can we say? You've rather sprung this on us. I, um, Amelia?" Nigel, feeling a mixture of panic, disbelief and hope, turned to Amelia for help. Her eyes conveyed that she, too, was feeling a mixture of panic, disbelief and hope.

"Well, darling, I think we ought to discuss it, don't you?" She glanced at Nick. "Alone."

"Well, there's grateful," snapped Nick.

"We thought you'd be over the moon," said Gabe, disappointment dripping from every word.

"Oh, Gabe," gasped Amelia, rushing up to him and hugging him. "We're delighted at the offer, really, but it's such a big thing, you know? And we've never run a hotel or restaurant, we know nothing about it. And, really, how can we afford it?"

Gabe frowned at her in confusion. "Afford it? I don't understand. Didn't you hear what we said? We're *giving* it to you! A fresh start for the pair of you and darling Chloe, plus the salary we've paid you to do the work here. You have nothing to worry about, honestly! All you need to do is hire some experienced staff, put your hearts and minds into the running of it, we'll even make sure you're supplied with our unique coffee beans, and I guarantee you, this place will *work*."

Nigel believed him; after all, how could a place that had come into existence the way this one had possibly fail? It had, literally, been touched by angels!

Nick turned to him. "Before we get carried away here, though, there's something you may be forgetting, Nigel. You're work for us isn't done yet. You are our Witness. Once Gabe and I leave here it is up to you to tell the world that I am no longer the Dark Lord of Hell. You—"

He was interrupted by the arrival of Uri. Uri looked from one to the other and took command of the room, which he was able to do despite being dressed in his handyman uniform of sharply creased red trousers and plaid shirt. "Nigel, Amelia, hello. Why don't you go back upstairs and talk things over in private. Nick, Gabe, let's go outside, I'd like to have another look at the waterwheel."

Nigel sensed that Uri had returned with the verdict, and watched with concern as the three angels left the restaurant, wondering what was going to happen. But Amelia took him by the hand and led him upstairs to talk about the possibility of leaving behind their grotty flat in London and the detective agency that Nigel hated to become top class restaurateurs with an exclusive boutique hotel and a luxury apartment in the country. It would be so good for Chloe. And deep down they knew it would work, because Gabe said so.

Amelia turned in a slow circle to take in every aspect of the space. "Can we do this, Nigel?"

A slow smile spread across his face and he replied, "I think we can, Amelia. Let's at least give it a try, eh? We'll have to think of a name."

"I think we should keep its original name, Angel Falls Mill. It's a wonderful name, and people are always attracted to things like converted mills, aren't they?"

Nigel, looking out of the window and down on the waterwheel, nodded his agreement, then said, "I think we'd better go out there," he said. "I can't wait any longer to find out what's going to become of those two."

They went outside, Amelia cradling Chloe in her arms, and joined Uri, Nick and Gabe in front of the waterwheel. Nigel searched their faces for some clue as to what had been decided. Surely, surely, the Great Swap would not take place now, as Nick had not played by the rules?

"Well?" he demanded. "You've been gone a long time, Uri. How did it go? What's going to happen?"

Uri answered, "Michael was furious, as you can imagine, and the arguments went on and on, with more and more of the Host getting involved and giving their opinions. In the end Michael had to order them all away – including these two – and he and I have been shut up in his chamber until today."

"And?" said Amelia, as impatient as Nigel just to *know*.

"And," replied Gabe, his voice soft with defeat, "Nick has won."

Amelia gasped and Nigel, stunned to hear that news, looked questioningly at Nick.

"What?" barked Nick. "Why that look? The Grand Plan was agreed aeons ago. The DISC was found. Okay, so I moved things along a little faster, but Violet and Lorelei would have succumbed eventually."

"You don't know that!" shouted Gabe, and Uri shushed him, told him to keep calm.

"Whatever," said Nick. "The point is, the Plan came into play because the DISC was uncovered, the rest of it is incidental and hardly of importance." He turned to Gabe and implored, "I've *earned* this, Gabriel, surely you can see that?"

Gabe, a picture of abject misery, merely shrugged one shoulder and stared down at his feet.

Nigel puffed out his cheeks and released the air slowly. He really hadn't expected this outcome at all. "But what of Lorelei?" he said.

Amelia joined in, "Yes, please tell us, what are you going to do about her? Hasn't she suffered enough? She can't stop eating, she's broken off her engagement… It seems so unfair."

Uri put his hand out. "It will all get sorted out, Amelia, please don't worry. Because of the way Nick forced Gluttony on her, Michael has agreed that it can be undone. I will see to it personally before I leave."

"Leave?"

"Our work is done, Nigel. I must soon return to Michael's side, and these two…"

"I'm off to Paradise," declared Nick, his decidedly devilish grin almost splitting his face.

"Gabe?" said Nigel, softly. "Are you okay?"

Gabe gazed into the distance over Nigel's shoulder. "Me? I'm off to merry old Hell, aren't I? Why wouldn't I be okay?"

Chapter 30
reconciliation (i)

Since the day Hartley had talked to Violet about the font, the day she'd brought the crazy ginger cat home, he knew Violet had been trying hard to make up with her sister. Now here he was walking slowly to Merryvale Farm with Violet clinging to his arm, saying vehemently, "I'm going to knock some sense into the bloody woman! 'Scuse my language, Hartley".

Hartley tried to pay attention to Violet as they went along, but he'd had a severe shock first thing that morning, and he was still reeling from it. Lorelei had turned up for their usual Tuesday morning coffee, before she went to take her classes at the college, and she had eaten an entire quiche that he was defrosting for his lunch. It was if she hadn't even known she was doing it. And when it was all gone, she'd leaned back in her chair and belched without so much as an excuse me. He'd noticed that her blouse was stained and her skirt was held at the waist with a large safety pin. Lorelei had become a stranger. A greedy, scruffy, inconsiderate stranger.

He made an effort to tune into what Violet was saying.

"...So I've been trying to make this proposal to her, you see, but she won't listen. I'm hoping that your presence will help."

Hartley murmured that he hoped so, too, then, "How's your cat, Violet, has it settled in?"

"Oh yes. Took a while, but with much coaxing and tins of tuna, I got Fudge to come out from the sofa after three days sulking under it. He still glares at me and twitches that tail sometimes, but I don't think it'll be much longer before he's sitting on my lap, purring away."

Hartley, who could not imagine that ginger bundle of fury sitting purring on anyone's lap, laughed. "I do hope you're right, Violet."

The farmyard was, as usual, wet and slippery, and they had to pick their way through the smelly mud and cow pat mixture to the kitchen door, where Hilda was waiting for them. She led them through the dank hallway to the front parlour.

"Why's it so dark in here?" said Violet, teeth clicking. "It smells damp."

Hilda replied softly. "Well it is damp. The whole place is riddled with it, it never dries out even in the summer."

Hartley knew she wasn't complaining, just stating the truth.

Violet muttered something like "Hmph!" and asked where they should sit. Hartley could see what could well be speckles of grey mould on the sofa cushions. Those were definitely blooms of black mould on the old flowery wallpaper.

Hilda, looking a bit bewildered, suggested they might be more comfortable in the kitchen. "I'm sorry, I never use this room and hadn't realised it was so…" she trailed off.

Hartley led the way back up the corridor and into the large kitchen, which smelled of fried bacon and chicken feed.

"At least it's warm in here," huffed Violet. "Honestly, Hilda, you should have told me ages ago that things were so bad."

"And when could I have told you that, Violet? We hadn't spoken until last week." There was no annoyance in her voice, no accusation, just a calm statement of plain fact.

"Now then, can I get you anything? Tea? It won't take a jiffy."

"No thank you," said Violet sharply, before Hartley could answer for himself. He was beginning to think she'd returned to her old ways, but then, even as he thought it, her face visibly softened and she said softly, "Not yet anyway, Hilda. Now sit down, please. You look—"

"Haggard," interjected Hilda.

"Tired, I was going to say tired."

Hartley looked from one to the other and marvelled that the sisters were in the same room together. Living in the same village and both attending St Peter's, they couldn't help but see each other often, but they hadn't spoken to each other in years, until very recently. And the estrangement was all Violet's doing; Hilda had tried and tried to get Violet to be friends with her, and she'd written countless letters saying she didn't want any rift between them. Sadly, Violet had remained adamant that she didn't want anything to do with her sister.

As far as she was concerned, Hilda had betrayed her by stealing Harry Merryvale from her. Violet would never admit, even to herself, that Harry had never actually declared himself to her. It was just that she had dated him first, just the once, actually, and been mortified by his obvious preference for Hilda the moment he met her. Nor did she melt towards Hilda when the marriage turned out to be a miserable one, because Harry had turned out to be a skinflint and a slave-driver. Everyone said that if she could have found it within herself to be totally honest, she would have had to acknowledge that Hilda had done her a favour.

At long last, though, she was now acknowledging that had she married Merryvale, she would be the one living in the damp old farmhouse, scrimping to make ends meet, and Hilda would be the one to have gained from the sale of the Mill.

Now, at last, the sisters were reconciled, but Violet felt she needed to make amends. She'd explained to Hartley as they'd strolled along to Merryvale Farm that when Hilda had gone to Violet's cottage the day she adopted the cat, Violet had offered her money to fix up the farmhouse so she could sell it and retire to a cottage elsewhere in the village. But Hilda had refused, and that was why Violet asked him to come along today, to try and get Hilda to see sense.

Violet was a certainly a changed woman. Among the good citizens of Ham-Under-Lymfold she was a constant topic of conversation. She'd stopped her daily spying vigils from the bench on the village green. She was polite to everyone she met, whether in the bakery, in the village store, walking along the street, or in the pub. She'd even bought a round of drinks during last Saturday's Irish night, when the pub was heaving with people drinking pints and half pints of Guinness, that black brew with its thick, creamy head. Everyone asked for whisky or double brandy when they heard Violet was treating them, but she'd paid up gladly, and blushed rather sweetly through her face powder when people raised their glasses and thanked her.

But still, although everyone said how pleasant she was these days, how generous with her money, many were wondering where the catch was, and Hartley couldn't blame them.

Hilda broke the silence. "I hear things are going really well at the Mill. Have you been up there?"

"No," said Violet. "They'll be having their grand opening soon, though."

"Oh yes," said Hartley, "and Nigel told me that everyone is invited. We'll all be getting our invitations soon, I'm sure."

"I won't be able to go," said Hilda.

"Of course you will." Violet grabbed Hilda's hand. "Hilda, when was the last time you went out anywhere other than to the church? When was the last time you got dressed up for a party, eh?"

"Well, I—"

"Hilda, please, when was the last time you had any *fun*?"

"I've nothing to wear to a place like that."

"Oh, for Heaven's sake!"

Hartley, his head going from side to side like a spectator at a tennis match, heard the exasperation in Violet's voice. But she swallowed it down and smiled, a warm smile that reached her eyes and softened her whole face.

"We will go shopping. I need a new frock, too, so we will go shopping together, Hilda, and get ourselves something nice to wear." She raised her hand as Hilda started to object. "And I will pay for it."

Hilda capitulated. "You're so kind, Violet, thank you. I shall enjoy a shopping trip, I think."

"Oh!" The breath seemed to leave Violet's body as if she had been punched.

Hartley leaned towards her in case she was about to faint, but she waved him away.

"Kind, Hilda? Me? Oh my goodness." Violet mopped at her sudden tears with her fingers.

"Are you ill, dear?"

It was a question Hartley had been asking himself, alongside the question of what he was doing there, as he didn't seem to be needed. It was too warm by the large kitchen range, but he daren't interrupt whatever was going on between the sisters by taking off his coat.

Violet took a deep, shuddering breath, "No, Hilda, I'm not ill. I'm not seeking to make amends before I die or anything like that. I'm not lonely. I'm here because I've been an absolute idiot all these years. Can you ever forgive me?"

"Forgive you?" Hilda stared open-mouthed. "Forgive you? Oh, Violet, what's to forgive? After all these years I just want us to be friends, to be sisters again. I've missed you so much." Now she was crying, and Violet was still weeping, and then the two of them were in an awkward hug across the table, talking over each other, and laughing through their tears.

Hartley pulled out his handkerchief, then didn't know which one to offer it to, so he mopped his own brow with it. He put it back in his pocket and waited for the two women to compose themselves.

Violet was the first. "Oh, I'm so sorry, Hartley. I didn't ask you to accompany me just to watch two silly old ladies. Now, as I explained on the telephone, I asked Hilda to give up this place and either move in with me or let me buy her a place nearby. But she won't budge, says she won't let me spend so much money on her." She turned to her sister. "Hilda, do you know that Wisteria Cottage is up for sale?"

Seeing Hilda was going to object to Violet's suggestions, Hartley cleared his throat and said, "Hilda, do you mind if I say what I think?"

"Of course not, Hartley. You know I'd always listen to you."

"Well, good. Because I happen to agree with Violet. You cannot go on living here, it's unhealthy and simply too much for you. If you really feel uncomfortable with Violet helping you financially, you could treat it as a loan. I would suggest that you move in with Violet while the farm is fixed up a little and sold, and then you can use the proceeds from that to buy Wisteria Cottage or some other house of your own."

"Yes!" exclaimed Violet. "That's perfect. Oh, I knew I could count on you, Hartley. Hilda? What do you say?"

Hilda looked down on her hands, turning them palm upwards, then over, then palm upwards again. Her hands were mottled red, her fingernails ragged, the result of all her years of sheer, unrelenting, hard work. "I think we all need a cup of tea," she said, shakily rising from the table and rattling the kettle to ensure there was enough water in it. She plonked it back down on the range and gathered things together to make a large pot of strong tea.

It took a moment for Hartley to realise that she was crying again. "Hilda?"

Clutching the old tin tea caddy to her chest, she wailed, "To be able to leave this place! Not to have to do backbreaking work day after day, come hail or shine! To live in a neat, warm little cottage in the heart of the village, and to have time to enjoy life! To be friends once again with my sister! Is it possible, or am I dreaming?"

Violet spoke then, her voice trembling with emotion. "It's no dream, Hilda. I've got lots of money, and I don't need it all. The Mill was your home too, so you should share in the proceeds from it. We'll get this old farm fixed up so it's ready to sell, and you'll stay with me until we find a suitable place for you. Near me, of course."

"Like Wisteria Cottage?"

"Exactly like Wisteria Cottage. It's perfect for you. We'll be close neighbours but not in each other's pockets. We've got years and years to catch up on, and probably not many years left in which to do it. I've been a terrible person, Hilda, and I want to make it up to you."

Hartley beamed at Violet, feeling she was, indeed a prodigal daughter.

Violet returned his look with humour gleaming in her dark eyes. "Don't worry, there'll still be enough in the pot to repair the font."

After they'd left Merryvale Farm, Hilda, still sniffling, Violet clutched Hartley's arm and warmly thanked him. "The loan idea was a stroke of genius. As long as she thinks that's what it is, we'll be able to get her out of there and into a comfortable place near me. When she tries to pay me back I shall simply refuse to take a penny."

To Hartley, it felt as if he'd witnessed a miracle. If only Lorelei could sort herself out and get back to normal, he'd be a very happy man.

Chapter 31
reconciliation (ii)

Stephen pounded on the door. "Let me in!"

There was no reply.

"Let me in, Lorelei, or so help me I shall stand here and shout all night." He hammered louder, alternating between the knocker and his fist. "LET ME IN, LORELEI."

He hadn't seen her for a few weeks, and not for want of trying, but this time he wasn't going to give in. Stella had said firmly that she couldn't stand him moping round the Heritage Centre any more, and even his students at the university were muttering about his lacklustre lectures.

"Go and sort it out, Stephen," Stella had told him. "Even if it means kicking her door down. And give her that beautiful amethyst ring back."

The ring was in his pocket, he carried it with him everywhere. He wouldn't have to go as far as kicking her door down, because Lorelei had given him his own key, but he didn't think it was right to make use of it. Unless, that is, she really gave him no choice.

The door remained closed. To give his fists a break, Stephen peered in through the window. There was no sign of life so he decided he would have to let himself in, just in case Lorelei was ill in bed or something. He yelled that he was using his own key and gave a shout of exasperation when he tried to push the door open and found it held by a safety chain.

"RIGHT," he shouted at the top of his lungs. "YOU GIVE ME NO CHOICE, LORELEI. I'M BREAKING THE SAFETY CHAIN AND I'M COMING IN."

By now a few people had come out of their cottages and were standing in their doorways watching the commotion unfold.

Stephen took a run at the door and slammed into it with his shoulder.

"You go, Stephen!" someone yelled.

Shoulder throbbing, he took another run at it, and this time heard the splintering as the chain gave way and the momentum had him hurling into the living room.

"Don't take no for an answer!" shouted another voice.

A smattering of applause met his ears and he felt relief that they were on his side and not calling the police.

Lorelei wasn't there, and Stephen tried not to react at the sight and smell of the dreadful mess. Dirty cutlery and fast food containers were scattered all over the carpet. Used plates were piled up haphazardly by the sofa and armchair. He knew the kitchen would be the same.

Slowly, he climbed up the stairs, but already sensed that Lorelei was nowhere in the house. He came down again and went back outside.

"Stephen!" It was the next-door neighbour. "I saw her sneak out the back door. I think she's heading for the church."

Thanking her, and not missing the sympathy and curiosity in her eyes, Stephen carefully closed the front door and set off in pursuit of Lorelei. If she had indeed gone to the church, she would either be inside it or at her Aunt Ottilie's grave. If not there, he would hurry on the vicarage and see if she'd gone to her Uncle Hartley.

Lorelei was the only person in the churchyard, sitting on a small plaid rug beside her aunt's grave. She was wearing a shapeless rain hat and a shabby coat Stephen didn't recognise. His heart turned over when he saw she was crying, tears pouring down her face. She talked softly through her tears, having a conversation with her beloved and much-missed aunt.

As Stephen stealthily crept towards her, trying not to alarm her, she pulled a large bag of crisps from her capacious bag, and it crackled loudly as she tore it open with her teeth.

Gosh, thought Stephen, even in her haste to get away from him, she'd managed to pack a picnic blanket and some food. "Lorelei, please don't eat those crisps!"

With a start, she turned her head, skewing her hat, as he now hurried towards her, but she ignored his plea and started eating. One by one, each crisp immediately following the path of the one before it went into her mouth with barely a pause for her to chew. Watching her hand move from packet to mouth over and over, his heart turned over at the silent tears that continued to course down her cheeks.

Gently, slowly, he lowered himself to sit beside her, and snatched the near-empty bag from her greasy hands. He peered closely at her face. What he saw there, deep in her green eyes that were reddened and puffy, saddened him beyond belief and he had to drop his gaze. She was begging for help.

Beneath the open coat, Stephen could see that she was dressed in baggy, stained clothes in dull shades of beige, muddy brown and black. Colours she would never have dreamed of wearing before. The old Lorelei had delighted in jewel colours, particularly her favourite purple, as well as ruby and emerald and sapphire. Now, the clothes that clad her plump body were ill fitting and tatty as well as drab, as if she'd raided someone's dustbin for them. The skirt, Stephen could see, was held together at the front by a large safety pin, filling the gap between button and buttonhole. She had gained so much weight her waist had disappeared and the tops of her arms strained the fabric of her blouse. The glorious red hair that had once shone and curled around her face and down her back was dull and unbrushed.

But he saw beyond all that. He cupped her face and whispered, "I love you, Lorelei. I don't understand what's happening, but I want to help you. Unless you can look me in the eye and tell me that you no longer love me and that you're happy the way you are, then I shan't leave until you agree once again to be my wife."

"I'm not happy," she whispered, firmly withdrawing her hand. "Who could be happy like this?" She grabbed a sausage roll, biting off another piece before she'd swallowed the one already in her mouth. Flakes of oily pastry fluttered onto her skirt, and she didn't bother to brush them away. Once she'd taken the last bite, she hauled her bag onto her knees and, after a bit of rummaging and muttering, she withdrew a family-size bar of fruit and nut chocolate, and impatiently ripped the paper and foil off so she could cram chunks of it into her mouth.

Distressed beyond measure, Stephen insisted, "Lorelei, my dearest love, you are clearly ill, so let me help you get better. Lorelei, I shall go on telling you that I love you and I want to marry you. I—"

He was interrupted by Reverend Cordwell coming towards them, his fine white hair ruffled by the rising wind, his kindly face riven with concern.

"I don't want to see anybody," cried Lorelei, her mouth full. "Please go away, Uncle! You too, Stephen, just leave me alone."

Shaken by the vehemence in her voice, Stephen rose and went to waylay Hartley on the gravel path.

"Stephen! I'm so glad to see you," said Hartley, then, in a quieter voice and trying to see past Stephen to where Lorelei sat disconsolately on her crisp- and pastry-crumbed rug, "she's been coming here every day to sit with Ottilie. How is she?"

Stephen shook his head. "She doesn't want to see anybody, I'm afraid. Including me."

"I can't understand what ails my niece, I really can't. She's had all sorts of blood tests, but they couldn't find anything wrong with her. There must be something wrong, though!

People don't eat like Lorelei unless there's something seriously the matter."

"I agree. I've thought about it over and over and I just can't pinpoint when everything changed."

"Whatever it is, I'm sure there's a remedy for it. You, for instance, Stephen." He clapped Stephen on the shoulder. "Standing by her. Good for you."

Stephen laughed mirthlessly. "I've just told her for the hundredth time that I love her and want to marry her, but she won't consider it. Just tells me to go away and find someone else. How can I find someone else? She's the only one for me."

"Then take her home, young man, and make her see sense."

"I will, though I don't suppose she'll come willingly."

"Victory comes not to the faint hearted! Look, I'll help you get her home, then I'll leave you to talk to her. Come on, Stephen, let's get her up."

They gently helped Lorelei up from the rug and packed the food wrappings into her bag. She was surprisingly complacent, for a while, but then Uri came through the lychgate and while they were momentarily distracted, she lunged for the bag and started to run.

"Lorelei! Please!"

She disappeared behind the tool shed.

"It's hopeless, Hartley. Perhaps we should let her go. I'll try again another time." Stephen sank to the ground and pulled the ring from his pocket, the specially-made amethyst ring that should never have been removed from Lorelei's finger. "I so want to give this back to her, to see her wear it. To know that she will be my wife."

Uri came up to them, nodded to Hartley, then turned to Stephen. "That's a beautiful ring. May I?" He plucked the ring from Stephen's hand and held it up to the sky, proclaiming it to be the loveliest engagement ring he had ever seen. "Go after her, Stephen. Go down on one knee and tell her again how much you love her. She's ready to listen, she just doesn't know it yet."

He handed the ring back, and it was so hot Stephen almost dropped it. But his mind was on Lorelei, so he wrapped his fingers round it and held it in the palm of his hand and headed for the shed, because the only place his beloved could be was behind it.

She was there, leaning against the shed wall, her bag at her feet, wolfing down another sausage roll and crying with each bite.

"Lorelei. Enough now." He took the remains of the food away from her, threw it on the compost heap, and knelt before her on one knee. Holding out the ring, still very hot, he begged, "Take this back, Lorelei. Promise to be my wife, and together we'll make you right again. Please, Lorelei, I love you with all my heart. Please."

She gazed at him, her eyes swollen and her face ravaged with tears. She'd pulled off the rain hat and her hair was a tangled mess, but to Stephen she was beautiful and he told her so.

Slowly, so slowly that Stephen had to hold his breath in case she bolted again, she reached out her hand, holding it so that he could put the ring back on her finger.

He slipped it on, feeling the tremendous heat coming from the metal band. It wouldn't go over her knuckle.

She bowed her head, and sobbed until Stephen thought his heart would break. He went to take the ring from her, thinking he would get it resized as soon as possible, then resized again when Lorelei was well and slim again. But as he touched it and Lorelei whispered how much she loved him the ring slid easily all the way onto her finger. He gathered her into his arms and they whispered to each other over and over, "I love you, I love you."

Eventually Lorelei lifted her head and gazed him, and he saw the old Lorelei in her eyes. She then looked down in wonder at the ring, sitting snugly where it should have been all along, and she melted into Stephen once more.

When eventually they left the churchyard, Lorelei made no objection when he threw the bag of food into the bin. When they reached the church, Uri was watching them from the porch. He gave Stephen a salute and a wink as they passed by, and Stephen grinned back.

Chapter 32
a new beginning

In London, early on a Friday morning, Nigel awoke to the smell of coffee as a steaming mug was placed on the floor just inches from his nose.

"Wake up, sleepy head! This is the last morning we'll be city dwellers, and no more private investigating for you! A shame it's raining."

Nigel sat up and groaned to hear heavy rain drumming against the windows. It would slow them down getting to Ham-Under-Lymfold, and they were both so very eager to be there.

Nigel took care of Chloe while Amelia showered, then he got himself showered and dressed and joined his family in the kitchen. Side by side at the stove, he and Amelia prepared a full English breakfast as they weren't sure when they'd get the chance for lunch, and they ate it without speaking much, both thinking about the momentous move they were about to make.

Nigel's newly-purchased car, chosen for its practicality and safety rather than luxury now Nigel had his precious daughter to think about, was fully packed, and after the breakfast things had been washed up and put in a box, Nigel carried the last few possessions they were taking out of the flat and added them to the rest of their things. A charitable organisation had come the day before to take away their sofa, dining table and chairs, bed, and a few other sticks of furniture that they didn't want, and they had spent an uncomfortable night on a duvet on the floor. But they didn't need to take much to their new home, because it was already fully furnished with the most elegant furniture, thanks to the angels.

They did their final check of the flat to make sure nothing was being left behind. Amelia hoisted her bag onto her shoulder. "I can't say I'm going to miss this place, but we have been happy here haven't we?"

Nigel kissed her. "I would have been happy in a hole in the ground, as long as it was with you and Chloe. But ahead of us is a beautiful apartment above a stunning restaurant – *our* stunning restaurant – in a fantastic village, so are you ready?

"Yes, I'm most definitely ready."

They set off, in teeming rain, through the back streets of north London, towards their new home in the country.

Nigel drove through the choked, narrow roads, aware when he had to brake that there was quite a bit of weight on the back axle, mainly because of all of Chloe's things. How could such a tiny baby require so much stuff? he'd asked, as they'd loaded the car. Then he became aware of how responsive the car was, how smooth its ride, and remembered that he was driving a quality car, not the old, rusting estate he'd had before. The sky was black with ominous, low-hanging clouds and rain came down in sheets, and the car responded with its automatic windscreen wipers working at their fastest speed.

The drive was slow going, but at last they reached the motorway, and the rain eased the further they got from the capital.

"Shall I put something on for Chloe? Will it distract you?"

"No, it won't distract me. Look, there's the sun coming out now, it'll be easy driving from here."

Amelia selected a CD and she and Nigel sang 'Old MacDonald Had a Farm ee-I-ee-i-o' in silly voices until Chloe was happily gurgling and blowing bubbles between her rosy lips.

After an uneventful journey, with a stop on the way for a quick cup of tea, they entered Ham-Under-Lymfold just after one o'clock.

The skies were blue and cloudless as they reached the old rusting petrol pumps that stood like sentinels at the entrance to the village, and it looked as if it had not rained there at all. Nigel wondered if the angels had something to do with the fine weather, just at the time of their arrival, or, rather, if Gabriel had had a hand in it, because he doubted that Nick would ever learn to be so thoughtful.

Nigel slowed as the road curved quite sharply at this point, then stamped his foot on the brake and pulled over to the side of the road. Amelia, who had turned in her seat to check that Chloe was okay, was jerked around by the sudden stopping of the car. She glared at Nigel, about to remonstrate, but he grinned and told her to look, for strung between two lamp posts just before the village green, was a large banner.

WELCOME NIGEL, AMELIA AND CHLOE!

The stone blind and the crab apple tree had also been bedecked with colourful bunting and the village green teemed with people. They cheered as one when they spotted the car.

"I think we'd better park here and join our welcome party," said Amelia, her eyes shiny with happiness.

Nigel lifted Chloe from the back seat and saw Gwen Perkins hurrying towards them.

"Hello, luvvies," she cried. "We won't keep you long, we know you're probably dying to get into that beautiful new home of yours, but we just wanted to give you a warm, Ham-Under-Lymfold welcome."

She led them into the throng to Cynthia, who was laying a tray piled high with food onto a table already loaded with sandwiches and drinks. Dazed, Nigel accepted half a pint of lager and Amelia chose a bottle of ginger beer.

"This is wonderful! Gosh, I… we… well, what can we say?" Amelia almost choked on her words.

Someone called a cheerful "Halloooooo," and Hartley Cordwell came forward with his hand outstretched. Nigel shook it, and Amelia reached up and kissed his cheek, making him blush to the roots of his dandelion clock hair.

"This is really so kind. How can we possibly thank everybody?"

Mr Fordingbridge, standing nearby, laughed and shouted so everyone could hear, "Free drinks at the restaurant would do it, I should think!"

Nigel spotted Stanley standing beneath the stubby little tree, a pint of milk stout in his hand, Digby sitting with dignity beside him. When Nigel reached him he said, "I knew ye wus destined fer 'am-Under-Lymfold the moment I saw ye. And roight glad I be that you'm be 'ere, that I am."

Careful to breathe through his mouth at such close proximity to the pungent old man, Nigel said, "Thank you, Stanley, that's very kind of you."

Nigel and Amelia walked slowly through the crowd with Chloe, enjoying the party atmosphere and deeply flattered that it was for them. In the unseasonal sunshine it was like a summer carnival, with flags draped around the Blind and trestle tables groaning with food and drinks. They were reluctant to leave it, but time was getting on and they needed to get unpacked and settled in before it got too late. They went back to the car and tooted as they drove beyond the green and the church, and round the corner out of sight. They suspected that their leaving would not bring the party to an end any time soon.

On the sweeping gravel area in front of the mill, Nigel performed a three-point turn and reverse parked to the side of the great stone building, close to the front door of their new apartment. Sitting on the drystone wall were Arnold Capsby and Glen Perkins.

Nigel got out of the car. "I wondered why I didn't see you at the welcome party."

Arnold climbed off the wall. "There'll still be plenty by the time we join them. Thought you'd need a hand to unload."

Amelia, Chloe in her arms, thanked the men who'd unexpectedly turned up to help, shaking her head in wonder at how kind everyone was being.

As they had done many times before, Nigel and Amelia took a couple of minutes to stand and gaze at the magnificently renovated building. But this time it was different. This time they were gazing at their new home. Their future.

A large wooden sign, hung by a thick black chain from an intricately carved pole, announced the name of the restaurant in gilded letters. Beneath the name was a small picture carved into the wood, a copy of part of the ebony section inside the restaurant, the part that depicted Gabriel and Lucifer peering into the pit. The two angels had taken a while to warm up to Amelia's suggestion that they keep the original name, but they had agreed to it in the end as it was undeniably right, and Uri had created the sign.

"Welcome to Angel Falls Mill, my darling," said Nigel.

Amelia laughed with sheer joy, then he took her hand and led her through their private entrance and upstairs to the luxurious apartment above the restaurant. Glen and Arnold stayed where they were, appreciating that the young couple needed space for just a few moments before they started unloading the car and carrying things in.

The apartment had been entirely furnished by the angels – another gift they said – and it was stunning in every detail. It was as if they'd read Amelia's and Nigel's minds and come up with every little thing they'd ever wanted. It wasn't filled with the red and white furniture they'd had, because Gabe had soon ascertained that red was not Amelia's favourite colour. Instead, they'd chosen exactly what Amelia would have chosen, the muted blues and greens and creams that she loved and had used a lot in her interior design business. Every room matched Amelia's and Nigel's ideal.

They ran quickly through the rooms, laughing and hugging each other, making Chloe gurgle and coo as she was squashed between them. When Nigel went back outside, the two helpers were already approaching the stairs with their arms full. With their help it didn't take long to empty the car, and the men refused Amelia's offer of refreshments and said they'd like to join the party on the green, if there was no more they could do for them. Nigel thanked them profusely, but they replied that thanks weren't necessary as they were more than happy to have been of help.

At last, Amelia and Nigel found themselves alone with their happily chuckling daughter, surrounded by their belongings in bags and boxes.

What had happened to the angels' living quarters they didn't know, and when Nigel had asked Gabe if the portal was still there and Gabe and Nick might appear through it occasionally, Gabe had just smiled enigmatically. Were they still here, he wondered, invisible, sharing the space like in a parallel universe? Nigel decided not to think about it too much, because thinking anything about the angels usually gave him a headache.

Amelia, Chloe on her hip, went into the gleaming kitchen. "I still can't believe this marvellous place is ours. And this kitchen, well! We've got every modern appliance we could wish for, and then some." She opened and closed some of the cupboards. "And even if we ever manage to fill all these, how will be able to find anything again?"

Chloe's room was a marvel too, its walls painted with beautiful landscapes peopled with fairy figures. When Amelia had first asked Lorelei to do it, she'd initially turned down the commission because she was still suffering from what everyone referred to as 'Lorelei's Little Problem'. But Amelia, as Nigel had known she would, had really taken to Lorelei, and had refused to take no for an answer. So Lorelei had come with her paints and brushes and worked for days to cover the walls in a beautiful fantasy land, and during those days, she and Amelia had become firm friends.

Exhausted by the excitement of their journey, Chloe soon fell fast asleep so Amelia put her in her carrycot and joined Nigel on the squashy sofa that was far more comfortable than their old one had been. She laid her head on his shoulder and he curled her silky chocolate-coloured hair through his fingers, asking himself what wonderful thing he had done in the past to deserve so much.

The restaurant was having its opening night the following weekend and would be full with invited guests. The gardens had been beautifully landscaped and planted with mature bushes and shrubs so visitors would think that they had been there for many years. The mill wheel turned and churned the water to a creamy, frothing foam. Ducks, moorhens and swans swam where the river was calm, and made their nests under the branches of the weeping willows on the opposite bank. It was an idyllic location. Uri's carving had been completed and installed and was magnificent, a triumph. Experienced staff had been appointed, including a chef who had been enticed from one of the top city restaurants. The wine cellar was full and the bar fully stocked. The brochures, menus, wine list and business cards had been printed. Invitations had been sent out to the locals and a chosen few from outside the village, including, at Nick and Gabe's insistence, Nigel's ex-wife Tansy. Finally, a journalist had taken photographs and written a glowing article about the place in the local press, so advance bookings for both the restaurant and the five luxury bedroom suites were already coming in at a very satisfactory rate.

They were ready.

Chapter 33
the grand opening

"It's going well, isn't it?" whispered Nigel to Amelia.

Amelia whispered back fondly, "Yes, and we've not got started yet!" She moved forward to welcome their guest of honour guests, the Mayor of the county capital of Wiltshire and his lady wife.

The restaurant was filling rapidly with their specially invited guests, and people were circulating, clutching the glasses of excellent champagne in one hand and shaking the hands of their fellow guests with the other.

Nigel and Amelia were stationed at the door, watching with nervous pride as car after car parked either in the Mill car park or in the newly surfaced Turnaround, as directed by young Freddie. It was a beautiful spring evening, so people stopped for a few moments as they walked across the bridge to admire the bubbling river and the magnificently restored mill. The old waterwheel turned, filling the balmy air with the happy, sparkling sound of fast-flowing water.

Nigel and Amelia said their warm welcomes and invited their guests to take a glass from the waiters and waitresses who moved sedately through the crowd with silver trays of champagne. They knew that in the kitchen, well out of sight and hearing of the guests, the chef and his staff toiled in the magnificently equipped kitchen to produce a menu worthy of royalty.

Nigel's stomach churned just like the water passing through the wheel, not only because of the excitement of their opening night, but also because… ah, well because of this particular guest. He wiped his suddenly sweaty palms on the back of his dinner jacket as a dark blue Rolls-Royce swept into view. Freddie, on loan for the event from Cynthia and dressed in a rather loose-fitting dinner suit and skewed black bow tie, directed the huge vehicle over the bridge to one of the reserved parking spaces. The chauffeur, haughty in his uniform and stiff peaked cap, climbed out and opened the rear door. A large man emerged first, then turned and held out his hand to assist his companion as she stepped elegantly from the car. And there she was. Tansy Hellion-Rees, formerly Tansy Wutherington-Parker. Nigel wondered fleetingly if she would have been interested in marrying him if he hadn't himself had a double-barrelled name.

Tansy took her escort's arm and swept up the curving stone steps. Swathed in a white furry stole, the collar held closed by a gloved hand at her throat, Nigel couldn't help but think of Cruella di Vil, though he knew even Tansy wouldn't be so witless as to wear real fur. She swung the stole from her shoulders when she arrived at the door and handed it disdainfully to Amelia, who was still next to Nigel. Nigel quickly intercepted it and gave it to a passing waitress, asking her politely to take it to the cloakroom.

Tansy's gown, now revealed in all its glory, was stunning and, Nigel knew, would have cost thousands. It had a tight-fitting, low cut bodice that moulded itself around her creamy bosom, then flowed down her tall, slim body to her spike-heeled silver sandals in swathes of sapphire blue scattered with hand-sewn crystals. A diamond-encrusted bracelet sparkled on her wrist, huge diamond earrings glittered on her earlobes as she moved her head. She was like a goddess that had just stepped from the sea.

She held out her left hand to Nigel, no doubt wanting him to know that she still wore the ostentatious emerald ring he had given her and intending that he kiss it. He merely touched the tips of her fingers with his own instead and looked over her shoulder at the man hovering behind her.

"I'm sure you remember Fenston Marlow, darling," Tansy drawled.

"How do you do," said Nigel, politely bowing his head to the lawyer who now stood before him with a smarmy, superior smile on his pudgy face. "Of course it was your father whom I had dealings with," he said politely, while thinking to himself how that man had royally screwed him when he and Tansy had divorced, "but I remember meeting you in the office once or twice."

Tansy continued, "Daddykins had to go to New York and I decided I really *had* to see your dear little restaurant when I got the invitation, so Fenston stepped in as my escort." She fluttered her false eyelashes at Nigel, annoyance flitting across her face when she realised it had no effect on him.

Amelia pasted a smile on her face and Nigel could feel that she was well prepared to speak politely to the enemy, no matter what it cost her. He beamed down at her with pride, delighted that she looked so radiantly beautiful in her own elegant, floor-length gown of beaded silk that was the colour of milk chocolate and set off her hair and complexion to perfection. Tansy, however, rudely strode past her as if she wasn't there, exclaiming, "Oh, do I see champagne? *Divine.*"

"God, Nigel, how did you ever end up marrying that woman?" spat Amelia, once Tansy was out of earshot.

"In all truth, I don't know. I really don't know." He was relieved to have another couple of guests arrive at the doors so he didn't have to give any more thought to how stupid he had been to be taken in by Tansy.

When everyone was inside, Nigel asked that the great oak door remain open so people could wander outside if they wanted to and the party got into full swing. Huge electric fans hanging from the ceiling, there to keep the restaurant to a pleasant temperature in the summer, were not needed on this balmy evening. The champagne continued to flow, and waiters and waitresses carried out tray after tray of dainty, delicious canapés from the kitchen. After half an hour, Nigel and the headwaiter circulated among the guests inviting them to take their seats for dinner.

Arnold Capsby puffed out his chest like a pigeon performing a mating ritual in Trafalgar Square when he found that he and his wife had been seated at the mayor's table.

The food was beyond excellent. The conversation flowed effortlessly. There were speeches. There was laughter. The grand opening was a resounding success!

When coffee and hand-made chocolates were being served, along with liquors for those who wanted them, Nigel and Amelia circulated among the tables, being heartily congratulated by everybody. They had so many friends in the village now, and they were all there, including the Capsby, the Perkinses, the Fordingbridges, the re-engaged Stephen George and Lorelei Dove, Reverend Cordwell, Violet and her sister Hilda, resplendent in new dresses bought specially for the occasion. Debbie, looking very pretty, showing off her considerable assets in a low-cut, knee-length cocktail dress, talked the ears off Freddie, who looked like a rabbit caught in headlights.

Stanley had refused his invitation, as Nigel and Amelia had known he would, but his eyes had filled with tears at even being asked. However, Nigel had seen him outside, proudly wearing the new coat, new fingerless gloves and new hat given to him by Violet and Hilda. Digby, sitting contentedly at his side, sported a new red leather collar with a nametag, also given by the sisters. Nigel had made sure they got plenty of goodies from the kitchen throughout the evening.

Now, Nigel and Amelia, working the room together to ensure everyone was having a wonderful time, stopped to talk to a local television celebrity, an eccentric explorer and adventurer who had been born in the village, left when he was two, and now lived in Salisbury when he wasn't roaming the globe seeking out remote and strange tribes in deepest Africa. He had come to the party dressed in an ill-fitting dinner suit, tartan bow tie and dirty trainers without socks.

After a while, Nigel felt it was time to excuse himself and go and talk to the mayor, but as he crossed the room he heard a 'pssst' in his ear. He looked around but couldn't see anyone, so carried on. There was another, louder, 'pssst', and this time he recognised its source even though he still couldn't see the person trying to attract his attention. Gabe waved, and Nigel diverted from his route to the mayor to go and talk to him. Unlike the explorer, Gabe was a vision of sartorial perfection.

"It's going brilliantly, isn't it?" whispered Gabe.

"Where have you been? Where's Nick?" hissed Nigel, trying to keep out of the way of the two-way swing doors through which waiters and waitresses were constantly, busily barging.

"We've been, y'know, *back*," answered Gabe without a hint of enthusiasm. "Supervising the packing and everything. Nick's still in He—" he couldn't even say it, "*down there*, doing some last minute sorting. We're ready to swap places, just about."

Nigel shook his head sadly. "You really don't want to do this, do you, Gabe?"

Gabe's mouth turned down at the corners. "No. No, Nigel, I don't want to do it. I don't want to be the Dark Lord, Prince of Darkness, the Devil, Satan, blah blah blah." He flapped his hand dismissively. "All that bother and brimstone. No, I want to go on being the Archangel Gabriel, bearer of good news and all-round nice guy. I love good people. I love everything about Heaven." His shoulders drooped. "I love being up there. My place is empty and bare now, ready for Nick to move his stuff in. But the DISC was found, Nick got away with his cheating, and I really have no choice in the matter."

Nigel felt so sorry for him. "Perhaps you'll have just as nice a room in He—, er, where you're going?"

"Hah," Gabe's tone was bitter. "You've no idea. And you'll never know, because you'll go to Heaven when your turn comes. I'll get the likes of Tansy Wutherington-Parker and her obnoxious lawyers for company. She's here, isn't she?"

"Yes, as a matter of fact, but I can't understand why you insisted that I invite her. And she's brought her shark along just to rub my nose in it a bit more." He gave a rueful laugh. "Of course you knew she'd do that. You probably fixed it. Anyway, it really galls me that she will benefit from this wonderful gift of yours through extracting more and more maintenance payments from me, but there you go."

"I know, Nigel. That's why I'm here. Unfinished business, you might say. That ex-wife of yours needs her come-uppance and I'm here to make sure she gets it."

Nigel laughed. "But Gabe, surely that's Nick's job?" Gabe's look was withering. "Ah, sorry, I suppose it's yours now. But what are you going to do? I don't want Tansy hurt or anything."

"I promise you she won't be. All I'm going to do is get her off your back. Release you from that ridiculously unfair divorce settlement you were pushed into accepting. And give her a taste of her own medicine. I think I might even enjoy it, as I like you, Nigel, and I'm sorry I won't see you and Amelia and Chloe again when all this is over."

"Oh, Gabe! I know how much this is hurting you, but surely you won't just disappear from our lives? And, remember, you didn't visit Gluttony on Lorelei, Nick did that, so you still haven't done anything bad."

Gabe smiled a smile that reached his eyes. "Oh, that lovely young lady! But she's better now, isn't she?"

"Yes, she's okay and getting her life back on track. She's over there, look, with her fiancé, and she's looking very well, don't you think? But why was she chosen, Gabe? Why her?"

"Why not her?" he answered bitterly. "It had to be someone, and Nick insisted it had to be done to the most generous and sweet person in the village. Thank goodness you and Amelia weren't living here then, he might have picked on her!"

He brightened then as he had another thought. "But his cheating worked out for Violet and Hilda, didn't it? Mind you, once he'd done the deeds, he wanted to work on more than just two people, but fortunately the tribunal put paid to any more messing with innocent folk. Besides, the ripple effect of our presence has made quite a few people better off, if you think about it. The Perkins family have done well with all the builders going to their café for lunch, and Glen's new range of bread and cakes just fly off the shelves, he can hardly keep up with demand. Stephen George proved just how deep his love for Lorelei is. And other locals have benefited by working with you on setting up the Mill, and those you'll employ to work here. I know it's hard for you to believe, but what was done to Lorelei was the kindest way, really, and the bad stuff has all been put right now."

"Well, if you say so. But thank goodness the spell on her was broken before the damage was irreversible."

"Yes," said Gabe, "but remember, Nigel, Lorelei discovered that Stephen truly loves her for who she is. But it was Uri who removed the curse of Gluttony, and he could only have done it with Michael's say so. I notice, though, that you never pleaded with us to turn Violet back to the way she was?"

Nigel could say nothing to that.

"Anyway, it's all done and I'll be leaving after I've finished here tonight." He hesitated, and needlessly adjusted the pale-blue silk handkerchief tucked into his dinner jacket pocket, obviously working up to saying something. "I really do hope you've forgiven us for getting you involved in all this. You will be happy here, though, you do know that, don't you?"

Nigel looked amazed. "Gabe! How could I possibly not be happy here? And of course I've forgiven you, if I really had any forgiving to do. This has been the most fascinating time of my life, Amelia's too, and every day this place will remind us of how far we've come, thanks entirely to you."

"Well, thank you for that, Nigel, I can't tell you how much that means to me. Now, you'd better get back to the party." He grinned. "You must trust me, now. When I arrive introduce me as your lawyer and enjoy the show as your ex-wife gets the shock of her life!"

Nigel, puzzled and not a little bit nervous about what Gabe planned to do, heard Amelia calling him, and Gabe didn't give him time to ask questions. He hurried back into the restaurant.

Amelia grabbed his arm as soon as he appeared. "Tansy's been looking for you," she hissed, and then noticed Gabe. "There you are!" she said warmly. She clasped his hand, but looked warily over his shoulder.

Gabe laughed, "Nick's not here, Amelia, it's just me."

"Well, in that case!" Amelia hugged him tight and kissed him on the cheek. "I'm delighted to see you. Come and have a glass of champagne."

"I'll have one with you later, Amelia. I just need to do something first, okay?"

Smiling her pleasure, she left to do some more mingling and Nigel worked his way towards Tansy's table. She was talking to the explorer in the tartan bow tie, probably telling him about her own adventures, which included having regular full body massages in five star hotels across the globe. Fenston, sitting across from her, was clearly bored, twisting his brandy balloon by the stem round and round on the table. There were coffee stains on the white cloth, which he had tried to cover with his linen napkin.

"Ah, there you are, Nigel," exclaimed Tansy, indicating imperiously that he should sit down next to her. "We need to talk, darling." She turned to the explorer and said rather rudely, "Would you mind? This is private business."

The explorer, relief written all over his face, hurriedly left the table, grabbed a glass of champagne, tipped it into his brandy balloon, and headed for the group clustered around the mayor.

"Well, thank goodness he's gone," drawled Tansy. "All he could talk about was some ghastly tribe who pierce their masculine body parts with porcupine quills, and then hang stones from them with raffia."

Fenston, seated to her left, chimed in, "If you can believe such juvenile twaddle."

But Tansy ignored him, and said with obvious relish, "Apparently it made walking mighty awkward, and tribal dancing nigh on impossible, but they proudly staggered around with their, er, *thingies,* somewhat… *stretched*."

Inwardly grimacing, Nigel sat.

Fenston removed a large Havana from a silver cigar box and, without offering one to Nigel, turned his gimlet eyes on him. "So you own this restaurant, then?" He puffed on the cigar until it was lit, and arrogantly blew smoke in Nigel's direction. Nigel, refusing to cough, just nodded. "Ah. So. You do understand, then, that Tansy is entitled to twenty per cent of your earnings from it?"

"Of course. She's had twenty per cent since the divorce, thanks to your father, I don't imagine she's going to be generous now and get out of my life altogether."

"Oh, darling, don't be mean," Tansy simpered.

"Having seen the restaurant," said Fenston, firmly bringing attention back to himself, "we are prepared to offer you another deal. Ten per cent ownership."

"Ownership? Are you mad? I—"

"Good evening," said a soft voice behind Nigel. Gabe swung into view in the periphery of Nigel's vision. The face was unrecognisable to Nigel, but he knew it was Gabe who pulled out a chair and sat down. The usually curly hair was sharply parted and plastered on Gabe's skull, the grey eyes were hidden behind tinted spectacles. Only the dimples were still evident as Gabe talked, but all of the other things taken together made him look very different, somehow darker and more sinister. The whole effect was, Nigel realised, a little more like Nick.

Gabe put out his hand to Tansy. "You must be Mrs Tansy Hellion-Rees? Or have you reverted to Ms Wutherington-

Parker?" The tone was surprisingly menacing for Gabe. He turned to Fenston, and Nigel had to hide a smile when he asked in a very insulting manner, "And you are?"

Fenston smoothly reached inside his jacket and withdrew a thick, white business card. "I am Mrs Hellion-Rees' lawyer," he growled.

Gabe bowed his head in acknowledgement and took the card. "Ah, yes. Fenston Marlow-the-second, your reputation goes before you. I knew your father well, you know. I trust he is enjoying his retirement in the Bahamas? Did I hear you just now offer a deal to my client?"

"Your client?" said Tansy and Fenston together.

"Indeed. My card," he handed over a business card with fancy raised lettering, thicker and whiter than Fenston's own.

The lawyer glanced at it, then fumbled for his reading glasses. Putting them on in what he hoped was an insouciant manner, Nigel could tell he was bewildered to find that he couldn't read the copper-coloured lettering. It would be too embarrassing to ask the man's name, so he handed it to Tansy in the hope that she would read it out loud. Tansy, the incredible blue of her eyes owing everything to contact lenses, couldn't read it either, no matter how she squinted. She put the card on the table with an irritable exclamation.

Fenston decided to take the initiative and command the conversation. "Yes," he said, "I have made your client an offer. I take it you are au fait with the terms of the divorce settlement?"

Gabe merely inclined his handsome head.

"Well then, I'm sure you will agree that ten per cent ownership of this business is a fair deal? This restaurant has success stamped all over it. Mr Hellion-Rees will do well out of it, and so will his ex-wife, who is clearly deserving of his continued financial support."

"Hmm," said Gabe, stroking his chin. "But what if it isn't a success? Then the first Mrs Hellion-Rees would surely lose out by changing the terms of settlement as you suggest?"

Chins wobbling, the lawyer puffed himself up. "The restaurant business may fail, certainly, but this building and the land it sits on is worth a great deal of money and has great potential to be something else. It would make a magnificent health spa, for instance. And the fixtures and furnishings would fetch a tidy sum too."

"Yes," said Gabe, "that's all very well, but according to the terms of the settlement, which you wish to change, the first Mrs Hellion-Rees is simply not entitled to anything from Mr Hellion-Rees, nor has she been for some months. Neither twenty per cent of earnings nor ten per cent ownership. Not even the shirt off his back, come to that."

"I'm afraid you have your facts wrong, sir," said Fenston stiffly. "Mrs Hellion-Rees *is* entitled to the lawfully agreed maintenance until she remarries. She has not, I assure you, remarried, nor are there any nuptials in the offing."

"Ah." The smile Gabe bestowed on Fenston and Tansy put Nigel in mind of a barracuda. "I suggest you read again the divorce documents. In fact," he reached into an inside pocket, "knowing you would be here and also being aware of what's been going on, I just happen to have a copy here." He opened out a sheaf of papers and spread them on the table. "Page 14, paragraph 3, clause 4ii, I think you'll find."

Fenston glared at Gabe and blustered, "What the blazes are you talking about, man?"

Nigel imagined Tansy's lawyer would be feeling an uncomfortable cold trickle down his spine faced with the implacable expression on Gabe's face. Gabe merely tapped the document.

Fenston reached for the papers and turned to the relevant page. Three pairs of eyes watched as he read the clause pointed out by Gabe. He read it again. He ran his forefinger inside his collar, as if it had suddenly become too tight. "There must be some mistake," he said, alarm making his voice sound like a teenager enduring the voice-breaking stage of growing up. "There's no way my father would have agreed to this!"

"Oh, there's no mistake," retorted Gabe coldly. "This is our own copy of the divorce agreement, signed and witnessed, and I appreciate that you must go to your office and check your copy."

Tansy was looking from her lawyer to Gabe, her face reddening.

"I can do better than that!" exclaimed Fenston angrily, pulling his slim mobile phone from his pocket. "We will settle this outrageous matter right here and now!"

Nigel, Gabe and Tansy listened with interest to the one-sided conversation.

"June, it's Fenston. Yes, I am in Wiltshire... Listen, I need you to do something for me... Well I'm sorry to interrupt your TV dinner and your romantic film, but this is important. I need you to go to the office and get the Hellion-Rees file out... I don't care if it isn't convenient, I need it now!... A taxi! Good grief, woman, you only live around the corner. Just get the file, and ring me back... What?... Yes, yes, double overtime, just get on with it, will you?" He ended the call and threw the phone on the table.

Nigel noticed that beads of sweat had formed on Fenston's brow and upper lip and was longing to know what was going on. What could Gabe possibly have done to the divorce contract?

Tansy could stand it no longer. Almost demented with rage, fear and confusion, she hissed, "Will someone please tell me what the *Hell's* going on?"

An appropriate choice of phrase, thought Nigel, and he didn't miss the fleeting smirk on Gabe's lips.

Gabe was totally unfazed by her outburst and turned to Nigel to ask after Chloe's health. Nigel replied, playing the game, despite not knowing what the game was, excitedly telling Gabe about the way she liked to curl her mother's hair around her fingers as she drifted off to sleep, how she loved it when he and Amelia sang lullabies together. Tansy glowered.

The wait before Fenston's mobile rang seemed to go on forever.

"Yes," he barked into the phone. He pulled Gabriel's document towards him as he listened. "Have you taken the document from the locked filing cabinet in my office? Turn to page 14, paragraph 3, clause 4ii and read it to me." He was getting noticeably paler as he listened to his secretary. "What? Read it again!" At last, he said goodbye and pushed his phone into the inside pocket of his jacket. From his breast pocket he pulled out a red silk handkerchief and mopped his face with it, looking deeply unhappy. Then he turned to Tansy, and took a deep breath.

"I think we should leave now, Tansy dear, and I'll explain things to you on the way."

"You will explain things to me right now," said Tansy icily enough to freeze freshly boiled water.

Fenston cleared his throat and ran his forefinger inside his collar again, skewing his bow tie. More beads of sweat rolled down the sides of his bulbous nose. "Perhaps you should read this for yourself." He pointed at the document on the table, swallowed hard. "Page 14, paragraph 3, clause 4ii."

"You know damned well I don't want to read it!" spat Tansy. "I don't understand lawyer-speak, and what does Daddy pay you for? Just explain to me what is going on and do it right now before you find yourself fired!"

Nigel, wondering if Fenston Marlow-the-second was about to be fired anyway, couldn't help stealing a glance at Gabe, but the angel's face remained inscrutable. Was he enjoying this? Was he managing to become a little Nick-like after all?

Fenston cleared his throat again. "According to the divorce document, and I don't know how this happened, I do assure you, only my father could shed light on this, the settlement ran until you remarried or, if Nigel should marry before you, it ran only until the day after the birth of his first child."

"That's nonsense, I—"

"Let the man finish, Tansy," interrupted Gabe, his voice like warm syrup, a smug smile on his face.

Fenston, shifting in his seat, continued, "It would seem that, not only are you not entitled to anything from him whatsoever, you owe him for anything he has paid you, either in cash or in lieu, from the day after his daughter's birth."

Tansy sat in stunned silence. For about two seconds.

"That's ridiculous!" she spat. "At no time has this *ever* been mentioned, and if it had been I'm sure Daddy would not have accepted it. No, he made it very plain what he required, and your father will answer for this, retirement or no retirement. It's outrageous, it's…" Sparking with fury, she was unable to go on.

Nigel knew it wasn't about the money. She had plenty of money from her doting father. But she wanted Nigel to pay for throwing her out over a couple of silly little flings, as she'd called them, and go on paying until she was tired of it and not before.

The lawyer wisely stayed silent. He knew his lucrative career was over. By the time Tansy's daddykins was through with him, even though he wasn't responsible for that reprehensible clause, he'd be lucky to get a job sweeping floors.

Nigel was as stunned as Tansy. He didn't remember that clause either! Surely he would have known that it was there, it would have been explained to him and he and Amelia would have had a double celebration on the day of Chloe's birth, knowing that freedom from the tyranny of the Wutherington-Parkers would be theirs the very next day.

But no-one had known about it, because it hadn't been there! Gabe had done this. Gabe had set him free!

Tansy marched out of the restaurant with her nose in the air, Fenston Marlow scurrying humbly in her wake. Nigel heard her bark at him to fetch her stole, and then they were gone. He turned to Gabe. "I don't know how to thank you. Yet again. You've done so much."

"Actually, it was Nick's idea, and he was going to do it. But then we decided it should be me. You know, the chance to genuinely practice being bad."

"It doesn't feel like a bad thing, Gabe."

Gabe gave a rueful grin. "No, it doesn't does it? We got you out of a situation you didn't deserve to be in, but I had to lie and cheat to achieve it. But there we are. As Nick said when we cooked this up, sometimes you have to do something bad in order to achieve something good."

"I can't wait to tell Amelia. Thank you again, a million times. Will you thank Nick on our behalf?"

"Of course I will. Nigel, I want you to know that you've done so much for me, too. It's been such a pleasure watching you and Amelia together, and then the little one arriving the way she did... Honestly, this was the least I could do."

Chapter 34
the fall of Gabriel

"I have one last favour to ask of you, Nigel."

"Gabe, you haven't asked any favours of me. You've done many favours *for* me, but all I've done for you is a paid job. Handsomely paid, at that. But anyway, ask away, my friend."

"I'd like you to be with me when I—" he hesitated and swallowed hard, "when I *go down*."

That was the very last thing Nigel had expected him to say. "But… but how can I do that, Gabe. Surely I'd have to be… well, dead, wouldn't I?"

Gabe managed a short-lived laugh. "No, no, Nigel. You've already been there, and you definitely weren't dead then."

"I have?"

"The office! The office where you came to see me. The upside down icicle, as you like to call it."

Nigel gaped. The Icicle was Heaven *and* Hell? When the angels had explained about portals, for some reason he'd only thought of Paradise. He felt a cold, tingling sensation run up and down his spine.

Hardly believing he was asking such a question, Nigel stammered, "So will I see the real thing when I go back with you this time?"

Gabe put his hand on Nigel's shoulder. "No. It pleases me that you said 'when' and not 'if', but you'll only see what your mortal brain can comprehend. I suggest you tell Amelia that you'll be gone for a little while. No, scratch that. She won't even realise you're gone. As you have already discovered, time isn't the same for us angels as it is for you humans."

"But aren't you going to say goodbye to her, Gabe? And to Chloe?"

Gabe's shoulders slumped. "Can't do it, Nigel. I'll only disgrace myself by bawling my eyes out. But I'll keep an eye on young Chloe as she grows up, I promise you. After all, I am her godfather."

Nigel wondered how they'd manage to make his godfathership official, as the christening wasn't for several weeks yet, and Gabe in his new guise as Satan could hardly turn up at the church. As he opened his mouth to speak, Gabe grabbed his arm and he was suddenly in the back of the dark grey limousine. When the weird fluttering sensation in his solar plexus subsided, he risked a glance out of the blackened windows, but there was nothing to see but a pearly, swirling mist.

When the car came to a halt in the parking garage beneath the Icicle, Nigel opened the door before the chauffeur could do it for him and stepped out. He turned and looked across the car's roof at Gabe, who was white faced, his grey eyes dark and shadowed. Neither of them spoke until they were inside the elevator heading upwards. There was no operator this time.

Nigel looked carefully at the polished brass panel of buttons next to the doors. They were in three uneven rows. In the centre row, bottle-green buttons were labelled *Parking Garage, Open Doors, Close Doors, Alarm*. The right hand row had nine buttons in a pretty shade of pale blue, but they weren't labelled numerically as for floor levels. Instead, they were labelled top to bottom in the ranks of the angelic hierarchy: *Seraphim, Cherubim, Thrones, Dominations, Virtues, Powers, Principalities, Archangels, Angels*. On the left row there was just one button. A black one. It was labelled 'Hell' in fiery letters.

Nigel remembered riding up very high that first time he had come to see Gabe, and surmised that each level of the hierarchy must have several floors. Then he mentally shook himself. Floors? Heaven didn't have floors. If it did, the Seraphim would be several hundreds of storeys up.

The elevator doors slid open, and Nigel was just a little relieved to see the same long corridor stretch out before them. Feet sinking into the thick carpet, he walked alongside Gabe, respecting his need for silence.

When they arrived in the office of his secretary, it was in a state of terrific upheaval. Sarah, not at all her usual calm self, was barking orders at the team of men who were packing things into boxes. It was only when she saw Gabe that she made an effort to smile and look cool, efficient and in command again.

Gabe went up to her. "Sarah, you know you don't have to come with me. Why don't you stay up here and work for Nick, hmm?"

Nigel saw the look of panic on Sarah's face, but it was there a mere moment before she recovered her poise. "No, Gabriel, my place is by your side."

Gabe patted her arm, and indicated that Nigel should follow him into his office.

That, too, was a mess of half packed boxes. Pale rectangles on the walls were sad reminders of where Gabe's glorious art collection had hung. The fantastic view through the floor to ceiling window was gone. All Nigel could see were grey clouds, like a storm was brewing outside. The whole scene was so surreal and Nigel, knowing that what he was seeing was only what his human brain could comprehend, practically felt his brain click and whirr until the cogs slotted into 'go with the flow' mode.

"So what now, Gabe?"

"I just have a few more personal things to pack, and then we'll be off. Oh, hi, Nick." The greeting was spoken, without an ounce of enthusiasm, as Nick sauntered in, a minion scurrying behind him with what appeared to be a very heavy box.

"Well, Gabe, the moment has come."

Nigel wasn't sure, but he thought he detected a hesitant note in Nick's voice. Was he a little reluctant now that the time had arrived? But as the soon-to-be-ex-Devil gazed around the walls, his demeanour changed.

"Gabe! You can't take the paintings. Put them back!"

"But—"

"No buts, bro. Your taste in art will look very out of place in your new home."

Gabe looked close to tears, but walked to the door and called that the pictures were to be put back up. Then he checked once more that the drawers of his vast desk were empty. He walked to the centre of the room and gazed about him, slowly turning 360 degrees, drinking it all in.

"You can't see what I see, Nigel. To you this is a large office, with desk and chair and all the officey things you expect. But that's not what it is."

Nigel, feeling Gabe's grief, stayed silent.

"I wish you could see it. I wish you could see Heaven."

"Yeah, but then he wouldn't be able to go home again, so let it go, Gabe." There was none of the usual drawl in Nick's words. Perhaps he, too, was aware and rather sad for his fellow angel's sorrow at leaving the home he'd lived in for thousands of years.

Gabe straightened his shoulders and clapped his hands. "Of course, brother, you're absolutely right and I'm being a sentimental old fool. It's not as if I'll never see this place again, it's just that it won't be *my* place."

"So, shall we go?" asked Nick, so softly, and in a manner so out of character, Nigel did a double-check. So did Gabe.

"*We*? Are you coming with us, then?" Gabe sounded surprised.

"I thought I would. You know, to show you round."

"I have been there, Nick, I don't need to be shown around."

Nick shrugged. "I'd just like to, that's all."

"Well I don't want you to!"

"Come on, Gabe, don't be like that."

"Okay, then, you win!" It was almost a shout from Gabe. "Let's get on with it."

The three of them went back to the elevator. Nick pressed the black button. The descent took a long time, and Nigel told himself firmly that the rising heat was just his imagination going wild. He expected Hell to be hot and so it would be. When they'd juddered to a halt – none of the smooth stops of the upper levels – Nigel hardly dared to look. What would he see? If he couldn't see the real Hell, how could it possibly be represented in a metaphorical office building?

The first thing to hit him was the blast of searing hot air as the elevator doors hissed open. The second was the cacophony of noise. So loud was the volume of chatter and shouting, of machinery, of ringing phones, it made his ears buzz. Then his eyes looked out in astonishment at a scene that was a cross between a gigantic call centre on a frantically busy day and the London Stock Exchange during a financial crisis. All seemed utter chaos.

"Let's go to my office," shouted Nick above the din. "Sorry, I meant *your* office, Gabe!"

They trooped along a narrow passage that edged the floor, then clattered up a spiral metal staircase. The banister was too hot to touch. Nigel, forced to wipe sweat from his face with his sleeve, glanced to his right, and every face he saw was glued to a computer, their frightened and desperate expressions lit by the eerie glow on the screens. Above their heads was a huge banner that read:

THOU SHALT LEAD INTO TEMPTATION

They all wore headsets and every now and again someone would stand up and yell, "SALE!" Or maybe it was 'SOUL'? The thought made Nigel shudder.

It was with relief that they reached an office with a very heavy door that shut out the sound, if not the heat. Gabe looked as shell-shocked as Nigel felt.

"It's not a call centre, Nigel, though I'm glad that's how it looks to you and you can't see what it's really like. I will certainly never get used to it," he said. "I think I'll have to wear ear defenders from now on."

Nigel looked around. The room was large, very similar to Gabe's in that there was a floor to ceiling window (how, he wondered, could he be looking at Alcatraz Island?), art on the walls, a vast, curved glass desk. The usual stuff. But on close inspection of the paintings, Nigel's nostrils flared in horror at the dreadful scenes depicted. Gore. Torture. Death. Destruction. He turned away, but was equally confounded by that view of that place that had once been a prison.

Behind him, the wall was also mostly glass, but this looked out over the bedlam they'd just walked through.

"One last time, just for the Hell of it, ha ha," said Nick as he walked to a microphone set on the sill of the window. "Number 14397, you're slacking!"

Nigel saw a flash of lightning, and someone, poor old 14397 he presumed, disappeared in a plume of black smoke. "What the—?" he exclaimed.

But when the smoke cleared, 14397 was still sitting there, looking right as rain, if a little singed, typing away very, very fast.

"I always enjoy that," chuckled Nick.

Gabe looked horrified, as well he might, and Nigel didn't think there would ever come a time that Gabe would be able to mete out arbitrary punishment like that.

"So, bro, our new Lord of Darkness as you now are, any questions?"

"Not really," said a visibly trembling Gabe. "But have you thought, Nick, what you are giving up?"

Nick's face looked thunderous. "Don't start that again!"

"But Nick. For thousands of years you have been the master of everything down here, only answerable to Michael. You have been able to do what you want, when you want. But up there you will be master of nothing. Uri is in charge there. All you will have to do is, well, um, read books, play music, be nice to the souls, ask the servants to dust the furniture…"

Nick laughed and clapped his hands. "Sounds wonderful!"

Nigel interjected, "But you did seem to enjoy that—" he flapped his hand at the workers outside, "that punishment thing."

"That was, as I said, just one last time. For luck, as you humans say."

Gabe's whole demeanour sagged. Clearly he had still held the hope, right up until this last minute, that Nick would change his mind and they could leave things as they were.

Nigel, watching him with sorrow and compassion, thought the angel looked as if his bones were melting, then found himself wondering if angels had bones. He knew they didn't have digestive systems, though they loved to scoff cake. What did they really look like? He was sure they weren't how he and everyone else who came into contact with them saw them.

Nick put his hand on the door. "Before I go, I would advise you *not* to try and turn Hell into another Heaven. I don't think Michael would take too kindly to that. Remember, *Gabriel*, that the souls are here to be *punished* and chintz furniture and pretty pictures do not create the right atmosphere."

Gabe's shoulders sagged even more, and Nigel wondered with alarm if he was about to slump to the floor.

"Oh yes!" exclaimed Nick. "One last thing. There is a code, a very specific one, that humans, usually calling themselves Satanists, can do to summon you. They have to get it *absolutely* right, mind, and some secret society in the depths of this place change it every so often, but when someone does get it, you *must* appear to them. In person. It's compulsory."

Gabe nodded his head. "The Summoning Spell, yes. I know about that."

"And, brother dear, if and when you do get that summons, please remember that you are The Devil. It's no good appearing to them in shining white robes with a halo above you and a smile on your face. Horns and hooves, that's what they expect. Billowing, high-collared cloaks. Black leather studded with metal spikes. Sharp teeth, black talons. Lots of growling. That sort of thing." Nick grinned at Nigel then and said, "You can tell it's been an awfully long time since anyone cracked the code, because I haven't dressed like that for, oh, centuries!"

Gabe's shoulders couldn't sag any more, so he collapsed into the nearest chair. Nigel went to him and put a supportive hand on his shoulder.

Nick opened the door. "Ah, another thing."

"Are you *ever* going to leave?" retorted Gabe, bitterly.

"I've left you all the wine in my cellar."

Gabe managed to say that it was most generous, but Nick spoiled the gesture by proclaiming, "Didn't see the point of taking it up there; I mean, I've always *said* it must be the best cellar in the cosmos, but I'm sure the heavenly stuff must be just as good, if not superior!"

Gabe suddenly leapt up to his full height and regarded Nick with flinty eyes.

"Will you GO!" he commanded.

Nick laughed, and he was gone with a breezy, "That's more like it! See you, bro."

Nigel didn't know what to do. Gabe was standing like a statue, in a state of shock.

The door opened again and Nick's head and shoulders appeared. "I almost forgot," he said, and threw something into the room.

It flew up to the ceiling, paused a while as if not wanting to come back down again, then tumbled over and over, glinting gold in the harsh office lights.

Gabe watched it impassively as it bounced twice on the carpet, spun seven times on its smooth edge, then tipped with the smallest *tink*. Nigel wondered how such a noise could be made on a carpet, but in view of everything else he'd seen and heard in the last couple of hours, decided it wasn't worth bothering about.

Suddenly the coin started to tremble, and a low rumbling noise could be felt as well as heard. The coin flipped itself over, and a low, dark cloud formed above it. Gabe and Nigel stepped away from it as the cloud billowed and grew in size. Slowly, slowly, with an ugly hissing sound, it formed itself into a… a… Nigel's brain scrabbled for the right description. A terrifying pterodactyl! It flapped its leathery wings and shrieked horribly. It glared malevolently at Nigel, then turned its great head and spotted Gabe. It shrieked again, and flew to Gabe's shoulder, talons gripping in what looked a painful manner.

"Ho hum," trilled Gabe with false gaiety. "The emblem of Hell is perched on my shoulder, so that's that." He picked up the DISC and put it in his pocket. "Um, Nigel… I want you to know how much I have appreciated your friendship, and I know you can hardly stay friends with me now…"

"What?" cried Nigel. "Why ever not? You'll still be the same Gabe."

"But I won't! Don't you see? This place will change me. I *have* to change, become more like Nick, or I won't survive it. Please, Nigel, if you just promise that you and Amelia will remember me as I was when I was Archangel Gabriel, it'll keep a little bit of my heart pure. Will you promise?"

"Oh, Gabe, of course I will! I don't ever want to forget you, nor this whole experience. And I know Amelia feels the same."

"Thank you. All I want for you and Amelia and beautiful little Chloe is for you to have a normal life. You deserve it. But you must never speak of it to anyone. Lorelei, Violet, Hartley, none of the villagers will remember us, only you and Amelia will remember, and I know you and your darling wife can be trusted. You must go now."

Throat tight with emotion, Nigel reached to squeeze Gabe's hand, but Gabe quickly pulled him into an embrace and whispered, "Goodbye, Nigel, my dear, dear friend."

Nigel heard Amelia calling him, and blinked hard when he realised that he was standing in the kitchen of his apartment.

Chapter 35
the last chapter, but not the end of the story

Nigel and Amelia strolled in the sunshine towards St Peter's Church. They carried Chloe between them in her carrycot, draped with white organdie and festooned with pale pink silk ribbons for the special occasion. Behind them Nigel's mother chatted animatedly to Amelia's mother, and the two fathers trailed behind discussing the latest Wales v England rugby match.

A whole crowd of people were waiting to greet them as soon as they'd passed through the lychgate.

"Hello, you two," cooed Gwen Perkins. She and Olive Capsby leaned over to gaze at Chloe. "Oh, will you just look at the little sweetheart," whispered misty-eyed Gwen.

Olive stroked Chloe's downy cheek and said in the sing-song voice adults used only when addressing babies and little children, "It's your special day, Chloe, oh yes it is, you delicious little thing you."

The other members of Nigel and Amelia's families, their friends and the invited villagers formed an untidy queue to congratulate them and to exclaim over the adorableness of Chloe in her long white christening gown.

Once everyone had had a turn, Nigel led them towards the church door where Hartley, resplendent in his official robes, waited to greet them. Stanley was there too, looking rather smart these days, but still smelling a little ripe, as if the pungent smell of so many years was too deeply ingrained in his skin to be washed out. The faithful Digby, washed and groomed by Debbie for the occasion and smelling of lemons as he usually did, sat by Stanley's side.

Nigel scratched the big dog's ears, enjoying that unique gruffling sound the dog made as it leant against him in ecstasy. "It's strange to see you here without your sandwich board, Stanley."

"Ah, well, sir, I do feel a bit lost without it, but y'see, I done a new one an' the paint ain't yet dry. Normal services will be resumed as soon as it be possible, though, an' I'll soon be walking around with a new an' important message."

"Are you coming inside, Stanley?" asked Amelia. "You know that you're welcome to join us. Digby, too, right Hartley?"

Hartley beamed and spread his arms. "He's one of God's creatures, Amelia."

Nigel almost laughed, knowing that Hartley would welcome the dignified Digby into his church far more willingly than the ever-pungent Stanley.

Perhaps Stanley realised that too, because he replied cheerfully, "Nay, Mrs Hellion-Rees, but bless you fer askin'. Me and my Digby will wait out 'ere like we always do. If the Reveren' would be kind enough to leave the door open, we'll be able to hear the service, so we will, an' that'll be pleasure enough."

"Okay, Stanley, but you will come to the Mill for a drink afterwards, won't you?" Amelia was daring the old man to say no.

Stanley grinned, a wide grin that showed the gold tooth at the back among the few blackened molars he had left. "To wet the little babe's head? Aye, ma'am, I'll certainly want to do that!"

The congregation filed in and Nigel's heart swelled as he looked around at his family and his friends, old and new. Among the new were Reverend Hartley, overjoyed to be conducting a christening after many a year, Cynthia, Lorelei and Dr Stephen George, soon to be husband and wife, though whether Lorelei wanted a church wedding was under debate. And, too, Violet and Hilda, who fought with young

Debbie Perkins for the pleasure of babysitting Chloe on the rare occasions he and Amelia went out without her.

Deep in thought about how he and Amelia had come to be part of this lovely village community, he hardly took any notice of the service until people were gathered around the font, newly repaired by a mystery benefactor, according to Hartley. He took Amelia's hand as Hartley called for the godparents to come forward, because he knew that she was missing Gabe's presence as well.

But a perfectly-behaved Chloe Gabrielle Lucy Hellion-Rees was duly christened, Gabe di Angelo pronounced godfather in absentia after the other godparents had pledged they would do their duty by Chloe, and they all gathered outside the church beneath cloudless skies for a few photographs to be taken.

Stanley had left his place in the porch and was nowhere to be seen, but Digby was still there. He trotted over and pushed his long, whiskered nose into Nigel's hand. Nigel looked down into the wise golden eyes, and Digby moved his head and looked intently at something in the distance. Nigel scratched his ears, but Digby nudged him again with his nose and took a few steps away, looking back over his shoulder as if willing Nigel to follow. "What's up, boy, what are you trying to tell me?" Nigel giggled, thinking he sounded like he was an actor in one of the old *Lassie* films, then he spotted a lone figure, almost hidden by the skirts of the ancient yew tree at the farthest edge of the churchyard.

Heart lifting, he whispered in Amelia's ear, and together they strolled over to Gabe, Digby following at their heels.

"I'm so glad you came, Gabe. We've all missed you so much."

"She's my goddaughter, Amelia, how could I not come?" He smiled, but his eyes were sad. Chloe's hand reached up to him and he leant forward to plant a kiss on her forehead. She clasped a curl of his hair making him chuckle with delight.

Digby wagged his whippy tail against Nigel's leg, which hurt somewhat, until Gabe called his name and he lolloped over to have his ear scratched. Gabe might now wear the mantle of the Dark Lord, but Digby still sensed the archangel within.

Amelia asked, "Are you all right, Gabe? Is it so very dreadful?"

Gabe sighed. "Yes, it's dreadful. But it's my duty, and an angel always does his duty." He suddenly perked up and said, "But Uri came to see me, and he said he's sure Nick won't settle in Paradise. He told me to be patient and maybe, just maybe, things will change back again."

"Oh, Gabe, that would be wonderful! I can't help agree with Uri that Nick won't like it. He's no more a good angel than you are a bad one. I think he'll soon be bored and hankering after his old position!"

"I'll drink to that," laughed Gabe. "But, here, Amelia." He handed her a small package wrapped in silver paper and tied with a white ribbon. "For Chloe. But remember, she is not to know my true nature."

"Your true nature will always be something wonderful, Gabe, and she would sense it, just like Digby does."

Nigel watched the gift change hands, wondering what story he could make up to tell Chloe about her absent godfather and curious to know what gift Gabe had chosen. Whatever it was, it would be special, something Chloe would treasure for always. Would she remember Gabe, Nigel wondered? How would they ever be able to explain it all to her? Amelia kissed Gabe and slipped the gift into her bag. "We'll open it later, Gabe, in private." Someone called her, then, and she walked away, Chloe in her arms still reaching for Gabe.

Gabe watched mother and daughter go, then turned to Nigel and said, "Just a few words before I leave, a couple of things to forewarn you of, if I may."

"Of course. Not bad things, I hope?"

Gabe shook his head. "Well, the first thing you'll not like too much. You see, you still need to prepare the completion of your job as Witness, so if Nick doesn't want his old job back, you'll be ready to do what you must.

"Oh", was all Nigel could say to that.

Gabe patted him on the arm. "The others things are nicer, Nigel. Violet is shortly going to ask you to do something for Hilda Merryvale, please help her. The other thing is, Hilda is selling her farm; you probably know about that. But it's in such a bad state she won't get much for it unless there's planning permission to knock it down and build something else. So I ask you to think about the possibilities. Apply your architect's skills. Trust me, you'll come up with a plan that will benefit the whole village in the long run, not just Hilda."

"Oh?" he said again, unable to think of anything else.

"Yes. You'll know just the thing to do when you put your mind to it. And you'll have the money to do it."

Nigel, brain already whirring, peered round the large tree to see if he could spot Hilda among the crowd milling around in front of the church. Digby barked then, a short, sharp woof, and when Nigel looked back, Gabe had gone.

Amelia came back to his side. "I feel so sad for him," she sighed. "He's really not cut out to replace Nick is he?"

Nigel took her hand and squeezed it. "No, he isn't, so let's hope that Uri is right. For my own sake as well as Gabe's, as I really don't know how I could possibly convince the world that Lucifer has returned to Heaven. Come on, we should get back to our guests." He called to Digby, "Come on, boy, Stanley will be wondering where you've got to."

The dog followed slowly, constantly looking back as if searching for Gabe.

Nigel was waylaid by Violet by the lychgate, who had obviously been waiting for him. Nigel wondered if she had seen who he and Amelia had been talking to behind the yew tree, but she gave no sign. Amelia said she'd go and encourage their guests to head to the Mill.

"Hello, Violet."

"I want to ask you something, a bit of a favour." She spoke in a whisper, her eyes darting around as if checking that they couldn't be overheard."

Nigel wondered if it was about Merryvale Farm.

"Did you know that Hilda has a son?"

Nigel nodded. "Yes. Maxwell, isn't it? He left the village when he was just a teenager, didn't he?"

Violet nodded. "And he's never been back. We know he visited Cynthia's son in Australia, because they'd been close friends at school. After that we know he went to New Zealand and worked as a shearer. He left there after a couple of years, though, and the trail went cold. Hilda doesn't know where he is, or even if he's still alive. Nigel," she put her gloved hand on his arm, "I heard you were a private investigator in London. Could you find him? It would make her so happy. I'll pay whatever it takes."

Nigel swallowed hard. So this was what Gabe meant. How kind of Violet to think of it, and what a wonderful thing it would be if Hilda could be reunited with her only child. "Of course I'll help, Violet, I'd be honoured."

"Good. But it'll be our secret. In case you don't find him. Or if he's—" She couldn't say the word, but Nigel knew what she meant. Violet slipped away and rejoined her sister, who was deep in conversation with Mrs Fordingbridge.

Nigel headed towards Amelia, who was talking to Stanley. She pointed to the sandwich board now strapped onto Stanley, new words painted in dark blue, streaky and uneven, on a pale blue background:

In the cherch be angels
to purk up your spirits

Nigel chuckled inwardly at Stanley's unique way of spelling, then looked closely at Stanley's guileless face. Surely he couldn't know about Gabe and Nick and Uri? "That's nice, Stanley, I'm sure Hartley approves?"

"I don't think he's seen it yet," Amelia interjected. "He's been too busy talking to everyone." She glanced at her watch, "I've been trying to chivvy people up, Nigel, and get them over to the Mill, or chef will be getting anxious his soufflés will sink. I hope you're still coming, Stanley?"

Stanley put his unlit pipe into his mouth. "Well, now, I'll not be comin' into your grand place, but I hope you don't mind if I wait around outside? P'raps ye'd be kind enough to send out a milk stout for me and a little something for Digby?" He adjusted the straps so they sat more comfortably on his bony shoulders.

Hartley came up to them and handed something to Nigel. "It's from Uri, for the little one. He left it with me to give to you today."

"Oh, it's exquisite!" Nigel turned the carved figurine in his hands. About six inches tall it was a beautiful piece, a man and a woman entwined around a tiny child. "Look, Amelia, isn't this lovely?"

Her eyes welled up and she whispered, "Yes, it is. Here, let me put it in my bag with Gabe's gift so we can look at them both properly when we're on our own."

At last they managed to round up all the guests and led them in cheerful procession to the restaurant, where drinks and a sumptuous buffet meal awaited.

But as they started the short walk, Stanley came jogging alongside them and, with another cheeky grin, stepped in front of them, so he was the leader. The back of his sandwich board could now be read by all:

Angel Falls Mill
will purk up your apetite

to be continued

Also by J Merrill Forrest

psychic dramas

'Flight of the Kingfisher'
ISBN 9780956795410

&

'Walk in the Afterlight'
ISBN 9780956795441

The Moon Tiger
2020

https://jmerrillforrest.com